BOOKS BY GILBERT MORRIS

THE HOUSE OF WINSLOW SERIES

1. The Honorable Imposter
2. The Captive Bride
3. The Indentured Heart
4. The Gentle Rebel
5. The Saintly Buccaneer
6. The Holy Warrior
7. The Reluctant Bridegroom
8. The Last Confederate
9. The Dixie Widow
10. The Wounded Yankee
11. The Union Belle
12. The Final Adversary
13. The Crossed Sabres
14. The Valiant Gunman
15. The Gallant Outlaw
16. The Jeweled Spur
17. The Yukon Queen
18. The Rough Rider
19. The Iron Lady
20. The Silver Star

THE LIBERTY BELL

1. Sound the Trumpet
2. Song in a Strange Land
3. Tread Upon the Lion
4. Arrow of the Almighty

CHENEY DUVALL, M.D.
(with Lynn Morris)

1. The Stars for a Light
2. Shadow of the Mountains
3. A City Not Forsaken
4. Toward the Sunrising
5. Secret Place of Thunder
6. In the Twilight, in the Evening

THE SPIRIT OF APPALACHIA
(with Aaron McCarver)

1. Over the Misty Mountains
2. Beyond the Quiet Hills

TIME NAVIGATORS
(For Young Teens)

1. Dangerous Voyage
2. Vanishing Clues
3. Race Against Time

9709

BEYOND THE QUIET HILLS

★ ★ ★

GILBERT MORRIS & AARON McCARVER

BETHANY HOUSE PUBLISHERS
MINNEAPOLIS, MINNESOTA 55438

Published by Bethany House Publishers
A Ministry of Bethany Fellowship, Inc.
11300 Hampshire Avenue South
Minneapolis, Minnesota 55438

Printed in the United States of America.

Library of Congress Cataloging-in-Publication Data

Morris, Gilbert.
    Beyond the quiet hills / by Gilbert Morris, Aaron McCarver.
       p.   cm. — (The spirit of Appalachia ; 2)
    I. McCarver, Aaron. II. Title. III. Series: Morris, Gilbert. Spirit of Appalachia ; 2.
PS3563.O8742B48   1997
813'.54—dc21   97–33829
ISBN 1–55661–886–7   CIP

Dedication

This book is dedicated with deep affection to two of the best friends anyone could have, my sisters, Marilyn Slatton and Ginger Bradford.

To Marilyn, thank you for always being there for me and encouraging me to strive for the best in every area of my life. You always made sure I had everything I needed, from money for school to a hair-combing to a special hug. Your example of how God brought you through difficult times to shining for Him will always be an inspiration to me.

To Ginger, thank you for your complete and total acceptance. Your steadiness in every part of your life, from spiritual to personal, is something I have tried to add to my life. Thank you for sharing your love of reading by giving me my first "grown-up" book. The other gifts that first book led to are immeasurable.

You both make me so proud! You have homes that are Christ-centered, and you put your families ahead of the things of this world. Thanks for the wonderful Christian examples!

I once heard it said that God made big sisters to take care of their younger siblings. Well, God certainly knew how much care I would need because He gave me the two best sisters ever!!! Thank you both for always watching out for me, for listening every time I have a problem, and for supporting me. But most especially, thank you for just loving me.

I love you both with all my heart!

Contents

PART III: BROTHERS

PART IV: THE YOUNG LIONS ROAR

Character List

They came over the Misty Mountains to forge new lives on the Appalachian frontier. They brought their hopes and plans to a land of freedom and opportunity. But they find they must deal with the past before they can build the future of their dreams . . . *Beyond the Quiet Hills.*

Jehoshaphat "Hawk" Spencer—He came west to escape a painful past and carved out a new life on the frontier. He must now use his newfound faith to face the past or see the life he has built destroyed.

Elizabeth MacNeal Spencer—After losing her first husband, Patrick, God has given her another love. She must now use her strong faith in God to bring two families together and make them one.

Jacob Spencer—Abandoned by his father after his mother died giving him life, he has been raised by loving grandparents. When his father comes back to Williamsburg to claim him, Jacob must deal with all the bitterness and anger he has harbored in his heart for a man who claims to be changed by God.

Andrew MacNeal—The death of his father brought his world crashing down, but a man of the frontier has restored his dreams. Now a jealous stepbrother tests his patience and his faith when both fall in love with the same girl.

Abigail Stevens—A lovely young woman of the frontier whose future is set with a childhood friend. Then his handsome stepbrother comes into her life and challenges all she holds dear, including her faith in God.

Amanda Taylor—Abused by her father, she longs for acceptance and love. But the one her heart secretly desires loves another.

Sequatchie—Torn between two worlds, this Cherokee chief may be the only one who can save the frontier settlement and help the troubled son of his best friend.

Zeke Taylor—He vowed to get even with Hawk for interfering with his family, but his wife's resilient faith in God halted his desire for revenge. Then he yields to old temptations and sets in motion events that could destroy them all.

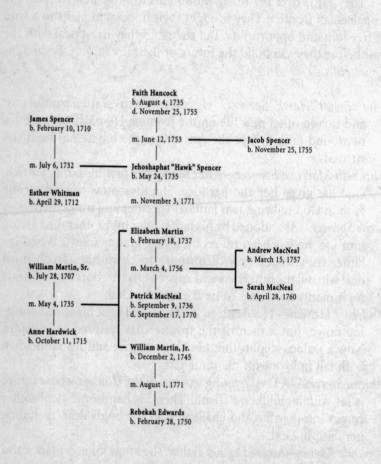

PART I

Hawk's Sons

November 1771 – December 1771

*The young lions do lack, and suffer hunger: but they that seek
the LORD shall not want any good thing.*

Psalm 34:10

Bride and Groom

One

$\mathcal{A}$s Elizabeth MacNeal stepped outside the small cabin, she took one startled look at the glistening black bear standing not ten feet away and froze in her tracks.

Hawk had warned her that the bears around Watauga were prone to wander close to the settlement, but she had only seen them at a distance since coming to the Appalachian Mountains. Now her heart leaped up into her throat at the enormous size of the bear. Suddenly he reared, his beady black eyes meeting hers. His coat was sleek and he was fat; thus she knew that most of his kind had already retreated into caves for the winter. A shiver of fear ran through her at the sight of the long claws and sharp white teeth as he slightly opened his mouth.

For a moment she could not think and had a sudden impulse to whirl and dash back into the cabin, but then she remembered what Hawk had told her. *The black bears around here aren't dangerous. Most of them are shy. All you have to do is clap your hands and shout at them and they'll turn tail.*

Abruptly Elizabeth swung the bucket she carried in her right hand, throwing it toward the bear and crying out loudly, "Shoo! Get out of here, you old bear!" Although the bucket missed, to her delight the bear uttered a startled *Woof!*, dropped to all fours, and scurried frantically away. As he disappeared into the timber among the scrub trees that lined the eastern border of their farm, Elizabeth clapped her hands together and smiled. "Now, that'll be something to tell Andy and Sarah!" she exclaimed.

Strolling across the open space, she bent down and picked up the bucket as she stared at the large bear tracks. She had wanted trees and grass close to the cabin, but Sequatchie, her Indian friend, had warned her, "That's for town people. Out here you don't need to leave any way for the enemy to creep up on you—and besides, when a forest fire comes you'll be glad of the open space."

Elizabeth strode purposefully along the worn path leading down to the creek that wound its way around the tall growth of walnut trees. She was not a tall woman, but very erect with a fully developed upper body and a tiny waist. Her thick blond hair bounced on the back of her neck, and as the morning sun struck it, brown highlights glinted as she swept it back over her shoulders from time to time. She had green eyes and a broad, well-shaped mouth. Her naturally fair complexion had been darkened by the sun so that now she had a rich golden tan, except for a few freckles, almost invisible, that speckled her nose. At the age of thirty-four Elizabeth was a beautiful and robust woman with a soft depth and a strong spirit. Those who knew her well admired the great vitality and keen imagination that lay beneath her calm exterior. Her firm lips and a determination in her eyes expressed the strong will and the deep pride that ran in her. As she moved along the path toward the creek, she exuded an air of serenity and happiness.

She threaded her way through a small clump of fledgling walnut saplings that were held in a crook of the creek's arm, until she came to the edge of the water. Stooping down, she reached forward with one hand and scooped up some of the clear water and tasted it.

"Better than Boston water," she murmured. As she stooped there beside the creek she thought how different her life was now that she had crossed the Misty Mountains, the Appalachians, and made her way into the uncharted wilderness of timber and streams and mountains. Lifting her eyes as though she could see the city she once called home, she thought about the greater change that was soon coming into her life.

Thoughtfully she held the bucket with both hands, then lowered it until the cold water filled it almost to the brim. Straightening up, she put it down on a patch of dead brown grass and stood for a moment, her clear eyes thoughtful and meditative.

"I'll have a new husband today!"

She whispered the thought aloud and then glanced around self-consciously, laughing slightly at herself. "I might as well talk out loud," she said, looking up at a woodpecker that was drumming industriously, seeking larvae in a towering chestnut tree. She watched as the bird extracted something and flew off. Her eyes followed him until he came to a hole in the top of a dead tree and disappeared. "I wonder if you've got some babies in there," Elizabeth said. She did not know when she had picked up the habit of talking to herself, but it had been since she had left Boston and spent long hours alone in the village of Watauga.

Finally she picked up the bucket, thinking suddenly of her first husband, Patrick. The memory of his face leaped into her mind, and her lips curved tenderly as she thought of him. When he had first been killed in an Indian raid on their journey west, she had thought sorrow would be her portion for the rest of her life. Slowly she had learned that God can even take away the sharp, bitter edge of grief. Now as she strolled along through the tall trees that stretched their arms up to heaven as if in prayer, she was suddenly grateful that she had Andrew and Sarah. Their looks and actions reflected so much of their father that he would never be forgotten, not as long as they were there.

A thought occurred to her and she put the bucket down and left the path, crossing rapidly into the thick canopy of trees. She reached a dying ironwood tree and put her ear to the slick surface. A pleased expression crossed her face when she heard the humming inside, and she whispered, "Honey in there! You just wait! I'll have Sequatchie get me some of that. Then we'll see some honey cakes!"

Leaving the tree, she turned to go back to where she had placed the bucket. Her thoughts were somehow still on her past. She had dreamed of Patrick sometime during the night, but it had not been a clear dream, for Hawk had been part of it, also. As she thought of the tall man she would be marrying in a few hours, she suddenly felt joy rise in her, and deep in her spirit she cried out, *Lord, thank you for sending two wonderful and good men into my life!*

Leaning over to pick up the bucket, she was slightly startled when a voice said, "Well, the bride's up early." Glancing swiftly across the opening she saw Hawk, who had emerged from the small cabin beside the larger one, where he had been staying since he had ceased his wilderness wanderings. A gladness filled her heart as he came to stand beside her, smiling down at her. As she gazed into his eyes, she could not speak for a moment, so happy was she.

"Nothing better for a bride to do than haul water?" Hawk

smiled, lifting one eyebrow. He reached out to put his hand on her shoulder and squeezed it slightly.

Even this light touch gave her pleasure. Elizabeth smiled up at him, thinking, *He's such a fine-looking man, but he doesn't know it. That's a good thing!* He was, she knew, exactly six feet tall and weighed one hundred eighty-five pounds. He was wearing buckskins, as usual, which were stretched tightly across his broad shoulders, and his wrists were thick and strong. His thick hair was as black as any man's she had ever seen. It had a slight wave in it as it fell forward over his forehead, and he had tied it behind in a queue with a rawhide thong. The eyes he put on her were very dark blue, the darkest she had ever seen. She knew also that when he was angry they looked almost black. Impulsively she reached up and placed her hand on his cheek. He had a square face with a strong cleft chin and a straight English nose. His skin was deeply tanned from years of being outdoors, and now he covered her hand with his, humor touching his eyes.

"You've got nothing better to do on your wedding day than to stand around and gawk?"

Elizabeth moved her hand back and shook her head. "You shouldn't see me before the wedding, Hawk. That's bad luck."

"Luck's got nothing to do with us, Elizabeth. I once put a lot of stock in luck and good fortune and things like that," he said quietly. His voice was a soft, pleasant baritone, and he kept his eyes fixed on her as he added, "But it was the Lord that brought us together, not luck."

At Hawk's words Elizabeth smiled, and a strange light came into her eyes.

"Why are you smiling?" he asked.

"It's just that it's so good to hear you talk about the Lord. There were times when I never thought it would happen. I suppose I don't have much faith."

Hawk's eyes clouded for a moment as memories swept over him. Long years of being alone had made him a rather quiet man who lived within his thoughts. He had lost his first wife at the birth of his son, Jacob, and the overwhelming grief that tore at him had driven him away from his home in Williamsburg. He had wandered west to the mountains of the frontier and had survived, becoming a skilled long hunter. Only recently had he returned to the Lord, and as he looked down at Elizabeth he felt a sudden gladness, knowing that his years of loneliness would end today.

Hawk put his hand out and ran it over her locks of blond hair and said nothing. It was strange, he thought, how the two of them did not always need to speak. Somehow she knew what was in his heart, as he knew the thoughts she pondered in hers. He suddenly picked up her hand and held it for a moment, then kissed it.

A flush came to Elizabeth's cheeks. It was a gallant thing for him to do, and one that he did rather awkwardly, but her heart warmed that he had within him what many men lacked—the willingness to show affection. She suddenly reached up, put her hands behind his neck, and pulled his head down. When his lips touched hers, she leaned against him and held him close. Then his arms came around her and she felt the love in his embrace and was glad, for she knew that same love herself.

"That's enough," she said, laughing breathlessly and shoving him back with a hand on his chest.

"Well," Hawk said, his dark eyes dancing, "you can say that now, but you wait till later."

"Oh, really!" Elizabeth teased saucily. "Well, we'll see about that!"

"Where do you want to have the wedding?"

"I think it would be nice to have it outdoors. It's such a beautiful day."

"A mite cold," Hawk suggested.

"That's all right."

"I suppose it is," Hawk said idly. He looked up and seemed to be studying a bird that was winging its way high overhead in the hard blue sky. "If you get cold," he said innocently, "it won't matter. You won't stay that way long."

Elizabeth's mouth dropped open, and she had a desire to giggle but held it back. "You are awful!"

"No, I'm nice," Hawk said. "I'll prove that to you very soon now." But he saw the humor rise in her eyes and was glad that he had found a woman with whom he could share a joke.

"I suppose being married under God's sky in this beautiful place is the best idea, since we don't have a church." He turned to her then, and a hesitation came to him. "Are you sure about this, Elizabeth?"

"Am I sure I want to marry you?"

"I mean, should we get married *now*? We could wait."

Elizabeth knew this was thoughtfulness on Hawk's part. He was really asking her if it was too soon after the death of her first husband. She warmed at his concern and said, "We've been over all this, Jehoshaphat."

Hawk could not help but smile. "You only call me that when you're upset with me."

"Jehoshaphat Spencer. I'll call you that when I'm upset with you. I'll say, 'Jehoshaphat Spencer, you stop that this minute!' "

"Well, we've got a preacher to marry us. Then I'll be taking Paul and Rhoda to Williamsburg so that they can be married, too."

"That's strange, isn't it?" Elizabeth said thoughtfully. "We've got a minister to marry us, but there's nobody to marry the minister."

"It is odd, I suppose." The two talked for a few moments about Paul Anderson and Rhoda Harper. They had come west at the same time as Elizabeth, when Paul was a minister-to-be and Rhoda was a tavern wench. It had been a source of wonder to everyone when Rhoda Harper found God's love and forgiveness and Paul Anderson asked her to be his wife.

"Come along. Let's go see the yearling," Hawk said abruptly.

"All right." She put her bucket down on the path, and the two circled the cabin, holding hands until they reached the small corral built of saplings and larger trunks. Matilda, the fine Jersey cow, looked up and mooed softly, then turned down to nuzzle her calf that was feeding greedily.

"There's something so beautiful about a young animal, Hawk." Elizabeth's lips were open slightly, and her eyes seemed to sparkle as she studied the animals. "I think almost any baby animal is beautiful."

"You ought to see a baby possum if you think that," Hawk grinned. "They look like rats." He watched the calf nursing and then said suddenly, "I'll have to be gone for a few weeks when I take Paul and Rhoda back to Williamsburg to get married." Something troubled him then, and he turned to her, saying, "We could wait until I return."

Elizabeth was surprised. "Don't you want to get married?"

"Well . . . yes, of course I do, but you know what it's like out here. Something could happen and you might be a widow again almost before you're a bride."

"We've talked about all that, Hawk," Elizabeth said quickly. She did not like to be reminded of the dangers that lay on the frontier. She knew they were there, yet still she pushed them into some distant corner of her mind and locked the door. Now she said, "We won't talk about that. We're getting married today, and you're not going to get out of it if I have to take a tomahawk to you!"

"Hold on, woman!" Hawk threw up his hands in mock surrender. "I give up!"

"Then hush! I don't want to hear any more about waiting longer." She reached out and smoothed the fringes on his buckskin shirt and was silent for a moment. Hawk studied her face, which somehow was in repose yet had an expression that puzzled him slightly. She was caught up in a woman's silence, which could mean many things. It was uncharted territory for Hawk Spencer, for though he had had a happy marriage with his first wife, it had been brief and was many years ago. Now as he studied Elizabeth, he wondered at the solemnness that showed in the smooth planes of her face. He had thought at times that this gravity was the shadow of a hidden sadness, but he knew that was not so, for she was a cheerful woman. And now she drew away the curtain of reserve and a teasing gaiety came into her eyes, a provocative challenge.

"You just wait," she whispered. "You're going to be all mine, and you'll never get away!"

"Don't intend to try." Taking Elizabeth's arm, he led her back to where the bucket lay on the path, and as he bent to pick it up, he was suddenly startled by a flash of movement. His reaction was so quick that Elizabeth gasped. He whirled and his hand went to the long knife stuck in his belt. It was in his hand before Elizabeth could move.

"What is it, Hawk?"

Hawk slowly relaxed. "Nothing," he said. "Just a deer."

Elizabeth glanced in the direction of his gesture and saw a beautiful ten-point buck that had stepped out of the timberline. He stood staring at them and seemed to be fearless.

"If I had my musket, I could get him," Hawk said, "but then it's getting harder and harder for me to kill deer."

Elizabeth knew that somehow deer had become a symbol to

Hawk. Twice in the past, at critical times of his life, he had seen a magnificent deer. These special visitations had helped bring him to God, and now his favorite Bible verse was, "As the hart panteth after the water brooks, so panteth my soul after thee, O God."

Hawk stared at the buck, not certain even now if this were a vision from heaven or a flesh-and-blood animal that stood before them. Then suddenly he lifted his voice and said, "I see you! Come on in for breakfast!"

At his call the deer whirled and disappeared into the thickets.

Hawk picked up the bucket and turned to go to the cabin, but Elizabeth said abruptly, "You've been thinking a lot about Jacob, haven't you?"

"Yes, I have." A smile turned up the corners of his lips, and he said, "You know me pretty well, don't you?"

"It will be all right. I know you're worried about him."

"I've given him a hard time, Elizabeth. Harder than any boy should ever have from his father."

The two of them stood there in the middle of the path, and far overhead a wavy "V" formation of Canadian geese beat their wings against the cold air. Hawk watched them for a long time, seemingly engaged by their pilgrimage to the south, but he was actually thinking of his son, Jacob, who was now fifteen years old, almost sixteen. A pain came to Hawk as he realized he had missed out on all of Jacob's boyhood. He had been so distraught by the death of his first wife that he had abandoned his responsibility, leaving Jacob to be raised by his grandparents, James and Esther Spencer. For years the thought of his son being raised without his help had deeply troubled him, but since he had found God so very recently the pain had been even more intense.

"I've been the world's worst father, Elizabeth," he said simply, his dark eyes filled with grief. "I don't think I can ever make up for it."

"Bring him back, Hawk," Elizabeth urged. "When you go to Williamsburg with Paul and Rhoda, go to him. Tell him you're sorry and that you love him."

Hawk Spencer was a man of rough, endurable proportions. There was little fineness about him. The years in the wilderness had made him a man of action. His mind was that way, too, for survival on the frontier meant living a life facing the hardships of that reality.

Each day brought the question, "Can I survive today?" and reaching nighttime was a small victory. After years of living like this, Hawk had somehow absorbed the struggle that ensues among the creatures of the wilderness and among the humans also. He had seen few happy endings to stories like his, and now there was a depression on him as he shook his head, saying, "I've only seen him once since I left shortly after he was born, and he hated me then."

"You're different now. We'll pray about it. God can do great things."

"I know that, but I can't force Jacob to come. That would turn him against me for good."

"With God all things are possible," Elizabeth whispered. She would have said more, but at that moment the door to the cabin opened and Andrew and Sarah came out.

"Ma, what are you doing out here on your wedding day?" Andrew asked. At the age of fourteen he had a stocky build and looked a lot like his mother with the same blond hair but worn short. He had the sparkling light blue eyes of his father. He was wearing buckskin like Hawk, and now he stood before the pair with his sister beside him, smiling at them.

"Hawk, you're not supposed to see the bride on the day of the wedding," Sarah said firmly. Although only eleven years of age, she had the temperament of a much older young woman. Her temperament was, in fact, much like her fiery red hair. She had her mother's pale green eyes and showed promise of being a tall beauty. She was very precocious and wanted her own way. She had it now as she advanced and pushed at Hawk. "You go away now!" she commanded. "You ought to know better!"

Hawk suddenly laughed. He was tremendously fond of Andrew and Sarah. By marrying Elizabeth he somehow felt that some of his lost years would be restored to him. Patrick MacNeal had been one of the best men Hawk had ever known, and as he had lain dying after an Indian attack, Hawk had made a solemn vow: "I'll take care of your family, Patrick...!" He had not known at that moment that he would fall in love with Elizabeth, but it had happened, and he knew somehow that God was in it.

Elizabeth turned and walked into the cabin, talking in an animated fashion with Sarah, who turned back over her shoulder to say, "You stay away, Hawk! You hear me, now?"

Hawk laughed and shook his head in wonder. "Andrew," he said as they walked away together, "you always have to obey a woman when there's a wedding in the air!"

Andrew MacNeal nodded happily. Whatever Hawk Spencer said was gospel to him, for he idolized the tall long hunter. He had loved his father dearly, and after his death had suffered greatly, as if an enormous emptiness occupied his whole heart and mind. But now, as he looked up at Hawk, although he said nothing, he was thinking how good it was of God to give him another father.

Two Become One

Two

Zeke Taylor tilted his chair back against the wall of his cabin and watched as two scrawny pigs fought over a rattlesnake they had managed to kill. The shoats were rather pitiful creatures with sharp backs and beady eyes now reddened with anger. One of them had the snake by the head, another by the tail, and with their hooves braced, they were pulling backward with all of their strength, grunting and squealing shrilly.

Taylor had watched the two kill the snake by stamping on it with their sharp hooves, but now he tired of the spectacle. Leaning over, he picked up a chunk of wood and heaved it at the struggling pigs, yelling, "Get out of here with that snake!" The stick struck one of the pigs on the snout, and with a startled squeal, the animal dropped his end of the dead snake and backed away. The other fled across the flat ground in front of the cabin, disappearing in a thicket, pursued by his companion, both of them squealing in a high-pitched fashion.

"Ugly pigs! Ain't good for nothin'!" Taylor muttered. Pulling a knife from his belt, he began shaving long, thin curls from the cedar stick he held. He never whittled anything in particular or made anything useful, but whenever he was at ease, he made a pile of curled, fragrant shavings.

"Ezekiel? It's almost time to go. Come on and put on your suit."

Taylor did not take his eyes from the cedar stick. He was of average height with a large paunch from years of heavy drinking, and now he muttered in a surly fashion, "Ain't goin'."

"Why, you've got to go, Ezekiel." Iris Taylor, at thirty-six, was fifteen years younger than her husband. She had dark hair and blue eyes and a thin face that retained some trace of a youthful beauty. Her loss of two sons and a difficult life with a drunkard for a husband had pared away all excess flesh and had quenched her spirit. At one time she would have taken the rebuke quietly enough, for Taylor had proved to be a brutal husband, often abusing her physically. Now as she stood there wearing a faded blue dress with white flowers, she hesitated, then said, "I wish you would go, Ezekiel. After all, they're neighbors."

Amanda Taylor, aged thirteen, had come to the door, standing behind her mother. She was a tall girl for her age, with long, straight, very dark brown hair and large brown eyes. She stared at her father, thinking, *He won't go because he hates Hawk.*

In truth, Zeke Taylor did despise Hawk Spencer, for the long hunter, on the trip from Virginia, had confronted Taylor after the shiftless man had beaten his wife and daughter. Taylor had drawn a knife on him, which Spencer had simply taken away from him, and then holding it to the throat of Taylor he had said, "If I ever hear of you touching your wife or daughter again, I'll take your scalp! I won't kill you, but you'll have a hard time without anything but skin on top of your head."

The memory was a raw wound in Zeke Taylor, and now as he looked up with his sullen muddy brown eyes, he said briefly, "You all go on. I ain't goin'."

"Please, Ezekiel. We need to be friends with our neighbors."

"Did you hear me, woman? You can go if you want to! Shut your mouth and stop naggin' me!"

"All right, Ezekiel." Iris nervously stepped back inside the cabin and saw that Amanda's face was pale. Going over to the young woman, she put her arm around her, whispering, "We'll have to go by ourselves, Amanda, but we'll have a good time."

"All right, Ma. I'm ready."

"And you look real pretty, too." Iris had worked long and hard making a dress for Amanda out of some material Elizabeth MacNeal had given her. It was a lightweight plum-colored homespun wool, with flecks of pink running through it. The dress had a high collar, long sleeves, a loose-fitting bodice, and a full skirt that came to the ankles. Black lace decorated the edges of the collar and the wrists of the sleeves. Reaching out, Iris stroked the girl's glossy brown hair and said with a half smile, "One of these days I'll be going to your wedding."

Amanda ducked her head. "I don't know who'd have me, Ma."

"Now, don't you talk like that, Amanda! You're a fine-looking young lady! By the time you get to be a full-grown woman, why, young fellas will be lined up to get to come courtin'."

Amanda did not answer. Her spirit had almost been broken by the brutal treatment she had received from her father. It was manifested in her every move. She walked with her head down as if she were afraid to look up, and her shoulders were often hunched as if she were expecting a blow. Still, on this special day she did look fresh and pretty, and now she managed a smile. "All right, Ma, if you say so."

"Come along. We'll have to hurry or we'll be late."

As the two left the cabin, Iris said, "We'll come back as soon as the wedding's over, Ezekiel." She received no answer, for her husband simply sat there adding to the pile of thin, curling shavings. Turning, the two hurried off, walking along the path that led to the eastern part of the settlement.

As soon as they were gone, Zeke stood up and stared after them. He slipped the knife back in his belt and walked aimlessly around the littered yard. A speckled chicken got in his way, and he swore at it, giving it a kick that sent it squawking through the air. This gave him some satisfaction, and he growled, "Get out of my way, chicken, or I'll wring your neck!"

As he wandered over the small farm, he thought back to the time when Hawk Spencer had held the knife to his throat and threatened to scalp him if he mistreated his wife or daughter again. It had gone hard with Zeke, for something in Spencer's dark blue eyes had warned him that he would do exactly what he said.

"Man can't do what he wants with his own family! Country's come to a pretty pass!" he muttered. A thought came to him and his muddy eyes lightened for a moment. Glancing around, he stepped more rapidly until he reached the woods that lay only a few yards past the front door of his house. He paused beside a hollow tree. Reaching carefully inside to the length of his arm, he grunted with satisfaction and pulled a brown jug from the hole.

"Now this is somethin'-like," he said with satisfaction. He had not been drinking so much lately. As a matter of fact, he had not had a drink for over three weeks. But something about the wedding sat ill with him. He was irritable and angry, and as he lifted the jug, a baleful light gave his eyes a hard glint. He swallowed the whiskey and stomped his feet as the fiery alcohol hit his empty stomach. Expelling a huge breath, he stood there for a moment blinking his eyes as the raw whiskey bit at him.

Taking a deep breath, he thought again of the knife at his throat, and the memory was as bitter as gall. "One of these days we'll see, Spencer! It'll be you that gets scalped and not me!"

———————

The small cabin that Hawk had made his home since coming back from his wanderings was no more than ten by twelve. The single room of the structure had a dirt floor, and only one window beside the door allowed in light and air. The furnishings were sparse and rough looking, handmade by Hawk himself. A table and two chairs were placed in the center of the room. A plain worktable with a shelf hung on the wall, while above, tin cups, plates, and a few pots and pans were suspended on pegs driven into the logs. One small bed was fastened to the back wall, bearing a corn-shuck mattress. The worktable was placed next to a small fireplace in which a fire crackled continuously, and over it dangled a cast-iron pot for heating water and cooking his meals.

Sequatchie was standing in the middle of the room dressed in full Cherokee chief regalia. At forty years old, this tall Cherokee had smooth bronze skin and dark eyes that revealed nothing unless he chose to let them do so. He had the typical square jaw and high cheekbones of his race. His face was long, but he had a broad forehead and an aquiline nose. His head was bald except for the topknot that hung down his back. The hair itself was jet black, and now there was a light of humor in his obsidian eyes as he studied Hawk Spencer, who was getting dressed.

Sequatchie had been Hawk's teacher in the wilderness, and now as he watched the tall man pulling off his buckskins and holding up the white shirt as if it were some strange, rather dangerous object, Sequatchie thought of how the two of them had become blood brothers. Sequatchie had saved Hawk's life, nursing him back to health with the aid of his mother, Awenasa, and he had never regretted it.

Andrew MacNeal stood with his back to the wall, also watching Spencer. "I've never seen you in a suit before, Hawk," he said.

"Well, you won't see much when you do."

Hawk slipped on the white shirt and then pulled on a pair of black broadcloth trousers. He picked up a string tie and stood before the small mirror and struggled to make it presentable. "I don't see why a man has to wear this outfit to get married."

"Why don't you just wear your buckskins?" Sequatchie asked. "It's *your* wedding."

"No, it's not. As far as weddings are concerned, as I've told Andy, a man doesn't have a great deal to say about it."

He finally completed tying the tie just as the door opened and three men walked in. The room seemed very small then as Hawk stepped back to make room for them. One of them was Paul Anderson, his childhood friend, who had followed him from Williamsburg. At no more than five ten, Anderson was the smallest man in the cabin, with sandy brown hair and light blue-green eyes. Now he said, with a mischievous sparkle in his eye, "I thought you would have run away before this, Hawk."

"Now, don't you start on me, Paul!" Hawk warned.

"All bridegrooms are fair game."

The speaker was George Stevens, a tall man, over six two, with gray eyes and reddish hair turning gray at the temples. He had come to Watauga as part of the Regulators who had left North Carolina, and he, along with his wife, Deborah, and their daughter, Abigail, had become close friends with the MacNeals and with Hawk.

"I thought you'd be on my side, George," Hawk said.

William Bean laughed aloud. A stocky man with a look of rough durability, Bean had founded the settlement at Watauga. Elizabeth had stayed with the Beans while Hawk had built the cabin, and now William said with a glint of humor in his gray eyes, "A bridegroom don't have any friends, boy."

Paul Anderson could see the respect that this leader of the settlement had for Hawk Spencer and was glad of it. "You look very nice, Hawk. I'd forgotten how you looked in regular clothes."

"I'm doing it to please Elizabeth. It's not my idea."

A touch of amusement illuminated the ebony eyes of Sequatchie, although he did not smile. "Cherokee women try to please the men," he intoned. "Not the other way around."

All the men laughed, and Paul said easily, "Well, I think people are basically the same everywhere."

"I'm glad we have a minister here to do the marrying." William Bean nodded toward Paul. "What we need is a church and a full-time preacher."

Paul shook his head and smiled briefly. He had heard this argument before. Both Bean and Stevens had tried to get him to stay and form a church, but he had felt the need to go with Sequatchie to preach to the Cherokee. Now he said, "Let's not argue about that again. This is Hawk's day."

"I wish you'd ask around in Williamsburg when you go with Miss Rhoda to get married," Stevens said. "Maybe you can find us a preacher there."

"I'll ask around," Paul agreed.

"It's not fair," Hawk complained. "I've had to take all the ragging from every man in Watauga about getting married, and you're sneaking off to Williamsburg. We won't even be able to give you a shiveree."

"That's why I did it," Paul grinned. "I *hate* those things." He grew serious then. "It's almost time. Hawk, you're new in your walk with the Lord. Would it be all right with you if we prayed for you to be the best husband"—his eyes then fell on Andrew and he smiled—"and the best father in all of Watauga?"

"I need it," Hawk said.

He stood there quietly while the men gathered around him. They put their hands on his shoulders, and Paul Anderson prayed a fervent prayer that Hawk would find the way of the Lord in raising his family on the frontier. After the amen, Paul took a deep breath and said, "Are you ready, Hawk?"

Hawk rubbed his chin and managed a slight grin. "Well, I'm as ready as I'll ever be. Come on." The men left as Hawk plunged out of the door, and William Bean said to his neighbor, "George, that's going to be a good family."

As soon as he was outside, Paul said to Andrew, "You go get your mother and bring her to her bridegroom."

"Sure, Mr. Paul." Andrew darted off, and the men made their way to the stream where the wedding was to take place.

———

Elizabeth's cabin swarmed with women. Her daughter, Sarah, was there, her eyes bright with excitement. Sarah stood by Rhoda Harper, Paul Anderson's bride-to-be. Deborah and Abigail Stevens were there, as were Lydia Bean and Charlotte Robertson, the wife of James Robertson.

The room was filled with laughter, and Elizabeth stood in the center of it, somewhat nervous but happy that she had such good friends. She had on a dress she had made herself out of a homespun wool dyed a very light misty green color. The square neckline had white ruching along the edges, the sleeves ended at the wrist with a small ruffle, and the tight-fitting bodice with embroidered white flowers decorating the front ended at the waist in a "V." The skirt was very full and also had white ruching and embroidery along the bottom edge.

"Rhoda, you're going to stand up with me," she said, reaching out to grab the woman's arm. "If I faint, you'll have to hold me up."

Rhoda Harper was, in one sense, completely different from any of the other women in the room. She was now thirty-six and had led a very difficult life, but her years as a tavern woman had not hardened her. She was very attractive with her dark brown hair and striking dark eyes, and now she reached over and hugged Elizabeth, saying, "You won't faint. You'll be just fine."

"What about your wedding, Rhoda?" Deborah Stevens asked. She was a shorter woman with thick sandy brown hair and greenish eyes. She and her husband, George, were leaders in the settlement, and Deborah had grown to love Elizabeth MacNeal and her children deeply. She had also learned to accept Rhoda, although the young woman's background had been a shock to her at first.

Rhoda turned to Mrs. Stevens and said quietly, "I wish you could all be there. I'll be a little bit lonely."

"Don't say that," Elizabeth warned, "or we'll all go back to Williamsburg with you." She knew this was impossible, of course, for the journey was long and arduous. "I wish we *could* go, Rhoda, but you'll soon be back with a brand-new husband." She giggled and put her hand over her lips, whispering, "We'll have to break them in together."

A knock at the door caught their attention. Rhoda was glad for the interruption. She had done her best to take part in the happy festivities, but despite her cheerful demeanor, she was not happy.

She had been filled with joy when Paul Anderson had asked her to be his wife, but now it seemed all wrong. He had always been a good man and now was a minister, while her own life had been dark and stained with the evils that come of a young woman growing up in a tavern, subject to the lust of brutal men. She was unsure about marrying Paul and felt completely unworthy but knew that she loved him and could only hope she would make him the best wife possible. Moving to the door, she opened it and smiled at once. "Why, Iris and Amanda, please come in."

Elizabeth hurried over to embrace the two. "How nice you both look," she said. "I'm so glad you could come."

"Did Zeke come with you?" Lydia Bean asked, her eyes sharp. She knew everything about everyone in the Watauga settlement, this Lydia Bean, and now she saw with one glance at Amanda Taylor's face that there had been trouble.

"No, he . . . he couldn't come," Iris said with a slight hesitation.

Elizabeth, seeing her pain, said quickly, "Well, I'm sorry about that, but I'm glad that you and Amanda could come. Don't you look nice, Amanda!"

Sarah MacNeal and Abigail Stevens had done their best to be good friends to Amanda. They were all close to the same age, and now the three of them drew together in a huddle. Amanda was shy, and it was Sarah MacNeal who said, "Come on. Let's go pick some flowers."

"Flowers in the winter?" Abigail said. "There aren't any."

"Oh, that's right. I forgot," Sarah said. "Well, we'll just have to have a wedding without flowers."

The three went outside while the women were helping Elizabeth, and Abigail, at once, began talking about weddings.

"I want a big wedding," Sarah said. Her fiery red hair had been tamed, and her pale green eyes glistened with excitement. "I want there to be songs and music and bridesmaids."

Abigail Stevens was the oldest of the three at the age of fourteen, and stunningly beautiful. She had thick honey-brown hair that fell in waves down her back, gray-green eyes, and a creamy complexion. "I want to wear a gorgeous dress when I get married, and I want a handsome man in a nice suit of clothes."

Sarah's eyes were full of mischief. "You'll only be happy if that's my brother, Andrew."

Abigail gave her a startled look, then flushed. "You shouldn't say that, Sarah!"

"Why not? You know you're sweet on him."

"I am not!"

Amanda stood back from the other two, smiling slightly, enjoying their fun and wishing she could enter into it. Finally Sarah turned and said, "What kind of wedding do you want, Amanda?"

For a moment Amanda was silent, and then she said very quietly, "It doesn't matter as long as he loves me and treats me nice."

The silence deepened, and Sarah exchanged a quick glance with Abigail. Both girls knew that Amanda had been abused by her father, for they had seen the bruises on her face before Hawk had put a stop to it. Sarah said quickly, "Well, I'm sure you'll get a nice husband." The girls entered the cabin together and for the next fifteen minutes watched as the older women fussed over Elizabeth. Finally there was a knock at the door and they all turned as Rhoda went to open it. Andrew stood outside, his hair pasted down with water.

"I think everyone's ready if you are, Ma," he said, looking at his mother.

At once Deborah Stevens said, "Come. Let's pray for Elizabeth." She said a quick prayer as the women gathered around, and then Elizabeth lifted her head and her eyes met those of her son.

"Give me just a minute with Andrew and Sarah, please."

Deborah Stevens hustled the women out of the room, and when the door closed, Elizabeth went to her children, who stood before her watching her carefully. She reached down and took each of their hands. "This is your last chance, Andrew, and you, Sarah. We must be one on this. I won't marry unless you are sure that you want to have Hawk for a father. Are you sure?"

"Of course I'm sure!" Sarah said. She hesitated, and then a worried look came into her eyes. "But will it be all right if we talk about our pa? I mean our real pa?"

"Of course," Elizabeth said instantly. "Hawk loved your father very much."

"It'll be all right, Sarah," Andrew said, patting his sister's shoulder. He looked at his mother and smiled. "It'll be great to have a pa again—and I know you've been lonesome, Ma."

Elizabeth suddenly leaned forward and kissed his cheek, and then did the same for Sarah. "Come now," she said. "It's time."

Stepping outside the door, they joined the women. They made a procession to the stream that Sequatchie and some of the men had cleaned out. It was free of brush, and now the brook murmured softly as the men and the women and the young people all met. Elizabeth looked up to see Hawk's eyes on her. She smiled as she met his gaze, and Andrew led her to him. He handed his mother to Hawk and whispered, "I love you, Mother." He looked at Hawk and said, "I love you, too."

Hawk looked away from Elizabeth long enough to smile at Andrew and then reached over and nodded toward Sarah, who was watching with large eyes.

Overhead the sky was a canopy of blue. Patches of clouds drifted along like white galleons on an azure sea. The day had turned warmer. The smell of the trees, the earth, and the babbling of the brook made it an idyllic setting.

Hawk held Elizabeth's hand. It seemed very small, but it was warm and strong, and as the two faced each other, he saw in her all that he had ever wanted from a woman. He knew there was a fire in her that made her lovely and brought out the rich and strong qualities of a spirit that sometimes remained hidden behind the cool reserve of her lips. She was his idea of a complete woman, and now as he stood there he felt the strange things a man feels when he looks upon beauty and knows it will be his.

As for Elizabeth, she felt secure. The tall man beside her represented safety and security and love, all of which she longed for. His face fell into sharp planes, and the strength that lay there drew her to him like a magnet. Her reverie was broken as Paul Anderson began to speak the words of the marriage ceremony. "Dearly beloved, we are gathered here today in the sight of God to join together this man and this woman in holy matrimony. . . ."

There under the open sky, Elizabeth MacNeal pledged her life to Hawk Spencer and knew the joy that comes to a woman who not only loves a man but is loved by him.

Departure

Three

The walnut bed made out of trees from Elizabeth's own land dominated the small bedroom, its four posters nearly touching the low ceiling. Hawk had made it for her for a wedding present. He had polished the dark, rich wood until it glowed with a warmth, almost as if it were alive. He had fastened it together to the side rails with ironwood pegs and had strung rawhides across the lower section of the rails so that they were as tense as a bowstring. On top of this lay a mattress made of light canvas and stuffed with corn shucks.

Elizabeth now lay snugly under the heavy blanket and the quilt she had brought with her all the way from Boston. Light crept in through the single window in the room, its feeble rays illuminating Hawk's face as he lay on his back beside her. Impulsively she reached out to touch his cheek but decided, *No, I mustn't wake him up.*

Even though the room was cold, she was deliciously warm under the bedcovers and intensely aware of the strength of Hawk's arm as it pressed against her. He had thrown it over her in his sleep, and now she reached up and held on to it with a light touch. Suddenly he turned his head toward her, and even in the early-morning darkness, Elizabeth could see the gleam in his dark blue eyes.

"You just can't keep away from me, can you?"

Elizabeth flushed and shoved at his arm, but he rolled over and pinioned her easily. His hair was ruffled, and a slight smile turned up the corners of his lips. He reached out and stroked the side of her cheek, then let his hand run down her neck and then down her arm. "You know what?" he whispered.

"What?"

"I've decided to keep you on. You prove to be a very satisfactory wife, thus far."

"Oh, Hawk!" Elizabeth turned to face him and put her hand on his neck. She felt the strength in the corded muscles and the skin toughened by countless days in the sun. A warm sense of possession came over her, and she reached up and pulled his head over and lifted her own so that her soft lips met his. She felt his arms go around her and reveled in the love and sense of protection. She felt almost like a child in his strong embrace, and her lips had a pressure of their own as she returned his kiss.

Suddenly she pulled back and shoved at his chest. "That's enough of that!"

"That's your opinion. It's not mine," Hawk murmured. He pulled at her again, but she shoved him over as she pulled away. "It's getting late."

Hawk turned over and glanced out the window at the sunrise that was beginning to touch the mountaintops with fire. "I don't think it's all that late."

Elizabeth caught the look in his face and said suddenly, "I like being married to you."

"So do I."

"Of course, it's only been a week." She smiled and added, "Say something sweet to me."

Hawk thought hard for a moment and then said, "Sugar candy."

Elizabeth laughed and slapped at him. "You are ridiculous!"

"A man in love is apt to be foolish."

"Are you really in love?"

"Why, I told you so, didn't I, when we got married? I thought that settled it."

Elizabeth stared at him. "Settled what?" she demanded.

"That I loved you. I didn't figure you'd ever want to hear it again. I figured that would do for at least forty or fifty years."

"Oh, you're impossible!" Elizabeth pouted. As a matter of fact, her demure way of pouting made her even more irresistible, and she surrendered as he kissed her and ran his hand down the back of her hair, then down the small of her back.

They lay there for a while, and then Hawk said, "You know what?"

"What?"

"The Bible says that when a man marries he's not supposed to do any work for a year. He's just supposed to stay home and keep his wife happy."

Elizabeth stared at him. "You made that up!"

"I did not! It's in the book of Leviticus or Exodus somewhere. I got it marked. I'll show it to you after breakfast."

"Well, if you don't let me up we won't have any breakfast."

Hawk reluctantly rose and got out of bed. He reached for the hunting shirt, pulled it over his head, and then stopped. "I should have shaved before I put this shirt on."

Elizabeth had slipped out of bed and was sitting before the small mirror brushing her hair. "Well, take it off again."

"Too much trouble," Hawk shrugged. "Nobody will be seeing us on the road anyhow except bears and wolves, maybe a hostile Indian."

Elizabeth looked up, anxiety on her face. "Are you really expecting trouble from the Indians?"

"Not really. Especially with Sequatchie along." He ran his fingers through his hair and began to pace the room anxiously. There was not much room, and his big form seemed to make it even smaller.

Elizabeth had already grown very conscious of Hawk's moods in the short time since they had been married. She had always been a sensitive woman, and now she looked up and saw that his face was tense. "What's wrong, Hawk?"

"Wrong? Why, nothing's wrong."

Elizabeth rose and went over to him. She put her hands on his chest and said, "Tell me."

Hawk covered her hands with his own and chewed on his lower lip thoughtfully. "I guess I'm worried about Jacob."

"I thought that might be it."

"It's almost his birthday. He'll be sixteen—no longer a boy." He stroked her hands and seemed to find comfort in them, but his eyes were troubled. "I don't know what to say to him, Elizabeth. I've treated him shamefully. If he never speaks to me, it will be just what I deserve."

"You mustn't think like that. You were wrong, and you confessed it to God, and now you need to make it right with Jacob."

"I know God's forgiven me," Hawk shrugged, "but I'm not sure that Jacob has. It's asking a lot of a sixteen-year-old to accept a father who abandoned him."

"We'll pray every day that God will work in Jacob's heart. He's your son," Elizabeth said firmly, "and God is able."

The two stood there for a moment, and Hawk put his arms around her, saying quietly, "I don't deserve a wife like you." He thought for a moment and then smiled. "No one else does, either, so I'm glad I got you."

He bent to kiss her, and she drew back, slapping at him playfully. "That's enough. I've got to make breakfast. I'm going to make you the best breakfast you've ever had."

She left the bedroom, followed by Hawk. He built a fire quickly while Elizabeth began to gather the ingredients to make breakfast.

Hawk went over to stand behind her, put his arms around her, and whispered, "I hate to leave you, Elizabeth." At that moment a knock at the door sounded, and immediately it opened. Sequatchie entered and stood still, looking at the two. He had spent the night in Hawk's old hut, and now he stood gravely studying the pair. Hawk was never quite sure what lay behind Sequatchie's impassive features. Most Indians could put on a poker face, and Sequatchie accomplished this better than most. Now Hawk thought he saw a gleam of amusement in the dark eyes of his friend.

"We can leave if you're ready," Sequatchie said.

"No, you're not leaving now," Elizabeth said, pulling away from Hawk. "You've got to have a good breakfast first."

The two men sat down, and Elizabeth, in her determined fashion, threw herself into the task of preparing the meal. Huge slabs of bacon were soon crackling and sputtering in the frying pan over the fire; potatoes and eggs were sizzling in bacon grease; corn cakes and fresh sourdough bread, which Elizabeth had prepared the night before, filled the room with the scent of baking along with the strong aroma of coffee. She began putting the food on the table, setting out fresh butter and honey for the bread.

They were halfway through the meal when the Stevens family arrived with Andrew and Sarah. The two youngsters had been staying with them for a week so that Hawk and Elizabeth could have, more or less, a honeymoon. They had seen the children every day, however, and now Elizabeth said, "Come in. There's plenty to go around."

The Stevenses sat down at once, as did Andrew and Sarah. The table was crowded, but a warm, pleasant air filled the cabin. As

Hawk ate, he thought how wonderful it was to have a family and good friends.

Andrew had plopped himself down next to Hawk, and now he said urgently, "Pa, please let me go to Williamsburg with you."

"Now, Andrew, we've been over that—"

"I know, Pa, but I would love to see it again."

"I'll take you some other time, son. Somebody's got to stay and take care of your mother and your sister." He turned to the boy and said seriously, "You have to grow up early out here. I know you're only fourteen, but you'll be the man of the house while I'm gone. Don't you understand that?"

Hawk's steady eyes held Andrew. The boy suddenly felt proud that he would be in charge, and he said, "All right, Pa."

"You're not bossin' me, Andrew!"

Sarah, always ready to defend her rights, glared at her brother from across the table. Her fiery red hair caught the gleams of the sun, and she stared at Andrew wickedly.

"Now, Sarah. You listen to your pa," Elizabeth said. "If he says that Andy's to take care of us, then that's the way it will be."

"I don't need any taking care of!"

The argument went on until the sound of approaching horses caught Hawk's attention. He got up and looked out the door, then said, "It's Paul and Rhoda."

Elizabeth got up at once and met Rhoda with a hug as she entered the door. "I wish I could be there for your wedding, Rhoda."

Rhoda whispered, "I wish you could, too." But there was something in her eyes that troubled Elizabeth; however, she said nothing and urged the pair to sit down and have breakfast.

Finally, when the meal was finished, Elizabeth said, "Come back in the bedroom. I have a present for you, Rhoda. Just for the new bride."

Rhoda followed Elizabeth, who showed her into the small bedroom, then shut the door. She waited until Elizabeth went to a chest, opened it up, and came back with a package wrapped in brown paper and tied with a red ribbon.

"Here, this is my wedding present to you."

"Oh, you shouldn't have done it! You've done so much for me already." Rhoda opened the package, and when the paper fell away, she gasped at the beautifully embroidered white nightgown. "Oh, it's so beautiful! Did you make it yourself?"

"Yes, I did, and I want you to have it."

Rhoda clasped the nightgown to her breast, and suddenly her eyes were pools of doubt. "I just don't think I can do it, Elizabeth."

Elizabeth knew at last that Rhoda had to speak. The troubles that weighed heavily on the young woman were obvious, and she said quietly, "I think you need to tell me what's bothering you, Rhoda."

"It's . . . it's Paul," she said, her head downcast as she stared at the gift she felt unworthy to accept.

"What about Paul?" Elizabeth urged. "Is he troubled about something?"

"No, it's not really him. He seems so happy. It's me, Elizabeth." Rhoda lifted her hand in a futile gesture, then dropped it again. "You know what my life has been. I'm just not a . . . a fit wife for a preacher."

Elizabeth had suspected that this was what had been troubling Rhoda, and now she went closer to her and said, "Here. Sit down on the bed. I want to talk to you, Rhoda, and I want you to listen very carefully." When the young woman sat down, Elizabeth began by saying, "We are all unworthy before God, every one of us. The Scriptures say there's not a just man on earth that doeth good and sinneth not—and that means women, too. And the book of James says, 'Whosoever shall keep the whole law yet offend in one point, the same is guilty of all.' Do you understand that?"

"No. What does it mean?"

"It means that some of us commit what people call the worst sins, but others commit those that aren't so looked down on in society. But in the sight of God, when we sin, no matter whether the sin is *bad* or *not so bad*, we've all broken God's law. So someone who commits murder is a lawbreaker, and someone who says an unkind thing about his neighbor is a lawbreaker. Do you see? We classify sins, but God doesn't do that."

"I . . . I don't understand. Aren't some sins worse than others?"

"I suppose some sins bring more disaster into our lives. If you murder someone, you're liable to get hanged for it. If you only gossip about them, or are unkind, that won't happen. But in God's sight, it all comes from a heart not right with Him. It's all lawbreaking and must be confessed to Him so it can be forgiven."

For a long time Elizabeth sat there speaking quietly to her friend.

She quoted many verses about God's love and abundant mercy to forgive and encouraged her. Finally she said, "Rhoda, remember. It was Mary Magdalene, a scarlet woman, no more than a prostitute, who brought the good news of the resurrection of our Lord Jesus to His disciples. Think about that."

As Rhoda listened, a ray of hope began to appear in her eyes, and she looked up, her hands clasped tightly together. "Oh, Elizabeth, I do so want to be a good wife to Paul."

"You will be."

"But all the men—"

"Don't think about that. Shut the door on it. If the devil comes to you and reminds you of your past, tell him he'll have to go to Jesus. You've given everything to the Lord. You truly are clean and forgiven now. He doesn't remember what is under the blood."

Rhoda's eyes became misty. "Can I really do that, Elizabeth?"

"Yes!" Elizabeth said firmly. "We'll pray that God will make you the best wife who ever lived—that you and Paul will have a wonderful family, and that you will never again go back and dig up these old things from your past." She bowed her head and prayed fervently, "Dear God, I pray you keep this woman safe. You have cleansed her as white as the snow through your blood, Lord Jesus. And now give her strength to be a good wife to Paul, who will serve you as your minister. In the name of Jesus, I ask it."

Rhoda reached over and clutched Elizabeth tightly. "Thank you, Elizabeth," she said in a choking voice. "I . . . I think I can do it now."

It took some time for Rhoda to compose herself, but finally the two women went out and Elizabeth saw that the men had been waiting for her. She went over to Hawk and said, "You take good care of these two, and of yourself."

"I will." Hawk looked at Andrew. "Son, remember. Take care of your mother and your sister while I'm gone."

"I will, Pa."

They stepped outside and Hawk, Sequatchie, Paul, and Rhoda mounted the horses. Rhoda Harper looked at Paul, who smiled at her, and then she turned again to Elizabeth. "Good-bye, Elizabeth . . . and thank you."

As they rode away from the small homestead, Paul finally asked, "What did you and Elizabeth talk about?"

Rhoda smiled mysteriously. "She was just giving me some sound advice on how to be a good wife."

Paul urged his horse closer to hers. He reached over and took her hand and held it for a moment. His plain face was wreathed with smiles, and a gleam of happiness sparkled in his eyes. "You're going to be the best wife a man ever had! You'll see, Rhoda. . . !"

Sixteenth Birthday

Four

*J*acob Spencer woke up with a violent start. He had been dreaming something and could not remember what it was—except that it was very bad. He shook his head and passed a trembling hand in front of his eyes. For some time he lay there, half opening his eyes as the familiar shapes of his room came into focus. He stared at the white ceiling, which sloped from one end of the room down to meet two small windows along the back wall. The dark blue and burgundy curtains stirred gently as the frigid morning air seeped into the small upstairs bedroom. He studied the burgundy wallpaper, decorated with tiny figures of animals in dark blues and greens, and his eyes swept around the room and took in the familiar images—the hardwood floor covered with the rag rug his grandmother had made, the oak tester bed that dominated the room, the walnut dressing table covered with a snowy white quilting, and the Chippendale easy chair covered with dark green horsehair.

"Sixteen years old."

Jacob spoke the words aloud and stretched, his lean body pushing against the top of the heavy bed frame, and thought about how he had looked forward to this day. Somehow, when he was just a child, he had decided that when he got to be sixteen he would be fully grown, a man, and had even announced this to his grandparents. His grandfather had smiled at him and said, "Sixteen seems a long way, Jacob, but it'll be here before you know it." Well, now it was here, and he tried to examine his feelings. From downstairs he could hear the sounds of people moving, and from the window, which was cracked open, despite the cold, he heard the clatter of horsehooves as a wagon rumbled by on the street outside.

Finally he threw the quilts back and shivered at the bite of the cold air. Quickly he dressed, putting on a pair of heavy wool pants and a cotton chambray shirt. He moved over to the washstand, added fresh water, bent over, and bubbled and spewed as he washed his face with the icy water. Then he straightened up and looked into the brass-rimmed mirror fastened to the wall beside the washstand. What he saw was a carbon copy of his father. His grandfather had told him that he looked almost exactly as his father had when he was a young man. He had the same dark, wavy hair and dark blue eyes that his grandmother had told him about. At the age of sixteen he was only an inch short of six feet. He was lean and wiry and had the same cleft in his chin that his father had.

He had noticed all the traits he shared with his father when Hawk had come last year to visit. Every moment of that single visit was etched in his memory. He remembered when his father had left again and had not offered to take Jacob with him. He remembered weeping bitter tears as he watched from his window that day. He had not wept since then, however, but the thought of his father always brought a mixture of anger and regret.

A knock at the door startled him. Whirling, he said, "Come in, Grandma."

The door opened and Esther Spencer stepped inside. She was a small woman of fifty-nine, and her brown hair was now streaked with gray. She had light blue eyes and a pleasant smile, as always. "Breakfast is ready, Jacob. But first I came to wish you a happy birthday."

"Thank you, Grandma." Jacob went over and put his arms around her. She was so small, she seemed almost like a child. He leaned over and kissed her cheek and squeezed her. "Sixteen years old! A full-grown man!"

"Well, we'll see about that. It's not a matter of years, but how you behave." Esther tried to be firm, but it was impossible for her to be very strict with Jacob. She reached up and stroked his cheek, murmuring, "You'll be shaving soon."

"I already have," Jacob grinned. "Last week. Feel the stubble?"

"My, think of that!"

"I think I'll raise a beard that will come down over my belt, like a mountain man."

As soon as he said this, he thought of his father, and some of the light went out of his eyes. Nevertheless, he pushed the feeling away. "I'm so hungry I could eat a horse!"

"We don't have horse this morning, but how about flapjacks and ham?"

"Sounds good. Let's go get started."

When they went down the stairs and into the dining room, they found James Spencer already seated at the table. He was sixty-one now, and his hair was silver. Still, there was a commanding presence about him. He was one of those men who, as he grew older, did not lose his physical strength nor his mental alertness. "Well, sixteen years old, eh? Happy birthday, Jacob!"

"Thank you, Grandpa." Jacob took his seat and waited until after his grandfather had asked the blessing. Then he reached over, speared three flapjacks, and plopped them down on his plate. As he was cutting them up, his grandfather lifted one eyebrow.

"With your hearty appetite, I doubt you will ever starve to death," he said, smiling.

Picking up the jug of maple syrup, Jacob poured a liberal stream on the flapjacks until all were soaked. He stuffed a forkful into his mouth, then picked up a chunk of ham and bit it off.

"I see your manners haven't improved," James said wryly. "Don't you want to cut that ham up into pieces?"

"Nope! It all goes to the same place, Grandpa. It doesn't make much difference how it gets there."

The two older people watched Jacob eat with gusto, and finally Esther asked, "Are you excited about the party this afternoon?"

"I guess so."

"What about your friend Tom Denton?" James asked. "Will he be there?"

"Oh yes. He'll be there."

Esther winked at her husband and then asked idly, "What about his sister, Annabelle? Will she be coming, too?"

Jacob glanced up, and seeing the smiles on the faces of both grandparents, he swallowed, and his face grew a dusky red. "Oh, I don't know. Maybe she will be."

Seeing the boy's embarrassment, Esther quickly turned the conversation to another subject. She thought of Annabelle Denton and for some reason was disturbed. For some time she had known of her grandson's attachment to Annabelle, the sister of his best friend,

Thomas Denton. The two had prominent parents, Edward and Phoebe. Edward was a wealthy planter with a fine house in Williamsburg, and his wife was a sweet-tempered lady but fully as determined as her husband to hang on to their money and spend it on the finer things of life.

Esther sipped the strong coffee from a delicate blue china cup. She did not like coffee very much, and as she studied the tiny scene painted around the edge of the cup, her mind was on Annabelle Denton. She looked up at her grandson and, as often happened, was struck again at how strongly Jacob resembled his father.

He looks exactly like Josh did when he was sixteen, she thought as her mind went back over the years. She remembered her son's sixteenth birthday. It had been in this very house, and he had had breakfast in this very room. With a start she realized that he had sat in the very chair that Jacob sat in now. All the similarities sent a shiver through her. She thought of Jehoshaphat, and, as always, a pang of regret washed over her. They had lost him sixteen years ago when he had fled Williamsburg and the bitter death of his wife to lose himself in the dark and wild world of the Appalachian frontier. Though he had visited once, she wondered how he was doing and longed to see him again.

Coming out of her reverie, she shook her shoulders slightly and said, "Jacob, you'd better hurry. You've got your chores to do before that party."

"Here, it's your birthday present," James said suddenly. He handed a small box to Jacob, who took it and stared at it.

"Thank you, Grandpa and Grandma. What is it?"

"All you have to do to find out is open it," James Spencer said, smiling slightly. He watched as the boy opened the box and saw Jacob's eyes fly wide open.

"Why, Grandpa," Jacob gasped, "you can't give me this!" He held up the gold watch with the gold chain. "You've worn this as long as I can remember."

"I've worn it longer than you can remember. My father gave it to me when I was twenty-one," he said. "But I thought you ought to have it."

Jacob ran his hand over the smooth yellow gold and stared down at the finely crafted watch. Lying in the bottom of the box was a small key that wound it. For a moment he could not speak. As he had done since he was a child, he opened the watch and looked at a miniature painting of a couple. They were his great-grandparents, he knew, the father and mother of James Spencer.

"They would have been very proud of you, Jacob," James said quietly, "as your grandmother and I are proud."

A lump formed in Jacob Spencer's throat, and he could not look up for a moment. He held the watch gently, running his hand over it, and finally whispered, "Thank you both. I'll keep it as long as I live." He turned and left the room hurriedly, and as soon as he was gone James said, "He's a good boy, Esther."

"Yes, he is." Esther turned her eyes to where Jacob had disappeared and had long thoughts, but she did not speak of them to her husband.

———

Jacob looked around at the spacious room where the ball was being held. It seemed to him rather frivolous to have a room in the house for nothing but parties, but the Dentons were proud of their ballroom and entertained lavishly. As Jacob surveyed the elegant surroundings, he had to admit that it was actually a rather beautiful place for a party. The rectangular room had gleaming white walls, and five floor-length windows lined each of the longer side walls. The windows were covered with fine lightweight white linen drapes that hung on gold rods and were held back by gold brackets. Gold sconces hung between each window to help illuminate the room, and paintings of landscapes decorated the bare spaces on the walls. The domed ceiling was covered with white punched tin panels edged in gold paint. A roaring fire in the white marble fireplace added a touch of warmth to the room, the flames reflecting their light across the highly polished black-and-white marble floor. Heavy mahogany chairs upholstered in dark blue silk damask encircled the room, and long serving tables laden with refreshments for the guests lined one side of the dance floor.

Jacob moved over toward the refreshment table where several of his friends were talking in an animated fashion. Tom Denton, a tall young man of sixteen with reddish blond hair and blue-green eyes, said, "Come and help me with these barbarians, Jake. You're practically a man now at the ripe old age of sixteen."

A laugh went around from the young men, and Jacob grinned

and shook his head. "I guess I'll hold off on that for a little while. What do you need help with?"

Tom Denton's eyes flashed. "I've been instructing these fellows in the meaning of the Boston Massacre."

"But that happened a year ago, Tom."

"Doesn't make any difference. England hasn't forgotten it. She won't, either. Mark my words."

Stephen Posten, a short, chubby young man of seventeen, shook his head. "England's too busy with her empire to fool with a little thing like a few rebellious colonists."

"Don't you believe it, Steve!" Tom exclaimed. "England never forgets *anything*. Why, she sent soldiers all the way to India to protect her possessions there. She's not about to lose the Colonies over here."

Posten came from a middle-class family. His father was owner of a small business that made shoes. "It'll pass away. Wait and see."

But Tom Denton was not a young man to be denied his strong opinions. His family was not only wealthy but strongly Tory and loyal to King George. When the Boston Massacre had taken place and the colonists had risen in arms, it had been Tom who had persuaded Jacob that the colonists themselves had been responsible for the so-called massacre. "I've been in Boston," he had said, "and you ought to see how the citizens treat His Majesty's soldiers! They throw stones at them and curse them and throw rocks at them in the street! They need to be taught a lesson!"

Jacob listened as the sprightly argument went on, but he said nothing. He was aware that his grandfather was not a Tory and had said on more than one occasion that this country will have to decide one day whether it will rule itself or will be ruled by a German king sitting on an English throne thousands of miles away.

Suddenly Thomas reached over and poked Jacob in the chest sharply. "I think you're wanted, old boy," he said, a broad grin creasing his face. He gestured with his head and Jacob turned. He saw Annabelle Denton standing there and at once grew more alert. Annabelle was the prettiest girl in Williamsburg and highly sought after by the young men, although she was not yet sixteen. Still, several young men had made it clear that they had set their sights on her for matrimonial purposes. Some of them simply wanted to align themselves with a wealthy family, but Annabelle was a beauty, and now as Jacob moved away from the young men, he took in her large clear blue eyes, the strawberry blond hair, and the trim figure. She was wearing a light rose-colored dress made of the finest silk trimmed with delicate white lace. The neckline was square, the sleeves loose and ending at the wrists in a dainty lace ruffle, and the snug bodice had small white ribbon bows accenting the front down to the waist. The overskirt was plain, worn over large hoops, and edged with lace, and the petticoat was made of white silk with small roses embroidered on it. She approached Jacob, smiling provocatively.

"I was wondering if you'd come and dance with me, Jacob."

The music was just beginning, and Jacob said, "I wouldn't miss it. As you know, though, I'm not the best dancer in the world."

"You will be after I get through teaching you. Come along, now."

Annabelle was an excellent dancer. She had given Jacob several lessons, and as the two moved across the floor, she nodded, saying, "You're doing much better, and don't you look handsome in your new suit!"

"I feel a little odd in it."

"Why should you feel odd? It's a beautiful suit. Your grandfather had it made at my father's tailor's shop."

The suit was made of a fine brown wool with the overcoat coming to his knees. The overcoat was worn open to reveal a waistcoat of the same material edged with a dark brown brocade, and a white linen shirt with ruffles down the front peeked out at the neck and at the wrists. Snug-fitting breeches came to below the knees and were held in place with gold buttons, and white silk stockings covered the lower part of his legs. Jacob was pleased that she liked it. As they danced, he was well aware that from time to time, Annabelle would press herself against him in a most alluring way. With any other young woman he would have known what to think of that, but he had long ago decided that this girl was willful and that she would do as she pleased. She was witty and talented, and Jacob was hopelessly in love with her. At times he would sink into bleak despair when she would provoke him by her flirtatious ways with other men, but he always came back when her coy attentions turned to him again.

"What are you thinking about, Jacob?"

"The next fifty years."

His rather sober answer caught Annabelle off guard. She suddenly laughed aloud and said, "Why, you can't think that far ahead!"

"It'll be here quicker than you think, Annabelle."

"Why are you so gloomy today? This is your birthday. Cheer up!"

"Annabelle, I think it's too early to think of it, but someday I'm going to ask you to marry me." He saw her eyes open wide and immediately urged, "When I get a plantation started, I'll need a wife. What would you say if I asked you to marry me?"

Annabelle smiled, her perfect white teeth showing beneath soft reddish lips. "Why, I don't know who else I would marry, Jake."

A thrill ran through Jacob Spencer, and he had the wild impulse to hold her close and kiss her. But she saw his expression and said, "Now, don't you hug me! You're holding me too tight!"

"One of these days I'll come see you, Annabelle, when I have something to offer you."

"Don't you go telling anyone what you just said, Jacob." She stepped close to him, and he felt the contours of her firm young body, and his face grew warm.

"I won't tell," he said.

"It'll just be between the two of us," she said. "Now, let's go get some punch. . . ."

———

James was sitting before the crackling fire in the large fireplace, soaking up the heat. He rose and poked the logs until they shifted with a hissing sound, sending myriads of sparks whirling up the chimney. Selecting another chunk of firewood, he placed it carefully on the fire and stood watching it for a minute. "There's an art to making a fire, Esther."

"I know. You always think of it as other men would think of a painting or writing a piece of music." Esther smiled and said, "But on these cold days, fires are better than paintings, aren't they?"

"Yes, they are." James straightened up, stretched, and arched backward, groaning, "I think I've got rheumatism or something."

"I hope not." Esther watched as he moved back and sat down. She was knitting, for she always had to be busy doing something. Now as the fire crackled and a wind swept the house, she said, "What do you think of Jacob and Annabelle?"

"I don't like it one bit."

Surprised at the brevity of her husband's reply, Esther looked up. Their eyes met, and she seemed to know his thoughts. It was that way with these two. They had lived together so long that many times they did not even have to speak to know what the other thought. "I know what you mean. She's a beautiful girl, and very clever, but . . ." Words failed her and she suddenly put her needles down in her lap. A troubled light came to her eyes. "The Dentons are not our kind of people, are they, James?"

"No. They're not. In the first place, they're Tory to the bone! If a war comes with England, they'll stand with the Crown, and I'd like to think that Jacob wouldn't do that just because he married into a wealthy Tory family."

"You don't really think a war will come, do you?"

"England's been unfair to the Colonies. If the prime minister could only see that America is the biggest prize England has! Far more valuable than India or any of the other possessions." His eyes grew warm, and he shook his head in disgust. "They try to rule us from thousands of miles across the sea and tax us without our consent. There's only one end to that, I'm afraid."

The two sat there quietly for a while, then Esther said, "The Dentons aren't godly people. They go to church on rare occasions, but it's just for the sake of appearance."

"I thought the same thing myself. And that girl, Annabelle—of all the flirts I ever saw, I think she's the worst! Only fifteen, and who knows what she'll be by the time she's twenty."

"She'll be married long before then, James."

"Jacob could get hurt. At the age of sixteen," James said, "it doesn't take much to hurt a young man." He started to speak, but Ellen, the maid, entered the room. "What is it, Ellen?"

"Someone is here to see you, sir."

"To see us? Who could it be at this time of the day?"

"You're supposed to go to the library," Ellen said. She had a half smile on her face, and Esther was puzzled by her behavior.

"Well, come, Esther," James said. "Let's go find out who this mysterious visitor is."

The two moved out of the parlor and down the wide hall. When they turned into the library, Esther gave a short cry and her hands flew to her lips. "Josh!" she cried and rushed over to throw herself into the arms of the tall man who was grinning broadly.

James moved forward, a smile on his face. He shook hands first with the Indian who stood watching him. "Hello, Sequatchie. It's been a long time."

"It has been a long time. I'm glad to see you, Mr. Spencer."

"If you can turn loose of my son, I'd like to at least shake hands with him," James said. Hawk did not release his mother but stuck out a tanned, muscular hand that gripped his father's hand hard.

"It's good to see you, sir," he said. "Very good."

"Why didn't you tell us you were coming?"

"You know the post. It's easier to come yourself than trust."

Josh looked down at his mother, and something moved in his face. "My favorite story in the Bible has always been the story of the Prodigal Son, Mother. And now I guess the prodigal has really come home."

Esther gasped and looked up. Her face turned pale and she reached up and touched Hawk's cheek. "Josh," she whispered, "you mean. . . ?"

"That's right. I went pretty far down, but I've returned to following the Lord now. I've accepted Jesus Christ as the Lord in my life."

"Praise be to God! My prayers have been answered," Esther cried out as James reached over to give his son a strong hug.

Sequatchie stood to one side, watching the joy of these two older people. James turned to him and said, "I assume you had something to do with this, Sequatchie."

"Jesus draws men to Him," Sequatchie said quietly. "But I have been praying a long time to see Hawk come back to God."

"Where is Jacob?" Hawk asked, and an anxiety came into his voice.

"I'll get him. He's up in his room," James said. He quickly left the room and went up the stairs and knocked on Jacob's door. "Jacob, come quickly."

The door opened almost at once and Jacob looked rather startled. "What is it, Grandpa?"

"It's your father. He's downstairs." He saw a strange look cross Jacob's face and wanted to say more, but he knew that he could not force this tall young man to accept the father he had never known. "Come along, son. He'll be glad to see you," he said gently.

Jacob followed his grandfather downstairs, his mind spinning. When he walked into the room and saw his father, he stopped dead still.

Hawk moved forward and said, "Hello, son. Happy birthday."

"Thank you," Jacob said rather stiffly and took the hand his father put toward him. An awkward silence fell over the room, and Hawk said, "It's not good manners to just drop in like this, but we had a purpose. You remember Paul Anderson?"

"Of course!" James exclaimed. "Is he with you?"

"He's here in Williamsburg, but he's come to be married."

"Who is he marrying?" Esther said.

"You remember Rhoda Harper. She's recently become a Christian, and I had to bring them all the way in because there was no preacher to marry them out in Watauga. Besides, Paul wanted to be married in his parents' home."

Jacob stood listening as his father spoke, his eyes fixed on his face. A turmoil of conflicting emotions grew in him and tore at his heart. For years he had longed for a father, but this was eclipsed now by the bitterness that arose when he thought of all the lonely years that his father had left him, even though he was with his grandparents.

Sensing that Jacob was uncomfortable, Hawk said quickly, "We'll have plenty of time to talk, son. I'd like to tell you about Watauga."

"Very well, sir. That will be fine."

"You can stay in the big room with the two windows, Josh," Esther said. "And you'll stay, too, Sequatchie."

"If that would be all right."

Sequatchie had sensed the difficult situation he had stepped into. In his mind Hawk had made a terrible mistake leaving his son to be reared by others, but now that he knew God, Sequatchie was hopeful that things would be better. As the two men ascended the stairs, he said, "Your son has become a man." He got no answer but saw a troubled look on Hawk's face and knew that things were not well with his friend.

"It's a new country over the mountains, Father," he said. "Nothing at all like you have here."

"It's very primitive, isn't it?" James asked, leaning forward. They were sitting in the smaller parlor where they had come after a lavish dinner that Esther had prepared. Now they were drinking tea, and Hawk was speaking of the events of the past year. He had told them of his struggles and how he had come to know the Lord, and Esther had not been able to keep the tears back. Finally James said, "I wish you could know Elizabeth and her children. She's such a fine woman."

At the mention of her son's new wife, Esther shot a glance at Jacob. He seemed paler than usual, and he had spoken very little. At the mention of Hawk's family, she thought she saw a somber flicker in his eyes and wondered what it meant.

As they talked, Sequatchie sat and observed, saying almost nothing. He had seen the happiness in James and Esther Spencer as Hawk told them of how God had healed his bitter and broken heart, but he was mostly concerned with the young man, for he was an astute student of human nature. *He's unhappy,* he thought to himself. *He doesn't like the idea of his father being married—which is strange considering that it will mean more of a family to him.*

Finally the conversation turned to the Spencers, and once again they were thrilled as Hawk told them how Rhoda had been converted and how she had grown in the Lord so rapidly.

"I hope Paul and Rhoda will come to see us while they're here, son," Esther said.

"Oh, I'm sure they will. Paul thinks the world of you two, and of you, too, Jacob."

Jacob started slightly. He remembered Paul Anderson well, and when he saw a reply was expected, he said, "I'd like to see him again."

Hawk was feeling as uncomfortable as he ever had in his life. He had tried to think of some way to express what he felt to Jacob, but everything he wanted to say sounded awkward and artificial. Now he cleared his throat and said tentatively, "I've been hoping, Jacob, now that I've got my life right with God and have a home, that you'd come and live with us."

"Live with you?" Amazement and shock ran across Jacob's face.

"Well, with me and Elizabeth. You'll like her very much—and her children. Andrew is two years younger than you, but I'm very proud of him. He's learned how to handle a rifle like a grown man. Brought down a ten-point buck just a few weeks ago." Pride filled

Hawk's voice, and he did not see the lips of the young man tighten.

Sequatchie saw it, however, and shook his head slightly, thinking, *He should not be boasting about his stepson. It is not wise.*

James and Esther were staring at Hawk. It was something they had never thought of, but now James said, "It would be very good, Jacob, for you to spend some time with your father."

But Jacob was staring at his father. Up until this moment he had kept his temper, but now he said coldly, "You left me here sixteen years ago, and now you come here unannounced and say, 'Come live with me,' and expect everything to be fine. I've got a life here with my grandparents, after I was abandoned by a father who obviously didn't care one bean about me." He saw his words strike against his father's face and took a perverse pleasure in hurting him. And then he did something that he regretted the moment he said it. "Besides, I'm thinking of getting married."

"Married?" Hawk said, his eyes opening wide with surprise. "But you're only sixteen."

"I don't mean right now, but I'm in love with a young woman named Annabelle Denton." In his anger he forgot his promise to Annabelle to say nothing about marriage. Curtly he ended by saying, "You're not really my father. I think you should go back to the frontier with your other family, especially the *son* you're so proud of. Forget about me, because I'm going to try to forget about you!" He whirled and left the room, and they heard the front door slam.

A silence reigned over the room for a moment, and James said quickly, "Jacob will calm down and probably change his mind. After all, it's a pretty big shock for him."

"Yes, it is," Esther said. She came over and touched Hawk's arm gently. "Don't be angry, son."

"I'm not angry. I understand, and really I deserve everything the boy said."

"I'll talk to him," Esther said.

"No, don't do that, Mother. I wouldn't force him to do something against his will. You two have been a real blessing in his life, actually his mother and father. I'll tell him I won't bother him again if he doesn't want me to."

Esther was closer to Hawk than the others. His face was turned slightly away, and for the first time since he was a very small child, she saw something that shocked her. This tall, strong man who had braved the wilderness and was able to handle anything that came his way had tears in his eyes. She reached out and whispered, "God has brought you back to Him, Josh, and now He's not going to forget you. You'll have your son again."

Jacob and His Father

Five

A fitful night's sleep had left faint dark circles under Jacob's eyes. As he left his room and moved down the hall to the landing, he felt miserable and discontented. He put his hand on the polished walnut, remembering his delight in sliding down the curving banister when he was younger. *I must have gotten in trouble a hundred times over this banister!* The memories of that time came back as he descended to the first floor, and he found himself longing for those halcyon days when life had been so much simpler. He was a thoughtful, introspective young man, at times retreating from reality into a secret world of dreams and longings. Now as he entered the dining room, he shook his shoulders, forcing himself to assume a more pleasant expression.

"Good morning, Grandpa."

"Good morning, Jake." James Spencer had been standing at the mullioned window looking out at the oak tree that had shed all its leaves and now appeared bare and dark against the gray November sky. A brisk wind was stirring the crisp leaves that lay around the base of the huge tree, catching them up into a miniature tornado that swept across the flat ground and dissipated as they collided with a green hedge of holly decorated with crimson berries. Clasping his hands behind his back, James commented, "It's going to be a cold winter. I knew that when I saw how thick the caterpillars' coats were last summer."

Jacob found himself smiling briefly. His grandfather put great stock in things like this. Taking his seat at the large oak table, he pulled his chair up close and looked up, saying, "And the acorn shells were thicker than usual this year."

"That's another sign. It's going to be bitter cold before we're out of this. You mark my words." Moving over to the table, James pulled out one of the Windsor chairs and sat down. He was a well-preserved man, firm and somewhat thicker around the middle than when he was younger. Still, there was an alert air about him as he studied his grandson's face. "How was the party?" he asked, watching the expression on Jacob's face carefully.

"Very good."

The reply was brief, and Jacob was relieved when his grandmother entered carrying a silver bowl with a cover. "Good morning, Grandma," he said. "Can I help you bring something in?"

"No, it's just oatmeal, bacon, and eggs this morning. How was the party?"

"Crowded." Jacob's brief reply brought a cautious look into his grandmother's eyes.

"Did you have a good time?"

"Yes, I did. The music was good." He looked around rather nervously and said, "Where's . . ." He started to say "my father" but could not bring himself to frame the words. After a noticeable hesitation, he said, "Where are our guests?"

"They've gone to see about Paul and Rhoda's wedding," James Spencer said. "I think you ought to attend. We'll be going."

Jacob desperately did not want to attend any function where he would have to look at his father. He had mixed emotions on finding out that his father and Sequatchie were gone. He did not want another scene with him, and yet there was something in him that drew him to his father. "If you say so, Grandpa."

The two waited until Esther had brought the rest of the food in, then James bowed his head and asked a blessing. He ended by saying, "We thank thee, O Lord, that you have brought our son back home, if only for a little while. In Jesus' name."

The meal was quiet. Jacob was depressed, not understanding fully why he felt so miserable. He knew his grandparents were puzzled, and even hurt at his behavior. Breaking the silence, he finally said diffidently, "I'm sorry that I have to disappoint my father." He said the word "father" this time with a distinct effort, then added, "But I don't really want to have anything to do with him."

A swift glance passed between the Spencers, and it was James who leaned forward and put his hands flat on the table as he stared at his grandson. "I think we need to talk about this, Jacob."

"There's nothing to talk about. I'm not going to live with him." There was a flatness to the young man's reply, and his dark eyes contained a stubbornness that the older people had learned to recognize. "He abandoned me, and he can't just come waltzing in here and expect to become a father to me as easily as if . . . as if he picked up a new puppy!"

"It isn't like that at all, Jacob," Esther protested. "Your father's had his difficulties."

"Yes, he has, hasn't he? But I haven't been one of them."

There was such raw bitterness in Jacob's voice that James involuntarily shook his head. He was totally devoted to this young man who had grown up in his house from the day he was born. He had pride in him, too, for he knew that Jacob had strengths that had been emerging all of his life. Now that he stood on the verge of manhood, James Spencer was pained and grieved to think that Jacob was hardening himself in this fashion.

"I think you ought to consider your father's invitation," he said as mildly as he could.

"Do you want me to leave?" Jacob demanded. He knew this was not so, and even as he saw the hurt leap into his grandmother's eyes, he hated himself for speaking like this. Somehow he seemed to have lost control of himself. His father's presence had disturbed the equilibrium of his life, and he sat at the table, his head up, with his backbone stiffened so that he was rigid and unbending.

"You know better than that, Jacob," Esther said quietly. "You know we would miss you terribly."

"I know that, Grandma," Jacob said, forcing himself to meet her eyes. "I didn't mean to speak that way. Forgive me, please."

"Of course, but at least think about it. You need your father."

"I don't need anyone except you."

"That's not true," James interjected. "Your grandmother and I are getting older, and you're a young man with a lot of life ahead of you."

"You're not old!"

James suddenly realized that there was fear in Jacob's voice. *We're all he has, really,* he thought. *He's afraid of losing us, and then he wouldn't have anybody.*

"I think I made a mistake," James said finally. "We haven't talked of your father enough all through these years that he's been gone." He looked down at the table, picked up the silver spoon in front of him, and held it lightly, staring at it as if it had some meaning. Then he looked up and said, "It was too painful for all of us, but I see now it was my fault."

"I think you're right, James," Esther said quietly. She was leaning back in her chair, and a sadness filled her eyes as she added, "I wish you could know how much your father loved your mother, Jacob. I've never seen a man so caught up with a woman. Why, he worshiped the ground she walked on! And when she died, her death literally destroyed him."

"That's right," James nodded grimly. "It was almost as if he took a bullet in the brain. He couldn't think straight, and he was like a crazy man."

From outside the window a mockingbird began singing, and the sound of it was cheerful inside the dining room. Jacob listened to it but was preoccupied with what his grandparents were saying. "I can't love him," he said. "I just can't forget how he walked away and left me."

The only sound in the room was the ticking of the small clock on the mantel, and the mockingbird throwing his song out on the morning air. The sunlight streamed in through the window, touching the table silver, transforming it from a dullness to a bright, glowing, warm color. "You can't live with bitterness," Esther said. "It will destroy you as it almost destroyed your father. If you don't deal with it, you will become the very thing you say you hate."

"The Scriptures are clear on that, and I think it's the most difficult thing in the Bible," James added. "Forgiving those who have wronged us probably isn't in our makeup. It's just not human. I think that's why the Bible says it is Christ in us who enables us to do things like that. Jesus on the cross looked down and said, 'Father, forgive them, for they know not what they do.'"

"That's right," Esther said quickly. "You must remember that, Jacob. Your father didn't know what he was doing at the time. He was distraught, half crazy with grief, and behaved very foolishly. But if you continue hating him, you'll be just as foolish as he was."

Jacob sat silently listening as his grandparents spoke. He knew very well that they had his good at heart and that they loved him without reservation. He also knew he was wrong for hating his father, but the cauldron of roiling anger was stronger than he was. Finally he forced himself to say, "If you force me to go, I will."

"No, that won't do," James said instantly. "You can't make people different in their hearts. It would do no good to force you to do something you hated."

"Your grandfather and I have been praying that you would change your mind and decide to go with your father—at least for a time. It doesn't have to be forever, Jacob, but you need to give God a chance to work things out between you."

Jacob found it hard to resist his grandmother, for her gentleness was one unchanging factor in his life. He looked up at her now and bit his lip as he thought hard, then said, "Don't get your hopes up. I don't think I can do it." He got up and left the table without another word, and behind him he left two people grieved over a young man they loved with all their hearts—and over the son they had never given up on.

———

The home of Silas and Martha Anderson was not opulent, but it was solid and well built. A single step led up to the large clapboard-sheathed saltbox home. It was painted a light brown color with mauve and light blue trim around each plank-framed window and had overgrown bushes on each side of the small landing. The windows were twelve-over-twelve sash with three on the top floor and two on the first floor, one on each side of the large oak door. A massive brick chimney made its way through the center of the dark brown shake roof that sloped sharply down the back. Through the large door was a foyer with hardwood floors and eggshell painted walls. The first door to the right led into the best parlor, a large room with chocolate brown-colored carpet with black diamonds running through it. The walls were painted a light slate color and had a border of various kinds of trees and animals edging the windows, surbase, and cornice. The small pine and pewter fireplace had a warm fire crackling, and the larger furniture had been moved to the hall outside and replaced with Windsor easy chairs standing in rows for the guests.

Rhoda stood beside her husband-to-be in the center of the room, and Reverend Joseph Jefferson, the local Congregational minister, stood before the couple. Rhoda was not wearing a bridal gown but had chosen a simple dress made out of sapphire blue handwoven light wool. It had a square neckline edged with black lace and long, tight sleeves that ended at the wrists in a small ruffle. The bodice was tight, and the stomacher was embroidered with black and gray flowers. The skirt was full, long, and had two small rows of the black lace along the edge.

Paul Anderson, standing beside her, had not even bought a new suit. He was wearing a charcoal gray woolen suit with an overcoat that came to below his knees, worn open to reveal a white linen shirt with ruffles at the neck and wrists, and a waistcoat buttoned to the top with black buttons and decorated with black brocade along the edges. His breeches were loose fitting and reached below the knees and fastened with large black buttons. His face was alight as he looked at Rhoda, for he was very much in love with this young woman. They were the same age, thirty-six, and while Paul was not a handsome man, there was a winsomeness about him that was very attractive as he looked his bride full in the face.

Standing beside Paul, Hawk had drawn himself up straight so that he could see the profile of the minister and the faces of the bride and groom. He had known Rhoda for years, and suddenly old memories of her past tried to surface and he quickly pushed them aside. Her new faith in Christ had grown so fast that she truly looked like a new person. She had a bright expectation in her dark eyes, and she looked young and beautiful as she was about to take her vows.

He let his glance lift slightly, taking in Silas and Martha Anderson, Paul's parents. He knew it had been a disappointment to them when Paul had not come into the family business. It had been the Andersons' dream that he would take part in the business with his brothers as they were older, but they had never rebuked Paul for it. They were very proud of their preacher son, and as the minister repeated the familiar words of the marriage ceremony, Hawk saw the elderly couple beaming with pride.

Reverend Jefferson was deliberate in his weddings. He never rushed through them but pronounced each word solemnly, almost lovingly, and gave to every wedding he performed a grace and dignity that never left the memories of the couples that stood before him. Now he was having the two repeat their vows, and as Paul promised to love and honor Rhoda as long as he lived, the tall minister's eyes were fixed on his face. He shifted his gaze, then said,

"Rhoda, repeat after me. I, Rhoda Harper, do promise to love, honor, and obey. . . ."

Rhoda repeated the words almost in a whisper, but they were audible throughout the room. For her, this moment seemed like some sort of fairy tale. For years she had felt as if a dark cloak had weighed her down. Now it seemed as if time stood still. She remembered the day Jesus had lifted her out of a dark and bitter past and forgiven her. She would never forget from where she had come, but her heart was filled with a deep gratitude and joy for the honor God was giving to her now. Looking fully into Paul's face, taking in the sandy brown hair, the plain features, and the total seriousness that now occupied him, she solemnly made her vows aloud to him, but inwardly she was saying, *Oh, God, never let me fail this man. . . !*

Finally Reverend Jefferson smiled and closed his book. "I now pronounce you husband and wife. You may kiss your bride, Paul."

Paul put his hands on Rhoda's shoulders and leaned forward. His lips fell on hers, and they were soft and warm and yielding. Then he heard her say as he drew back, "I'll always love you, Paul!"

And then they were surrounded by family and friends congratulating them.

After the wedding refreshments were brought in, Hawk made it a point to go up and stand beside Rhoda. She had served everyone, and now they were isolated in the room, as much as was possible.

Rhoda looked at him and said abruptly, "Hawk, you've never faulted me about my past. You don't know how much that's meant to me."

"Well, I understand that's what Christians do," Hawk remarked. "You look beautiful, Rhoda," he said. "You and Paul are going to have a fine life."

At that moment Paul came up and slapped Hawk between the shoulders. "Now I'm an old married man just like you."

"That you are," Hawk grinned. "And you can start learning how to be a good husband."

"Maybe you can give me some lessons."

"Not me," Hawk protested, a wry grin touching his lips. "I'm still learning myself."

"What about Jacob?" Paul asked and noted at once that Hawk's mood changed. "Is he going back with you?"

"No, he won't be going back with us to Watauga."

"Oh, that's too bad," Rhoda said. "I know you're disappointed."

"Yes, I am, but it's his decision."

"Do you think if I talk to him it might help?" Paul asked anxiously.

Hawk hesitated and then said reluctantly, "No, perhaps that might be too much pressure."

Paul, however, could sense the longing in his friend's heart to have his son go back with him.

"How long a honeymoon will you two need?" Hawk asked.

"When were you planning to go back?" Rhoda asked.

"Will three days be time enough?"

"Oh yes." Paul stepped over and put his arm around Rhoda and winked at Hawk. "You understand, I'm not settling for a three-day honeymoon. Our honeymoon will continue on the journey back, and after we get there."

"How long of a honeymoon do you *have* to have?" Hawk smiled.

"Oh, I think ten or fifteen years ought to get us off to a good start." He leaned over suddenly and kissed Rhoda's smooth cheek and saw happiness wash across her face and joy light her eyes.

"All right," Hawk said. "Come to my parents' house in three days. Sequatchie and I will be ready.

———

As soon as Hawk stepped inside the door, he knew he had to speak with Jacob. It brought him no joy, for his son had left no doubt about the way he felt. Nevertheless, his years in the wilderness had taught Hawk Spencer never to turn his back on trouble. If there was an unpleasant task to be done, he went to it immediately. In his heart, he knew this might be his last opportunity ever to talk to his son. Moving to the library, he found Jacob sitting at the large rosewood desk staring at a book before him. "Am I interrupting, Jacob?"

"Why . . . no. Just reading a little."

"What is it?"

"*The Odyssey.*"

Hawk looked over and saw that the book was not in English. "Is that Greek?"

"Yes, sir."

Hawk stood loosely before the desk, looking down at his son. Regret touched his eyes, and he shook his head in a gesture of sadness. "I was exposed to Greek once, but the last fifteen years I lost what little I had. I hope you don't do that."

"No, sir."

The brevity of Jacob's reply told Hawk that the boy was still adamant. "I can understand why you feel as you do about me, Jacob. I think I'd probably feel the same way if my father had treated me as I have treated you."

Jacob blinked with surprise. There was a mildness in his father's manner, a quiet sorrow that he recognized instantly. He had thought of him for years as a wild mountain man, but now he saw a sensitivity in the man that matched his own.

"I really don't think there's much more to be said," Jacob finally spoke up.

"Probably not, and I won't bother you for long. I want you to come to Watauga more than anything, but I can't force you. I . . ." For a moment Hawk hesitated, and his eyes dropped to the polished pine floor beneath his feet. He knew how to stalk an animal in the forest and had the best skills of any frontiersman, but he had no power to put in words the feelings that were in his heart. Finally he said, "I had hoped that even after all these years we might become close. I realize it's my fault that we're not, and I again tell you how sorry I am and how foolishly I behaved."

Jacob, for that one moment, felt himself drawn to the tall man who stood before him. He was a lonely young man who had felt himself cut off by the death of a mother he had never known and the abandonment by his father. All of his life he had envied those young people around him who had a father and a mother, even those whose parents were not completely admirable. Even though he had the love of his grandparents, who had been like a mother and father to him, the knowledge that he had been abandoned—in his mind, discarded—tore at his heart. Now as he stared at his father something rose in him, and he found himself drawn to the idea of doing what his father asked—but then the years of bitterness and loneliness bound his heart.

"I appreciate your offer," he said, keeping his voice toneless, "but I want to stay here in Williamsburg."

Hawk studied the youthful face before him, and it was in some ways like looking into a mirror. At one time he had been this young, this vulnerable, but his own childhood had been happy and untroubled. Now the grief that stung him for what he had done to his son was bitter and sharp, and he knew he had failed.

"We'll be leaving in three days, Jacob," he said quietly. "If you change your mind, it would make me very happy. But you're a man now and must make your own life." He turned and left the room, closing the door softly behind him.

Jacob stared up from the book and felt his hands trembling, and he clasped them hard to hold them still. Slowly he leaned forward and put his forehead on his clenched fists and was shocked to find that his eyes were burning with unshed tears. He thought he had cried himself out on this matter long ago, but the shock of looking at his father, of seeing him, and of finding in him a man whom he had not known really existed had shaken him. He had built up a picture in his heart and in his mind of a ruthless, harsh, and uncaring man, but he knew now that this image was an invention stemming from his own hurt and pain. For a long time he sat bent over, his forehead pressed against his fists. He was being torn by the events that had come so abruptly into his life, but he knew he could not bring himself to agree to his father's proposal. The wound was too sharp and bitter, and the long years had left a deep scar. Finally he sat up, rubbed the heels of his hands into his eyes, then straightened up, his mouth a thin line. He pulled the book forward and stared at it blindly, not understanding a word he read, but continued doggedly to pursue the ancient history of Greece.

Betrayal

Six

*U*nable to get the memory of his last talk with his father out of his mind, Jacob Spencer found himself in a strange emotional state. At times he felt he was a fool for refusing the obvious offer of love his father had made, but he had been unable to shake off the bitterness that had hardened him over the years. He kept to himself a great deal of the time, throwing himself into his studies, but his father's words echoed in his mind, coming again and again to interrupt. *I'd like nothing better than for you and me to become close.* Somehow those words could not be buried deeply enough, for they kept rising to the surface of his mind, until finally in desperation he left the house and spent long hours walking the streets of Williamsburg.

Finally, late Thursday afternoon, after two days of uncertainty, doubt, and anger at himself, he decided to visit Annabelle. The sun was dropping toward the hills in the west, but there was still plenty of daylight as he walked along the neatly paved streets until he reached the Denton house. For a moment he hesitated, then walked firmly up to the door and tapped the brass knocker.

"Why, Mr. Spencer!" the maid exclaimed. Her name was Margaret, and she smiled, tilting her head to one side as if she knew a secret. "You came calling on Mr. Tom?"

Knowing he was having his leg pulled, Jacob managed a smile. "Is he home, Margaret?"

"Yes, sir. He's in the library. I'm sure he would want you to go right in."

Stepping inside, Jacob moved past the diminutive maid down the long, broad hallway. It was a high-ceilinged house, and the walls were adorned with rich pictures, which he did not notice as he moved along. Turning into the library, he saw Tom Denton lying on his back on a horsehair couch. His eyes were closed and a book was unfolded on his chest.

"Hard at work, I see, Tom," Jacob said and grinned as Denton came awake with a snort and stared wildly around.

"You're a fine friend waking me up like that! I'll have you know I was meditating!"

"I can see that," Jacob said. He moved around the library, admiring the leather-bound books, all expensively and tastefully done. He had a suspicion that Edward Denton had bought them by the yard and imagined him saying, "I'll take three yards of Homer, two feet of Montaigne, and whatever you have in a businesslike green color for this space here." Jacob had availed himself of some of the books, but he always felt guilty leaving a gaping hole in the line. Sometimes it looked to him like a man whose front tooth had been knocked out. However, he sat down and watched as Denton ran his hand through his hair, trying to smooth it down.

When it was roughly in order, he said, "Your father left yet, Jake?"

"No. Not yet."

"He's quite a sight. Fine-looking man. A little rough after all his years on the frontier but very handsome."

"Do you think so?"

"Why, certainly." Young Denton stretched, arching his back, then shrugged. "Do you suppose he's ever felt any regrets about leaving a good life here and throwing himself away in that wilderness over the mountains?"

"I don't know. I doubt it."

"He could have been rich by now if he had stayed here and applied himself."

"I suppose."

Denton stared suddenly at Jacob. "What's the matter?"

Jacob had not intended to mention his father's invitation, but the two were good friends. Tom was, as a matter of fact, the only close friend Jacob had, and now he heard himself saying, "He wants me to go back to Watauga with him."

"What?" Denton sat bolt upright and stared at his friend with consternation. "Well, he doesn't want much, does he? Here he goes off and leaves you when you were a baby. Now he pops up and says

'Come on home, sonny. Time for me to be a daddy again.' "

Since Jacob had more or less said the same thing to his father, he could not argue his friend's comment. Nevertheless, put in those terms, it made him feel uncomfortable. He rubbed a hand across his cheekbone, then shook his head doubtfully. "He thinks he's doing the right thing."

"The right thing? To take a budding young man like you out and bury you in the wilderness! The next thing I suppose he'll want you to marry some Indian maiden!"

"I don't think he'd go that far, Tom." Jacob was wishing he had not brought the matter up and tried to change the subject, but Tom was not through with it.

"You're not thinking of going, are you?"

"Oh no. Nothing like that."

"Well, that's a relief. You're not given to rash gestures, Jake, but I suppose there is a certain romance in going over the mountains." He grinned abruptly and added, "I think you'd get tired of sitting around in moth-eaten furs and scratching fleas." He stood suddenly and came over and clapped Jacob on the shoulder. "You gave me a fright there, old friend." His expression changed slightly, and he motioned with his head. "Arthur Horton is here."

"Arthur? What's he want?"

"Well, I suspect he wants Annabelle," Tom shrugged.

Resentment flared in Jacob Spencer momentarily. Arthur Horton was nineteen, the son of a wealthy Williamsburg family, even wealthier than the Dentons. Jacob had never liked him, for Horton was an impertinent snob. He was not particularly bright, and his dislike of Jacob was long-standing, since at one of the local affairs, where the young men had tested their strength in wrestling, Jacob had put the older boy flat on his back twice, the second time so firmly that it knocked the breath completely out of young Horton's body. Since that day a coolness had hung between them that mattered not at all to Jacob Spencer.

"Perhaps I'd better go out and head him off."

"I think it might be best." A light of humor touched Tom's eyes, and he said, "You know, if he weren't so rich, Arthur would be quite a bore."

Jacob grinned. "Yes, he would. It's amazing how riches make people charming and interesting, isn't it? Well, I'll see you before I go. Are we still on for the hunt tomorrow?"

"Sure. I want you to see that new gray mare I bought."

Jacob nodded, then turned and left the room. He made his way down the hall, which made a sharp turn to the left and led to an outer door. Stepping outside, he found himself in an elaborate flower garden and arbor. Tall hedges now formed walkways, and he could hear the murmur of voices. The air was cool, but the sun was bright, and he was actually looking forward to putting Arthur Horton in his place. It amused Jacob to poke fun at the slow-witted young man. Annabelle, who was *not* slow-witted, had often giggled with Jacob later, saying, "You shouldn't make fun of Arthur like that!" But she had enjoyed it, too.

He reached the end of one hedge and stepped into the gap. The voices were plainly audible now, and he stopped suddenly. As he looked into the open area he saw Annabelle being embraced by Arthur Horton. He was surprised, for Annabelle had always made little of Arthur's attentions, yet Jacob knew she did like to be courted, and Arthur, despite his lack of brilliance, was certainly a fine catch. Annabelle, of course, was only fifteen and was flattered by the attentions of young Horton.

Jacob started to call out when suddenly he heard Arthur say, "I want you to marry me, Annabelle."

"Marry you? Why, Arthur!"

"It can't come as a surprise to you." Young Horton was tall and thin and had to look down on Annabelle. He was wearing an expensive suit made out of the finest dark blue wool that money could buy. "You must know what I feel for you. I've told you often enough."

"You say that to all the girls, Arthur."

"Why, I certainly do not!" Horton exclaimed indignantly. "I never said it before to any girl!"

"What about Mary Mullins?"

"What about her?"

"Why, you were chasing her with all your might just last year before she married Henry Ellis."

"I was amusing myself, but what I feel for you is different."

Jacob stood silently staring at the two, who had not heard his approach. He felt awkward for eavesdropping, but somehow he could not bring himself to make his presence known. Finally, after

Horton kept urging Annabelle, he heard her say, "Why, who else would I marry but you?"

Who else would I marry but you?

The words were echoed, the exact cadence and slight lift of the voice at the end. She had spoken these very words to him, and he had taken it to mean they were committed to each other. And now she was saying the same thing to another man!

Jacob Spencer was not an impulsive young man as a rule, but a sudden anger at the girl, who stood looking up so bewitchingly at the tall man who held her, boiled over. He stepped out of the hedge, and the sound of his heels striking on the pathway startled the two and they jumped apart.

Without hesitation Jacob moved forward and struck Arthur in the face with the palm of his hand.

"Jacob, what are you doing?" Annabelle cried.

Jacob Spencer knew at that moment he had struck the wrong person. Arthur Horton had every right to his feelings for Annabelle, but *she* was the one who had betrayed him. He stood staring at her for a moment, forgetting Arthur, who was sputtering and whose face had turned pale. Jacob did not see the blow that was thrown at him by the tall young man. It caught him in the temple, and for a moment the world seemed to turn into stars that flickered and sparkled. He felt himself hit the ground but at once came to his hands and knees, then struggled upright. He had time to block a second blow, but the third one caught him flush in the mouth.

The two young men began trading blow for blow, and Annabelle circled the two, begging them to stop. More than once they fell to the ground, rolling, kicking, and striking at each other. Horton was the older of the two, and much taller, but Jacob was stronger. He was more of an outdoorsman, and long hours of riding had hardened him. He slowly began wearing his opponent down, and then he felt his arm grabbed and, out of breath, turned to see Tom Denton, who had come to step between the two of them.

"Have both of you lost your minds!" Denton exclaimed. "What do you think you're doing, Jake?"

"He came bursting in here like a madman!" Horton gasped. His breeches were stained with dirt, and he had the beginnings of a bruise over his right eye. He was furious and said, "What sort of a crazy man are you? Did you get this from that frontier father of yours?"

Jacob tried to pull his shirt closed where it had been ripped. "Keep my father out of this!"

"I think you'd better go, Jake. Cool off, and we'll talk about it later."

Jacob turned and said, "Annabelle, is that what you want?" Annabelle's eyes were bright with excitement, and he thought with astonishment, *Why, she's enjoying this!*

She saw his sudden understanding of the situation and caught her breath for a moment. "It might be better if you both left."

"No need for him to leave," Jacob said stiffly. He turned, pulled away from Tom, and walked rapidly away. He heard Tom calling him, "Wait, Jake!" but broke into a half run. He did not go through the house but circled by the walkway, ignoring Tom's call and the high-pitched voice of Annabelle as he hurried down the street. Bitterness rose to bite at his throat like bile, and unbidden, the thought came, *It seems like I was born to be betrayed. First my father, and now Annabelle.* He shook his head to clear it, for bitterness and anger enveloped him like a dense fog. He knew he could not walk away from this forever, but he didn't have the will to handle it right now.

When he arrived at his house, he hoped no one would see him before he could change his clothes. He opened the front door very cautiously so that it would not squeak. He closed it and tiptoed as quietly as possible to the stairs. He was startled when Sequatchie suddenly appeared. The Indian took in the torn shirt, the swollen lip, and asked, "What happened to you?"

"Nothing!" Jacob said shortly.

"That nothing must have packed a pretty big punch. Did you lose any teeth?"

"Never mind. You can go ahead and tell my father now. I'm sure that's what you'll do."

"It's not for me to tell," Sequatchie shrugged. When the young man turned, Sequatchie followed him up to his room and stepped inside. "Are you hurt?"

"No!"

"You're angry, though. I can see that."

"You'd be angry, too, if—" He halted abruptly, for the whole story of his betrayal had been on his lips. He turned and went over to the window, staring down bitterly. He was trembling with anger and did not want anyone to see him. "Why don't you leave me alone?" he said.

"Sometimes," Sequatchie said quietly, "it helps to talk things out. Who did you fight with?"

"A fellow named Arthur Horton." He turned and stared at Sequatchie, anger flaring in his eyes. "If you think I look bad, you ought to see him!"

"What did you fight about?"

Jacob found himself suddenly pouring out the whole story. He knew he could not tell his grandfather or his grandmother, and he certainly would not go to his father. Somehow the impassive face of the Indian who spoke gently encouraged him. Sequatchie stood like a statue, not a flicker of emotion in his eyes, as Jacob poured out his story, and then the boy flung himself into a chair and passed his hand across his face. "Now you can go down and report it all to my father!"

"Why would I do that? It would only hurt him. But if you would tell him, it might be good."

"Stop trying to force my father on me! I'm sick of it!"

"No matter what you feel now," Sequatchie said calmly, "Hawk is your father. And if you want to become the man that God has made you to be, you're going to have to accept that."

"I can't do it! How would you feel if you were forsaken by your father?"

"I *was* forsaken by my father," Sequatchie said flatly.

Startled by the simple statement, Jacob looked up and stared at the face of the Cherokee. He saw then, only for a moment, a break in the expression of the tall Indian and knew that he was not the only one who had suffered in this way.

"Sorry," he muttered. "I didn't know."

Sequatchie did not answer right away. He stood looking down at the young man and thinking how much he looked like his father. Finally he said, "Only God can help you do that."

"Do what?"

"Accept your father and love him."

Jacob pulled his lips together in a straight line and said shortly, "God has never helped me."

"You sound like your father did at one time."

Jacob's head jerked at this. He did not want to be compared with his father, but Sequatchie was looking at him with a peculiar expression. He then said to the young man, "I'll make a pact with you."

"A pact? What kind of a pact?"

"I don't know what you call it in English. If you'll do something for me, I'll do something for you."

Curious, Jacob studied Sequatchie's face, then said, "All right. Tell me what's on your mind."

"If you'll go back to the frontier with us, I promise to bring you back if you don't want to stay—after a reasonable time."

Despite himself Jacob burst out, "A reasonable time? What's a reasonable time?"

Sequatchie did not answer. Although the boy did not know it, he was praying for this young man. He had learned to pray as he moved through life, and now he was asking God to do a miracle in Jacob's life. "Think about what I've said."

"Well, all right. I'll think about it."

"You'd better do something about that ripped shirt. Don't know what you can do about that lip."

"You're not going to tell?"

"No. Change your shirt."

Sequatchie left the room and immediately Jacob slipped out of his coat. His shirt was torn right down the front, and he walked over to study himself in the mirror. His lip was somewhat swollen, but perhaps he could get by with it. He slowly picked a light tan shirt off a peg and put it on. He thought about what Sequatchie had said. He buttoned the shirt slowly, thoughtfully, and realized that the last hour had changed his whole life. He knew now, with a dead certainty, that he could never feel for Annabelle what he had *thought* he had felt before. He was young and had little to do with girls, but he knew that he would be a long time forgetting her words, *Who else would I marry but you?* He had taken her for a flighty young woman, but now he knew that he had been mistaken. He shoved his shirt down in his pants and then stood uncertainly in the middle of the room.

"I don't have anything to stay in this place for," he spoke aloud, and bitterness tinged his voice. A thought began to grow in him, and he had a logical mind that began putting things in order. *Maybe that Indian's right. If I leave with them, I won't have to say anything to anybody about Annabelle. Then I can come back one day, and by that time she'll probably be married to Arthur or some other dolt.* He moved around the room restlessly, thinking, *It doesn't have anything to do with my father.* Deep down he knew this was not altogether true, but he came to stand at the window and the thoughts moved slowly through his mind. *I don't want to go with him, and I'll never accept him as my father, but I'll at least get out of here until I get over Annabelle.* Somehow he knew that he was not being honest even with himself, for despite all that he had said and thought, there was a longing in him for a father. He buried this, however, and said aloud, "All right. I'll do it. But it's just for my own convenience. Not for *him!*"

───────

A sadness lurked in Esther Spencer's eyes as she served supper. She had heard, of course, about Jacob's fight with Arthur. That could not be kept secret, and now as Hawk and Sequatchie sat down across from James, she wondered where Jacob was. She had seen him only once that day, and he had said nothing at all about his father.

James was feeling much the same way, and now he said quietly, "Perhaps we ought to try to talk to Jacob again. At least maybe we can convince him to come to you later."

"No. I don't think so," Hawk said quietly. "I believe we ought to leave the boy alone." He tried to put a good face on it and added, "I know he's well cared for here. After all, that's about all I have a right to ask."

He had no sooner spoken than Jacob entered the room. Hawk saw a strange expression on his son's face. He sat up straighter and his eyes narrowed as the boy, instead of sitting down, planted his feet and locked his hands behind his back.

"I've changed my mind," Jacob said in a strange tone. He avoided his father's eyes and instead watched his grandparents. "I've decided to go to Watauga for a time." Shock ran across every face— except that of Sequatchie. A slight smile turned up the corners of his mouth as he watched Hawk, who was staring in disbelief at his son.

"Well, I'm glad to hear that, son," he said quietly.

Jacob said, "I won't be with you too long. Just for a while." Then he turned to his grandmother, as if unwilling to face his father, and said, "Would you help me pack?"

"Of course I will. Come along."

As soon as the two were out of the room, James said, "Well, miracles do happen."

"I wonder what changed his mind?" Hawk asked quietly.

Sequatchie never said a word. He sat at the table smiling quietly and thinking about how God could change the hearts of young men.

———————

"I'm going to miss you both."

Now that the hour to leave the only home he knew had actually come, Jacob found it difficult to maintain his composure. All night long he had tossed on his bed, wondering what had possessed him. Several times he had actually made up his mind to go down in the morning and say that he had changed his mind again—that he actually did not want to go to the far valley of the Watauga.

Now, however, he found himself unable to do anything but stand before the two who had played such a large part in his life and struggle not to let the tears appear that burned in his eyes.

"It's going to be harder on us than it is on you, Jacob," Esther said. She found it difficult to speak, for her throat was choked with emotion. She and James had talked until long in the night and prayed, hopeful that they were doing the right thing to encourage their young grandson to make such a drastic change in his life. Now that the morning had come and they were faced with the actual separation, it was almost more than she could bear.

James Spencer stepped forward and put his arms out, and Jacob embraced him quickly. He felt the quick strength in the young man's arms, and also the frustration and doubt that he was feeling. "I couldn't love you any more and couldn't be any prouder of you than I am. Just take care of yourself, Jacob."

Jacob turned to his grandmother, embraced her, kissed her cheek, and then stood awkwardly in the center of the dining room. The remains of the breakfast were on the table, and he had been unable to eat more than a few bites.

"You must go now," Esther said quickly. "They're waiting."

The three made their way outside where Sequatchie and Hawk stood holding the horses. Jacob's own mount, a rangy old gray mare named Queenie, pranced impatiently, pulling against the bridle that was held firmly in Sequatchie's hand.

Over to one side Paul and Rhoda stood holding their own horses. They came forward now, and Paul shook hands with the two, while Rhoda was embraced by Esther.

Hawk stood watching all this, keeping his eyes on his son's face. Finally, before he swung into the saddle, he went forward and embraced his mother, then his father. "I'll watch him carefully."

"Take care of yourself, son. And may God keep both of you," James said.

Hawk moved back to his horse, slipping astride. He turned to Jacob, and the two regarded each other silently. Then Hawk said, "Let's go home, son."

He got no answer, for Jacob's throat was too full to speak. As the small procession moved away from the Spencer house, Jacob turned back for a last look at the only home he had ever known. He waved at his grandparents and saw that his grandmother was being held tightly by his grandfather, as if she were too weak to stand. He turned his head away, unable to watch it more, and then the five clattered down the streets of Williamsburg, heading for the wilderness that lay across the misty mountains.

The New Family

Seven

"Are you getting pretty tired, Jacob?"

Shifting back and forth in his saddle, Jacob turned quickly to see that Rhoda had pulled her mare up even with his own. She was smiling at him, and he took in the clean sweep of her chin and the brilliance of her eyes, thinking, not for the first time, that she was very attractive for an older woman. He had expected to find a woman of thirty-six rather dowdy and had been slightly shocked by her attractiveness—and also by the liveliness of her mind. He had heard something of her past from his grandparents and from common gossip in the community, but looking at her now, as the afternoon sun filtered through the towering chestnuts and beeches overhead, he decided he liked her.

"I'm all right," he said. He hesitated for a moment, then said, "I'm not used to riding this long at a time."

"I know. It makes you numb, doesn't it?"

Jacob grinned at her and said, "I wish I *was* numb. It wouldn't hurt so much, then."

The small party had been two and a half weeks out of Williamsburg. Jacob didn't realize that Hawk and Sequatchie had deliberately slowed the pace, knowing that Jacob would not be able to keep it up without showing the strain. All in all it had been a rather pleasant journey. The fall colors were fading now, but still the air was fresh and crisp with the ending of the season. Winter lurked over the low-lying hills ahead of them, and both Hawk and Sequatchie knew that in one night the cold breath could descend, paralyzing the land and freezing the grass into a crisp brown ash.

The days had been exciting for Jacob. He had somehow put behind him the apprehension that arose at the difficult adjustment he would have to make on the frontier. He found himself talking more and listening with fascination as Sequatchie would speak of the legends of his people at night around the campfire. Jacob had a faulty concept of what Indians were like. Instead, he saw quickly that Sequatchie's mind was quicker than his own. Though the tall Cherokee was uneducated in books, he knew every tree and animal, what the weather would be the next day, and how to find water. All the things that a lifetime of experience had taught him were there for Jacob to see. He listened avidly as Sequatchie told the history of his people and once said, "You ought to put this all down in a book so it won't be lost."

"It will not be lost. We do not have books—not yet," Sequatchie said, "but it is all in the stories of my people. They are told around campfires and will be as long as the wind blows and the waters flow."

Paul had also watched Jacob Spencer carefully. He had some apprehensions, for he knew the bitterness that lurked below the surface of the young man's polite manners. Of all the men he knew, Hawk Spencer was the one he admired most, and it was imperative to Paul that he do all he could to help restore the relationship between the two. He had not spoken of this to Hawk, for the two men understood each other. However, one night as he slept beneath warm blankets with the campfire crackling, he asked, "What do you think of Jacob, Rhoda?"

Rhoda moved against him, holding him tightly. "I think he's a very troubled young man, Paul. He speaks so stiffly to his father."

"Yes," Paul whispered. The wood crackling in the fire punctuated the silence of the night, and overhead a ghostly form crossed the skies, blotting out the moon for a second, a great hunting owl out for his prey. Paul watched it as it disappeared, then put his lips on Rhoda's smooth cheek. He had not gotten over the marvel yet of the love that had come to him, and now forgetting the conversation, he whispered, "I love you, Rhoda."

"I love you, too, Paul."

———

"Well, there it is. There's Watauga, son."

Jacob looked up quickly, taking in the small collection of rough cabins that followed the bend of a creek. There seemed to be no pattern in the town, and he was somehow troubled by what he saw. His concept of a town was Williamsburg, all laid off in neat, geometrical streets, each house taking a certain amount of space, and each street intersected by others with different names.

What lay before him was nothing like that. Smoke curled up in a haphazard, twisting fashion from almost all of the chimneys, and between the cabins only a few figures could be seen moving. Somehow the picture in his mind had been of a well-organized village. Watauga was nothing but a scattering of rude cabins punctuated with small out-buildings, all very roughly built.

"It doesn't look much like Williamsburg, does it?" Hawk said wryly, noting the look of surprise on Jacob's face.

"It's so small!"

"The biggest settlement this side of the mountains," Sequatchie said. "Look, there's our welcoming committee."

As the procession wound its way around a crooked trail into the village, two men advanced to meet them.

As soon as they were close enough, Hawk said, "Hello, William. How are you, James?"

William Bean and James Robertson stopped, and Robertson smiled slyly, saying, "Welcome back, Reverend—and you, too, Mrs. Anderson. I want to wish you a happy marriage. Wish I could have been at the wedding."

William, with his wife Lydia, had established the settlement. He and Robertson were two of its prominent leaders.

Rhoda had wondered how she would be accepted as the wife of a minister, but the teasing smile in the eyes of Robertson gave her reassurance. She returned the smile, then listened as Hawk introduced his son to the two men. She was thinking, *I wonder if the women will be as kind as the men. They usually aren't.* She thought, however, that she knew the women of the Watauga settlement, and a glance at her new husband gave her a sudden sense of joy and acceptance. *It will be all right,* she thought, *as long as I have Paul.*

"What's been happening since we've been gone?" Hawk asked, slipping off his horse. He slapped the animal on the neck and listened as William Bean spoke. He noted a rather worried look in Bean's eyes.

"Well, Hawk, there's a man come here named Alexander Cameron. You know of him?"

"Can't say as I've heard of him."

"He claims to represent John Stuart, the Indian superintendent for the south."

"I know Stuart. He is a good man," Hawk replied. His mind suddenly flashed backward to the time when he had been with John Stuart. Stuart had been the British captain who had led the force to recapture Fort Loudon. For just one moment he seemed to hear the explosion of muskets and the screams of the dying and the wounded. Hawk had this strange characteristic of re-creating involuntarily scenes from his past, so that now it seemed as though he could smell the burning gunpowder and feel the slippery body of the Indian under his as they struggled for life. All these came back to him in a flashing, dynamic moment. Shaking his head slightly, he listened carefully as Bean continued.

"They've been surveying the whole area, Hawk."

"What are they doing that for? It's already been done."

James Robertson spoke up almost angrily. "They say there's some kind of discrepancy as to who has the rights to the land settlements. We told him the settlements are on the land that was promised, and what remained was for the Cherokee."

"Stuart negotiated a treaty with the Cherokee after they were defeated in 1761," Hawk said. "What are the settlers doing?"

"Nothing much. Waiting to hear from the results of this survey. It's called a Donelson Survey. I guess that's the name of the fellow who's drawing it up."

Hawk and Paul listened closely, well aware that this could mean serious changes in all of their lives. If the government decided that the former survey was wrong, all the work they had done on their homesteads could be lost.

Hawk shook his head, saying, "I've got to get home. We'll talk about this later."

"Come along, Rhoda," Paul said. "It's time for us to set up housekeeping."

Rhoda smiled as he drew his horse around, and she followed him.

"We fixed their cabin up for them real nice while the preacher was gone to get married, Hawk," Bean said. "The women cleaned it up, and we've got plenty of meat in the smokehouse. I wish they'd stay there permanently and start a church here."

"They won't do that," Hawk said firmly. "They'll stay there this winter, but in the spring they'll go to the Cherokee, preaching the gospel to them. Isn't that right, Sequatchie?"

"Yes. My people must hear the Word of God. I'll spend winter in Hawk's old cabin, and I will go with them in the spring." His eyes followed the couple as they left, and he was thinking, with joy, what it would be like to have a minister among his people who so desperately needed the living God in their midst.

———

Andrew MacNeal was splitting red oak firewood as the sun sank down behind the low-lying western hills. It was a chore he liked a great deal for some reason. Sawing the trees off into lengths with a buck saw was not as enjoyable. That was pure work, but now he planted his feet firmly, lifted the heavy ax, and, after measuring the distance to the chunk of wood before him, brought the ax down smartly. The blade struck the upright wood with a *chunking* sound, and the two fell splinterless like two pieces of cloven rock. This gave Andrew a great deal of satisfaction. Reaching over to pick up another chunk, he began to sing under his breath a snatch of a song he had heard at one of the rare dances held in the settlement. His blond hair fell over his forehead, and he brushed it back, then split another block of wood. As the two pieces leaped to the side, he heard a voice and turned quickly with an alertness that had not been there. Automatically he moved toward his left, reaching for the musket that was leaning up against a sapling, his clear blue eyes attentive and watchful. Then he saw the two tall men exiting from the patch of woods on the east of the farm and cried out, "Hawk!" Dropping the ax, he stepped forward, his face alive with pleasure as he waited. He took in the third rider and thought, *That's got to be Jacob. Ma said that Hawk might bring him back to live with us.*

"Ma—Sarah, Pa's back!"

Almost at once the cabin door swung open, and Elizabeth came out. She was wearing a simple gray dress with a white apron, and her hair was bound up and crowned with a small white cap. Andrew grinned at the expression on her face and watched as she flew across the yard to where Hawk came off his horse in one smooth movement. He moved over toward Sarah and nudged her in the ribs. "I think he's glad to see her, wouldn't you say?"

"Hush, Andy!"

Elizabeth was a loving woman and usually more conservative in physical demonstrations of her affections. Now, however, she threw herself into Hawk's arms, reached up and pulled his head down, and kissed him firmly. The lean strength of his body was something she had longed for, and she had not realized until this minute how deeply her life had become one with this tall man.

"I missed you," Hawk whispered tenderly. Then he seemed to be the one embarrassed by the embrace. He glanced quickly at Jacob, and with his arm still around Elizabeth, he said, "I brought Jacob back with me. Jacob, this is your family. This is Elizabeth, and this is Andrew and Sarah."

Jacob nodded and murmured a vague greeting and then watched as his father threw his arm around the blond-headed young man. Somehow the action stirred a displeasure in him. It was not that he himself would have endured the same kind of caress from his father, but deeply seated was the resentment that another was getting the affection he had been robbed of all of his life.

As Hawk put his arms around Sarah and whirled her around, laughing as she squealed, Andrew came forward with his hand outstretched to Jacob, putting a big smile on his face.

"Glad to have you, Jacob. Welcome to Watauga."

A perverseness seized Jacob, and he held his hand out limply and allowed Andrew to shake it. He felt himself taken by an instant dislike for his stepbrother.

He doesn't mean all this, he thought. *He doesn't care whether I'm here or not. I never could stand a phony!*

Andrew seemed unaware of any coolness on Jacob's part. "It'll be good to have another fellow around my age," he said. "Especially since we'll be brothers now."

At the use of the word "brothers," the dislike that Jacob had first felt intensified. He opened his lips to say, "We'll never be brothers," but then clamped them together firmly.

Sequatchie, standing off to one side, had observed all this without moving. His quick mind understood at once, and he felt a disappointment that Jacob had so hardened himself against the family that was so willing to receive him. *He will have to learn better,* he thought silently. *He can't live by himself. No man can do that.*

Elizabeth, without turning loose of Hawk's arm, said, "Now, you come right in the house. It won't take long, and we're going to have a welcome-home dinner."

"I will come later. Perhaps tomorrow," Sequatchie said. He turned and walked away without even another word, and Elizabeth looked toward Hawk with a question in her eyes. "What's wrong with him?"

"I guess he's been in civilization long enough," Hawk said quietly. "I know how he feels. I never saw so many people in all my life. For a while all I want to see is trees and mountains—and you, of course."

Reaching up, Elizabeth grabbed a handful of his hair and yanked his head. "You better put me on that list!" Her eyes sparkled and she leaned against him, reveling in the touch, and then said briskly, "Well, come along. It'll be ready soon."

An hour later Jacob was sitting at the table, which was loaded with food. A large venison roast had been cooking slowly over the fire all day and was now placed on a large platter and sliced into juicy, thick slabs and put on the table. A pie tin containing a large beefsteak pie, with a flaky crust and flavored with parsley, marjoram, savory, thyme, and butter, had been made the day before and was now served cold along with the rest of the meal. Bowls of sweet potatoes covered with slices of tart apples, and green beans in a cream sauce decorated the table with their bright colors, and a brown crock of baked pumpkin pudding filled the air with its rich aroma. Freshly baked bread was served with thick butter and preserves, and mugs were filled with steaming hot tea.

Jacob had been bombarded with questions about "civilization" by Sarah and Andrew and had been unable to avoid answering them. He felt awkward and ill at ease, and now as they began to eat, he was glad they were listening to Hawk as he spoke of the trip.

"Oh, I have letters from your family," Hawk said. "You want them now or after supper?"

"Let me read them now. I've been worried about them."

Hawk rose and went over to the pouch he had tossed down beside the fireplace. Opening it, he removed an oilskin package, took out several letters, and moving back, he handed them to Elizabeth. She began reading as the others went on speaking, mostly Hawk relating to Sarah and Andrew the wonders of Williamsburg. The first letter she read was from her father. It was very brief, and the handwriting was shaky. It said basically that he missed her and prayed for her every day, and that he hoped she could come back for a visit.

The letter from her mother was much longer. Elizabeth's mother, Anne Martin, wrote well, and with a certain verve:

> *My dearest daughter, Elizabeth. As you know, we were taken by surprise to learn that you were to be married again. So often when a woman has a good marriage she will marry again, and I know you and Patrick were completely happy with each other.*
>
> *I still grieve over the loss of Patrick, and I am certain that you do also. But I hope both of us will remember that he is with the Lord Jesus Christ now and in the presence of God, as we both shall be someday. And he would not have us to grieve, but to go on with life until that day when we will all be in our Father's house.*
>
> *I wish I could bring you better news about your father, but William is not doing well physically. He has had several bad spells over the past few months, and each time leaves him a little weaker. I pray that God would let me keep him for as long as it is His will, for I would be lost without him.*
>
> *I cannot tell you how proud I am of Will, and how happy I am that he married Rebekah. . . .*

Elizabeth's mind went back to the time when her mother had not felt that way. Her brother, Will, had been engaged to marry a young woman named Charlotte Van Dorn. Rebekah was a servant in her father's house, and never once had it occurred to any of them that Will would do other than marry Charlotte. It had been through Rebekah that the plan hatched by Charlotte and her father to take control of the Martin shipping business had been revealed. During this time, Anne had disliked Patrick MacNeal, and when Patrick had been implicated in the scandal fabricated by the Van Dorns, she had been extremely harsh to him. It had been Rebekah who had discovered the scheme and had told Elizabeth and Patrick. Elizabeth remembered how hurt Will had been at the treachery of the woman he had planned to marry. After the storm had broken and the Van Dorns had left, it had been Rebekah who had been there to listen to Will. The young man had fallen in love with her, and now the two had married, and Elizabeth was filled with gratitude that her mother had someone there who loved her and whom she trusted.

> *Your father and I are so pleased with Rebekah's growth. She is*

a godsend to your dear father, seeing to his every need, and she and Will are so much in love that it is a joy to observe them. I think God has sent her to us to take care of us and to cheer us in our loneliness since you are so far away. I love you, my daughter, and pray that God will bless you in every way. You live so far from this place that I do not know if I shall see you again on this earth, but we can be certain that we will never be separated in the day of Christ Jesus.

Your loving mother, Anne

Elizabeth's face had grown sober as she had read the letter, and Hawk had not missed this.

"Bad news, Elizabeth?"

"No, not really. It's good news, as a matter of fact. Will and Rebekah are doing splendidly."

Hawk had not been a husband long to this woman, but he had learned to know her well. Now he leaned forward and said, "You miss your family, don't you?"

"Yes, I do."

"Well, it couldn't be otherwise. We'll pray that God will work things out so you can see them again."

Elizabeth smiled at her husband and took his hand in a gesture of gratitude at his understanding.

Andrew had listened to all of this, and finally when the conversation had changed, he said, "Hey, Jacob, tomorrow I can't wait to show you some of the things to do around here."

"What sort of things?"

"Well, hunting and fishing. We'll go fishing tomorrow, if you want to."

"I think that would be a good idea." Hawk smiled. "Andrew's one of the best fishermen around here."

A flash of resentment came to Jacob. He could not seem to control it. "I'm not sure," he said coolly. "I'll have to see."

Andrew's face showed the disappointment, and he said, "Well, anytime you want to I'll be ready."

"I know one thing you can do tomorrow," Sarah said, an impish light in her eyes. "You can ask Abigail to go fishing with you. But you wouldn't want another fellow along, then, would you?"

"Who's Abigail?" Jacob asked, seeing the flush rise in Andrew's face.

"Abigail Stevens," Sarah grinned. "Andy's sweet on her."

"I am not! You hush up, Sarah! We're just friends, Abby and me."

Hawk, Elizabeth, and Sarah laughed at Andrew's discomfort, but then Elizabeth grew more serious. "I do want you to meet all the young people in the community. Why don't you ask Abigail to come over tomorrow, and Amanda Taylor, as well."

As she said this, her eyes suddenly went to Hawk, and an unspoken communication passed between the two. He understood at once that there was something she needed to say that could not be spoken in front of the children, and he knew that she would speak of it later.

————

It had been a tiring journey, and the family went to bed very early. Sarah was in her room, Andrew and Jacob slept in the main room, and in the larger of the two bedrooms, Hawk and Elizabeth were stretched out in bed. He put his arm around her, and she turned and moved close to him, stroking his bare chest as she asked, "Tell me how the trip went. I was so glad that Jacob came back with you."

"He refused to come at first. I didn't think he would."

"I was a little surprised. What changed his mind?"

Hawk reached over and stroked Elizabeth's glossy hair gently. He knew she had bathed today, for she always put lilac in the bath water, and then he could smell it in her hair as well. "You smell good," he said quietly.

"Never mind my smell. What made him come back?"

"I don't know. I think he had some kind of a disappointment in love."

"Love! Why, he's only fifteen."

"No, sixteen now. He's had another birthday, and anyway, if I remember when I was sixteen, love affairs were mighty important."

"How many did you have when you were sixteen?"

"Must have been dozens. Can't keep track of 'em all."

She was accustomed to his mild teasing and reached up and tapped his nose. "Don't tease me. What happened? Why did he come?"

"I think God worked a miracle. He was very cold toward me from the day I arrived, and I couldn't, of course, blame him for that.

And then out of nowhere he marched in and said he had decided to come and live with us for a while." He hesitated, then added, "He made that pretty plain. It's only for a while."

"I think he'll like it here. He and Andrew are about the same age. They can be real brothers."

"I hope so." He thought again of her look at the table and said, "What were you going to tell me about the Taylors?"

"Oh, it's not good news. Zeke's drinking again!"

"You've seen him?" Hawk was surprised, and the motion of his hand on her hair stopped.

"No, I haven't seen him, but there are rumors. Besides, Iris and Amanda aren't coming around. I haven't seen them since the wedding."

"That may not mean anything."

"I think it does. Iris was coming by very often to visit and to talk to me about the things in the Scriptures, and she was bringing Amanda by. That girl needs all the friends she can get. She and Sarah get along well together. You'll have to see to it."

"Who made me a keeper?"

"I did. You do it because I say so."

Hawk smiled, then rolled over on his side and pulled her closer. He had not known how much he would miss this woman that lay beside him. Long years of loneliness had hardened him, but now that they had married, he discovered, to his shock and amazement, that he was not the same man. Always before he did as he pleased, and now he found himself trying to find little things that would please Elizabeth.

"Did you miss me?" he whispered.

"Oh, were you gone?"

Hawk squeezed her suddenly, his strength driving the breath out of her. "I'll have to remind you what you've been missing since I've been gone."

Elizabeth reveled in the strength of his arms. She put her arms around his neck, pulled him closer, and kissed him firmly.

"Remind me," she whispered. . . .

———————

Jacob and Andrew had already fallen into bed. Jacob was almost blind with fatigue. The trip had been hard on him, and he had not known how tired he was until he had stretched out on the corn-shuck mattress. Andrew was saying something vaguely, and turning his attention with an effort, Jacob heard the younger boy say something about what a wonderful man Hawk was and how thankful he was that God had sent him into his family's life. "There's nobody like him, not in all these mountains," Andrew said. "He can shoot straighter and run farther and is stronger than any man in the whole settlement."

"I suppose so."

Andrew said, as he had before, "I guess I didn't say it very well, Jacob, but I'm really glad you're here. I get lonesome sometimes. Sarah gives me a hard time. She's always teasing me. Now maybe with you here we can give her some of what she's been dishing out."

"All right."

"Can't wait for you to meet the other young people, especially Abby."

This caught Jacob's attention. "Is she pretty?"

"Oh, she's all right." The brief reply covered up more than Andrew wanted to reveal. "I know it'll be different for you here, but you'll like it. I came from Boston myself, you know, and I had to learn everything. But we're going to have a great time." He seemed to sense then that the visitor was not saying much and said quickly, "Well, good night, Jacob."

Jacob closed his eyes and after a hesitation said, "Good night."

As the silence grew, he thought about what he had seen on his journey from Williamsburg. It had been exciting to him, moving through the mountains. The danger of it was merely an added enticement, and he felt a stirring in him that he had not felt in town. He knew he was green, however, and resented the fact that Andrew MacNeal had already had his training under Hawk Spencer.

I'll learn, he thought. *I bet I'll shoot better and run farther than Andrew after I've been here awhile.* He thought of his father, and as he did he heard Andrew mumbling a prayer and was slightly shocked by it. He knew that Elizabeth was a Christian woman, and now his father had given his life to God, or so he said. *But they're not going to force their religion down my throat!* he thought with a surly attitude. He lay there quietly, exhaustion causing sleep to come quickly. As he drifted off, his last thought was of the face of Annabelle. She seemed to be smiling at him and holding her arms out, inviting him to come back, and he fell asleep crying her name in his dream.

The Young Lion

Eight

*E*lizabeth awoke to the sound of a voice, muted but clearly audible, directly in front of her. Opening her eyes to slits, she pulled the quilt down and caught sight of Hawk, his back to her, peering into the tiny mirror over the washstand and raking his face with a straight razor. A smile touched her lips as she heard his grumbling and the rasp of the razor as he pulled it across one cheek. The room was cold, but despite that, Hawk wore only a pair of buckskin trousers. *I don't think many men back east could break the ice in a basin and then shave in freezing water,* she thought and snuggled down in the bed, savoring the warmth.

She ran her hand over the quilt that was made up of large butterflies of varying hues—brilliant reds, cool greens, yellows, and all the other colors of the rainbow. She remembered making the quilt when she was no more than six or seven years old, learning to sew under her mother's tutelage. They had sat in the large parlor listening to the ticking of the grandfather clock as they made the tiny stitches that put the butterflies together. The scene was so clear to her that she almost seemed to see the woman and the small child peering at the colorful cloths and patterns as they sewed side by side. That had been over twenty-five years ago, and the thought came to Elizabeth, *I wonder where the little girl is now? The little girl that I was? She was so alive and vibrant and full of life, and now she's become part of my past.* She knew, with a sudden flash of insight, that not all of that little girl was lost, for part of her still remained in the grown-up woman.

Elizabeth turned her attention back to Hawk and watched as he finished his shave. Bending over, the large muscles of his back and shoulders flared out—a contrast to his rather small waist and lean hips. He had long muscles rather than bulky ones, and as he ruffled his hair, threw the water in his face, bubbling as he did so, she took a pride in his strength. He was built for hard usage, and the land had tempered him, stripping away every ounce of excess weight, so that now all was bone, sinew, and muscle. He turned and caught her watching him. Grinning, he came over and sat down beside her on the bed.

"You going to sleep all day?"

"Yes."

"Then I'll come back to bed with you."

"No," Elizabeth protested, putting her hand on his chest. She felt the strong, vibrant muscles beneath her hand, and she felt safe and secure with this man, for she knew that whatever could be done to protect her and her family, Hawk would do it. "I'm getting up," she said.

Hawk winked at her, saying, "That's a pity!"

"Never you mind that!"

Elizabeth shivered as she got out of bed. Reaching over, she grabbed a wool robe and shrugged into it, then slipped her feet into the moccasins that Hawk had given her. The fur was turned inside and they immediately warded off the chill of the room. Rising, she went over to the washstand, poured the water out of the basin, and filled it with fresh water. "I wish we could have hot water every morning."

"We can. All you have to do is heat it."

"I mean, I wish that someone would do it for me," Elizabeth smiled archly. "I'd like to have a little bit of luxury."

Hawk came over and stood behind her, putting his arms around her waist, pressing her soft body back against his firm strength. He had put on his hunting shirt now and leaned down and whispered against her fragrant hair. "You smell mighty good," he said.

"How good?"

"Better than most things out here. Better than a black bear, I'd say."

"Oh, get away, Hawk!" she protested and pushed away from his embrace.

As she washed her face, she was aware that he had sat down on the bed and was watching her. It was something he did every time he got a chance, and Elizabeth found it pleasing. She had not known exactly how her second marriage would work out. She had been so happy with Patrick, who had loved her dearly, and she had returned his love. One of her friends had said a second marriage could never be as happy as the first if you had a good man the first time. But now Elizabeth knew this was not so. As she brushed her hair, she said, "Christmas is coming."

"Well, don't get excited. You haven't been good enough to get any presents."

"We'll see about that." She continued to stroke her hair with the brush. It was thick blond hair with brown highlights, and it sprang back into waves as the brush passed over it. "What about Jacob?"

"He's trying. It's a big change for him."

"Do you think he likes it out here?"

"I'm not sure. He likes some of it, but so much of it's so strange to him. He has to get used to a new family, and our ways are different."

Elizabeth put the brush down and turned to him. She raised her arms and began to pin her hair up with hairpins. "You know, I have an idea. Why don't we have a big dinner? We'd all like it, and we could go to special pains for Jacob, making him feel at home."

"That's not a bad idea. Who would you have?"

"Well, I would like to have—let me see." Her lips pursed, and her eyes half closed as she went over the neighbors in her mind. "I'd like to have the Andersons and the Stevenses and the Beans, of course." She thought awhile longer, then said, "Would it be too many to have the Robertsons and the Taylors?"

"If you like crowds, that ought to do it."

"It'll be fun." She came over, put her hands behind his neck, and looked down at him. "Would you go with me to invite them all?"

"Sure. Why not."

"It'll be a good chance for us to check up on the Taylors. I'm not happy about the way things are going over there. Could we go this morning?"

"Sure. We'll go right after breakfast."

She leaned down, kissed him, then smiled brilliantly. "You are a fine husband. Most men would hate doing something like that."

"I'm a wonder, I am," Hawk shrugged. "I'm glad you're learning to finally recognize it."

They left the bedroom, and Elizabeth fixed breakfast while Hawk went outside to do a few of the chores. When he came back, Andrew and Sarah were up and already seated at the breakfast table. Jacob had joined them, and Hawk said cheerfully, "Good morning. I think it's going to be a great day. Did your mother tell you what we're going to do?"

"No," Sarah piped up and looked at her mother. "What is it, Ma?"

Elizabeth was bringing a pan of biscuits from the hearth, holding them with a thick cloth. Setting them down, she examined the golden tops and shook her head, saying, "I think I got these a little too done." Then she smiled and said, "Your father and I have a surprise for you. We're going to have an enormous Christmas party." She went on to describe the event that was to come, then said, "We're going out today to visit everyone and give invitations. I'd like for you all to come."

Sarah and Andrew were anxious to go, but Jacob said quickly, "If you don't mind, I think I'll stay around here. I don't feel too well."

Elizabeth glanced at Hawk, for both of them knew that this was an excuse. Nevertheless, they sat down and, after the blessing, enjoyed the good breakfast. After they had cleaned up and gone out to make their visit, Hawk paused by Sequatchie where he was standing idly in front of the small cabin watching them leave. "Watch out for Jacob while we're gone."

"I always will, friend."

———

The sun had risen, and although it was cold and a brisk wind bit at their faces, the family had an enjoyable time. They had visited all of the prospective guests except the Taylors, and now they wound around the crooked path that led to the Taylor farm.

Sarah was sitting with Andrew on the brown mare, and as she swung with the rhythm of the animal, she said, "What am I going to get for Christmas, Pa?"

"You're not going to get anything," Andrew answered before Hawk could speak. "You haven't been good enough to get a present."

"I have so!" Sarah began to beat on Andrew's back, and he hunched his shoulders.

"Stop that or I'll throw you off!"

"Well, you won't get any presents by beating up on your brother, Sarah," Elizabeth rebuked her daughter.

Immediately Sarah stopped and sat sullenly, but before they had gone another quarter of a mile, once again she was pleading to know what her presents would be.

Elizabeth was amused and irritated at her daughter, whose impetuousness matched her fiery red hair. *She's not like me. I don't know who she's like,* Elizabeth thought as she took in the pale green eyes and the fair skin under the bonnet that shaded her forehead and eyes. *She's not like Andrew. He's like his father. There must have been some wild man or wild woman back in my family tree.* She was concerned about Sarah, for despite a basic sweetness in the girl, there was a rebellious streak that surfaced from time to time.

"There's the Taylors," Hawk said, interrupting her thought.

As they moved up to the small cabin across a yard cluttered with trash, Iris Taylor stepped outside the door to greet them. Instantly Elizabeth saw that she looked unhappy and apprehensive, but she smiled as she dismounted and went over and embraced the woman. "It's so good to see you, Iris. How are you?"

"Fine," Iris said, but her eyes were fearful, and something in the tone of her voice was not right. She cut her eyes back to glance at the cabin, then made herself smile. "I'm glad to see you all. Won't you—" She broke off abruptly and Elizabeth knew she had been about to say, "Won't you come in," but something had stopped her.

"We've come to invite you to a big Christmas party," Sarah burst out. "We've asked everybody to come, and now you've got to promise, Mrs. Taylor."

Iris hesitated. Most women would have answered in the affirmative at once, but at that moment Zeke Taylor came to the door. He was wearing a pair of shabby trousers, torn and ragged at the cuffs, and a heavy wool shirt missing several buttons, exposing dirty underwear, and the man had not shaved in several days. His eyes were hooded, and he said gruffly, "Hello." He did not ask them to dismount and come in but stood glowering at them.

"We're having a big Christmas celebration, Zeke," Hawk said easily. He sat on his horse loosely, his hands resting on the saddle horn. "We'd like to have you and your family join us."

Taylor's eyes were filled with suspicion and something else.

"Thank you," he said shortly. "I reckon we'll be spendin' the holidays at home."

"Oh, please, Mr. Taylor, won't you come? At least let Amanda come. Is she here?" Sarah asked.

"She's busy," Zeke Taylor responded harshly. "Can't come to the door." Taylor shifted his feet impatiently, and once again put a hard glance on Hawk, then muttered, "We've got things to do." He turned to enter the door, then paused and swung around to face Iris, obviously waiting for her to join him.

At one time Iris Taylor would have instantly walked inside, but on the journey from the East she had gained some measure of self-confidence. It was not much, but from the time Hawk had held a knife to her husband's throat and threatened to scalp him if he ever laid his hand on his wife or daughter, a tiny spark of independence showed, as it did now.

"I'll be in in just a minute, Zeke."

Zeke Taylor stared at her, and his body stiffened. "Hurry up, then," he muttered. He wheeled and walked inside, slamming the door.

Iris swallowed hard. It had taken all of her courage to stand up to him, for he was a volatile man. "I thank you for your invitation, but I'm sorry, we can't come."

Elizabeth instantly took Iris's hand and asked gently, "What is it, Iris?"

"It's . . . nothing. Just pray for us, will you?"

Hawk said instantly, "You know where to find me if you need anything, Iris."

She cast a quick look at Hawk's face and murmured, "I thank you," then turned and walked back inside the cabin, closing the door quietly.

Hawk and Elizabeth exchanged concerned looks, then it was Elizabeth who turned and said, "I guess it's time to go home."

———

As the sun rose in the sky, pale and without much heat, Jacob wandered aimlessly around the homestead. During the weeks that he had been here, he had learned to know the farm and the surrounding woods very well. Now he paused to stare at the place where Hawk had told him a new barn would be built in the spring to house a cow and maybe some pigs. A brief flicker of interest came to him, and he found himself considering which direction it should face. Then he abruptly pulled his mind away, thinking, *I won't be here to see it,* and walked quickly down across the open space and into the woods of second-growth oaks and elms.

Reaching the small stream, he halted and stood looking down into it. He had enjoyed catching the fat pumpkinseed perch and now considered going back for a line and some bait. Finally he decided against it, then moving close to the stream, he reached down and let the force of the water form a furrow across his knuckles. It was icy cold, and on the sand just beneath the water's surface, a school of minnows remained suspended almost motionless, their shiny bodies flashing like raw silver. A sudden movement of his hand, and then they were all off, turning as one animal. *How do they know how to do that all at the same time?* Jacob wondered. *They always go the same way quicker than you can think.*

He rose and turned to go down the stream and then halted abruptly, fear leaping into his throat, for a man stood there. For a moment Jacob froze, and then he recognized Sequatchie. It irritated him that he had not heard the man, although he knew the Indian could walk silently, even through woods where his own feet crunched dried twigs and crispy leaves that had fallen earlier.

Sequatchie did not move for a time, and then finally he said, "How are things with you, my son?"

"All right."

"They are not good between you and your father."

"He's not my father!"

"Don't be foolish! He *is* your father! I'm surprised at you, Jacob!" Sequatchie's dark eyes took in the rebellious expression of the boy's face. "I thought you would gain some wisdom out here."

Jacob shifted and was unable to meet Sequatchie's piercing eyes. He let his glance turn and studied a tall dead tree where a redheaded woodpecker clung to the side drumming. After a moment he turned and answered, his voice low and somewhat uncertain. "Nothing can ever give me back the years I lost. He owed them to me, Sequatchie, and he didn't pay his debt!"

"You must learn to forgive."

"But he left me without a father!"

"You always have a father," Sequatchie replied instantly. He felt the boy's gaze return and held Jacob's eyes as he pointed up, saying, "Your heavenly Father never changes. The Bible says that He is the Father of the fatherless."

Jacob shifted nervously. He reached down, picked up a stick, and threw it in the water, watching as the concentric waves spread out. "How do the Indians know what the Bible says?"

Sequatchie shrugged slightly and spoke evenly. "A long time ago a man named Elmo McGuire came to my people. He brought a book with him, and many, including myself, learned to know the God of heaven and His Son Jesus Christ."

"What happened to him, this missionary?"

"He died, then all we had left of him was the book, but no one could read it."

"That must have been hard," Jacob murmured.

"Yes, it was hard, but then something happened." Sequatchie's face broke for a moment from its customary impassive cast, and a smile spread across his bronzed face. "Your father came along. He was running from God, but he could read the Book, and we made a pact, your father and I. I would teach him the ways of the forest, and he would read from the Bible to the Cherokee."

Jacob was shocked but impressed. He had not known this part of his father's story. "Do you think God was in all of that?" he asked.

"Yes. I know it to be true." Sequatchie went on to tell how on two occasions Hawk had been impressed by a vision of a deer. "But it may not have been a vision," he said. "Whatever it was, God has used your father to help my people."

Sequatchie seemed to be finished as Jacob stood in silence, thinking over what he had said. Finally Sequatchie added, "You may not like to hear all of this, and it was wrong of Hawk to leave you. But God used him, even when he was not obedient, to help my people."

"I didn't know this," Jacob murmured. Somehow the Cherokee's words troubled him. He had his mind made up to dislike his father, but the open honesty of Sequatchie and his obvious admiration of Hawk stirred him. As he stood there, a shrill scream split the air, and Jacob flinched and whirled to face the source of the sound. "What was that?" he gasped.

"That is what your people call a mountain lion."

Even as Sequatchie spoke, a tawny flash caught Jacob's eye, and he saw a large cat leave the shelter of the trees. It was visible only for a second before it disappeared back into the brush.

"What's he screaming about?"

"It is a female. She has missed her kill, and her cubs will go hungry."

"How do you know all of that?"

Sequatchie shrugged. "That is the way of the Cherokee." He saw Jacob's eyes mirror disbelief and then added, "Your Bible will speak of this."

"What do you mean? About a lion?"

"Yes. In the book called Psalms, one verse says, 'The young lions do lack and suffer hunger: but they that seek the Lord shall not want any good thing.' Hawk has told me that the lions in the lands where the Bible was written are different, but to me God is telling us about lions. If you would turn to God for your needs," he said abruptly, without warning, "you would not feel so empty inside."

Startled, Jacob demanded, "How do you know how I feel?"

"Because my father died when I was very young, so I grew up without a father also."

"That's different. Your father didn't run away and leave you!"

"No, but losing a father leaves an empty place in your heart." After a pause, Sequatchie continued. "And the Bible tells you what happens to these young lions in another place. It says, 'The young lions roar after their prey and seek their meat from God.' If you would seek God, you wouldn't need anyone else to fill the emptiness of your heart. You must learn, in any case, that no human being can take the place of God. Only God can fill that place."

Jacob was angry as he listened. He did not want to hear about his father, and he did not want to hear about God. "You just don't understand, Sequatchie."

When Sequatchie did not answer, Jacob grew calm. He scratched in the dirt with his feet, then shifted nervously. "I wish I knew the frontier and the woods."

"I will be glad to teach the son of Hawk as I did his father."

"Really? Would you do that for me, Sequatchie?"

"Yes." Sequatchie nodded, and then his lips turned upward in a smile. "There is a price, of course. Just as there was for teaching your father."

"A price? I don't have any money."

Sequatchie stared at the young man and seemed to be thinking hard. Finally he said, "It is time to discuss our first agreement."

"Which agreement is that?"

"About how long you will stay here in this place."

"I'm only going to stay until spring, until the warm weather comes."

"If you will stay longer, I will teach you as I've taught your father. You will become a true long hunter, a man of the woods. You have the makings of a great hunter in you, but you will need a teacher."

Jacob considered his words of encouragement but said nothing. Now he asked quickly, "How long would I have to stay?"

"Until," Sequatchie said evenly, "you become a man."

Overhead a red-tailed hawk soared, looking for his prey. Jacob looked up and watched as the magnificent hunter suddenly banked, folded his wings, and dropped. He disappeared behind the trees, but somehow Jacob knew that he had made his kill. He turned to Sequatchie, who was watching him, and said abruptly, "All right. If you will teach me, I'll stay."

"Good. We are agreed."

Sequatchie spent the rest of the day with Jacob. He had formed a genuine attachment to the young man, and when Hawk and the others appeared and Jacob went to meet them, Sequatchie leaned back against a towering hickory tree and lifted his gaze upward, praying for God to touch the son of Hawk.

Christmas Surprise

Nine

*R*ising before dawn, Elizabeth prepared a quick breakfast of eggs, ham left over from supper the night before, and bread served with apple butter. As soon as it was ready, she sent Hawk, Sequatchie, Jacob, and Andrew out to find a Christmas tree, while she kept Sarah beside her to help with the cooking.

After the men had left, Elizabeth began cooking all the food for the enormous dinner she had planned. Her mind raced ahead, counting the guests and arranging, in her own imagination, how everything would take place.

An hour later she heard the sound of voices and stepped to the door. It was cold outside, although December had been warmer than usual. She saw Hawk carrying a perfect Christmas tree.

"We got some mistletoe and red berries," he called out as he approached the door.

"Bring it inside."

"Going to be crowded enough with all this company," Hawk warned.

"I can't help it. We've got to have a tree. Sarah, make a place for it over in the corner."

Jacob was surprised to discover that he could take part in the festivities. He joined in with Sarah and Andrew, who were stringing popcorn with needles for decorations, and soon after, the guests began to arrive. The Andersons and the Stevenses came first, and Deborah had done a great deal of cooking. Opening up a basket, she began taking out pie tins of chicken pudding, a large plate of almond tarts, and Sally Lunn bread. Joined by Abigail, the women all helped pull the meal together.

Paul Anderson and George Stevens stepped outside to join the other men while the women worked on the meal and talked about the news in the settlement.

Elizabeth took a quick break from the cooking to inspect the tree and laughed at the decorating job. "You men can do better than that."

"Why, it looks all right to me," Hawk said with surprise.

"It takes a woman to decorate. Sarah, you and Abigail do it right. You can get Jacob and Andrew to help you."

Jacob kept back, but he could not help noticing how attractive Abigail Stevens was. He admired the thick brown hair that fell down in waves and the cool gray-green eyes. Most of all he noticed the smooth complexion and trim young figure. *She's going to be a beauty when she grows up*, Jacob thought. He was, at sixteen, a year and a half older than Abigail, but there was a precocious quality about Abigail Stevens that caught his attention.

As Abigail decorated the tree, she was well aware that Jacob Spencer was gazing at her. He was very tall, she saw, with the same wavy black hair and dark blue eyes of his father. She held his gaze for a moment, then smiled at him, and at once he came to stand beside her.

"I'm not much on decorating," he said. "How do you do it?"

"Why, it's easy. I'll show you."

The two seemed to be preoccupied with each other, and then Sarah called out, "Andrew, you and Jacob hang the mistletoe."

Jacob, being the tallest, reached up and fastened a sprig of mistletoe to the ceiling of the cabin. As he did so, Abigail walked by, seemingly by accident.

"Jacob, look at Abigail," Sarah said. "She's right under the mistletoe. You know that means you must kiss her."

Jacob grinned abruptly, reached out, and kissed Abigail on the cheek very near her lips. "I suppose if it's the custom, I must do it," he said. He kissed her again on the other cheek and Abigail flushed, but her bright eyes were laughing.

Andrew said abruptly, "There's no time for this foolishness!"

Sarah looked at her brother with a demure smile and, knowing him well, poked him in the ribs. "You'll have to be quicker than that if you're going to hang on to Abigail," she said.

Jacob overheard her and turned away so they would not see the smile that had come to his face.

––––––––––

The rather small cabin was soon crowded, for William and Lydia Bean and James and Charlotte Robertson had arrived. The Beans brought their children, including Russell, who had the distinction of being the first white child born in the area in 1769. The Robertsons had a baby born that same year, but a little later. They had brought the child when they had come west.

The meal was a great success. Something about being packed in so closely added to the fellowship, and the room resounded with laughter. Finally, as Elizabeth directed the women in bringing out the gooseberry and blackberry pies, the talk turned to the Donelson Survey.

"I don't know exactly what we're going to do," William Bean said fretfully. "We may have to leave our lands."

"I don't agree with that," Hawk said quickly. "A line on a piece of paper isn't going to drive me off this place."

James Robertson leaned back, chewed thoughtfully on the pie, and shook his head. "I'm with you, Hawk. I don't like the sound of it, but we'll have to wait until spring."

After the meal was over, the Beans and the Robertsons left to visit brothers and sisters who had settled in the area. The Andersons and the Stevenses stayed a little longer to help clean up. While the adults were busy, Andrew took the opportunity to pull Abigail aside. "Let's go outside a minute, Abigail. I . . . have a present for you."

"Oh, Andy, I don't have anything for you!"

"That's all right. Here, I hope you like it."

Abigail's eyes were warm as she opened the brown wrapping. When she took out the object that was inside, she squealed with pleasure. "Oh, it's a muff!"

"Yes. Mother made them from the pelts I caught and cleaned. That ought to keep your hands warm."

Abigail reached out and touched him on the chest gently. "That was very thoughtful of you."

As the two stood together just outside the front door of the cabin, Jacob suddenly appeared. "There you are!" he said. "I wondered where you two had gone. I understand we're going to sing carols around the tree. Come on in!"

Jacob took Abigail's arm and pulled her back inside. She glanced back at Andrew with an apologetic smile and a shrug as she disappeared through the doorway. Andrew followed the two but felt somehow that he had been cheated. "Jacob could have waited," he said. "He didn't have to come butting in like that!" While the singing went on, Andrew himself mumbled the words but could not help but notice the admiring looks Abigail gave to Jacob, who had, indeed, a fine singing voice. A thought came to Andrew, but he pushed it down and shook his head slightly, then tried valiantly to join in with the celebration.

———————

" 'And it came to pass in those days that Caesar Augustus sent forth an edict that all the world should be taxed. . . .' "

Elizabeth sat quietly as Hawk read through the Christmas story. Her glance went around at the children, and she noted that Jacob somehow managed to separate himself so that he sat with his back against the cabin wall.

When Hawk finished the story he looked up and said, "Elizabeth, you made it a wonderful year for me." Turning to the children, he said, "And you three. You give a man a reason for living. Now," he said, "it's time for Christmas gifts." He moved out of the room and came back with a cotton sack and pulled out several packages, handing them out. "I guess I'm Santa Claus," he grinned.

Sarah opened the package and gasped when she saw the beautiful new dress her mother had made. It was made out of a royal blue silk with a square neckline edged in white lace, and elbow-length sleeves that ended with a large band of royal blue brocade and a large white lace ruffle. The bodice had an edging of brocade following all the way down the front and onto the plain overskirt, and the stomacher had been delicately embroidered with white thread in the pattern of snowflakes. The petticoat was made of the same material and had no decoration, but a pretty pinner cap of white linen and lace and a beautiful blue silken cord with a drop pearl completed the outfit.

Andrew found a coonskin cap inside his package and instantly clapped it on his forehead.

Sarah was intrigued with the music box that Hawk had brought back from Williamsburg and put her ear down close, her lips moving in time with the music.

But it was Jacob who was surprised. There had been nothing in the sack for him, and he had felt left out. Then suddenly Hawk had stepped back into the room and come out with a rifle in his hand. "This is for you, Jacob."

Jacob was speechless, for he saw at once that it was a new Kentucky long rifle. He had heard of the weapon before but had only seen one on rare occasions. He let his fingers slide over the gun, then looked at his father, unable to speak.

"Do you like it, Jacob?" Hawk asked quietly.

"Oh yes! It's wonderful, but you shouldn't have done it!"

"Why, of course I should have done it." He clapped the boy on the shoulder and said, "You might need a lesson or two. Be glad to teach you what I know."

Jacob had been open and felt pleased with the gift, but the deep resentment he had kept bottled up over the years came out, and he heard himself saying, "That's okay. I think I can handle it." He saw that his father's face broke, and there was a hurt look in his eyes. He glanced over and saw Sequatchie staring at him with a frown, so he said, "Well, maybe we could all go out together."

Sequatchie had sat back, not taking part in the gift exchange, and now he rose and left the room. Jacob said, "I'll get some more wood." He hastened out of the cabin and caught up with Sequatchie. "I guess I didn't handle that very well, did I?"

"No. Not too well. Your father deserves better."

"I'll . . . I'll try to do better. I'll talk to him."

Jacob picked up a few sticks of firewood and went back inside. Several times that evening he tried to get Hawk alone, but the house was small, so finally he went to bed without saying a word. He looked over at his stepbrother and thought for an instant of telling him that he enjoyed the Christmas, but instead, "It was a good celebration."

"Yes, it was. Good night."

Surprised by Andrew's rebuff, Jacob stared at him, then he recognized that Andrew had barely spoken to him since he had kissed Abigail under the mistletoe. He lay back and shook his head, thinking, *I'm not doing too well. I'll have to do better than this.*

Hawk and Elizabeth were preparing for bed, and when Elizabeth had put on her nightgown, she turned to him and said, "I've got a present for you."

"Do I have to wait for it until Christmas morning?"

Elizabeth had a strange expression on her face. She put her hands on his broad chest and for a moment said nothing. Her eyes were glowing. "You'll have to wait a little longer than that. As a matter of fact," she whispered, "you'll have to wait seven months."

Hawk blinked with surprise, then suddenly her meaning came to him. A light of pure pleasure leaped to his eyes, and he put his arms around her, looking down. "Are you sure?"

"As sure as a woman could be at this point." Elizabeth reached up and put her hands on his lips but merely shook her head. "God has blessed us." She savored the feel of his strong arms around her and ran her hand around the planes of his jaw. There was a joy in her that she had never known before, and now to cover up the tears that threatened to come, she said, "Well, God's blessed us even if you are an old man."

Hawk laughed and held her tightly. "You're right about that. I got me a child bride."

"Hawk, are you happy about it?"

"Yes. Nothing could have made me happier. It's a miracle from God." He held her close, put his lips on hers tenderly, and then she buried her face against his chest. The two stood there completely and totally happy for that moment, and Elizabeth wished that nothing would ever change.

———————

The morning dawned and the cabin was filled with the sound of laughter. There was no time for breakfast, for there were other presents to be exchanged, including sweets made by Elizabeth and Sarah, and handmade things that Hawk, Andrew, and Sequatchie had created themselves.

After the presents were opened, Hawk suddenly said, "Elizabeth has one more present to give us all."

Everyone turned to Elizabeth and she suddenly flushed. "It's . . . it's really a present for all of us from God."

Sarah immediately squealed. "Am I going to have a baby sister?"

As soon as his mother nodded, Andrew shook his head. "No, it's going to be a boy, isn't it, Pa? Isn't that what you want?"

"A son would be nice, but a daughter would be all right, too." He grinned at Sarah and then went over to put his arm around her, saying, "I like girls mighty well, Sarah. They're nice and they smell better than boys. Maybe it will be a girl."

Everyone was excited, but only Sequatchie noticed that Jacob was saying little. He watched the young man and suddenly knew what he was thinking as clearly as if he had spoken it. *Hawk is going to have a son, and he'll be left out again. He's already envious of Andy's relationship with his father, and now once more he'll feel on the outside.*

Jacob Spencer would have resented Sequatchie's saying such a thing. He sat back, watching the happiness in the faces of everyone, and tried to make himself smile, but, indeed, he did feel left out—an outsider in his own family.

PART II

Watauga

April 1772 – April 1774

For the LORD thy God bringeth thee into a good land,
a land of brooks of water, of fountains and depths that spring
out of the valleys and hills.

Deuteronomy 8:7

Meeting at Chota

Ten

Sequatchie had risen before dawn, as was his custom, and made his way down to the creek that meandered across the valley. For some time he stood quietly, motionlessly watching the sun shake off the night and cast its rays over the eastern hills. Most men would not have noticed the details of the landscape that absorbed the pale crimson rays of the great sun, but the Cherokee was alert, and his obsidian eyes missed nothing. His quick eye caught the flash of a white tail as a deer a hundred yards away stepped out of the brush and dropped her head to drink. Sequatchie took pleasure in the beauty of the animal, watching the doe as she stepped across the creek, lifting her head from time to time, alertly searching the landscape for possible danger.

The water at his feet bubbled over rounded stones, some of them covered with green moss. Once a large fish broke the water, his huge mouth open, as he enveloped a smaller fish, then fell back with a noisy splash.

"The big fish eats the little fish," Sequatchie murmured. "That is the way of the forest." His eyes narrowed, and for a moment he was moved by a black depression that sometimes came upon him. "And that is the way it is with men, also," he spoke his thought aloud. He knew the history of his people better than most and had the vision to see that there was no stopping the white man. He knew that the ancient ways of the Cherokee were doomed, and he had spent many hours trying to find some way to make the passing of the nation less painful to the tribes. Nevertheless, as he stood soaking in the early beams of the morning sun that now began to throw a long light across the top of the eastern hills, he could find no answers. *A man must do what God has put in his way. The way of the Cherokee is passing, and now we will see what the white man will do to this world.*

When the sun had cleared the ragged tops of the hills, he turned and slowly made his way to the Spencers' cabin. Hearing the sound of voices inside, he called out. At once the door was opened and he was greeted warmly by Elizabeth.

"Come in, Sequatchie. You're just in time for breakfast."

Hawk was already seated at the table. His face was glowing from a fresh shave, and he looked happy and contented. "You have a positive gift for arriving whenever there's food to be had, my brother," he grinned.

A light of humor touched Sequatchie's eyes as he sat down across from Hawk. "It would be bad manners not to accept an invitation."

"Well, you have good manners, then. But I think we'd better eat hearty. It's going to be a hard trip."

Elizabeth moved quietly around the cabin as the two men talked. She stirred the mush until it was bubbling hot, poured three bowls full, then set them on the table, along with a bowl of fresh butter. Setting down a platter full of fried venison steaks and warmed biscuits, she remarked, "You'd better eat while it's hot."

Hawk bowed his head and asked a brief blessing. This simple act had been hard for him at first, but he had quickly learned to pray aloud without feeling awkward. Now as he picked up a biscuit and split it with his knife and layered it with the yellow butter, he asked Sequatchie, "How do you think the meeting will go?"

"We will know when we get there."

After breakfast the two were to be joined by James Robertson and John Bean, William's brother, to leave on a trip to meet with the Cherokee chiefs. The land problem had grown more serious for the Wataugans, and the leaders had felt it wise to make a special quest to speak with the chieftains. Sequatchie had been included to act as an intermediary.

"Have you thought what you will say, Hawk?" Elizabeth asked as she tasted the mush and added a little salt.

"I am leaving that mostly to John and James. From what Bean says, it would be best to ask the Cherokee to sell or to lease the land around the Watauga River." Chewing thoughtfully on a biscuit, Hawk was silent for a moment, then he lifted his eyes to Sequatchie.

"What do you say, friend? What will the Indians do?"

Sequatchie lifted a cup of cider, drank some of it, then shook his head doubtfully. "In every tribe there'll be hotheaded young warriors—and I'm afraid that's what we'll encounter. Even the chief's son, Dragging Canoe, and other braves like him will want to keep the old ways. They will attempt to sway the nation to fight—to kill the white man if necessary."

"Are there many of them?"

"I'm afraid there are enough to cause trouble, but a lot of the older chiefs I have already spoken with have more wisdom." Sadness clouded the dark eyes of the Cherokee, and he added quietly, "I have convinced them that it would be best to adopt the white man's way of life. Most of them see that we must do this, for more and more white men are going to come. In a way," Sequatchie said suddenly, "as tragic as it is in the eyes of some of my people, some good may come out of this."

"How is that, Sequatchie?" Elizabeth asked quickly. She had known little of Indians before she moved across the mountains, but this one godly man had changed her entire concept. She knew there were none more loyal or more honest than this tall man who sat across from her, and now she leaned forward to hear his answer.

"Why, as more white men come, the more they will spread the word of the Lord Jesus."

"Not all the white men who come will be good," Hawk warned.

"I know, and I hate what those who are greedy and selfish will do to my brothers—and to the land. The time will come when this land will not be what it is now, for the Indians honor the land, but the white man will cut down the trees, plow up the forest floor, kill off all the animals, and one day all this will be gone." He would have said more, but at that moment Jacob, Andrew, and Sarah entered the room, so he fell silent.

"Pa," Andrew demanded at once as he plopped down into his chair, "please let me go with you! Maybe I can be of some help."

Hawk shook his head at once, saying, "Andy, it seems like we go over this every time I leave the house. I need you to stay here and watch out for your mother and your sister."

"Jacob is here. He can do that."

"It will take both of you," Hawk said. "I know things have been quiet lately, but that's exactly the time when you need to be alert.

You never know when a hostile raiding party might come through, so I need both of you."

Jacob had said nothing, but now at these words he felt some resentment. He wanted Hawk to say that *he* alone could take care of the family, even though in all reality he knew this was not true.

Actually, Hawk was doing his best to keep both Andrew and Jacob out of danger, for he knew that the trip he and the others would endure would not be easy. He was slowly learning how to be a father, and he and Elizabeth had talked this over the previous night, agreeing that it would be safer for the two boys to stay on the homestead.

After breakfast the two men rose to leave, and as Hawk pulled his gear together, he mentioned, "Paul and Rhoda must miss having Sequatchie with them on their travels with the Cherokee, but this time I'm glad he's going with us." He said this more to change the subject, for he could tell that Elizabeth was worried about Jacob's sullen attitude lately.

"I'll be glad when they can come for a visit. I've learned to love Rhoda so much, and of course it's always a joy to have Paul around."

Hawk came over to her, holding his rifle in his right hand, with a bag slung over his shoulder. He put his left arm around her, drew her close, and ran his hand along her back. They were silent for a moment, and he whispered, "I still liked the idea about a man staying home for a year and pleasing his wife. Those Old Testament Jews had the right idea there."

Pulling his head down, Elizabeth kissed him fervently, then whispered, "Oh, be careful, Hawk!"

"I'm always careful. I'll be back as soon as I can."

When the two stepped outside, he found the three youngsters standing beside the cabin and Sequatchie already mounted and holding the lines of the two packhorses.

Hawk turned to Andrew, slapped him on the shoulder, and said, "Good-bye, son. Take care of things." He reached down, picked Sarah up, and twirled her around until she squealed. "Don't you get any prettier until I get back. You hear me?"

Jacob had watched this, and when Hawk turned to him, he had a momentary desire to go to him, but the same perverse spirit still kept him back.

"When I come back, Jacob," Hawk said, "we'll have some time together."

"Good-bye," Jacob nodded briefly, then watched as Hawk turned to Elizabeth and hugged her again.

"Take care of our little one," he whispered so quietly that only Jacob, who was standing closer, heard it, then he turned, swung onto his horse, and took the lines from his own packhorse. The two men swung away, and as the family watched them disappear, the last thing they saw was Hawk, who turned and waved to them with his free hand.

As soon as the cabin was out of sight, Sequatchie said, "It's hard to leave your family."

"Yes, it is. I haven't had one for so long, I'm having to get used to it."

The two men said little as they made their way to their rendezvous at William Bean's homestead, both filled with their own thoughts. When they reached the clearing around the Bean cabin, James and John were there waiting.

William Bean had come out to see them off, and now he said nervously, "I wish I was going on this trip. I didn't see how I could make it, though."

"That's all right, William," Hawk said. "We'll do the best we can without you."

"All right," William shrugged. "Get back as quick as you can. Cameron's not going to be put off too much longer. As soon as you return, we'll have to make some decisions about what to do. Off with you, now, and God be with you!" He stood and watched as the four men disappeared into the forest, leading their packhorses. Worry shaded his eyes, and he shrugged his shoulders impatiently, wishing that he could go. Finally, he turned and moved back toward his house.

———

"There it is. That's Chota, the sacred town of the Overhill Cherokee."

Sequatchie had pulled up his horse as the four men had topped a long crest. Hawk, Bean, and Robertson dismounted and stared down at the village. "It's not much, is it?" Robertson murmured, shading his eyes with his hand.

The village itself was made of longhouses that consisted of uprights of saplings buried in the ground, forming structures some fifteen feet wide and as long as forty feet. Dogs wandered among the children who were playing, and several Cherokee women were smoking meat over a large fire.

"It's been a hard trip," Hawk murmured. "I don't think my horse could have made it much farther." He turned to look up at Sequatchie, asking, "Do we just ride in?"

"Yes. You have not noticed our escort?"

"Escort?" Hawk said with surprise and looked around. "You mean we've had folks watching us?"

"For the last ten miles. You've grown careless living in the settlement."

"I reckon you're right," Hawk admitted with chagrin. He strolled ahead, his eyes more alert. As they made their way down the slope toward the longhouses, he indeed saw signs of life that he had missed before. *I'd better open my eyes*, he thought grimly. *I don't want to lose my scalp just when I'm starting to live.*

By the time they reached the heart of Chota, a crowd had gathered. Advance scouts had obviously brought word that they were in the vicinity. Most of the men bore arms of some sort, many of them holding ancient muskets, while others kept their tomahawks and bows ready.

"You must be patient," Sequatchie murmured. "My people are not in as much a hurry as white men."

Though the party was received well enough by the older chiefs, it was late that afternoon before any sort of formal meeting could take place. After a meal that consisted mostly of roasted venison, the chiefs arranged themselves in front of a large fire the young braves had built up, and a small, unimpressive Cherokee rose to make the welcoming speech.

"That's Chief Attacullaculla," Sequatchie whispered. He was sitting between James and Hawk and kept his voice only loud enough to be understood by these two and John, who was next to Robertson.

"The one they call the Little Carpenter?" Bean asked quickly.

"Yes. They call him that because he fits together peace treaties as a carpenter fits pieces of wood together. He is a wise man, and I'm hoping that he will be able to keep the wild young braves from violence."

The preliminaries took some time, for it included the smoking of the peace pipe and long speeches by several of the older chiefs.

All the time this was going on, however, Hawk was watching a fierce-looking warrior who sat directly across from him. He was very tall, and his muscular arms and powerful torso revealed a brute strength that must have been phenomenal. His smoky eyes were narrowed to slits, and as the Little Carpenter and others spoke of peace, the grim look on his face clearly showed he was opposed to it.

"Who's that? The big man right across from me?" Hawk whispered to Sequatchie.

"That is Akando."

"He looks like a firebrand."

"He is the strongest among the Cherokee, and the one most likely to cause trouble."

"What does he want?"

Sequatchie hesitated for only a moment, then said, "He wants all the white men in this country dead."

"Why does he hate white men so much?"

"Because, my friend, the maiden he wished to marry chose a white man who was traveling through. He took her back to his people to live. Her name was Awinita."

"He's got an unforgiving look about him," Hawk whispered.

The negotiations dragged on for some time, but finally a fierce argument broke out between Little Carpenter and Akando.

Neither Bean nor Robertson understood the language of the Cherokee enough to follow it all, but it did not take a language expert to understand that Akando was in favor of war and the Little Carpenter's caution was for peace. At one point Akando jumped to his feet, yanked a glittering tomahawk from his belt, and glared across the fire at the two white men. Hawk's hand went to his knife and he felt Sequatchie stiffen, for there was a maniacal gleam in the eyes of the tall warrior.

Little Carpenter leaped between Akando and the white men, speaking rapidly, and was soon joined by two of the older chiefs.

The visitors watched, almost holding their breath, and finally Sequatchie breathed more easily. "It will be all right. Little Carpenter has persuaded enough of the chiefs to go along with the white men."

"What will they agree to?" Robertson asked.

"The land will be leased for ten years. Little Carpenter will go to Watauga shortly to work out the final terms and the final payment."

"Akando, will he go along with the decision of the chiefs?" Hawk demanded.

"Until he is strong enough, he will."

"I'd just as soon leave here in the morning," Robertson said. "I'd like to get back. William says we need to make some decisions."

"Yes, we will not linger," Sequatchie agreed at once, knowing that it would be dangerous to keep his white friends in the village.

As the four left at dawn the next morning, they saw no sign of Akando or his faction, but as they left Chota all were firmly convinced that the tall Cherokee would not accept the decision made by the older chiefs. Hawk remembered the fierce look of hatred in the brilliant eyes of Akando, and his eyes moved ceaselessly as they pulled out of Chota and drove their horses at a fast gallop until the village was far behind them.

For two days the party traveled hard. The horses were tired, and finally they had to slow down to a more reasonable gait. As they moved along on the third day, Hawk finally turned and stared back at the trail, his eyes drawn down to narrow slits. "Sequatchie, I feel that we're being followed." He waited, but Sequatchie only shook his head, saying nothing.

"Maybe we're just being escorted," Robertson offered. "Just to make sure we leave the area."

"No. Hawk is right. We are being followed."

"You think we'll be attacked?" Bean shot back quickly.

Once again Sequatchie did not answer, but his silence was enough to make the other three men more alert. All day they moved as quickly as the tired horses would carry them. Finally, they pulled up and made camp that night, and it was Sequatchie who said, "A cold camp. No fire."

They took turns sleeping, leaving one to keep guard throughout the night. When they pulled out the next morning at daybreak, all of them felt a sinister quality in the silence that hung heavy in the woods.

They had not gone more than a half mile from their camp when the trail led between a gap formed by two masses of rock. Sequatchie was in the front and his alert eyes suddenly caught a flash of movement. At once he pulled his horse up and cried out something in the Cherokee language that neither Robertson nor Bean caught.

Even as his warning was in the air a shot rang out, and Hawk felt the wind from a musket ball on his cheek. At once he jerked his horse to the left, shouting, "There's cover over there! We can make a stand!"

The four men drove their horses toward a rise of ground that was capped by a grove of towering walnut trees. Hawk said, "James, give me your musket! John, tie up the horses in the grove. We'll need them to get away from here."

"You have chosen well, my brother," Sequatchie said, coming to stand behind a tree with Hawk. He glanced at the wall of rock at their backs and nodded with satisfaction. "They can only come at us from this direction."

At that moment a series of wild cries broke the air, and the Cherokee began advancing, waving their muskets in the air. Hawk drew a bead on one of them but paused to say, "If we kill them, it may kill the treaty as well."

"No, shoot to kill!" Sequatchie said sternly.

At his word, Hawk pulled the trigger, and a short, heavyset Indian was driven off the back of his horse. He cartwheeled, fell to the dust, and his legs kicked spasmodically, then slowly grew still.

Hawk picked up Robertson's weapon and without hesitation took another shot. This time the Indian was not killed, but he let out a yelp. As he did, Sequatchie's musket exploded and the horse of the leader, whom they all recognized as Akando, suddenly collapsed. Akando was thrown to the ground and dropped his weapon. He was unhurt, however, and shouting commands, he drew the warriors of the small band off.

"They'll be back," Hawk said as he rammed a musket ball in on the charge. "You load, James, and let Sequatchie and me do the shooting."

Knowing the deadly accuracy of his two companions, Robertson obeyed. Soon the firing began to die down. The Indians were not particularly good shots, and although their musket balls came close, none of the men were touched.

The unerring fire of Hawk and Sequatchie, however, was more potent. More than one of the renegade Cherokee were struck by the two who fired carefully until the battle settled down and no sign of the enemy was seen.

"They'll be waiting for night," Sequatchie said. "Then they can come in with knives and tomahawks. Muskets won't help us then."

"Then we'll have to make our break as soon as it gets dark," Hawk said.

"Yes, that's our only hope."

The four men settled down for a siege. Fortunately they had water in their canteens. As the hot sun rose, they portioned it out sparingly.

As the afternoon sun began to fall, Hawk, who was watching the land below carefully, asked, "What do you think, Sequatchie?"

"About what?"

"About our chances of getting out of here."

"That is as God wills. If He wants us to get away, we shall. If it is our time to die, then so be it."

Hawk turned and grinned at his friend. "That puts it on pretty plain terms," he said. There was a relaxation in Hawk's strong form, despite the danger. He had learned to live with danger, mostly beside this tall Cherokee who stood a few feet away from him. "I feel a little bit differently now," he said. "Always before, when we were in a spot like this, I was pretty scared of dying—because of what might come after."

"I knew that, but now you will be in the hands of Jesus if we die here. But I do not think we shall. Do you hear something?"

Hawk turned his head to one side and listened. "No. What is it?"

"Horses coming."

Robertson and Bean grew more alert then, and finally Hawk said, "I hear them."

"It's from over there. Many horses."

Five minutes later Hawk exclaimed, "It's Little Carpenter!"

It was indeed the Cherokee chief, Attacullaculla! He was accompanied by a band of some thirty warriors, and from their vantage point, the four men could see that he had surrounded the smaller band of Akando.

"Let us go down. I think we will be all right now," Sequatchie said.

Quickly the four men piled on their horses, rode down the hill, and sat quietly as the Little Carpenter and Akando had a violent conversation. Once again neither Bean nor Robertson understood enough of the language, but it was clear that the Little Carpenter had the upper hand. He spoke harshly, and Akando clamped his lips together. His eyes were filled with rage, but the party of armed warriors surrounding him and his followers clearly outnumbered them.

"These men will be dealt with," Attacullaculla stated flatly. "They have broken the treaty, and they will pay for their actions."

"I thank you, Chief," Sequatchie said. "It is bad when brothers cannot be trusted." He put his hard glance on Akando, who returned it defiantly.

"I will send two of my warriors with you while we take these back to Chota to deal with them."

Hawk spoke up, thanking the Little Carpenter, and the chief listened and said briefly, "I will see you in Watauga."

As the Little Carpenter led his men away, surrounding Akando and his band, James Robertson drew a shaky hand across his forehead. "A mite close," he said rather fearfully. "Let's get back while we still got our scalps." Glancing at the impassive faces of Hawk and Sequatchie, he looked at John Bean and rolled his eyes as if to say, "These two ain't got any nerves! Wish I didn't. . . !"

The Watauga Association

Eleven

The bitter winter broke off short, and by May 1772 the entire land was splashed with wild flowers, making the hills garish with color. Mild winds blew and a beneficent sun beamed over all the land so that the settlers' gardens seemed to spring up almost of themselves. It was a time of peace and harmony—which most felt could not last.

Hawk looked up from hoeing his garden to see Jacob and Andrew, who were listening to Sequatchie carefully. He felt a sense of satisfaction as he watched the two boys; they had protested against working, wanting to go fishing instead. Now Sequatchie was explaining something to them in a voice so low that Hawk could not hear it. He thought back over the weeks that had passed since he had returned from Chota, and a sense of apprehension rose in him that had become familiar of late.

The Little Carpenter would indeed come, and the terms for the peace treaty would probably be met, but Hawk had not forgotten the hatred of Akando. He knew the wily and vicious warrior was doing all he could to stir up ill feelings for the white settlers. *Sooner or later he'll break out, and when he does, there'll be blood flowing.* Anxiously he glanced toward the cabin, thinking of Elizabeth and the child that was to come, but then the sound of approaching horses came to him faintly. He turned and waited until three horses appeared, then recognizing Paul and Rhoda, he stuck his hoe in the ground and moved over to greet them. He noted the third rider with surprise and a feeling of pleasure.

"Hello, Hawk!" Paul grinned. He had grown tan and fit from his journeys to the Cherokee, and his teeth flashed whitely against his brown skin. Stepping from the saddle, he turned to help Rhoda, but she slipped off in her own independent way and the two came to stand before him.

"How are you?" Hawk said. "You're looking fit." He took their greetings, then put his hand out to the man who stood aside watching him with a smile. "Daniel," he said. "I'm pleased to see you, and a mite surprised."

"How are you, Hawk?"

Daniel Boone and Hawk were old friends. The famous long hunter was a spare man with light blue eyes that seemed to take in everything. He had a narrow face and now was in need of a shave. He wore the familiar fringed buckskin shirt of a long hunter and moccasins on his feet.

Aware that Sequatchie had approached with the two boys, Hawk said, "You haven't met my son Jacob. Jacob, this is Daniel Boone."

Jacob blinked with astonishment. Boone's name was famous throughout the seaboard, for he had been one of the first to cross the mountains and bring back word of the rich country that lay beyond. Now, somewhat awkwardly, he put his hand out and found it held firmly by the older man. Boone smiled and said, "You'll never be able to deny this one, Hawk. Spittin' image of you."

Jacob flushed with pleasure. He was proud that Hawk had introduced him as his son, but then he heard Hawk say, "And this is my other son, Andrew," and some of the pleasure went out of the moment. He stood there listening as the men talked and could not take his eyes off of Boone.

"What are you doing in this part of the world, Daniel?"

"I heard there was going to be a meeting pretty soon for the Wataugans, and I figured I ought to be there."

"I'm glad you came," Sequatchie spoke up. He and Boone were old friends, and he had great respect for this white man's opinions. "What do you think of the treaty?"

Boone shifted his feet. His eyes moved constantly, now on one of the men in front of him, then moving from point to point, never stopping. He was alert to his world in a way that few men were, and finally he said, "I think you did the right thing going to the Cherokee. I'd rather have them as landlords than most white men I could mention."

"The English want the Cherokee to force the settlers out," Sequatchie observed.

"I know they do, but they ain't always going to get what they want," Boone said.

"It's not official yet," Hawk said.

"If the Little Carpenter gave his word, then the thing is over." He looked to Sequatchie for confirmation, and the Cherokee nodded silently. "I heard about the trouble that you had on your last trip," Boone said abruptly.

Hawk glanced at the cabin and said quickly, "I didn't tell Elizabeth anything about that. As a matter of fact, I don't tell her *everything*."

Andrew and Jacob grinned, and it was Andrew who said, "If *we* don't hear *everything*, we might let something slip to Ma that says she doesn't know everything."

Hawk groaned and looked up at the heavens. "Later I'll tell you all about it. Come along, now—Elizabeth will be pleased to see you all. . . ."

Only rarely did the entire body of settlers along the Watauga River come together. True, some of them were collected into the small settlement, but others were in far-flung parts of the area. However, word sent out by James Robertson and William Bean had its effect, and the largest structure available was utilized for the meeting. This proved to be the cabin where they stored powder and other essential supplies. All these were cleaned out and set outside while the crowd gathered.

Hawk took a stand along the wall and cast his eyes around the crowded room. He noted Sequatchie, Paul Anderson, and George Stevens grouped together, while Zeke Taylor, James Robertson, William and John Bean, and John Carter, of the Carter Valley settlement, were at the other end of the room. He was glad to see Jacob Brown of the Nolichucky settlement and Daniel Boone standing close together by a large window.

The women were there, too, and even some of the young people, but they were set apart by themselves, more observers than anything else. Andrew stood beside his sister, Sarah, but his attention was mostly on Abigail Stevens.

Jacob had noticed Abigail, too, thinking how pretty she was. She had worn a dusky rose-colored cotton dress decorated with white lace and pretty pink rosettes on the elbow-length sleeves, and her complexion seemed to have matured even more during the brief time since Jacob had come to the settlement.

William Bean rose to call the meeting to order, and after asking Paul Anderson to lead them in prayer, he launched into a brief discussion of the necessity for a meeting. "We're isolated out here," Bean said, "with no protection whatsoever. We need to have a system of law and order, and this meeting is called to see that that is provided."

Bean spoke the truth concerning the isolation of Watauga. The settlement was outside the jurisdiction of Virginia and located far enough from North Carolina that it seemed to be in another world. A vast forest wilderness and a towering range of mountains separated the small community from the Colonies, and it was not only a matter of geography. The Wataugans were classified by the British government as mere squatters on Indian land, and sooner or later, as Bean pointed out, the British would send troops to force them off of their land. "We are not part of the Colonies," Bean said firmly, "and out here we are as little protected by the government as the bears in the forest."

James Robertson spoke up. "I agree with all that William says—and there's another matter." Robertson was an impressive man with a full voice and a tall, commanding figure. "We're in danger of becoming a haven for every debtor and felon who flees from the Colonies. We all know that many of them have already headed in this direction, and I for one want to make it clear to men such as these that Watauga will not be such a settlement."

The meeting went on for some time, and finally William Bean said, "We are determined, then, to form our own association for governing the area. Since we have proposed our own agreement to lease the land from the Cherokee, we feel that we are able to do our governing better than anyone back in Virginia or North Carolina."

At this moment a loud voice rose and everyone turned to see Zeke Taylor, who had lurched to his feet. His face was red and his eyes were bloodshot. He was obviously drunk, or close to it. Always a surly man, and with no ability to put his views forward in a mild fashion, he shouted, "I'm against it! I wouldn't trust these dirty Indians as far as I could throw one of them! We've got to stick to our own kind, and do away with the redskins!"

Hawk glanced immediately at Sequatchie, who remained leaning stoically against the wall. His face did not change, but Hawk knew his friend well. He saw a glint of anger in Sequatchie's usually placid eyes.

"I say Zeke is right."

William Isaac Crabtree of Wolf Hills was a tall, rawboned man with a full beard. His brother had been killed on the frontier, and he never let an opportunity slip to blame the Indians and vent his hatred upon them. For some time he stood, trying to remain calm as he spoke against the Cherokee, but finally his anger boiled over like bile, and he shouted, "I say we've got a right to this land, and I ain't payin' a penny to any redskins for it!"

"I think you're wrong, Crabtree."

Daniel Boone suddenly stepped forward and everyone in the room fell silent. His reputation was beyond measure, the most respected in the valley. Indeed, he was the one man west of the Appalachian Mountains—the Misty Mountains as he called them—who was known throughout the Colonies. He had left his musket inside the door, as had all the other men, and Hawk thought he looked almost naked without it. But still there was a power, almost a dangerous aspect, to Boone as he glanced at the faction that had obviously been brought by Zeke Taylor and William Crabtree. When he spoke his voice was quiet, but there was a strength like a band of steel in it.

"You were right in settling with the Cherokee. It was their land, and we can't steal it from them." Boone saw agreement go through most of the men and the women who were listening and continued. "Leasing from the Cherokee is the best way to stay in the area." He spoke persuasively and swayed the crowd, finally ending by saying, "If we treat the Indians fairly, they'll treat us fairly. Eventually I think they'll sell the land, then it'll be yours without question."

A fierce argument began then—Zeke Taylor and Crabtree maintaining vehemently that they would never cooperate with the Indians. Boone, Robertson, and Bean held to a more moderate course and insisted that the pressing need was for an association to band themselves together.

It ended abruptly when Taylor and Crabtree left the meeting. Taylor forced Iris and Amanda to leave with him, and Elizabeth watched with concern as the family left. She leaned over and whispered to Rhoda, who was sitting beside her, "I'm worried about Zeke's family. They look so fearful." But there was nothing to be done for it, although she had purposed in her heart at that moment to be more careful to visit the Taylors regularly.

After Taylor and Crabtree had left, the meeting went smoothly. William Bean nominated John Carter as chairman of the court of the association, and he was duly elected. The other four members were James Robertson, his brother Charles Robertson, Zachariah Isbell, and Jacob Brown. Bean himself declined to serve.

Quickly two officers of the court were appointed. Long hunter James Smith was named as clerk. Then to Hawk's astonishment he himself was nominated and quickly elected as sheriff of the association. Hawk stood up to say quickly, "I don't have any experience as an officer of the law."

"Then you'll get it as you go along." Robertson smiled at him, and a murmur of approval went up from all those gathered.

This ended the formal meeting, but very quickly the "Written Articles of the Association" on which their government was based were set down on paper.

Hawk sat through all of this, and Elizabeth whispered to him, "I'm so proud of you, Hawk, that you're the sheriff of the Watauga Association."

"I could have done without it," Hawk murmured. He was aware that his sons were watching him with pride, but he was thinking, *I might have to sit down hard on Zeke Taylor, and I don't know exactly how to handle that.*

Daniel Boone stepped forward, his hand out to Hawk. "Couldn't have been a better choice for sheriff," he smiled.

"Don't know about that, Daniel," Hawk said. "I'll do my best."

"Reckon your best is all the men want—and it'll be prime, Hawk. You can do 'er!"

The meeting was adjourned, and as the settlers of Watauga left, there was a new feeling of unity. All of them felt that somehow their precarious position as squatters had been improved. To-morrow might bring the British to run them off their land, or they might be attacked by marauding Indians, but these brave settlers had learned to live one day at a time. Now that they had law, government, officers—men of honor—the sun seemed to shine on the Wataugans.

A Little Fishing

Twelve

Spring of 1772 proved to be a gusty season, bringing mild sunshine and an explosion of greenery throughout the valley. Everywhere plows were pulled by mules, oxen, and horses, turning over the rich loam and laying it in neat furrows as the ground was prepared to receive the seed. It was a time of peace, something that came rarely to the frontier. The Indians were quiet, at least for the time being, and no wandering bands of Choctaw or Chickasaw had come close to Watauga.

The homestead that Hawk and his family claimed as their part of the wilderness burst into blossom. Elizabeth had put out the flower seeds that Hawk had brought back from Williamsburg and tended them carefully. When the first yellow and red blossoms appeared, her cries of delight had brought Andrew around the side of the house. He had been working in the garden with Jacob and Sarah, and now he said anxiously, "What is it, Ma?"

"Look, Andrew," Elizabeth breathed, bending over to touch one of the tender blossoms. "Aren't they beautiful?"

Andrew's eyes lit up with amusement. "Oh, Ma . . . I thought it was more than an old flower! I thought at least the pigs had gotten into the cabin."

Elizabeth paid him no attention for a time. For her, the flowers represented civilization. She had grown up with flowers and knew their names, their odors, and when they would bloom, whether to plant them in the shade or the sun. Now as she stroked the blossoms her mind was back in Boston where she had grown up as a girl with a garden that included whole banks of flowers such as these. Turning, she smiled, saying, "It makes me feel like home, Andrew. Don't you remember the garden there?"

"Why, sure I do, Ma," Andrew said quickly. Truthfully, the past was fading quickly for him, for his whole life was taken up with the homestead and the surrounding wilderness. He had quickly become a son of the frontier. To him, the world to the east of the Misty Mountains was becoming more vague and more indistinct with each passing day. From time to time, he had a fleeting desire to return to see his friends, his grandparents, and other relatives, but the mountains had captivated him.

"They're very pretty, Ma. I'll help you get the weeds out of them after I get through in the garden."

"Thank you, Andrew."

Moving back around the cabin, Andrew strolled toward the garden patch, which was much larger than any of the neighbors possessed. Hawk had insisted, "We're going to have vegetables to give away this fall, and we'll have the biggest garden in the whole settlement."

Now Andrew lifted his eyes and saw that it was, indeed, a large garden for such a small family. He ticked off in his mind the various vegetables: two full rows of potatoes, a row of sweet potatoes, corn, okra, squash, peas, green beans. Closer to the outer limits grew the salad vegetables: radishes, carrots, onions, and other succulent plants. They were already pushing their way through the soil, and it was Andrew and Jacob's job to keep the deer and the rabbits out. The dogs did that pretty well, but Andrew knew they would have trouble with the raccoons when the corn began to tassel.

He moved over to where Jacob and Sarah were hoeing weeds in a leisurely fashion, and for a while he joined them. He and Jacob laughed as he dug up a juicy, fat, wiggling worm and ran over, threatening to put it down Sarah's dress. She squealed, dropped her hoe, and fled, but he caught her easily and pinioned her with his strong arms, saying, "You'll have to give me your piece of pie tonight if you don't want this worm down your dress."

"You let me go, Andy!" Sarah's eyes were bright and flashing, and although she was not strong enough to break his grip, she suddenly raised her foot and stomped on his bare toes with all her might.

"Ow!" Andrew yelped, releasing her at once. He stood on one foot, rubbing the injured member, and said reproachfully, "You shouldn't have done that, Sarah!"

"Then you keep your old worm to yourself!"

Jacob, standing back leaning on his hoe, found the scene amusing. He had an analytic mind, and without meaning to do so, he studied the nature of people. Andrew had drawn his special attention because of the close relationship Andrew enjoyed with Hawk. Jacob could see that Andrew was an easygoing young man, with a temper that was rarely aroused. There was no guile in him, Jacob well knew. It was not as if Andrew had deliberately intended to supplant Jacob's place with Hawk Spencer. The two simply shared an easy camaraderie, born out of Andrew's genuine friendliness and openness, which Jacob envied. *He wouldn't be quite so easygoing if his pa had given him away,* he thought, and a cloud passed across his face.

Sarah came back, picked up her hoe, and said, "Jacob, if Andy does that to me again, I want you to whip him!"

"You do, do you?"

"Yes. He's so mean to me, but he won't do it in front of Pa. So you'll have to whip him for me." A small silence ensued, for Andrew had come back in time to hear this. He stared across the row of sweet potatoes at Jacob, and for a moment the two boys were solemn. Each was measuring the other, and Jacob, though over a year older and two inches taller than Andrew, did not have the strength of the younger boy. Andrew had been subjected to the rough frontier life for longer than he, and there was a promise of growing strength in his shoulders and chest.

"I'm not going to whip anybody because of a thing like that," he said mildly and was relieved to see Andrew's face relax. "What about if we go fishing after we get the garden tended?"

"Yes! Let's do!" Sarah said at once. She loved to fish better than any other activity, and while the boys were often gone hunting in the nearby woods, she would sit for hours by the small beaver pond a mile and a half from the cabin. "This is close enough. Let's go now."

Andrew shook his head cautiously. "We'll have to ask Ma."

"She won't care. I'll go ask her. You two dig some worms and get the poles."

Flying toward the cabin, Sarah tossed her hoe toward the house, where it fell with a clatter. It was typical of her, instead of placing it on the peg that Andrew had driven into the side of the cabin to hold the gardening instrument. He himself always hung his hoe up carefully and neatly, but there was none of this precision in Sarah, who was quick and rather slapdash in most things.

Bursting into the cabin, she found Elizabeth mixing dough for baking and cried, "Ma, can we go fishing? We got the garden finished. Please, can we?"

"Are you sure you're through?"

"Well, *almost*—and we can finish when we come back. It's the best time of the day to fish, Ma."

Looking down at her daughter, Elizabeth was very much aware that very soon Sarah would pass out of childhood into early adolescence and then into womanhood. This daughter of hers had a tempestuous quality in her that Elizabeth had never been able to trace. She reached out and smoothed Sarah's hair, thinking of Patrick, as she often did, with a faint feeling of regret, and yet with pleasure that some of him remained in the two children he had left behind.

"I suppose so, but you'll have to finish the garden when you come back."

"We will, Ma."

"And don't be too long."

"We'll come back as soon as we get plenty of fish for supper." Sarah whirled and left the cabin at a run. She saw the boys digging worms, and she stopped long enough to pick up a rusty tin pail that they used for fish bait, then hurried down to where the boys were turning over rich, loose soil at the corner of the small barn.

"I wish we had night crawlers. They're better than these red worms," Andrew complained.

Sarah bent down, and when Andrew turned over a spoonful of dirt, she immediately grabbed a long, wiggling worm and dropped it into the bucket. "These'll do good! I'll bet I catch more fish than either one of you!"

"Bet you don't!" Andrew grinned. "What do you think, Jacob?"

"I don't know. She's a pretty good fisherman."

Gratefully Sarah looked up at Jacob. Since he had come to live with them, she had been aware that he was uncertain and had done her best to make friends with him. He was, to her mind, a strange young man, not at all like her brother, Andrew. There were long periods of time when he would say practically nothing to anyone, and she had asked her mother why this was. Her mother had simply replied that he was different from other young men, more sensitive, and perhaps pondered things a little more deeply.

Jacob was well aware that Sarah was watching him carefully. He liked the bubbling girl a great deal. All throughout his life he had missed having brothers and sisters, and something about the girl's rather fiery behavior appealed to him. Indeed, he often wished he could be as outgoing as she was, but he knew that would not do. A man had to be more thoughtful. He envied the sense of security she exuded, and when he questioned her once about her father, she had said, "I miss him every day, but we've got a new pa now. I'll never forget my real pa, but one day I'll see him in heaven." Her calm confidence had impressed Jacob, and he now teased her mildly as they filled the pail with worms.

Finally they had enough bait, or so Jacob thought. "This will be enough, I guess."

"I was thinkin'. . . ." Andrew said and then halted.

"What were you thinkin', Andy?" Sarah demanded.

"I was thinkin' we could go by and see if Abigail might like to go."

"She doesn't care anything about fishing! She's afraid she might get dirty." Sarah pouted, for she wanted the two boys all to herself. In truth, she liked Abigail Stevens very much, but she was well aware that if Abigail were there, she would not get her share of the attention.

Jacob said quickly, "I think that's a good idea."

Instantly Andrew glanced at Jacob, seeing nothing but agreement in his face. "All right," he said, "we'll go. Let's go wash these worms off our hands."

Twenty minutes later they were on their way, Andrew swinging a small box tied by a string containing a lunch he had wheedled out of his mother. He was whistling tunelessly, and there was a pleased expression on his face as they made their way down the path that wound to the Stevens' place. When they arrived, they called out, "Hello the house!" as was customary, and he was pleased to see Abigail come out at once. She was wearing a pale blue dress with small white flowers, and her hair was tied back with a yellow ribbon.

"Well, hello," she said when the three stepped into the yard. "Going fishing?"

"Yes," Andrew said quickly. "Come with us."

"I'll have to ask my folks."

"We've got a picnic lunch here," Andrew said to entice her more strongly, "and I expect your folks could use some fresh fish."

"Come with me, Andrew, while I ask them."

Andrew stepped inside the cabin, where he found George and Deborah Stevens sitting in front of the window cracking walnuts and preserving the nutmeats in a glass jar. "Mama—Papa. Can I go fishing with Andrew and Sarah and Jacob?"

"I suppose so," Deborah replied, "but you'll have to come back early."

"Oh, I will."

"And we'll bring you some fresh fish, too, and I'll clean them for you, Mrs. Stevens."

"Why, that would be nice, Andrew. Don't wear that dress, Abigail. You might fall in the creek." George Stevens smiled.

"I'll change it."

Abigail at once climbed the ladder to the loft, which was her room, and soon came down again wearing a worn brown dress. It was too small for her, being an older dress, and her father remarked mildly, "You won't be wearing that dress much longer. It's too little for you, or maybe you're too big for it."

Abigail pouted, which Andrew thought was very attractive. She went over, kissed her parents, then said, "Come on, Andrew."

The two went out the door, and Abigail asked, "Where are we going?"

"Down to the beaver dam," Andrew said.

As they started off, Jacob said suddenly, "You know, the Taylors' place is right on the way. Why don't we ask Amanda to go?"

"All right," Andrew said. "The more the merrier."

Fifteen minutes later they stopped by the Taylor cabin and found Iris outside weeding her small, scraggly garden patch. She appeared haggard and worried, and Andrew said, "We're going fishing, Mrs. Taylor. We thought Amanda might like to go."

For a second Iris hesitated, then she nodded and said, "Why, I expect she might." Lifting her voice, she called, "Amanda, come out here!"

Almost at once Amanda stepped outside of the cabin door. Her head was down, and she appeared discouraged. But Andrew said cheerfully, "Come on, Amanda. We're all going fishing over at the beaver pond."

"Sure, come with us," Jacob encouraged. He felt sorry for the girl, for he knew she had had a rough life.

"Is it all right, Mama?"

"Why, I reckon it is."

"We'll bring you back a load of fish, Mrs. Taylor," Andrew said confidently.

Jacob grinned, saying, "You're giving away these fish pretty generously, Andy. We better catch 'em before we give 'em away."

But Andrew would not be denied his boasting. "You don't know who you're talking to, Jacob!" he said. "When I catch fish, I catch fish!"

As they left the yard, Sarah said, "Where's your pa, Amanda?"

"He ain't home."

Sarah turned to look at her friend quickly, but when Amanda offered no more information, Sarah was bright enough to understand. Wherever Zeke Taylor was, Amanda was glad he was not at home.

Half an hour later, after following the stream that wound through first-growth timber until it emerged on a meadow sprinkled with yellow and white wild flowers, they reached the beaver pond.

The dam itself was a hodgepodge of logs, sticks, and saplings that blocked a narrow outlet. The water from the stream was captured in a shallow pond, and in the center, a domed structure rose up, which they knew to be the beaver house.

"I hope we see some beavers today," Sarah said. "I think they're cute."

"Well, they're worth money, that's for sure," Andrew nodded. "I'm going beaver trapping next year up in the mountains. Pa said he'd take me."

At this remark Jacob's face changed slightly, but he said nothing. Hawk had said nothing to him about going trapping, and he felt a moment's resentment but managed to shove it away, saying, "Let's go fishing."

Jacob set the lunch up in the crook of a tree, and when he got back, he found Abigail unwinding her line.

"Let me put the worm on that hook for you, Abigail."

Abigail turned and smiled at him. "Would you, Jacob?"

"Sure."

"Good, I hate that part of fishing."

Andrew was baiting his own hook at this time and looked up with surprise. He had been fishing with Abigail before, and she had never seemed to mind baiting her own hook. His eyes narrowed as he watched Abigail smiling at Jacob in an open fashion. However, he baited his hook, threw it out in the water, and then turned to Amanda, saying, "Can you bait your own hook, Amanda?"

"Yes, I can, Andrew."

Sarah, on the other side of Amanda, was holding firmly to a wiggling worm. She skewered it on the hook, then said, "I wonder if it hurts. When you put the hook in them, I mean."

"Why, of course it does!" Amanda said with surprise.

"How do you know?" Sarah demanded.

"It just stands to reason. They're alive, and when you stick anything that's alive with something sharp, it hurts. Didn't you ever stick a hook in your finger?"

"Yes, but I'm not a worm! I don't think it hurts them a bit!"

"Don't bother trying to educate Sarah, Amanda," Andrew grinned. "When she gets an idea in her head, she doesn't want to be confused by facts."

Sarah argued cheerfully, but almost at once her line straightened out, and she yelped, "I got one!" Her eyes glowed with excitement, and she hauled back on the pole. The fish shot out of the water over her head, and with a squeal she pounced upon it. "Look, I got the first fish!"

"Not big enough, Sarah," Andrew protested.

"It is, too! I'll eat it myself!" Sarah hated to throw any fish back, and in truth this one was a borderline case. She stepped on the fish, extracted the hook, and then put it on the stringer that Jacob had made out of a strip of rawhide. "Let's have a contest," she said, "to see who catches the most fish."

"I'll win," Andrew laughed. "You wait and see!"

The sun was hot on the young people, but they were accustomed to the heat. The fish were biting well, and the stringer rapidly grew heavier and heavier. Finally, after two hours, Jacob said, "I'm hungry. Let's eat."

"Yes, I'm starved," Amanda said.

"You'd better wash all that worm and fish off your hands, Abigail," Jacob said. "I wish I'd brought you some soap."

"Oh, I'll be all right," Abigail said. She knelt down to wash her hands, and Jacob knelt beside her, talking cheerfully. He made a slight joke, teasing her about something.

Andrew, who was ten yards farther down the stream beside the other two girls, turned his head in their direction and called out, "How many fish did you catch, Jacob? I caught twelve."

Jacob flushed, for he had had bad luck. "Just three," he muttered.

"Well, I guess that makes me the champion fisherman."

"I caught more than you did!" Sarah protested.

"But I caught the biggest ones."

The argument went on until finally they spread the meal that Elizabeth had provided and Jacob sat down beside Abigail. As they ate the food, he described a play he had seen in Williamsburg. His eyes sparkled and he was witty enough, so that soon the three girls were laughing at him. Andrew smiled slightly, but there was a troubled light in his eyes. He had not resented Jacob for being smarter than he was, but somehow he felt left out. Jacob was charming when he chose to be, and he was obviously showing off for Abigail. Andrew grew quieter and quieter, and finally lapsed into total silence.

Amanda Taylor said little herself. She rarely had anything to say. Now she took in the situation before her, and when she got up to get a piece of the cake that Elizabeth had packed, she sat down beside Andrew, trying to make it seem almost accidental.

"Tell me about the beavers, Andrew," she said.

"The beavers?" Andrew took his eyes off of Jacob and Abigail, and seemingly grateful for an excuse, he began to tell the slender girl beside him what Hawk and Sequatchie had taught him. He had actually trapped a few with Sequatchie once, and when he described how it was done, he noted that Amanda was listening intently. "Are you really interested in beavers?"

"I guess I am. I'd like to have a coat sometime made out of beaver. It's so soft and smooth."

"Maybe we'll catch enough to get skinned and you can have one."

Amanda smiled and her large eyes looked very pretty at the moment.

Sarah had eaten heartily and suddenly she asked, "What about your birthday, Abigail?"

"I want to have a party," Abigail said, "and then all the girls can stay all night."

"Can I come?" Sarah demanded.

"Why, of course you can, and you, too, Amanda." The girls began to talk about the birthday party, while Andrew and Jacob said little to each other. Finally, after they had eaten, Andrew said, "I guess we'd better head for home."

"It's too early!" Sarah protested.

"We've got to clean the fish, and it's a long way."

Somehow the fun had gone out of the fishing trip for Andrew, and he did not say half a dozen words on the way home. When they reached the Taylors' they left a third of the fish, which Andrew and Jacob cleaned. When they left, Amanda came and whispered to Andrew, "Thanks for taking me fishing. It was fun."

"Why, sure. You're welcome, Amanda."

They reached the Stevenses house shortly thereafter, where they again divided the fish and the boys cleaned them. When they got ready to leave, Abigail was standing close to Jacob. She smiled up at him. "Thanks for coming to bring me fishing."

"Well, actually it was Andy's idea," Jacob said.

Abigail turned her smile on Andrew and said, "Thank you very much, Andrew. It was thoughtful of you."

Suddenly Jacob reached down, took Abigail's hand, and kissed it. Abigail, taken off guard, flushed, her neck and cheeks growing crimson. It was the first time anything like that had happened to her, and she did not know what to say.

Andrew was taken by surprise, also. His jaw tightened, and he whirled and stalked away.

Sarah followed him quickly, and she said, "Did you see Jacob kiss her hand?"

"I'm not blind!"

"You're mad, aren't you?"

"No, I'm not mad! Now, will you leave me alone!"

"You are mad! Do you think I can't tell?"

Andrew said nothing, and Sarah, who had known her share of teasing by her brother, could not resist saying, "Well, you won the fishing match, but it looks like Jacob seems to have done a little of his own kind of fishing! I think he caught Abigail."

Andrew gave her a furious look, then twisted his head. Jacob was still standing in front of Abigail, and Andrew could see that Abigail's eyes were alight and her lips were smiling. He whirled and said, "Come on! You don't have to talk so much!"

———————

Jacob leaned over and blew out the candle, then lay back on his bunk exhausted. After they had returned from the fishing trip, they still had to finish the garden, then clean the fish for their own family and do a number of other chores. Now the corn-shuck mattress felt inviting as he relaxed and thought back on the day's activities. At the supper table Sarah had given Hawk and Elizabeth a full recital of the fishing trip—including Jacob kissing Abigail's hand.

Jacob squirmed slightly, for he had been embarrassed. Neither Hawk nor Elizabeth had teased him about it. Hawk had merely said, "I guess young men will do things like that."

"Yes, you might learn a few manners from Jacob, Andy," Elizabeth had said. She had meant it innocently enough, but Andrew had taken it ill and had dropped his face toward his plate, saying not another word.

Jacob knew that Andrew was upset, and somehow it pleased him that he had evened the score. Andrew was a better fisherman, but he knew that he had won the day with Abigail. He turned his face toward Andrew, who was lying in the other bed, and grinned with satisfaction. "Hey, Andy," he said. "I guess it'll be a good party. Abigail's, I mean."

"I wasn't invited," Andrew said.

"Why, you know she'll invite you."

"No, I don't know it."

Usually Andrew was cheerful, but there was a surly quality in his answer that Jacob could not fail to notice. However, he continued to talk about the party until finally he grew sleepy. "Well, I'm looking forward to the party," he said, then closed his eyes and smiled as thoughts of the day faded into dreams.

Sleep did not come as easily to Andrew. As he lay there he, too, could not help reviewing the day. It had been a bad day for him— one that had started out well but had fallen apart. Now he tried, unsuccessfully, to put it out of his mind and go to sleep. He kept seeing the scene over and over again of Jacob reaching for Abigail's hand. He could not forget how she had flushed prettily, and her eyes had lit up at the gesture. Andrew was an imaginative boy, and he lay there wondering how he could have made the day different. Obviously Abigail had been much taken with Jacob's wit, and for the first time since Jacob had come, Andrew resented his stepbrother. He thought of Jacob, who was taller, with rather dramatic good looks, and he felt homely and awkward.

Outside he heard night noises, the cry of a night bird far off, and then later the lonesome wail of a coyote that always made him slightly sad. Just as he was about to drop off, he had a sudden picture flash into his mind of Jacob leaning over and kissing Abigail's hand, and he gritted his teeth and wished that he had never agreed to a fishing trip!

The Little Carpenter and
The Carpenter

Thirteen

As the warm days of summer fell upon Watauga, Elizabeth felt the clock of the seasons moving slowly. She had walked through the garden and reveled in the herbs that were growing, and the blossoming of the flowers brought a new joy to her.

One morning when Sarah was away visiting Abigail, Elizabeth said, "It's time for you boys to have a bath."

"Aw, Ma!" Andrew grumbled. "Who needs a bath? Indians never take baths!"

"That's their business," Elizabeth said firmly. "Now, you go down to the creek, both of you, and see that you wash off good." Moving over to the cabinet, she produced an old stoneware mug and filled it with a handful of soft soap. "Mind you wash good!" she warned them.

The two boys actually welcomed the trip to the creek. They had found a favorite spot to swim—a wide, deep hole with a sandy bottom where they could dive from an overhanging tree trunk. Now they made their way there, carrying the stoneware mug and coarse towels made of tow. Soon they reached the creek and for half an hour splashed and yelled, falling in head first, then feet first, turning flips as they laughed and shivered in the cold water.

Finally, after their swim was over, they rubbed their bodies with the soap Elizabeth had made. It was a gray jelly of a soft texture, and they worked it into a lather with the cool water of the creek. Then, having lathered all over, they splashed again until the soap washed free. Overhead a red-tailed hawk circled, seeming to eye them curiously, and from far off came the high-pitched cries of plovers. It was a plaintive cry, and one that always made Jacob feel peculiar, but it was a fine day, and finally the two dried off and headed back toward the cabin.

Back at the house, as soon as the boys had left, Elizabeth had carried hot water to her room in a wooden keeler. She brought some of the soft soap in a mug and opened the window so that a breeze came through with a fine tang to it. Outside she could hear the pleasing sound of martins, the birds she loved the most. They were building in the birdhouse that Hawk had built at her request. For a while she watched them—sleek purple and black communal birds that loved each other's company.

Then, standing by the keeler, she began to bathe, spreading the soft, delicate lather over her body. She caressed the growing mound that was the miracle she was so thankful for. She thought again of how happy she was to be having a child that was Hawk's and hers. This little one, to her anyway, represented the bringing together of the two families into one. She seemed to wash away the weariness that had come from all the work of spring. When she was completely covered with a spongy coat of foam, she dipped one foot and then the other in the keeler. She let the drops fall off, and she rinsed carefully with the water that had grown warm. She took a towel and rubbed herself into a rich glow, feeling exuberant with excessive health and the fine day.

When she had finished cleaning up after her bath, she went about her chores until she heard men's voices. Looking out the window, she saw William Bean and James Robertson talking with Hawk and Sequatchie. Moving outside, she listened as they spoke urgently. Bean seemed agitated.

"Chief Attacullaculla came into the village yesterday, Hawk."

"He's come to negotiate the final settlement?"

"Yes," Bean nodded. "It's been put off too long for my liking."

"I think you're right, William," James Robertson said. He stood half a head taller than Bean and a couple of inches taller than Hawk himself. His lean body seemed to sway in the light breeze, but he displayed a solemnness that caused men to trust in him.

"You'll have to go, Hawk."

"Why do I have to go?" Hawk said. "I don't have any business there."

"Yes, you do," Robertson nodded. "You're an officer of the court of the Watauga Association."

"That's right, and you'll have to be there. As sheriff, it's your job," Bean seconded. He glanced over and added, "Sequatchie, we'll ask you to come, too, to serve as an interpreter."

"When is the meeting?" Hawk asked.

"Tomorrow. Try to be there early."

Hawk shifted restlessly on his moccasin-shod feet. He had no interest in politics, but he knew it was necessary to settle the business of the ownership of the land. Glancing at Sequatchie, who nodded slightly, he shrugged, saying, "All right. We'll be there."

―――――――

By the time Hawk and Sequatchie had arrived at the meeting place in the center of the Watauga community, the other officials were already there. There was a hum of voices as Hawk and Sequatchie entered, and men greeted them warmly. It was an informal meeting, and none of the men had worn other than their everyday garb.

"It's a far cry from a meeting of the House of Burgesses," William Bean said to Hawk. "We'd all be wearing boiled shirts and top hats there." He looked around, seeing nothing but hunting shirts, woolsey trousers, and the rough clothes they were all accustomed to. "I like it better like this myself," Bean said. "Who was it that said, 'Beware of any enterprise that demands the buying of new clothes'?"

"I don't know," Hawk murmured, "but he was right, whoever it was. How long do you think this will take?"

"Got no idea. Look, I think we're about ready to start."

The meeting began almost at once, and to Hawk's surprise it was a rather brief meeting. The Little Carpenter, as Chief Attacullaculla was called, had already worked out the details with his own people. They were generous terms, far better than anyone in the settlement had expected. The Little Carpenter was an unobtrusive, even unimpressive figure as he stood up to give the terms. He had a smooth face, as all Cherokee did, but was much smaller than others. His voice was surprisingly deep for a little man, and his eyes moved from point to point, touching on every face in the room as he spoke of what his people had agreed to.

"These terms will be called the 'Articles of Friendship,'" he said, his voice carrying well to all the listeners. A silence filled the room for a moment as the settlers waited. It would have been within the realm of possibility for the Cherokee to demand an exorbitant sum, and failing to get it, to have brought war against the settlers. William Bean and James Robertson sat there, almost holding their breath, waiting for the terms.

"You will receive a ten-year lease of the lands around the Watauga River," the Little Carpenter said. "You will pay the Cherokee six thousand dollars merchandise and trade goods, plus muskets and household articles. . . ."

William Bean expelled his breath with an expression of relief. His eyes met those of Robertson, and the two nodded in a pleased manner. Hawk took this in and knew that the Little Carpenter had indeed made good terms insofar as the settlers were concerned.

Sequatchie was pleased, also. He knew that the Cherokee could have asked for more, but he also knew that if they had demanded too much the settlers might simply have refused. That would have caused such bad feelings that it was almost certain a war would have taken place, for the young, hotheaded braves among the Cherokee were longing for a reason to declare war.

Finally the meeting ended, but William Bean suddenly turned to Paul Anderson and said, "Reverend Anderson, some of us would like to see a meeting for the entire community tomorrow. It's the Sabbath day."

"Why, certainly," Paul agreed at once. He had no official post in the association, yet his stature as a minister was growing, and both Bean and Anderson knew that it would be well to draw the people together by ending with a service. Besides that, they all admired and respected Paul Anderson, and most of them still nurtured the idea of having him start a church and become their full-time minister.

"That's fine, Reverend," Bean said. "I'll be sittin' right in the front row. You can start on me, and then that would give the rest of the transgressors a break."

———

The service the following day was held outdoors in an open space in the middle of the settlement. It was a place the women often used to come to grind their corn in a huge iron pot with a suspended block of wood that could be lowered to crush the grain. The area was filled, and Hawk had brought his family, as had other settlers who lived some distance away from the settlement. He stood beside Elizabeth and glanced down at Jacob, Andrew, and Sarah, who stood beside her. A feeling of pride went through him as he looked at them. It had been something he had missed during his days of solitary wandering through the forest as a long hunter. Now he had a homestead, a warm, tight cabin, a fine, loving wife, three growing, healthy children, and another on the way. *God has been good to me*, he thought as the congregation began to sing another song.

They sang many songs that morning, all standing, but no one seemed to grow tired. Hawk noticed that Jacob had a fine singing voice but Andrew did not. Hawk especially reveled in the words of the hymn *Great God of Wonders* by Samuel Davies. His voice rose as he sang the second stanza:

In wonder lost with trembling joy
We take the pardon of our God;
Pardon for crimes of deepest dye,
A pardon bought with Jesus' blood;
A pardon bought with Jesus' blood.

Glancing over to the other side of the crowd he saw Sequatchie standing close beside Paul Anderson. He was wearing his full regalia as a chief of the Cherokee and looked statuesque and colorful. Others in the crowd had on their Sunday best. It was a time out from work, from labor, from the incessant driving chores that consumed all of them six days of the week. This Sunday was an island on which they could all gather and rest and hear the Word of God proclaimed.

Paul Anderson was wearing a simple dark suit, and his sandy brown hair caught the light as the sun broke forth from the fluffy clouds overhead and spread itself gently on the congregation that waited for him to begin the sermon. Rhoda stood with the other women to his right. When his eyes touched on her with pride, she smiled slightly. He knew her smile meant, "I'm proud of you, Paul," and thus encouraged, he began to speak.

"We are happy to have in our midst," he said firmly, "Chief Attacullaculla, and I have been interested in his other name, the Little Carpenter. I've been impressed this morning to speak of another man who was called a carpenter. I speak, of course, of the Lord Jesus. As you all know, He was, when He was here on this earth, a real carpenter. We have little record of His activities, but it was very likely that He was a good workman, able to use the adze, the plane, the chisel, the hammer. All that a skilled craftsman following the trade of carpenter would use. . . ."

The minister's voice rose clearly above the sounds of the birds and the rustling of the green leaves in the trees that surrounded the clearing. There was a warmth in Paul Anderson's eyes that communicated itself well to his hearers. Here was a man who loved people and who had proved it by going to the far-off reaches to preach the gospel to the Cherokee. He also had proved it in his daily life in the community by his good-heartedness and willingness to get his hands dirty and to help, but now he was doing that which God had called him to do, speaking of the great gospel, and excitement tinged his talk as he continued.

"And so Jesus lived with an earthly father, and in the midst of a family, until at the age of thirty He began His ministry. We have little record of that, but I've often thought that His father, Joseph, must have been an extremely good man, and, of course, His mother was a woman filled with faith, as we have record in the Scriptures. Joseph we know less well, but I've often thought that when Jesus said, 'Our Father,' speaking to His Father in heaven, of course, He must have been very conscious of His earthly adopted father. I think it is correct to say He loved His earthly father and honored him with obedience, with love, and with devotion."

As Jacob listened, he began to grow very uncomfortable, for he was forced to think about his own father. He glanced over to the side and saw his father's profile, strong and firm, his eyes fixed on the minister. As usual, Jacob thought instantly of the years he had had no father, and resentment began to stir within him. But still there was a feeling of guilt. He had held his father at arm's length, even though these past months Hawk Spencer had done everything a man could do to show his affection and his willingness to give of himself. Jacob thought of the many instances he'd gone on hunting trips, the fishing expeditions, the long hours when Hawk had spoken not only to Andrew but to Jacob of his days as a long hunter. All of these acts of kindness now came back to Jacob in a rush, and he lowered his head. A feeling of shame came to him as he thought how he had responded with nothing but a surly attitude.

Paul Anderson had moved the crowd, and now he said, "Jesus

had to obey His heavenly Father as we all do. When He became a man, He was fully required to do all that men must do, and yet He said of God, 'I do always those things which please Him.' It was His joy to be obedient to His Father—to serve Him and to obey Him. That is the glory of the humanity of the Lord Jesus—that though He was God, He was at that same time a man, and the Scripture says, 'He was in all points tempted like as we are yet without sin.' Part of this was the temptation, no doubt, to go His own way, but He never did." Paul lifted his voice then, and it came like a trumpet. "He always pleased God, and He always loved His Father. God is our true Father, who loves us more than anyone."

Jacob found himself trying to deny this. *No one loves me like that,* he thought bitterly, but then he heard Paul beginning to speak of the cross, and somehow just the mention of the word "cross" seemed to pierce him like a sharp knife. He felt ashamed and humiliated as Paul began to speak of Jesus dying on the cross.

"When He hung on the cross He suffered physical pangs, but it was not that which was the worst," the minister called out in a strong voice. "The worst was that His Father had forsaken Him. Do you not remember how He cried out, 'My God, my God, why hast thou forsaken me?'"

The truth of those words struck Jacob Spencer for the first time. He suddenly realized that Jesus had been forsaken by His Father, even as he himself had been!

"God had *not* forsaken His Son ultimately. He allowed Him to suffer the agony of the cross, for He had agreed with His Son before the foundation of the earth that this was the price that had to be paid for sinful man. As Jesus hung there dying, He was saying, 'Yes, I will obey my Father, even though He seems to have abandoned me. Even at this moment, when I feel alone and cast away, destitute, a foreigner, yet will I still cling to my Father.'" Paul hesitated for a moment, and there were tears in his eyes as he looked over his hearers. His eyes were not the only ones touched with tears, for many were moved by his words.

"God knows what it takes to bring His children back to Him," Anderson said in a voice little louder than a whisper. "And He knows that we feel forsaken at times, but I'll tell you that God is with us whether we see Him or whether we do not. He loves us when we do not feel His love. He cares for us, though His presence may seem blotted out for a time. We may go through a dark night of the soul and doubt whether there even is a God. But I remind you, God puts His children through the valley of affliction more than anyone else. If you feel afflicted, forsaken, and unloved, I urge you to look at Jesus as He cried, 'Why hast thou forsaken me?' " Then, with a ringing voice, Paul said, "We are *never* forsaken by God. Let us look unto Jesus, the author and the finisher of our faith. . . !"

Jacob's head, by this time, was bowed and he felt miserable. As the service closed, many went forward to kneel in prayer, to ask for the prayers of the pastor and of other believers. For one moment he had a wild impulse to join them, but that soon passed. A hardness and stubbornness rose again as it always did. He turned to go, well aware that Hawk was watching him, as was Elizabeth, but he could not help himself. He left the meeting feeling forsaken by his earthly father and also by his heavenly Father.

Presents for Abigail

Fourteen

*L*ife was hard, as a rule, in the Watauga settlement, and when the rare excuse for a holiday came it was followed by excitement. The birthday of Abigail Stevens, which fell on June the seventeenth, had been anticipated with excitement by the young people for days. Now the Stevenses' homestead was swarming inside and out as guests came pouring in from the outlying settlements. The cabin itself, of course, was too small to hold all of the guests, so a natural division took place. The men who had dropped by gathered outside, squatting on the ground, whittling, and speaking of crops, dangers with Indians, and neighbors. Farther off, the young people had come together in a cleared area, their laughter and shrill voices filling the air. The weather was mild with a benevolent yellow sun pouring down warm rays on the green fields and forest, and a gentle breeze stirred the tender shoots of grass, making a ripple as if the fields were pools of green water.

Inside the cabin the women were gathered, so that one could hardly turn around without running over another. Rhoda Anderson, who was helping Deborah Stevens with the cooking, turned to Iris Taylor and asked quietly, her voice below the hubbub of voices, "Zeke didn't come with you?"

"No, he couldn't come." Iris's answer was brief, and as usual, when her husband was mentioned by another woman, she seemed embarrassed. She lifted her eyes and added, "I wish he had come to be a better neighbor."

Rhoda said no more, for she knew it was not likely. Along with others in the community, she had heard rumors that Zeke Taylor had returned to his old drinking ways. She let her eyes fall on Iris's face but could see no signs of bruises. *He's too afraid of Hawk to abuse his wife, but if Hawk weren't here, I'm afraid to think what would happen!*

Elizabeth was chatting happily with Betty Foster, a newcomer to the settlement. The Fosters had moved in from Virginia and were better off than most of the settlers. Charles was a short man with blue eyes and blond hair. His wife, Betty, was even shorter— a diminutive woman with china blue eyes and a ready smile. Their two children, Joseph and Leah, ages fourteen and twelve, had been a welcome addition to the community, especially for the young people.

"Having babies is exciting," Betty said, her eyes running quickly down Elizabeth's figure. "How far along are you?"

"About seven months." Elizabeth hesitated, then asked, "Did you have trouble with your babies?"

"Law, no!" Betty scoffed and laughed merrily. She laughed easily, and there was a prettiness about her, not yet hardened by the rough life on the frontier. "They both came so quick I was surprised both times. How about you and your two?"

"It wasn't that easy."

"Well, maybe it will be this time."

Deborah Stevens, who had been sitting across from Elizabeth, asked, "Are you feelin' all right? Having babies should be a natural thing, but sometimes it's hard."

"I think Hawk's worried about it more than I am."

"He lost his first wife in childbirth, didn't he?" Deborah inquired. She actually knew little of the history of Hawk, nor did anyone else in the community, but somehow she had picked up on this bit of information, and now she saw that the thought troubled the young woman. "Sometimes it frightens a man to have his wife bring a child into the world."

"Men aren't worth anything at a birthing," Betty Foster shrugged. "I told Charles to go hunting when mine came."

"I wouldn't want that," Deborah said.

"No, I wouldn't, either," Elizabeth smiled. "Not that there's anything they can do, but I'd feel better if Hawk were around."

As the hubbub of talk swarmed about her, she was thinking of how Hawk had treated her during her pregnancy. It had been almost ludicrous the way he had refused to let her work, even during the early months of her time. Once, when they had walked a little farther than he thought right for her, he had simply scooped her up in his arms and carried her back to the cabin as if she were a small child. Remembering that now, she thought how his strength had brought a comfort to her, and she glowed with pleasure at the thought of having a strong man at her side. But Hawk had been worried, she knew that. It was not that he said much, but she could tell. Many times she had tried to assure him that she was not afraid, but it had not soothed his nerves.

She looked up to watch Rhoda, who was chatting now with two of the other women, and wondered how long it would be before she and Paul would have a child. When Deborah Stevens questioned her again about how she felt, she said quietly, "It's all in God's hands. We will be all right, Deborah."

Deborah nodded with satisfaction. She knew Elizabeth Spencer to be a sensible woman, not flighty like so many she had known, and now she raised her voice and asked, "How are the cakes coming, Rhoda?"

"Just fine."

Rising to her feet, Elizabeth moved over to stand beside Rhoda. The other women had gone to the door for a moment, to step outside and cool off while watching the children play. Elizabeth sensed something was troubling Rhoda and asked quietly, "Is everything all right?"

For a time Rhoda did not answer, then she turned her eyes on Elizabeth. She had very attractive eyes, large and well shaped, but now there was a cloud in them, and she said, "It's the same thing. I don't ever feel quite right."

"About being married to a minister?"

"Yes. I . . . I just don't know if I can do it, Elizabeth. I can't help Paul the way I should." She clasped her hands nervously and dropped her head. Her shoulders drooped in an attitude of doubt, and Elizabeth put her arm around her, saying, "Of course you can help him."

"I just don't know. I wish I'd had a different kind of life."

Iris Taylor had been standing in the doorway, and now she turned and said in a strange tone, "Just be glad and thankful you got a man who loves you."

Rhoda shifted quickly to face Iris, realizing how much better off she was than this poor woman. "I reckon I shouldn't ever complain," she said.

"God knows all about you and the Reverend," Iris said. There was a sudden strength in her voice, a quality that had not been there months before, and now she said evenly, "God will be with you in everything and through everything."

"That's right," Elizabeth echoed quickly. She hesitated for one moment, then said, "Has Zeke . . . been abusive to you or Amanda?"

A sigh shook Iris's thin body and she shook her head. "No, he's just yelled at us a lot. Sometimes I'm afraid that he will hurt us, though. I know that God's with me, and I'm trusting Him to keep me and Amanda safe."

"I think the three of us all need to pray for one another," Elizabeth said. She put her hands out, and each was taken by the women. She prayed quickly but fervently for Iris, that her home would be made whole, then for Rhoda and Paul. When she was finished, Rhoda, in a halting fashion, prayed for her, and then Iris said a brief prayer. When Elizabeth looked up, her face was glowing. "Isn't it wonderful that we can take these things to God?"

"Watch your hand, Joseph! You're cheating!"

The young people who had gathered for the party were all in an irregular circle around Joseph Foster, who was kneeling and had one eye shut as he squinted at a group of marbles inside a roughly drawn circle. He was a strongly built lad of fourteen with a shock of dark hair and light green eyes. His tongue was slightly extended as he concentrated on the marbles, murmuring, "I'm not, either. I'm right on the line."

He propelled the marble strongly with his thumb, and at once Andrew shouted, "You hunched! You got your hand half a foot over the line!"

Grinning broadly, Joseph shook his head. "You're just a sore loser, Andy." He picked up two of the marbles that had been knocked out of the ring and then proceeded, despite Andrew's frequent protests, to drive the rest of the marbles out. He had a light touch and was the champion at marbles in the settlement. Picking up his winnings, he put them into a leather bag and winked at Abigail. "I guess we know who the champion marble shooter is, don't we, Abigail?"

Abigail was wearing a new dress for her birthday. It was an off-white lightweight cotton with pale pink roses running down the dress between alternating lines of small pale green leaves and a single yellow stripe. It had elbow-length sleeves that ended in a fabric ruffle and had pink lace edging the sleeves and the neckline. Her rich brown hair was carefully arranged in curls that fell down her back, and she smiled at Joseph Foster winsomely. "I don't think anyone doubts that, Joseph."

"Let's race," Andrew insisted. He had lost all his marbles in the game and now wanted to do something at which he was more skilled.

"We'll have the girls' races and then the boys' races," Sarah said.

"Of course we will," Andrew said. "Girls can't race with boys."

The girls' race was between Sarah, Abigail, Amanda, and Leah Foster. Although the other girls were older, it was Sarah who came flying in to win the race. Her eyes sparkling, she turned around and shouted, "I win! I win!"

"You can run faster than any girl I ever saw," Amanda said. At the age of thirteen, she was two years older than Sarah but had come in last. The other two girls, Abigail and Leah, were stronger and more vibrant with health. "I wish I could run as fast as you could."

"Come on. Line up," Andrew shouted. "Come on, Jacob."

Jacob shook his head. "I don't want to race."

"You're not afraid, are you?"

Jacob glared at Andrew and without another word went over to stand between him and Joseph Foster. There were two younger boys there—really too young for the party but had come anyway.

Jacob crouched down and waited for the signal. It was Abigail who shouted, "Go!"

The boys raced toward a tall maple tree at the end of the clearing. There and back was the race, and by the time Jacob made his turn, he knew he was going to lose. Both Joseph and Andrew were well ahead of him, and he was gasping as he reached the finish line, but Andrew had already come in one step ahead of Joseph Foster.

"You win, Andrew," Abigail said.

Andrew's eyes were glowing. He was scarcely breathing hard, and he winked at Joseph. "If you're the marble champion, I'm the running champion."

"I guess you are," Joseph admitted. He was basically a good-natured boy, though rather stubborn at times, wanting his own way.

"Come on. Let's roll hoops," Abigail said.

The group spent the next hour playing with hoops in various forms of games. The hoops themselves had been bought to make barrels with, and the young people rolled them along the ground with sticks. Strangely enough, it was Amanda who was the most adept. She somehow had the ability to run and to keep the hoop spinning by touching it lightly at the back. When she won the race, Abigail hugged her and said, "You've got a light touch, Amanda. I think you're the hoop champion."

At this moment Deborah Stevens came outside with a pitcher and several mugs. "Anyone for fresh apple cider?"

The response was instantaneous, and as soon as Mrs. Stevens left, Abigail poured the clear cider into the mugs, serving herself last.

"This is good," Joseph said, wiping his brow. "I could drink a barrel of it."

"Well, we don't have a barrel, and we have to divide it evenly," Abigail said.

They all had walked over to the tall hawthorn tree at the edge of the field, enjoying the shade. Far away to the north, the land seemed to rise up as the foothills made a jagged outline on the horizon. In the other direction, the forest lay quiet and thick, filled with game of every kind and waiting the advent of the settlers. Soon it would be fields and trails and cabins, but now it was dark and brooding, the habitat of deer and bear and raccoon rather than of man.

After the cider was gone Abigail said, "Let's sing."

Joseph shook his head. "No, let's play ball."

But Abigail insisted, and soon her clear voice rose and the others joined her.

Finally Abigail said, "I wish we could have a big ball here where all the ladies could dress up in pretty dresses, and the men could wear suits and ties, and we could have music and dance."

Sarah agreed with this, for there had been many splendid balls at her home in Boston. "Oh, that would be wonderful!" she said, clapping her hands in delight. She described a ball she remembered, then added wistfully, "There'll never be anything like that around here."

"Have you ever been to a ball, Jacob?" Abigail asked.

"Why, of course. We had them all the time in Williamsburg."

"Do you like to dance?"

"I sure do. As a matter of fact, I think we could have a dance right here."

Abigail looked at him skeptically. "We don't have any music."

"We've got singing, though. Come along. You and I'll show them how to do it, Abigail."

Andrew muttered, "What fun is there in dancing?" He was scowling as Jacob went over and pulled Abigail to her feet.

Leah Foster's eyes gleamed with fun, and she began singing a familiar tune. Those who knew it joined in, and Abigail felt Jacob's arm go around her. She took his hand and the two began to move around under the shade of the trees.

The sunlight filtered down through the leaves, forming a pattern of light and dark, and Sarah laughed, saying, "Why, it's as good as a ball!"

Amanda smiled, but she glanced over and saw that Andrew looked perturbed.

Abigail was enjoying the dancing. She had attended several as a girl in North Carolina, of course, but there was something grown-up about the way Jacob held her and watched her. She tried to draw back after a while, but he only pulled her closer, laughing at her.

Finally Jacob stepped back and bowed, and then with a gleam in his eye, he moved over and pulled Amanda out in the clearing. She was protesting, but he shook his head. "I'm going to dance with every pretty girl in this crowd," he said.

Sarah was standing beside Andrew, watching the two go around. "You ought to dance with Abigail, Andy."

Abigail, hearing this, turned to Andrew and smiled with invitation.

Andrew did not want to confess that he did not know how to dance. He had never learned and had, indeed, not wanted to. Now he stared at the two dancing, shuffled his feet, and then blurted out, "Dancing is foolish!" He turned and walked off stiffly.

Sarah moved over closer to Abigail and whispered, "I think he doesn't know how to dance, Abigail. Don't be mad at him." She turned and ran off, and when she caught up with her brother, she scolded, "You shouldn't have said that!"

"Well, it is foolish!"

"No it's not! Don't you know how to dance?"

"No, I don't, and I don't want to learn."

"*That's* foolish!" Sarah said. "I'll teach you how. It's not hard."

The two went on toward the cabin, and at that moment Deborah stepped outside, saying, "Come on. It's time to eat."

"Go tell Abigail you're sorry," Sarah commanded. She reached out and jerked at Andrew's sleeve. "Don't run off like this! You'll spoil her party!"

"All right," Andrew said. "I'll apologize." He waited until Abigail approached. She was standing beside Jacob, and Andrew wished that he were alone with her, but it was something that had to be done, and he said, "I'm sorry I acted like I did, Abigail."

"Why, that's all right, Andrew," Abigail said quickly. She studied the face of Andrew MacNeal, and then her eyes went to Jacob Spencer, who was watching all this with interest. Turning back to Andrew, she said, "Let's go in and eat. We'll play some more games later."

The meal had to be served both outdoors and indoors. The young people ate inside at the tables since it was Abigail's birthday. The men took their food outside, carrying their plates and mugs out to sit under the shade of the trees.

After the meal was over, Abigail opened her presents. Sarah handed her a package, and when Abigail opened it, she said, "A bonnet. I bet you made this yourself." She held it up for everyone to see. It was made of white cotton, with a small edging of white lace along the wide brim, and a light blue ribbon between the crown and the brim that extended down the sides, long enough so that it could be tied under the chin.

"You're so clever, Sarah. Thank you so much."

The rest of the gifts were small and inexpensive, most of them being handmade. From Amanda she received a sampler with a picture of a small church in the center surrounded by flowers, birds, trees, and animals, all worked in brightly colored thread on a heavy cotton background.

Andrew gave her a small wooden trinket box with flowers carved on the lid.

"Oh, it's beautifully done! You do the best carving, Andy!"

Andrew's cheeks glowed at the compliment, and then he watched as Abigail opened another package. She pulled out a pair of beautifully made mittens of rabbit fur. Laughing with delight, she stuck her hands inside and turned to say to Jacob, "I'll bet you didn't make these, Jacob."

"I shot the rabbits, and Sequatchie showed me how to tan them."

"Look, everyone!" Abigail handed the mittens over to the girls, who were watching avidly. "Won't these be nice and warm this winter? They're so beautiful!" She rubbed her hands over the softness of the fur, smiling demurely at Jacob.

Jacob grinned and said, "If I had known you were going to like them so much, I would have made you a cape and boots to go with it."

"Well, there's always Christmas," Abigail teased.

"I'll start trapping rabbits tomorrow," Jacob promised.

Abigail opened the rest of her presents, but it was obvious the mittens were her favorite. She scarcely put them down, and from time to time, she rubbed the softness of the fur against her cheek. Jacob was pleased, for he had spent a lot of time making them under Sequatchie's careful instruction. Now he thought he had seldom seen anything prettier than Abigail Stevens as she touched the soft fur to her silky cheek.

––––––––

Abigail, Sarah, and Amanda were all sitting around in a circle in Abigail's room. The girls were too excited to sleep and for an hour had relived the party.

"It's the nicest party I've ever been to, Abigail," Amanda said. She did not add that she had only been to one or two in her whole life, mostly when she was younger. It had been a fine day for her. She had come outside the shell that she had built around herself, and now she was content and happy, wishing that the party could go on forever.

Sarah reached over and picked up the mittens, saying, "These are the prettiest things I've ever seen."

"They are beautiful, aren't they?" Abigail nodded.

Sarah put her hands into the mittens. "They're so *soft*. I'm going to ask Jacob to make me a pair." She rubbed the fur against her cheek, then said with an impish look in her eyes, "It looks like Andy has competition."

Abigail flushed. "There's no competition."

"Why, sure there is," Sarah said. "Jacob and Andy are both after you."

"I'm not a . . . a *prize* to be won, Sarah. Besides, Andrew and I are just good friends."

Amanda had listened to this carefully. "What about Jacob?"

"Well . . ." Abigail said and then halted. She flushed slightly, saying, "He's a good friend, too."

"I hope you don't fall in love with Jacob. I always thought when you and Andy grew up you could get married, then we'd be sisters."

"Why, you'd still be sisters even if she married Jacob. He's your brother," Amanda said.

Abigail was flustered by this sort of talk. At the age of fourteen, she was on the brink of young womanhood. Girls married young on the frontier, sometimes only a year or two older than she herself, but now she was confused and pleased at the attention from both of the young men. Somehow this seemed wrong, but she did not know why. "I've always been fond of Andrew, but I just want to be good friends with him and Jacob both."

"I think that's the way you should be," Amanda remarked. "They are both such good boys."

"If you had to choose between them, which one would you take?" Sarah asked. "I mean, if you had to choose right now."

Abigail reached up and grabbed a pillow and threw it at Sarah. It caught her in the face and she threw it back. Finally they grew so loud that George Stevens' deep voice bellowed up the stairs, "You girls be quiet up there and go to sleep!"

"I guess we'd better," Abigail said. She lay down on the bed next to Sarah, who was sharing the bed with her, while Amanda slept on a thick bearskin on the floor. Abigail had the mittens in her hand, and she ran her hand over them, stroking the fur continually. A thought came to her, and she leaned over and picked up the trinket box and traced the flower carvings in the top of it. Long thoughts came to her then, and finally she put the box and the mittens down, lay back, and went to sleep almost at once.

Sheriff Spencer

Fifteen

A haze had gathered over the meadows as Hawk made his way out of the deep woods. He had been gone only two days, yet it seemed longer than that to him. As he passed into the broken ground dotted with scrub oak and hackberry, he suddenly was aware of an anxiety to be home again.

Home!

The word had taken on a new meaning since he had married Elizabeth. He had not known a settled place of abiding in all the years of wandering through the mountains. His first marriage he remembered from time to time, but the years had caused many of those memories of his first wife to fade. Before that, his boyhood stretched back to the time when he could not remember at all.

This was different, however, and he realized it was not the cabin or the barns or the pastures of the homestead, but the woman who waited for him that made the place draw him like a magnet. Even as he thought of Elizabeth, he quickened his pace, and a smile turned his mouth upward. At times he could not understand her, and yet during their brief marriage, he had become part of her in a way he had never imagined a man could know a woman so deeply. He knew her ways now, as she knew his. He knew how her face would change when he said something to her that pleased her—a slight brightening of the eyes, an upward turning of the corners of her lips, bringing the small dimple in her left cheek. He knew also how a cloud could come across those green eyes of hers, so expressive, when trouble came. Not that she complained, but he knew she was unhappy, and somehow this made him determined to do those things that pleased her.

Now he crested the rise of the hills that held the homestead down in the valley. Stopping, he took a deep breath and looked up for a moment at the hot July sun that beat down upon his head and his back and shoulders. But the house drew his attention again, and something rose in his chest as he studied the lay of it. *I'd never find a place like this one,* he thought as his eyes went over the cabin with a small tendril of smoke curling lazily upward in the still air. The horses grazed placidly in the green grass beyond the cabin, and he saw Elizabeth outside washing clothes in a wooden washtub. The sight of her stirred him and he kicked his horse in the side anxiously. "Come on, Red," he said urgently, "show a little spirit here!"

The big stallion moved forward wearily, quickening his gait to a gallop, and when Hawk was in shouting distance, he lifted his voice, calling her name, "Elizabeth—Elizabeth!"

Elizabeth looked up at once, and even at a distance he could see her shoulders straighten as she threw the garment she was washing into the soapy water. Leaving the washtub, she came forward to greet him, and something in her eyes caught him and held him. She lifted her head, took his kiss as he put his arms around her, then she embraced him, hugging him tightly, her hands locked behind his back.

"Well, I'd say offhand you're glad to see your old husband."

Elizabeth could find no words for the overwhelming love that had come to her. She wanted to tell him how much she had missed him, how the farm was not the same when he was not working nearby in the fields. Somehow she wanted to say how lonely she felt at night, though the children were there as she sat out on the porch after the day's work was done, but the words would not come. All she knew was an emptiness and a loneliness when he was gone that nothing else could fill.

Looking into his face then, she reached up and ran her hand along the edge of his lower jaw, noting the scar that ran up into his hairline from an old battle. "I missed you," she said finally.

"I hurried back as soon as I could." The touch of her strong, round body beneath his hands stirred him, and he held her tightly, whispering, "A man needs a woman. That's something I found out since we've been married."

"Have you?"

"You know it. You can draw a man against his wishes, Elizabeth. Did you know that?" He thought hard for a moment, then said,

"Yesterday I nearly gave it up and came on in, I was so anxious to see you."

Elizabeth was pleased. She knew many men who would never think of saying such a thing to their wives, and she was glad now that he had come to that point where he could admit freely how much he missed her. It had come as a surprise to her, for he had been a man of few words, but during their hours alone, especially lying in bed talking of the affairs of the day or early in the morning when they first woke, he had said endearing things that most men could not express. They were not eloquent but simple, and even now he said, "I guess I'll have to tell you again how much I love you, wife."

"Both of us?" she said, pointing to her expanded middle and smiling.

"Both of you. Are you all right?"

"Yes. Everything's fine. The children will be glad to see you. Come on in and I'll fix you something to eat."

"Good. I'm starved to death."

Half an hour later Hawk was leaning back from the table talking to the four who listened to him. He had been on official business as sheriff of the Watauga Association, and he laughed aloud when Andrew asked, "Did you have to shoot anybody, Pa?"

"No. Old Mrs. Montgomery said that she sold Lawrence Satterfield some ducks and Lawrence wasn't satisfied with them, so he tried to make her take them back. She said they were his ducks now."

"What did he want you to do? Force the old woman to take them back?" Elizabeth said indignantly.

"Something like that. You know Lawrence. He's not happy unless he's arguing with someone."

Jacob had been listening to this story, then suddenly lifted his head. "Someone's coming," he said.

Surprised, Hawk looked across the table. "I don't hear anything."

"I do. It's a horse coming across the path, I think."

For a moment Hawk sat very still, then he said, "You've got sharp hearing, like a fox, Jacob. That'll help you out in the woods."

"Who can that be coming this time of the morning?"

The answer to Elizabeth's question came when Sarah moved to the window and looked out. "It's Reverend Anderson," she said.

Hawk's face brightened, for he was always glad to see Paul. "Better cook up some more of those eggs and pork chops. I never saw a preacher who'd pass up a free meal."

Anderson dismounted as Hawk stepped out on the front porch and greeted him.

"Hello, Paul. You're up and about pretty early." Anderson tied the bay to a hitching post, then came over to shake Hawk's hand. "Are you all right?"

"Been gone a couple of days." The tone of his voice was uneasy and Hawk did not miss that. He noted the horse lathered with sweat and knew that it was not the minister's custom to run a horse that hard. Something in Paul's face also caught his attention. "What's wrong? Is there trouble? Indians breaking out?"

"Nothing like that, but there is trouble."

Elizabeth had come outside to hear the last of this. "Is it something I can hear?"

"Hello, Elizabeth. I suppose so. A man can't have any secrets from his wife." He smiled and his plain face lit up with a mischievous look. "A man can't have any secrets at *all* from a wife. I'm finding that out."

"You come on in and I'll feed you while you tell us what the trouble is."

Anderson entered and took his seat, speaking to the children individually. As Elizabeth brought the meal, he said, "I hate to be the bearer of ill tidings."

"What is it, Paul?" Hawk asked.

"John Sevier came to see me last night. He asked me to come and tell you about Honey Shoate."

Instantly Hawk straightened slightly and frowned, so that his dark blue eyes were hooded. "Shoate? What's he done now?"

"Who is he, Hawk?" Elizabeth asked. "I don't know him."

"A bully boy," Hawk said. "He always wants to use his fists on someone."

"I heard he killed a man before he came to Watauga," Paul said. "George Stevens said he got him down and kicked him to death in a tavern back in Carolina."

"I can see Honey would do a thing like that."

"Well, do you know a man named Noah Leary?"

"Don't know him."

"He just moved in about a month ago. Hasn't been around the

settlement much. Got a wife and two small children." Anderson picked up the mug in front of him and drank the coffee, shuddering slightly. "That stuff's strong enough to float a horseshoe nail, Elizabeth!" he protested. Then he smiled and said, "But I guess a man needs strong coffee." He turned the cup in his hands and saw that the whole family was watching him. He spoke slowly, searching for the right words, for he was a man careful of his word. "Honey Shoate's got a horse he's proud of, a quarter horse, and him and Leary worked up a horse race. According to Sevier, Shoate's horse won the race and that's when the trouble started."

"What kind of trouble?"

"Shoate claimed that they had put their horses up for a stake—that the winner would take the loser's horse, but Leary says it wasn't so."

"Did Sevier hear the bet made?"

"No, but he saw what happened. It was a brutal thing. Leary argued with Honey Shoate that there was no bet made, and when Shoate just laughed at him and started away with the horse, Leary lit into him. He's just a small fellow, and you know what Shoate is."

"A bully boy," Hawk murmured. "Did he beat him pretty bad?"

"He was beat up worse than any man I ever saw."

"Did you talk to him?"

"Well, such as I could. He was in bed by the time I got there. His jaw was broken, and he lost some teeth, and both eyes were closed all the way shut. He had ribs busted where Shoate kicked him." A look of pain crossed Anderson's eyes, and he shook his head. "His wife was all shook up, and the children were crying. I don't know how they'll make it. He won't be doing any work on his place, but we can help with that," Anderson said quickly. "I've already talked to some of the neighbors, but Sevier said he thought Shoate was going to kill Leary. He finally had to pull a gun on him to make him stop kicking him. Shoate went off threatening to kill John, and I think he might do it, too."

"Any other witnesses?"

"Zeke Taylor was there and William Crabtree."

"What did they say?"

"They didn't actually hear the bet being made, but they hold with Honey Shoate. The three have been running together, drinking a lot, causing trouble wherever they go."

A silence fell over the room and Hawk did not move. His face was bronzed from the sun and an elusiveness enveloped him as he sat in his chair. Elizabeth knew him well, however, and asked at once, "What will you have to do?"

"Shoate will have to stand trial on the charge of stealing a horse and attempted murder."

"Stealing a horse? Haven't there been men hung for that, Pa?" Andrew spoke up. His eyes were wide as he studied Hawk's face, carefully searching for some answer.

"He may hang," Hawk said. "That'll be up to the members of the court, but I'll have to go bring him in."

"Take somebody with you," Paul said quickly. "Shoate is a wild bull. He doesn't care for any man's life. John said he would have killed Noah Leary sure if he hadn't stopped him."

"I'll take Sequatchie with me."

"I'm going, too, and we'll pick up John Sevier."

"Don't see as I need all that help just to get one man."

Elizabeth said at once, "Don't be foolish! Take all the help you can get!" Suddenly, a fear gripped her heart, and as the two men left to go to Sequatchie's cabin, she felt a tremor begin in her hands. She held them tightly, but Sarah had noticed and came to stand beside her.

"Pa will be all right, won't he?"

"Yes. He'll be all right. Don't worry, Sarah," she said, trying to sound calm, but in her own heart she knew Hawk would be in danger. She was aware of how closely her life was tied with this man who had no fear and would not turn back one moment from any danger. She began to pray for God to protect the man she loved dearly.

The sun was almost down by the time Hawk and his party reached the Shoate homestead. It was far out away from the settlement, and as they approached down the scarcely worn trail, John Sevier cautioned Hawk. "I ain't sure you know about what a bad man Honey Shoate is." He thought for a moment, then added, "He'd just as soon shoot a man as look at him."

Hawk glanced at Sevier and said, "We'll have to see what he does. He's going in for trial whether he likes it or not."

Sequatchie had said little on the journey. Now he nodded, saying, "The cabin's up there. Do we ride up or take him by surprise?"

"We'll give him a chance." He glanced at the four men, saying, "When we get there, spread out. Don't bunch up. I'll ride up close to the house and give him a call."

Paul Anderson did not like this. He held a musket over the pommel of his saddle and wondered if he would be able to use it to shoot at a man. "I hope he goes in peacefully."

"Not likely," Sevier said curtly. "You don't know Honey like I do. You should have seen him. He was crazy when he got Leary down. He would have killed him sure. He won't be going in for any trial—not of his own free will."

Hawk said nothing, but when they reached the opening in the trail leading to the cabin that sat almost in the shadow of a tall grove of hickory trees, he motioned for the others to move out. When they were positioned, he lifted his voice. "Hello the house!"

Instantly a challenge came. "Who's there? What do you want?"

"Hawk Spencer! I want to talk to you, Shoate!"

"What do you want?" The voice was slightly blurred, but Hawk saw a rifle suddenly appear in the window. It was aimed directly at him, and he did not move.

"Come out, Shoate! We've got business!"

"I got no business with you! Get off my place!"

"Put the gun down!"

"You come any closer and I'll shoot you, Spencer!"

Slipping off his horse, Hawk laid his rifle down and advanced several steps. "I'm leaving my gun here! Come out, Shoate! We've got to talk!"

"I told you! Stay away or I'll shoot! Now git!"

Hawk heard Shoate talking to someone else and wondered how many men were in the cabin. "Who's in there with you?" he asked. There was no answer and Hawk hesitated. "If you don't come out, I'll have to come in after you!" he called finally.

Even as he ended his threat he saw the rifle shift, and raw instinct caused him to throw himself, with a violent motion, to the left just as the explosion rocked the silence of the homestead. His horse gave a scream, and as Hawk rolled in the dirt, he saw that his mount was down and kicking. Anger raced through him, and he did not stop moving. He knew it would take time for Shoate to reload unless he had another rifle handy, which was always possible. He never stopped his motion but made a dive back to where his musket was, grabbed it up, and then made a zigzag run toward a log that lay fallen in the yard. Even as he fell behind it, another explosion came, and he yelled, "I'll have to take you in, Shoate! Dead or alive, it's your choice!"

At that moment Shoate suddenly appeared in the doorway. He was a huge man with bulky shoulders and a neck so short that he appeared to have none. He was wearing a dirty hunting shirt, and in his hand he carried a hatchet. His eyes, Hawk saw, were wild, and he had one chance to throw up his rifle, but he did not want to kill the man.

Shoate, for all his size, moved quickly, and he seemed to ignore the gun in Hawk's hand. He hurdled forward, and Hawk, choosing not to fire, reversed the musket and struck out. The musket missed striking his head but struck Honey in the chest. The man's burly strength was too much. With a roar he brushed it aside and suddenly was on top of Hawk.

Hawk was bowled over backward, and the rank smell of Shoate filled his nostrils. He saw the hatchet rise and desperately tried to throw the man's weight off but he could not. For one brief moment he thought, *Getting killed by a drunk. What a waste.* The hatchet was over Shoate's head, and his eyes were wild with rage.

But the hatchet never descended. Something struck Shoate in the back of the head and he suddenly collapsed, falling loosely over Hawk.

Hawk rolled the heavy body off and sat up to see Sequatchie standing beside him, holding his musket. He looked down at the barrel and shook his head regretfully. "I think I bent it," he said. "I should have shot him."

Shoate was rolling on the ground, but his brute strength was so great that even being struck by a heavy musket on the head was not enough to put him down.

Quickly Hawk rolled him over, pulled his arms behind him, and pinioned him with one of the strips of rawhide he always carried. Seeing the massive strength of Shoate's arms, he wound two more strands around, then came to his feet. He turned just in time to see William Crabtree and Zeke Taylor come out of the cabin, both carrying muskets and both obviously half drunk.

"Stop right there and drop those guns!" Sevier cried out. He had come to stand beside Hawk, and Paul Anderson had taken position over to their left. The two men stared wildly at Honey, who was moaning but getting to his knees awkwardly.

"Don't shoot!" Taylor cried out.

"Lay those guns down," Sevier said. When they had laid them on the ground slowly, he advanced and took them. He turned them to wait for Hawk to speak.

Hawk jerked the huge man to his feet and said coldly, "You're under arrest for horse stealing, Honey."

"You won't never hang me!" Blood ran down Shoate's head, but his thick skull had cushioned the blow. His eyes were red rimmed, and despite his hands being tied, he threw himself forward like a maniac, shouting, "I'll kill you, Spencer!"

Hawk simply swiveled and struck the huge man on the back of his neck. The blow drove Honey sideways, and, off-balance, he fell to the ground.

Hawk picked up his musket and put it right against the big man's temple. "If you'd rather get shot than hang, it's your choice."

Anderson drew a sharp breath, wondering if Hawk would pull the trigger. Finally he was relieved to hear Shoate begin cursing but not showing resistance.

"Let's take 'em in. We'll have the trial as soon as we get the association together," Sevier said.

"We didn't have nothin' to do with it!" Taylor cried out.

"You saw him nearly kill Noah Leary, didn't you, Zeke?"

"Wasn't none of our affair. You don't bust into another man's quarrel."

Hawk stared at the two and shook his head. "You'll be at the trial," he said. "If you don't tell the truth, I think we can string you up along with this one." He turned then and said bleakly, "Let's get him back to the settlement."

———

It was five days after the arrest of Honey Shoate that the Watauga Association court convened. Some of the members of the court had gone on a salt-hunting expedition, and it was necessary to await their return before the trial could take place.

Finally, on a Thursday morning the court met in the accustomed place, and the room was packed. It was the first real test of the power of the court to enforce laws.

Honey Shoate stood in front of the members of the court sullen and belligerent. He refused to have anyone defend him and continually interrupted the court with blasphemy and cursing.

"Doesn't he know he could be hanged?" Paul whispered to Hawk, who stood beside him, both of them with their backs to the wall.

"I reckon he does, but he doesn't care much."

After Sevier had given his evidence, and Noah Leary's wife had testified that her husband was not a betting man and would never have bet his horse, Shoate fell into a rage, cursing Mrs. Leary until Hawk had gone to him and said, "Shut your mouth or I'll put a gag in it!"

Honey Shoate had gazed balefully at Hawk, and even with the shadow of a hanging over him, he was not daunted. "I'll kill you, Hawk!"

"I expect you'd like to try."

"There's lots of places. I'll get you! You ain't gonna live long!"

John Carter, head of the court, said, "Shut your mouth, Shoate!" He turned to Zeke Taylor and said, "Did you hear a bet being made?"

Taylor swallowed hard. He was rather pale, for he knew it was entirely possible he could be hanged because he had ridden off with the horse, as well.

"No, I didn't hear that."

"How do you know the bet was made?"

"Why . . . why, Honey told me. He said Leary bet his horse against his'n."

"It was all hearsay?"

"I reckon so."

William Isaac Crabtree had nothing else to add. He told his story, and finally James Robertson said, "Why didn't you stop him from kicking Leary?"

"Why, it wasn't our fight," Crabtree said indignantly. "A man minds his own business."

Carter stared at the two and appeared to be pondering what action he'd be taking against them, but finally he shrugged and said, "Let's get on with the trial."

Honey Shoate's defense was nonexistent. He swore that Leary had bet his horse despite the testimony of the man's wife and brother that Leary never bet anything. It was against his principles, they both said, and neither had ever known him to make a bet of any kind.

Finally John Carter ended the session, saying, "Take your prisoner away while the court comes to a verdict."

Hawk cleared the room but then went back inside as the men talked about the verdict.

"I don't see we need to take a lot of time," Robertson shrugged. He made a tall shadow as he stood beside the window gazing out, then turned and said, "He's guilty as sin. I vote for hanging."

"So do I," Carter said and shook his head. "He's a mad dog, and he'll kill somebody else."

Hawk hesitated. "He didn't actually kill Leary."

"He stole a horse," Carter said shortly. "You're not gettin' tenderhearted, are you, Hawk?"

"Hate to take a man's life. You can't give it back to him."

"He would have killed Noah if Sevier hadn't stopped him," Robertson said, "and he'll kill you if we let him go."

"I'll take my chances on that."

But the verdict was quickly reached. Hawk hesitated, then when asked by Carter, made it unanimous.

The court was reconvened, and when Shoate was brought in, John Carter announced, "You're guilty, according to the association. I sentence you to be hanged by the neck tomorrow until you're dead."

Hawk examined Shoate's face. It was a brutal face without a redeeming social kindness in it, and the verdict seemed to enrage him. He cursed and had to be restrained from attacking Carter, and when Hawk took him out and locked him up in the powder house, he said, "You'd better think about God and your soul."

Shoate only cursed him and Hawk turned away sadly.

The next day the sentence was carried out at dawn, and Hawk, who had seen his share of dead men, felt a chill as Honey Shoate went to his death cursing man and God. When it was over, Hawk said to Paul Anderson, "I hate to see a thing like that."

Anderson had tried to speak with Shoate earlier, but he had been cursed, as well. His face was pale, and he said, "He seemed to think there was no judgment."

"He knows better now," Hawk said grimly, then turned and walked away.

————————

That evening Hawk was quiet all during supper, and afterward he walked out and did not appear until after the children had gone to bed. Elizabeth, knowing him well, came to him and touched his arm. "Did it have to be done?"

"The court thought so."

"But what about you?"

"I wouldn't hang a man for stealing a horse. For killing a man, yes. But he didn't kill Leary."

"He would have, though. That's what Sevier said."

"I suppose so. And we do have to make sure the area stays safe to live in."

A bleakness clouded Hawk's face, and Elizabeth put her arm around him as he stood at the window staring out into the darkness. "What about his soul?"

"Paul went to see him, but he wouldn't listen to him."

"I was surprised at Paul, being a minister and all."

"What else could he do? He says the Bible upholds capital punishment. We had a long talk about it," Hawk said. He turned and faced her, and spoke slowly and thoughtfully. "We don't have much law out here, and we get some mighty hard men. They've got to know that when they break the law they'll have to answer for it. It's a hard way, but that's the way it must be."

"I hope it doesn't happen again. Another hanging, I mean."

"It probably will," Hawk said almost bitterly, then he shook his head and with an effort put the events of the day away from him. "We won't talk about it anymore."

"No, let's talk about your daughter."

"Daughter? How do you know it's not going to be a son?"

"Because I just know. Will you mind too bad not having another son?"

"No. I hope she looks like you." He laughed and drew her close. "Be terrible if she looked like me."

The two stood there holding each other, and finally as Elizabeth turned and headed for the bedroom, he followed her. The door closed, shutting out the world outside so that all they had was each other.

A Brother's Choice

Sixteen

*H*awk?"

"Yes, what is it, Elizabeth?"

Elizabeth was lying in the bed, unmoving. When she turned her face to Hawk, he saw that her lips were pressed tightly together and alarm ran through him.

"Is it time?"

"Yes. I think you'd better go get Deborah."

Hawk leaped out of bed, pulled his pants on, and left the room. He called out, "Andy—Andy!"

A rustle came from where the boys were sleeping, and then Andrew's tousled head appeared in the opening. "Yes, Pa. What is it?"

"Quick, son! Run and get Mrs. Stevens."

"All right, Pa."

"And don't tarry. You hear me?"

Hawk turned to see Sarah, who slept in the large room, and at once she asked, "Is Ma going to have her baby?"

"Yes." Hawk's answer was terse as he looked at the door to the bedroom. The muscles of his jaw grew tense and he swallowed convulsively. He seemed to have forgotten Sarah, who came and stood by him, frightened by his expression. "She'll be all right, won't she, Pa?"

Hawk shook his head nervously and then turned to look down at her. "Yes. She'll be all right, Sarah. We'll just have to pray for her and the new baby."

———

The rifle cracked and Andrew lowered his musket. "Look, Pa, dead center!"

Hawk had been staring back at the cabin where Deborah Stevens was with Elizabeth. Sarah and Abigail were inside the kitchen in case they needed any help. Hawk had offered to stay, but Deborah Stevens had said, "You'd just be in the way. Now, take the boys and go off somewhere, but not too far."

Hawk had gathered up the two boys, telling them to bring their muskets, and they had gone two hundred yards past the house, just over the rise where he could still keep an eye on the door. Sequatchie sat with his back against the tree, watching as the boys took their target practice.

"Your turn, Jacob," Andrew grinned. "I bet you can't top that shot."

Jacob had loaded his rifle. He had been inordinately proud of the weapon Hawk had given him for Christmas and had spent some time practicing. Now, however, he seemed preoccupied, and when he shot he merely clipped the bark on the tree where the target was pinned.

"You're not paying attention, Jacob!" Hawk said with some irritation. He hardly knew what he was saying, for his mind was back in the cabin, and he did not see the hurt look that crossed Jacob's face. "Try it again!" he said impatiently.

Jacob bit his lip and loaded the rifle. He had gotten to be quick at this, pouring the black powder into the pan, then a measured amount down the long barrel, followed by the musket ball, and then a wad on top, all shoved down with a ramrod. Replacing the ramrod in the clips on the stock, he took careful aim but missed again by a greater margin than before.

Hawk had been watching and now said, "Why don't you listen to what I'm saying? Look, I'll show you!"

Jacob, however, whirled and walked away angrily.

"Wait a minute, Jake!" Hawk halfheartedly called after him, but Jacob paid no attention.

Andrew looked at Hawk and said, "I think you hurt his feelings, Pa. I'll go talk to him."

As Andrew ran after Jacob, Sequatchie spoke for the first time. "That was not well, my friend."

"No. I shouldn't have shouted at him."

"I know you are worried."

"Any man would be worried, I suppose."

"It is not just Elizabeth you think about."

Hawk blinked in surprise, thinking he had misunderstood. "What do you mean by that?"

"You are thinking of your first wife."

Hawk had long ago given up trying to figure out how Sequatchie could read his thoughts. There was something almost eerie about the way the tall Cherokee could often tell what he was thinking.

Hawk moved restlessly, his eyes troubled. "I thought it would be all right, Elizabeth having a baby, even though Faith died. I thought it would be different this time."

"But it is not?"

"I keep thinking about how Faith died. I thought I'd be able to trust God. I know He's able, but, Sequatchie, now that the time is here I . . . I remember how happy I was when Jacob was on the way, and then when Faith died I just went crazy. It keeps coming back into my mind. I can't put it out."

"Elizabeth is in God's hands. That is the best place for anyone to be."

Hawk nodded but still looked apprehensive. He stood uncertainly, not knowing whether to go talk to Jacob, but then Sequatchie spoke up.

"I think someone else is thinking of your first wife, too."

"Of Faith? Why, who could that be?"

"I think her son may have her on his mind. Didn't you see his face and how his hands are not steady? He can shoot better than he did today."

"I never thought—"

"He's probably hurting on this day just as you are. I think you should go speak to him."

"Yes. I will." Hawk nodded, tried to smile, then left the hill at a run. He found the two boys at the well outside the house, and he heard Jacob saying, "Leave me alone, Andrew! Just get away from me!"

"Andrew," Hawk said, coming to a stop, "let me talk to your brother alone."

"All right, Pa."

Waiting until Andrew had gotten out of hearing, Hawk turned to face Jacob. He hesitated, awkward and uncertain. With part of his mind he was listening to the faint cry that he heard inside the cabin, but he said slowly, "It seems like I have to spend most of my time apologizing for things I do to you, Jacob." He waited for the boy to speak up, but Jacob said nothing. "I know you're thinking about your mother."

Surprise filled Jacob's eyes, and he turned quickly to look at Hawk. His eyes narrowed, but he did not speak, waiting for Hawk to say more.

"You know, son, even though I love Elizabeth very much, I still think about your mother. And I know that Elizabeth still thinks of Patrick, too. That doesn't mean we love each other any less. I can't understand why your mother died, but the only way to handle something like that is just to trust God to do what's best for His children."

Jacob had a bitterness that came to his lips almost unbidden. "Was it best that I be left alone for most of my life?"

With anguish in his eyes, Hawk shook his head. "We've been over this. I told you how it grieves me, son, the things that I've done. I turned my back on God and behaved very foolishly. All I can say is that I know I love you, and I'll do the best I can for you now and all the rest of my life."

At that moment Deborah Stevens suddenly appeared at the door. "Hawk!" she cried out, and when he turned he saw that she was smiling. "You'd better come inside and see your wife and your new daughter."

Hawk let out a whoop that carried over the yard and clear away to where Sequatchie heard it and appeared, running toward the cabin. Hawk started past Jacob and said, "Come on. You can see your new sister."

"No. You go on in. I'll come in a minute."

Hawk barely heard, so frantic was he to see Elizabeth, and he disappeared at once. Sequatchie came running up to Jacob and asked, "The baby's come?"

"Yes." Then Jacob suddenly asked, "Sequatchie?"

"Yes?"

"Do you remember you promised to take me back whenever I asked? Well, maybe it's time."

"Why would you say it is time now?"

"Things aren't working out."

"Why would you say that? You are becoming a good hunter, but it takes time to become a long hunter. Another year and you will be as good a man in the woods as your father."

"I don't know. I just know I can't stay here."

"Maybe it's because you don't want it to work out," Sequatchie observed. His keen eyes were glowing, and he said, "It would crush your father and the rest of the family if you left now. You would miss seeing your new sister grow up. You need a family. You didn't have anyone for so long, and now you have a father and a mother and a brother and two sisters." He laid his hand on the boy's shoulder. "And you have me for an older brother—or another father, if you would have it so."

Jacob stared at the bronze face of Sequatchie and could not answer. Uncertainty ran through him, and he finally mumbled, "I just don't know, Sequatchie."

"Wait a few days. If you don't change your mind, I will honor our agreement. Now," he said urgently, "go inside and see your new sister."

"All right, I will." Jacob turned and entered the cabin, followed by Sequatchie. He found Deborah Stevens washing her hands in a basin, and she nodded at them.

"You can go in, but not for long."

Jacob wanted to turn and run from the cabin, but Sequatchie was there with him, his dark eyes fixed on him. Stiffly he walked inside the door to the bedroom and then stopped dead still.

Elizabeth's face was pale, and lines of strain marred its smoothness. But after one glance at her, Jacob stared at his father, who was sitting on the bed beside Elizabeth holding a tiny bundle. The eyes of Hawk Spencer, Jacob saw, were filled with love. His face, which could be so stern in times of danger or of trouble, was now gentle, and a smile softened the hard lines of his mouth. Looking up and seeing Jacob, he held the baby up and said, "Come and greet your sister, Jake."

For a moment Jacob just stood there, then Hawk said, "Come. Take her."

Jacob moved forward awkwardly and took the tiny bundle. The baby was wrapped in a linen towel, and looking down at the red face, he stroked the soft hair as he studied the infant. "She's so little," he whispered. He held the baby as if she were a fragile and very precious burden. He could not stop looking at her face. Until this moment the baby had not been real to him, but now he knew that this flesh and blood was *his* flesh and blood. He even imagined that she looked somewhat like the Spencers, but with honey-colored hair, and the same shaped face, in miniature, as his father and he himself had. He was unaware that everyone in the room was looking at him—Sequatchie standing just inside the door, Sarah and Andrew off to one side, Elizabeth from her bed, and Hawk, as he stood looking down at him.

"Your sister's name is Hannah Faith Spencer," Hawk said quietly.

Jacob looked questioningly at him. "After my mother?"

"It was Elizabeth's idea to name her Faith."

Somehow this touched Jacob more than anything had in his memory. Suddenly, without warning, two things happened. He could not help smiling down at the baby, and at the same time he felt his eyes suddenly overflow with tears. Strangely enough, for all his pride, he did not care that the tears ran down his cheeks. He stood there holding the child, totally oblivious of the smiles on the faces around him.

"She'll need a big brother to watch out for her," Elizabeth said.

Sequatchie looked at Jacob carefully. He saw something in the youthful face that pleased him, and he thought, *This will keep him here. He has found out what it means to have a family.*

Bread Rounds

Seventeen

*T*he winter of 1772 to 1773 had been mild. Spring had come now with all of its softness and gentleness, erasing from the memory of the settlers the light snows and the one hard freeze. As always, the spring seemed to bring a new time of hope, and a spirit of expectation had come to the dwellers at Watauga.

The Spencer cabin was now enlarged. Hawk had added another full-sized room, joining it by a walkway through the middle of the two structures. Since the dogs slept in it, it was called the dog trot, and oftentimes at night the sleepers inside would awaken to hear the dogs' claws scratching on the board floor between the two rooms. It had a loft, the same as the first structure, so that now Andrew and Jacob shared it, while Sarah had the old room over the original structure.

Paul and Rhoda Anderson had come for supper on Friday night. They had just returned a week earlier after spending all winter preaching the gospel among the Cherokee. Rhoda was holding the eight-month-old Hannah Faith in her arms and cooing down at her.

"She's got her mother's green eyes," she said, smiling up at Elizabeth. "And look, her hair's the color of honey." Elizabeth, who had just taken a pie out of the Dutch oven before the fireplace, smiled. She was content now. The baby was healthy and already filling the cabin with her meaningless sounds that she thought was talk.

Across the room Paul and Sequatchie were speaking with Hawk. It was Sequatchie who said, "Some of the Cherokee are still not happy about the leasing of their lands."

"Been peaceful enough."

"Yes, but some of the younger warriors don't want it that way,

Hawk," Paul said. His eyes now on Rhoda, he thought, *I wish Rhoda and I could have a baby. It's done so much for Elizabeth.*

Hawk did not miss the wistful look in his friend's eyes, but he said nothing of it. "We'll talk to the leaders of the community and see what can be done."

The men sat there talking until the meal was set on the table. They plunged into the fried chicken, biscuits and gravy, sweet potatoes with sliced apples on top, and early peas from the garden, and afterward when Rhoda and Elizabeth were cleaning up, Elizabeth asked, "Tell me more about your trip. Were the Indians receptive to the gospel?"

"Oh yes. Some of them were. It's hard to tell," Rhoda said. "They come and they sit. Some of them like the singing, but their way of life is so different from ours." She was putting mugs back on pegs in the cabinet and said, "I'm still having a hard time, Elizabeth."

"You mean about being a preacher's wife?"

"Yes. I still don't feel worthy."

"Have you talked to Paul about it?"

Rhoda turned and said with exasperation, "I've tried, but he thinks I'm wonderful!"

"Well, that must be awful, having to listen to that kind of talk all the time."

Rhoda caught the grin on Elizabeth's face and could not stop the smile that came to her own lips. "I should be thankful for what God's given me, and I am, but I feel so inadequate."

Elizabeth was quiet for a moment. She was a thoughtful woman who liked to hold things in her mind for a time, and she had thought often of what Rhoda had said about feeling unworthy. She had prayed about it, and now she said firmly, "I think what you've just said is against God." Seeing Rhoda's shocked look, Elizabeth said quickly, "I think that when someone gets down on themselves, that's a form of pride, and the Bible says that God hates that worse than any sin."

"Why, I'm not prideful! I've got nothing to be prideful about."

"I don't think you mean to be, but you're always talking about the things you say you lack. Do you think it was God's will, Rhoda, for you to marry Paul?"

Rhoda was still now, caught by what Elizabeth had said. She had thought this over many times, and Paul had helped her with it. "Yes," she said. "I really believe it was."

"Do you believe, then, that God's called him to be a minister?"

"Of course I do."

"Well, certainly you don't think God would give Paul a wife who would be a hindrance. He would give him one who would be a helper." Wiping her hands on the towel, she came over to stand beside Rhoda. She studied the strong features of her friend for a time, then said, "Rhoda, God has forgotten your past, and the people on the frontier, including the Cherokee, have no problems with it."

Rhoda stood quietly as Elizabeth talked to her, and finally she grew encouraged. "You've been such a help to me, Elizabeth. Paul tries to help me, but women need other women, don't they?"

"Yes, and they need the grace of God so they can do what He wants them to do."

Rhoda smiled openly and with relief, and the two pulled up chairs and sat down, talking for a while. Afterward they each prayed for God to bless the other and to be wives who would be pleasing to God.

———————

The Watauga Association Court had rarely met during the winter, but now Hawk sat back and listened as Carter, Robertson, and others went over the problems and the plans of the group. He had little to say, for these two men were far more able than he, he felt, to take the lead in this sort of thing. Finally, however, when there was a pause and John Carter said, "Is there any other business?" Hawk did speak up.

"I think we ought to do something to help our relationships with the Cherokee."

James Robertson stared at him for a moment with surprise. "What were you thinking of, Hawk?"

"I've been talking to Elizabeth, and we came up with the plan to give a feast to honor the Cherokee." He ran his hand over his coal black hair and added, "You remember your history. The Pilgrims did that for their Indian friends."

"That's not a bad idea," Carter said.

"No, it's not," Robertson added quickly. "We could have a feast and games and races. . . ."

After some talk it was decided, by general consensus, to have the meeting a year later, for it would take time to spread the word to all the Cherokee and to the settlers, and to provide enough food to go around.

"Sequatchie and Paul will spread the word to the Cherokee," Hawk said. "Daniel Boone's in the area. He travels everywhere, and he can spread the word to the settlers wherever he goes."

At this moment Sequatchie walked in with George Stevens. Stevens was holding a young man by the arm, and an odd expression was on his face.

"What's this, George?" James Robertson asked.

"This is Hiram Younger. He just moved into the community last week."

Younger was a very small young man of some seventeen or eighteen years of age. He had carrot red hair and pale blue eyes that he lifted nervously to watch the men of the court.

"I expect this is a job for you, Sheriff," Stevens said, looking at Hawk.

"What's he done?" Hawk demanded. "He doesn't look like a very bad sort." He saw the relief that crossed the young man's features and wondered what sort of a crime he had committed.

"Well," Stevens said, "this morning Deborah baked some pies and bread. She put them outside to cool, and when she heard somethin', she went to the window. She saw Hiram running away. I was right there and I caught up with him. Brought him right here."

Robertson tried not to smile, but he could not help it. "Well, Younger, did you do it?"

"No, sir. I didn't do it. I was just passing by."

Hawk was amused, as were the other men. "Why were you running, then?"

"I . . . I was just in a hurry."

"A hurry, were you? What about those bread crumbs on your mouth?"

Hiram Younger's eyes flew open, and he swiped his hand across his mouth.

"You didn't even have time to wipe your face," Hawk said.

"I didn't mean no harm. I was so hungry and it smelled so good."

Robertson winked at Hawk and Carter. "I think stealing pies and

BEYOND THE QUIET HILLS

cakes and bread is a pretty serious offense. Hanging, wouldn't you say?"

"Oh no! Don't hang me!"

"Well, a whipping at least," Carter said.

George Stevens saw that the young man was distraught. "I don't want that to happen. It was just one loaf of bread, really. I just want him to stop stealing."

Some discussion went on about a fit punishment, and finally Carter said, "What do you think, Sheriff?"

Hawk looked over at Sequatchie, seeing the light of humor in the dark eyes. "What do you think, Sequatchie?"

"I think you can just spread the word among the community. Tell them there's a bread thief loose."

Hawk grinned and said, "All right, Younger. You got a new name."

"A new name?"

"That's right. Your name is Bread Rounds Younger. I hereby make it official. Now, get out of here."

Younger immediately whirled as soon as Stevens released him and fled through the door. The men all laughed, and as he disappeared they all called out, "Good-bye, Bread Rounds!"

"I wish all crimes were that minor in this part of the woods," Hawk murmured. It had been a time of relaxation, and he made a note to find the young man and let him know that he had at least one friend in the community.

———————

A few weeks after the Bread Rounds incident, Hawk and Sequatchie were helping George Stevens build an addition to his cabin. It was Stevens who said, "I haven't seen Bread Rounds much lately."

Hawk was helping to lift a log into place and waited until the ends fell into the notches they had made with their axes before answering. "He left the settlement."

"Left? I didn't know that," Stevens said. He took his neckerchief out of his hip pocket, wiped his face, and grinned. "He didn't steal any more bread."

"No, but everybody called him Bread Rounds. I don't think he could take that."

"It wasn't much of a punishment," Sequatchie observed.

"Among my people it would have been worse."

"I expect so," Hawk said, "but all the young people took to following him around and calling him Bread Crumbs and offering him crusts of bread, even the little ones."

George laughed and shook his head. "Well, I guess Hiram learned his lesson."

Sequatchie picked up his ax and started notching the next log to be fitted into place. "It is good that we have law in Watauga, even for things like stealing bread."

Iris and Amanda

Eighteen

Shifting Hannah from one hip to the other, Elizabeth glanced down at the infant and smiled. *Ten months old,* she thought, *and it seems like only yesterday that she was born. But time has gone by so quickly.*

Spring was slipping away and summer was fast approaching. Rumors from the coast had brought ill tidings, or so it seemed. The patriots in Boston and New England were taking more stringent action against the British. War talk drifted over the Misty Mountains, but by the time it reached Watauga, all of the action on the coast seemed as distant as if it were in China.

"Doesn't seem a year since Abigail's fifteenth birthday, does it, Elizabeth?" Rhoda Anderson was walking alongside Elizabeth, and now she reached over and said, "Let me carry Hannah for a while."

"She's heavy as lead, Rhoda," Elizabeth warned but gladly surrendered her burden. She smiled as Hannah crowed and reached up to pull Rhoda's hair, which was hanging freely down her back. Getting a fistful she gave it a hearty yank, and Rhoda said, "Ouch! That hurts!" She leaned over and kissed the baby and, with admiring eyes, said, "She's the most beautiful child I've ever seen."

"She looks like her father, I think. Don't you?"

"Her face is shaped like his, but I can see you in her, too—especially around her eyes."

Deborah Stevens, who was walking behind the two women, accompanied by Sarah MacNeal, disagreed. "I don't think she looks like either one of you."

"She does, too!" Sarah protested. "She looks like Ma!"

The argument went on for some time until finally they turned on the path that led to the Taylor place. As usual, Elizabeth was depressed by the homestead, for Zeke Taylor did no work on it that was not actually required. Several pigs were rooting in the yard, and there was only a small bed of flowers that brought a bit of color to the dilapidated landscape.

"I wish Zeke would take more pride," Rhoda murmured. "Iris loves nice things, and yet she never has anything."

"No, and it's hard to help them," Elizabeth said. "Zeke gets angry. He says he's not going to take charity."

The group had approached the cabin, and it was Sarah who said, "I think I hear something."

Elizabeth cocked her ear as they approached the door but shook her head. "I don't hear anything." She knocked, and even as she did her ears caught a faint sound. "That sounds like someone crying," she said.

"It sounds like Iris," Abigail Stevens said. She had been tagging behind picking flowers and now had a small bouquet in her hands, but her eyes were troubled. Deborah looked at Elizabeth and said, "Maybe you and I ought to go in alone."

"All right," Elizabeth said. She pushed at the door, found it open, and when she stepped inside, was shocked to see the furniture scattered wildly about, overturned, the chairs upside down, and broken dishes on the floor. She paid no heed to that, however, for her eyes fell on Amanda, who was kneeling beside her mother, who was obviously unconscious.

"Amanda!" Elizabeth cried. "What happened?" She rushed up and knelt beside the unconscious woman and noticed that Amanda had a big raw welt on her cheek.

"I been trying to get her to wake up, but she won't," Amanda said, tears streaming down her face.

Deborah Stevens said, "I'll get some water." She moved outside to the pump, picking up a tall pewter basin on the way. When she came back, she snatched up a towel, dipped it in the water, and kneeling beside the unconscious woman, she began to dab at Iris's face. Her lips grew tense, for Iris had obviously taken a severe beating. Her eyes were swollen, and a cut on her mouth was bleeding. Anger welled up inside Deborah, but she said nothing, for she knew, as well as Elizabeth, who was responsible.

Elizabeth was struggling with her own feelings. She had grown very close to Iris Taylor, and Amanda, as well, over the long months on the frontier. During the trip out she had felt a sympathy for the woman and the child being tied to such a man as Zeke Taylor, and now as she half supported Iris, anger built up in her. *I'd like to see Zeke Taylor beat with a blacksnake whip!* she thought. But she said none of this. "What happened, Amanda?" she asked.

Amanda dropped her head. It was a customary gesture with her. She had formed the habit when she was but a child. Elizabeth believed it was a reflex action to avoid meeting the eyes of her father, and now she reached her hand out and took the girl's hand. "What is it? Tell me about it."

Rhoda stepped inside the door at this time and came to stand over Iris. Her back straightened and her eyes glowed with a sudden anger. "Who did this?"

"It's all right for you to tell, Amanda. Was it Indians?"

Amanda shook her head. "No," she whispered. "It was Pa."

Deborah nodded as if her thoughts had been confirmed. "Where is he, Amanda?"

"I don't know. He left."

"We've got to get Iris and Amanda away from here," Elizabeth said.

Rhoda and Deborah agreed, and they continued to minister to the injured woman until she regained consciousness. "You've got to come with us, Iris. You can't stay here," Elizabeth said firmly.

Iris Taylor was dazed. She could barely see out of her eyes, and she lifted one hand as she shook her head. "No . . . I can't—!"

"Yes, you can," Rhoda said firmly. "You get her things together, Deborah. I'll go hitch the horse up to the wagon. She's not able to walk."

"Yes," Deborah nodded firmly. "We'll make a pallet for you in the wagon."

Iris protested faintly but could not stand up to the determination of the three women. Half an hour later she was half carried out to the wagon by the three women. They helped her into the wagon, and she slumped back faintly as Amanda got in beside her and whispered, "Don't worry, Ma. It'll be all right." She looked at the cabin with fear in her eyes and reached up and touched the welt on her face. *I hope I never have to come back here,* she thought, and bitterness rose to her throat. Shutting her eyes, she lay back and put her arm around her mother and held tightly to her as Rhoda spoke to the horses sharply and the wagon lurched off.

"Can you tell us what happened, Iris?"

Elizabeth was sitting on the bed beside the injured woman, her eyes troubled. She had decided to bring her to her own home, and Amanda had stepped outside with Sarah and Abigail. They were in the next room, and Elizabeth heard them trying to distract the girl with talk of Abigail's upcoming sixteenth birthday party.

Elizabeth reached out and took Iris's work-hardened hand, and compassion filled her heart as she studied the battered face. "What happened to make Zeke do this, Iris?"

For a moment Elizabeth did not think Iris meant to answer. She sat quietly holding the thin hand until finally Iris moved her head from side to side. She spoke in a half whisper, saying, "For a time Zeke's been good—he changed after Hawk had his talk with him. And I been prayin', Elizabeth, and tryin' to live for the Lord so that I could be a witness to Zeke."

"Did he show any signs of really changing? I mean deep down?"

"Well, he treated us better." Iris paused, then added, "I tried to talk to him about Jesus, but the more I talked, the more he sort of pulled away."

"He's been running around with Crabtree and other men like that."

"That was the trouble," Iris said wearily. "He began to drink. Not in front of me and Amanda at first, but I found out about it. Then I told him that he didn't need whiskey. It made him do bad things. He told me to just leave him alone. No one was going to tell him what to do anymore." She hesitated, then said, "He cussed Hawk and said not even Hawk Spencer was gonna tell him what to do."

Elizabeth sat quietly listening as the frail woman spoke of how she had prayed harder and harder, and wondered why she had ever married such a man. She tried to imagine a youthful Zeke and Iris, but her imagination couldn't seem to picture it with the disturbed feelings she had at the moment.

"One day," Iris continued, "a few months ago he came in drunk. He was all mad because the crop was bad. At least that's what he said." She turned her head from side to side, her lips twisting with the pain. "I hate to say it about my own husband, but it was his own fault. He didn't work the crop right, but he blamed me. That was when he hit me for the first time since Hawk warned him."

"What did you do, Iris?"

"Well, I stayed away from him, and the next day he told me he was sorry."

"Why didn't you leave him?"

"I . . . I couldn't do that. I married him and promised to stay with him," she said simply. "I wanted him to come to know the Lord so bad, and I thought maybe if I stayed it would help."

"Did he hit you after that?"

"Yes, he did. Every once in a while, and he finally stopped even apologizing."

The windows were open, and just outside the sounds of the cow lowing out in the pasture floated in. The small bedroom was growing hotter now, and a buzzing fly flew in and lit on Iris's face. Quickly Elizabeth brushed it away and asked, "What happened today?"

"He came in drunk and he hit me, and then Amanda told him to stop. He turned around and hit her with his fist. It was the first time he ever hit her since Hawk told him to stop, and he was going to whip her with his belt. I pulled him away and told him to leave. That was when he beat me up. I don't remember him leavin', Elizabeth." Tears filled her eyes and rolled down her cheeks. As Elizabeth wiped them away, Iris said, "I don't know what to do . . . I just don't know what to do. I've got to get away from him. I could stand it myself, but I ain't gonna let him hurt Amanda."

"You can stay with us," Elizabeth said firmly.

"Oh, we couldn't—"

"Don't argue with me, Iris. It's all settled."

———

As soon as Hawk entered the cabin with Sequatchie at his heels, he saw that Elizabeth's face was drawn. "I have to talk to you."

"I couldn't find Zeke," Hawk said. As soon as he had heard what had happened, he had set out to find Taylor. He and Sequatchie had gone to the Taylor homestead, but there was nobody there. The cow had not been milked, and there was no sign of Taylor. They had made a swing around the settlement, but nobody had seen the man. Now he asked, "How is Iris?"

"She'll be all right, but that man—he ought to be whipped!"

Sequatchie lifted his eyebrows. It was the first time he had ever seen Elizabeth so angry. "I think he will be," Sequatchie remarked in a mild tone.

Elizabeth looked over at the passive face of the Cherokee and knew that something was going on inside his mind. She shifted her eyes to Hawk and saw the same sort of expression. "You won't hang him, will you?"

"That will be up to the court, but what about Iris and Amanda? They can't stay with that skunk."

"I told her she could stay with us for a while. Is that all right?"

"Sure. We'll make plenty of room," Hawk said.

Elizabeth had it all figured out. "Yes. They can take the boys' room, and the boys can sleep in the living area downstairs until we can figure out something."

"No," Sequatchie said quickly. "They can have my cabin."

"We couldn't put you out like that!" Hawk exclaimed.

"Do you think I'm a white man that I have to have a roof over my head?" Sequatchie said sharply. "I'll make a hut close by where I can watch out for them." He smiled suddenly, but it was a grim smile. "I wish Taylor would come to visit them. I'd like to have a talk with him."

"That might be better at that," Hawk said. "They'll have a place all their own and won't feel they're an imposition."

"Come along. We'll tell her." She led the two men into the bedroom and saw their faces harden at the sight of her battered face. Quickly she said, "It's all settled, Iris. You're going to live in Sequatchie's cabin. He's going to build another hut to stay in where he can look out for you."

"Oh, I couldn't do it!"

"Yes, you can," Sequatchie said. He went over and said, "Anywhere is my home as long as God is there, and He's everywhere, isn't He?"

Iris reached her hand out and Sequatchie took it, saying quietly, "It will be all right. God has not forgotten you."

Dancing Lessons

Nineteen

A delicious aroma of food arose from the pots and kettles in the fireplace of the Spencer cabin. Elizabeth and Iris were doing the cooking, and it seemed to Elizabeth that Iris had cheered up considerably. *It's helped her,* she thought, *to have her own place, but I don't know how long it will last.*

At that moment Sarah came in and asked, "Where's Amanda?"

"I'm not sure," Iris said. "Probably in the cabin."

"Sarah, you need to watch the bread. I don't want it to get burned."

"All right, Ma," Sarah agreed, and at that moment Jacob and Andrew stepped inside. Andrew said at once, "Could I have something to eat, Ma? I'm starving!"

"No, you'll have to wait for a while. Now, don't bother us. We're too busy with the cooking."

Sarah grinned at Andrew and Jacob. A mischievous light danced in her eyes, and she moved over to stand between the two. "Which one of you two is going to dance with Abigail when the dancing starts?"

"I will," Jacob grinned at her. "But," he added quickly, "I'll have to dance with all the other girls so they won't be disappointed."

"You are the most conceited thing!" Sarah exclaimed, but she was amused by Jacob's foolishness.

Andrew had drawn himself into a stiff upright posture. "I think it's silly to have all this nonsense at a party!" he said. Whirling, he marched back outside.

"What's wrong with him?" Sarah asked with surprise. "You're supposed to be foolish at a party, aren't you?"

Jacob reached over and ruffled Sarah's hair, which always irritated her. She slapped his hand away and he laughed. "Andy knows all the girls will be falling over me instead of him." Suddenly he reached out and put his arm around Sarah, took her hand, and waltzed her around the room. Elizabeth and Iris watched them with a smile, and Sarah laughed aloud. "You're crazy, Jacob!"

"No, I'm just charming and good-looking."

Elizabeth was happy that Jacob seemed to be feeling so much more at home over the last several months. She watched as he teased Sarah and thought how good it was for her to have another brother. Then she said, "You two get out of the kitchen. We've got work to do here." As the two left, Elizabeth looked outside and a thought came to her about Andrew. *I wonder what's bothering him. He doesn't seem himself lately.*

As soon as he had left the cabin, Andrew walked slowly toward the nearby creek. The big woolly dog that had taken up with them came to bark at him and suddenly reared up. He was a large dog of a reddish brown color, and his paws were muddy.

"Get off of me!" Andrew exclaimed, shoving the dog away. The dog barked happily, not at all offended, and ran out in short, sweeping runs as Andrew continued on the way.

Finally he came to the creek and stood for a while, silently staring down at the water. Bending over, he picked up some flat rocks and began skimming them.

"What are you thinking about, Andrew?"

"What?" Andrew whirled quickly to see Amanda, who was sitting in the shade of a big hemlock tree. He took a step toward her, scowling. "You shouldn't scare a fellow like that!" His feet hit a slick spot of mud, and he called out, "What—!" but he lost his balance and fell back as the other foot slid out from under him. He sat down in the mud with a splatting sound and Amanda laughed.

"You're so graceful, Andrew."

"Well, you're not all that graceful, either!" Andrew had not intended to speak so roughly, but he was embarrassed by being taken off guard and by his rather awkward fall. When he got to his feet, he began wiping the mud off of his trousers, then realized that Amanda had not answered. Looking over, he saw that her face was pale, and she half turned away from him.

"Hey, I'm sorry, Amanda. I didn't mean that."

"I'm sorry, too. I didn't mean to make fun of you."

"Well, it's not you. I'm just upset."

Amanda looked over and studied Andrew's face. The sun had tanned him now, although he still had freckles. He looked strong and healthy and fit, but there was a misery in his eyes that she could not mistake. "What's the matter, Andrew?"

"Aw, it's just that, well—everyone's talking about Jacob and this party, and I think it's all silly."

"I don't know why you'd think that. I think it's nice." She hesitated, then said, "You really like Abigail, don't you, Andrew?"

"Never mind that!" Andrew snapped sharply.

Rising from her place under the tree, Amanda came over and stood beside him. "What's wrong? You can tell me. I know something is the matter."

Andrew hesitated and shook his head. "Nothing that you could fix."

"Well, tell me what it is."

Andrew shoved his hands in his pockets, kicked at a stone, then muttered, "I can't dance. That's what's wrong."

At once Amanda understood clearly. She knew he liked Abigail more than any other girl, and she also knew that Andrew had become jealous of Jacob. Jacob was a fine dancer, and Andrew would have to sit on the sidelines.

"You could learn to dance."

"I'm too clumsy!"

"If I can learn, then you can."

Andrew turned to face her, a thoughtful look on his face and a faint eagerness in his eyes. "Do you think so, Amanda?"

"Yes. It's easy. Look. Put your arm here." She put his arm on her waist. "And hold this hand right here. Now we'll take one step back, and then one step to the right."

The brilliant sunlight filtered down through the leaves of the hemlock, creating patterns of alternating light and shade on Amanda's face. Andrew moved awkwardly enough, stepping on her toes more than once, but she only laughed and her brown eyes glowed with pleasure. She was a tall girl, slim, and her straight dark brown hair was tied back with a blue ribbon. She was usually quiet, but now as they moved around under the shade of the tree on the dry grass, she laughed more than once.

"You're not going to have any feet left," Andrew said after stepping on her foot.

"Oh, that's all right. It doesn't hurt. You're doing so well. You'll do fine when you dance with Abigail."

Andrew stopped and dropped his hands. He looked off into the distance, chewing on his lower lip, then finally muttered, "I can't dance like Jacob."

"Jacob is Jacob, and you are you," Amanda smiled. "Abigail will like you for yourself. So you should be yourself and not Jacob."

But still her words had not comforted Andrew. He turned to face her, saying, "But Jacob's so good-looking . . . and . . . well, he's good with girls. I guess he's what you'd call gallant."

"Yes, I think he is all those things."

Andrew glanced at her quickly. It was hard to know what was going on inside this girl's head, for she had learned to cover up her true feelings.

Finally Amanda added, "Have you ever thought that Jacob might be jealous of you?"

"Are you crazy? Why would he be jealous of me?"

"Why, you're good at so many things."

"What kind of things are you talking about?"

"Well, at hunting and finding your way in the woods. You know how to live in the wilderness. You can make things on the forge. You can do all kinds of things."

"Jacob doesn't care about those things." Andrew shook his head.

"I think you'd be surprised at what Jacob cares about way down deep inside."

Surprised, Andrew gave her a sharp look. "You know a lot about people, Amanda." He smiled then and said, "Thanks for helping me learn to dance."

"We'll practice some more. You'll be as good as anybody at the party. All right, now one step back, then one to the right. . . ."

An Uninvited Guest

Twenty

*H*awk and Elizabeth dressed carefully for Abigail Stevens' sixteenth birthday party. It was to be held in the center of the Watauga community. A platform had been laid out for dancing, and musicians were coming for the special occasion. It had actually turned out to be more of a community gathering than a girl's birthday party, but things were hard on the frontier, and any occasion for a get-together was always welcome.

"I don't see why I have to dress up like a Philadelphia lawyer," Hawk complained.

"We've already been over that. Now, you be still and let me fix your tie."

Elizabeth arranged his tie and then looked down at her dress. "Do you like this dress?"

"I like the woman that's in it," Hawk grinned.

Elizabeth pushed his hands away and shook her head, but she could not keep back a smile. "I'll have to go get Hannah ready."

Hawk watched as she dressed the baby. She said, "I'm worried about Iris, and nobody has seen Zeke since he took off after beating her. I hope she'll go to the party. It'll do her good to get out. She was ashamed of her bruises, but we told her that everyone would understand and that she had nothing to be ashamed of. I don't think she'll go, though."

"I talked to Sequatchie about this," Hawk said. "He's taken a real interest in Iris and Amanda. He had a pretty determined look in his eye." He laughed shortly and said, "Whatever that Indian sets out to do pretty well gets done."

At that moment Sequatchie was knocking on the door of the

cabin that he had given up for Iris and her daughter. When the door opened, he said at once, "I've come to take you to the party."

"Why, thank you, Sequatchie, but I'm not going."

"I think you should go for Amanda's sake," Sequatchie said. "You've done nothing wrong. Your husband did all the wrong that was done. If you hide, people might think differently."

"Do you really think so?" Iris asked anxiously.

"Yes. When people are not ashamed, then they hold their heads up high. You get ready. We will go."

"All right," Iris said. "It'll take a while."

"I will wait, and I'll promise not to step on your feet if you'll dance with me."

Iris suddenly smiled, and it made her look much younger.

"Give us a few minutes to get ready," she said.

————

The party had brought out more people than usual for a community gathering, and the village was packed with both adults and young people. Elizabeth and Iris were helping Deborah set out the food. Sarah and Amanda had gone to find Abigail, who was primping in the cabin used for community events.

"How do you like my new dress?" she asked, looking at herself in the mirror.

The two girls admired the dress, which was indeed beautiful. It was made of soft white cotton, loosely fitted and surrounded at the waist with a delicate flowered sash trimmed in light blue ribbon. It had a rounded neckline edged with white lace, and the sleeves stopped just above the elbows with a light blue ribbon between two rows of white lace.

Sarah said, "It's fun having parties and getting to dress up."

"Let's go outside," Abigail said. "It's too hot in here. Besides, we're going to play some games before we eat."

The three returned to the party, where they found Elizabeth, Iris, and Deborah greeting Rhoda Anderson and a woman they had never seen before. As they approached the group, Rhoda was introducing the woman to everyone. Diana Baxter was a slender woman in her mid-forties. Her light brown hair and blue eyes set off a face that was very attractive. Her dress and demeanor revealed a past that included higher social circles, but she showed no signs of feeling superior to those around her.

Rhoda continued her introduction. "Diana and her husband, Arthur, and their son, Philip, moved into the area a couple of months ago. Paul and I met them as we were returning from our last missionary trip."

"It is so nice to meet you," Elizabeth said as she took Diana's hand in a gesture of friendship. "What brought you to this area?"

"Well, I guess you could say that Arthur and I got a little restless. Our two older daughters are married and settled in homes of their own back in Virginia. We were tired of the 'single' society circle in Richmond and decided to see what was over the hills. Philip was only too glad to leave the city to come out to the 'wild' frontier. I was a bit nervous at first, but I'm really starting to fall in love with the area now."

"It is special here, and the people are wonderful, for the most part," Deborah said. "George and I feel that this is home now." She then turned to the three girls and said, "Why don't you three see if you can round everyone up to eat while we finish getting the food ready to serve."

As the girls moved away, Deborah said to Diana, "Come join us. We have all learned to just pitch in and work together here on the frontier. It makes everything more enjoyable that way." A sly smile crossed her lips as she added, "And while we work, we can fill you in on all the 'news' of the area."

Diana laughed along with the women and replied, "It sounds good to me!"

The women finished putting the food out on the tables that had been set up. People crowded around and served themselves from the heaping platters of cooked wild game and fresh garden vegetables. Some ate at the tables, while the overflow sat in homemade cane-bottomed chairs and used their laps as tables.

After the meal was over George Stevens said, "All right. Let's have some music." Soon the air was filled with the sound of music, which included a banjo, a fiddle, a mountain dulcimer, and a flute. The sun shone down on the group, and George Stevens at once advanced toward Abigail and said, "I claim the first dance by right of being your father."

Abigail's eyes danced with pleasure and she put her arms up. The two of them waltzed around on the dance platform, and soon other couples began to join in. When the dance was over, George said, "Now you can go have fun with your friends and not have to put up with an old man like me."

"There's nobody here that'll be a better partner than you, Pa."

"Well, I see you're learning to tell the type of lies that sound good to an old man."

He moved over to where Hawk, Sequatchie, and Paul Anderson were talking to Arthur Baxter. Baxter, a large man with thinning black hair and brown eyes, was telling the others about their decision to come to the frontier.

"I found myself heading toward fifty, and I was bored out of my head with 'civilized' life. I had it rough growing up and wanted my son to experience a bit of rough life himself. I must say it has invigorated me and Diana, and Philip seems to love it, too."

"We are glad you came, too," Paul replied. "It is always good to have another fine, God-fearing family move into the area."

"Speaking of God-fearing, is there a church in the area? I'm proud to say that all of my family have accepted the Lord as Savior, and we are hoping to join in and worship with others."

"We don't have a church yet," Hawk answered. "We have tried to talk Paul here into becoming our pastor, but he still feels called to preach to the Cherokee Indians. He does lead us in worship services as often as he can when he is in the area."

"Well, be sure to let me know about those services."

On the other side of the dance platform, Jacob and Andrew were talking to Philip Baxter, Arthur and Diana's son. Philip, a tall, slim young man of sixteen, had lots of questions for Jacob and Andrew about life on the frontier.

"Are there lots of wild animals? Do Indians attack a lot?"

Andrew could see by the look on his stepbrother's face that he was about to launch into many hair-raising stories about frontier life to have a bit of sport with Philip, so he quickly answered, "There are lots of wild animals, but they leave you alone if you don't bother them. And as for the Indians, the Cherokee do live not too far from here, but they are friendly for the most part." He pointed toward Sequatchie and said, "There's one talking to your father. He's a close friend of my pa. He taught me a lot of things about how to hunt and fish and live in the wilderness. He's really a great man. Most of the Indians that I've met are like him. I think you'll like living here. I certainly do. I used to live in Boston, and I wasn't too sure I'd like it when we first moved here, but now I wouldn't want to live anywhere else."

Philip turned to Jacob. "Do you like it, too?"

Jacob didn't want to say too much about his real feelings about living in Watauga. "I haven't lived here as long as Andrew, but it is a pretty good place to live." He saw Abigail, Amanda, and Sarah approaching and took the opportunity to change the subject. "Philip, meet the three loveliest ladies in all of Watauga. This is Abigail Stevens, Amanda Taylor, and my sister, Sarah MacNeal."

Sarah found herself at a loss for words as she looked upon Philip Baxter. She took in his slim yet muscular build. She especially liked the handsome face framed by dark hair that curled slightly around his ears and neck. His brown eyes seemed to sparkle as he smiled at her. Sarah vaguely heard Abigail telling Philip that they had met his mother earlier and were glad to meet him now. She barely noticed that the band had struck up another song, until she heard Philip speaking to her.

"Would you like to dance, Sarah?"

Sarah finally found her voice enough to say yes. She allowed Philip to escort her to the dance floor. She had dressed with particular care today. Her dress was light green cotton with gray stripes. The square neckline was edged with white lace, and the sleeves ended just below the elbow with a white cotton ruffle. The dress set off her fiery red hair perfectly. She was delighted when Philip complimented her appearance. As they whirled around dancing, Sarah felt like one of the beautiful ladies she used to see in her home in Boston during one of the many balls held there. She lost herself in the wonder of the dance in the arms of Philip Baxter.

"Come on, Abigail," Jacob said impatiently. "Let's dance."

As the two went off, Amanda said, "Andrew, why didn't you ask Abigail to dance?"

"She wants to be with Jacob."

"You don't know that." Amanda had hesitated about coming because her face still showed the mark that her father had left there, but she had put aside her reservations and now was wearing her prettiest dress. The dress was made of light mauve cotton with a square neckline edged in a white ruffle. The dress itself was rather plain, but Amanda had added a "pinner"—a flowered apron that was pinned to the dress. The pinner had a white background with small mauve, blue, and yellow flowers decorating it.

"If you don't mind dancing with a girl with a black eye, Andrew, you could dance with me."

Andrew swallowed quickly and took his eyes off of Abigail and Jacob. "Why, sure," he said. He made an effort by saying, "I'd like to dance with one of the prettiest girls here."

After the dance was over, the girls all gathered together and the boys went for lemonade as Abigail said with some surprise, "I didn't know Andrew could dance."

"I didn't know it, either," Sarah said. "I wonder how he learned." With a quizzical expression, she asked Abigail, "I wonder why he didn't ask you to dance?"

Sarah now drew aside with Amanda and whispered, "I think Abigail just wants to be with Jacob."

Soon the music started up again, and Abigail was aware that Jacob was heading toward her, about to ask her to dance again. Quickly she turned to Andrew, saying, "Aren't you going to ask me to dance?"

"Why sure, Abigail."

Philip Baxter grabbed Sarah by the hand, and soon the two of them joined the dancers as they whirled around the platform. Jacob and Amanda were left standing alone. He was watching Abigail and Andrew, and suddenly Amanda asked, "Are you having a good time, Jacob?"

"Sure," Jacob mumbled, not even turning his eyes around.

Somewhat embarrassed by his answer, Amanda asked, "Do you like the frontier now? Are you feeling more at home?"

Again Jacob mumbled something absentmindedly, his thoughts on the dancers.

"Do you see that bear around behind you there?"

Unthinkingly Jacob mumbled, "Yeah, sure."

Amanda gave him a rather sad look. Hurt by his attitude, she turned and walked away.

Suddenly Jacob realized he had been speaking in monosyllables, but he couldn't bring himself to apologize to Amanda. He watched her leaving, then turned back to gaze longingly at Abigail.

Sarah had taken time out from the dance to get some refreshments from the long table. She had observed all of this, and now she walked over to Jacob and said, "You are awful!"

"What?" Jacob stared down at her. Sarah usually admired him, but now he saw that she was furious. "What are you talking about?"

"You're the rudest human being I've ever seen! What made you treat Amanda like that, especially after what she's gone through?"

Abruptly Jacob swallowed hard and shrugged his shoulders. He was really a sensitive young man, and it hurt him to think that he had behaved so badly. "You're right, Sarah," he nodded. "I'll make it up to her." Turning, he walked over to where Amanda was standing watching the dancers and said, "I'm sorry I was so stupid, Amanda."

"That's all right."

"No, it isn't, but I'll make it up to you. How about a dance?"

"I promised this one to Joseph Foster."

At that moment Joseph came up and smiled. "Are you ready, Amanda?"

"Yes. Thank you, Joseph."

Jacob suddenly felt alone and left out. All the others were dancing, including Sequatchie, who had escorted Iris to the dance floor, and Helen Foster, who was dancing with a young man Jacob didn't know, so he flopped down under a nearby tree to sit by himself.

Having spotted Jacob looking a little forlorn, Elizabeth came over and said, "Maybe you ought to ask Amanda for the next dance." She had not missed the exchange between them and said quietly, "I think she needs all the encouragement she can get."

"All right, I'll do it."

Moving across the yard, he approached Amanda. "If you're not busy, I'd like to dance with you."

"All right, Jacob."

As all the couples began the next dance, no one noticed Zeke Taylor emerging from the shadows. Over to his left he saw his daughter smiling and dancing with Jacob Spencer. Anger seethed within him as he rushed forward and grabbed Jacob's arm, spun him around, and shoved him into a table laden with food.

"You get your filthy hands off my daughter!"

Whirling around, Zeke saw Iris and Sequatchie, and his bloodshot eyes filled with fury. "I can't believe you'd dance with a filthy Indian! You're just a common woman! That's all you are!"

Taylor had grabbed Amanda's arm and now was twisting it. Jacob was furious at the man's attack, and rage boiled over in him. He leaped at Zeke before anyone else could react and struck him a blow to the jaw.

Zeke Taylor was driven backward a step, but he planted his feet and threw a punch that caught Jacob on the forehead. Everything seemed to spin, and Jacob felt himself going backward. He struggled to get up, but his head was still spinning. He felt someone kneeling beside him, touching him, and knew it was Amanda. When his eyes cleared he sat up, shook his head, and saw that Zeke had thrown himself at Hawk. It was a futile effort, however, for Hawk stood off while Taylor windmilled a few blows, then stepped in and struck him in the stomach. Taylor's face turned pasty as he doubled over. By now the crowd was standing in stunned silence, hearing only Zeke's painful attempts to catch his breath.

Hawk reached down, jerked Zeke to his feet, and said, "You're not fit to be loose." Hawk's eyes were filled with a warning, and Taylor tried to speak.

"Shut your mouth, Taylor!"

Everyone's eyes were on Hawk as he hauled Zeke down the dirt road leading away from the village square to the community jail, keeping a firm hold on the back of Taylor's neck.

———

After her father was arrested, Amanda had immediately gone to her mother. The two had taken refuge inside the nearby community cabin for a time, where Amanda comforted her mother as best she could. Stepping outside, she saw Jacob and walked up to him quickly. "Thank you for taking up for me." She looked up and her eyes were brimming with tears.

"It was nothing," Jacob said. "I didn't do a thing."

"It wasn't just nothing. I'll always be grateful." Without thinking, she lifted her hand and touched his face where her father had hit him.

Jacob blinked with surprise and looked down at Amanda, who flushed and snapped her hand away. "Well, now we'll be a matched set." He touched his bruise, then reached over and touched hers and smiled at her.

Amanda could not help smiling, despite the turmoil that boiled in her heart.

"I'm sorry we missed our dance, but we'll make it up the next time."

"All right, Jacob," Amanda whispered.

As she returned to her mother, Jacob watched her go. "I can't figure that girl out," he whispered to himself, shaking his head. "Or maybe it's me I can't figure out."

By this time Hawk had returned and said, "I guess we're all ready to leave."

Philip Baxter turned to say good-bye to Sarah. "I hope I get to see you again."

"I hope so, too," Sarah said.

Deborah Stevens put her arm around Iris Taylor's shoulder and said, "Don't think about this, Iris. It wasn't your fault."

"I can't help it," Iris said. "I just wish I hadn't come."

Abigail had moved around, thanking the guests for coming, then she turned to Jacob and Andrew. "Thanks for making my party so special."

As the Spencers were leaving, Deborah turned and put her eyes on her daughter. "Did you enjoy your party, Abigail?"

"Yes, I did, Ma."

"Our little girl's all grown-up," George said fondly.

"Oh, Daddy!"

"Got two fine young men chasing after you. This time next year you'll probably have lots more."

"Don't tease me, Daddy!" Abigail had a faraway look in her eye. She turned and looked to the square as they were leaving, and her thoughts were on Jacob and Andrew. "We're just good friends," she murmured.

The next morning William Bean rode up to Hawk's homestead and pulled his mount to a stop. He was flushed and out of temper. As he slid off his horse, he turned to Sequatchie and Hawk, who had come out to greet him. "Taylor busted out of the jail."

"How could he do that?" Hawk asked.

"I think William Crabtree had something to do with it. Several people said they saw him hanging around the jail last night."

Hawk spoke his thoughts quietly. "Those two will probably turn up again, and I don't think it will be for good."

"No," Sequatchie said. "Two bad men. I wonder sometimes why the good men die and the bad ones live, but it is all in God's hands."

Upcoming Events

Twenty-One

*H*awk straightened up and arched his back, then glanced over at the two boys who were working alongside him in the field. A week had passed since Abigail's party, and he had heard no further news of Zeke Taylor. Secretly he wished the man would just disappear, for he was nothing but a drunk and a troublemaker and probably would never be much more. He worried about what would happen to Iris and Amanda if they went back to the man, and his bronzed forehead furrowed as he considered ways to put a greater fear in Zeke Taylor than he had before.

Andrew was moving evenly beside his father, weeding the grass out of the garden. He was good with the hoe, wasting no motion but moving steadily, the keen blade clipping the grass and weeds off even with the top of the soil. Andrew felt a secret sense of satisfaction as he saw Jacob, who was on his right, struggling. Once Andrew said, "You're gonna cut all the vegetables down, Jacob. You're supposed to be cuttin' the weeds down, not the squash and tomatoes."

Jacob paid no heed but moved along, well aware that he was not as expert at this as Andrew. He had tried hard, but still it seemed that Andrew had a natural gift for living on the frontier that he would never be able to emulate. It grated on him and made him exercise the greater gifts he had, such as singing and dancing and taking over in social situations.

"It looks like we planted too big a garden, Pa," Andrew said, stopping to look over the large garden that was now green and rich, with the vegetables plumping out. "We'll never be able to eat all this."

"Don't plan to, but you remember I told you about the celebration day we're going to have for the Cherokee, don't you?"

"That's right. I forgot that. When is it, Pa?"

"Probably next April. The word is pretty well out now," Hawk added. "Daniel Boone spread it to some, and Paul and Rhoda, on their travels, I think, got the word to most of the Cherokee."

"There'll be horse races, won't there?"

"I expect so. Indians love those," Hawk smiled. "You planning to enter, are you, son?"

"Enter? Why, I plan to win!"

"I wouldn't be so sure of that," Jacob said. Hawk had recently given him a fine young mare, which he had named Molly. When Abigail had asked him if he had ever known a girl named Molly, he had just winked and said, "I don't kiss and tell, but I always liked Molly for a name." Now he glanced over at Andrew and added, "My Molly and I figure on taking the prize for the horse race."

"You seem pretty sure of that, Jacob," Hawk put in.

"I promised Abigail I'd win it for her."

Hawk shot a quick glance at Andrew, for he and Elizabeth had often talked of how jealousy had arisen between the two boys over Abigail Stevens. He could not blame them much, for she was, without a doubt, the prettiest girl in the settlement. Not just his own boys, but all the other young men in the settlement and the outlying districts found occasion to stop by the Stevenses' place. Oftentimes they made an excuse, claiming a horse had strayed or asking if the Stevenses needed fresh-killed squirrels when they had shot a great number. Now he saw that Andrew was silent, and it troubled him. Hawk felt caught between the two, and rather than hurt the feelings of either one, he simply decided to stay neutral. "Well," he said, "I guess it's time for a break. I sure could use some water."

"I'll go get a bucket, Pa," Andrew said and ran off. He was growing more muscular, and yet he was light on his feet.

Hawk watched the boy go and said, "He sure is like his father. I wish you could have known him, Jacob. He was a fine man."

Overhead, sturdy clouds were beginning to gather. The tops were pure white, but underneath they were streaked with dirty gray, and Hawk observed, "I think we're going to get some rain out of those clouds. The crops could use it." When he got no response he felt awkward, and finally he said, "I haven't had a chance to talk to you since the party, son." Jacob did not answer, and Hawk found himself having a difficult time forming what he wanted to say. He was basically a man of few words, but he longed to break through the shell that Jacob had built around himself. He turned and said, "I haven't had a chance to tell you how proud I am of you for the way you stood up for Amanda."

A sudden touch of joy came to Jacob Spencer then. He wanted his father's approval more than he would admit to himself, and now he basked for a moment in the compliment before saying, "It was nothing."

"Yes, it was something," Hawk said at once. He stepped forward and put his hand on Jacob's shoulder, noting that the muscles were growing and that the boy was taller than he had been when they had left Williamsburg. "I want you to know that I'm mighty glad to have a son willing to stand for somebody who needs help." He would have said more, but at that time Andrew came back with a bucket of water and a dipper and he ended the conversation.

As they went back to work after their drink, Jacob thought, *Things have changed between me and Pa since I came here. It's getting better.* At the same time as this thought warmed him, he was aware that he was still not able to totally accept Hawk Spencer as a father. However, he was beginning to think of him as a friend, and now the thought came to him, *He's a good man now, even if he wasn't all the time I was growing up. Maybe someday I'll be able to forget all the old memories about how he left me.* The thought cheered him, and he began to whistle cheerfully and moved faster to catch up with Andrew, who decided to make a race of it.

Hawk watched as the two boys worked down the rows, raising a cloud of dust, while overhead the clouds grew darker. Soon it began to sprinkle, and at the first drop Hawk said, "Let's get in out of this rain, boys."

―――――――

At dinner that evening, Elizabeth listened as Jacob described how he had crept up on a buck and shot it. It was his first deer kill all by himself, and he had been inordinately proud to bring that doe home and dress it himself. When he had finished telling the story, she smiled and said, "That was real good, Jacob. You've become quite a hunter."

"Sure have," Hawk said. "Couldn't have done better myself."

"Well, I couldn't have done it if you hadn't taught me, Pa. You and Sequatchie."

"We all have to learn. Sequatchie taught me the same things. Why, I couldn't hit the broadside of a barn when he first got ahold of me," Hawk smiled. He leaned back in his chair and thought of those days when Sequatchie had saved his life and then promised to teach him the ways of the forest if he would stay and read the Bible to his people. *Best day's work I ever did,* Hawk thought as he looked around the table studying his family. *If I hadn't met up with Sequatchie, I wouldn't have all this now.*

As she fed Hannah, Elizabeth said, "Sequatchie is eating with Iris and Amanda tonight."

"Yes," Hawk nodded. "He's really looked out for those two." Glancing at the boys, he grinned and said, "He's so busy with them, some of the work is piling up. I think we'll all have to pick up the slack when Sequatchie goes with Paul and Rhoda on their next trip."

Sarah perked up and said, "When are they leaving, Pa?"

"I'm not sure. It won't be long, though."

"No, it won't," Elizabeth said, and a strange expression came to her eyes, and her lips turned upward in a smile. "They won't be gone long this trip."

Surprised, Hawk looked up. "Why do you say that? They usually stay for months."

"Not this time."

Now Elizabeth had everyone's attention, and Hawk looked at her and said, "What's in that head of yours, wife?"

"I suppose," Elizabeth said after pausing, "it's all right to tell you." She smiled broadly then and clasped her hands together and squeezed them. "Paul and Rhoda are going to have a baby, and Paul wants to get back before Rhoda's too far along."

"Well, how about that!" Hawk exclaimed.

"They're so happy," Elizabeth said. "We'll have to pray that the baby comes and that Rhoda will be all right."

For some time talk ran around the table, mostly about the baby that was coming, and Paul and Rhoda. Finally Elizabeth spoke up and said, "I have some more news for you."

"What's that?" Hawk asked. He had half risen and now sat back down in his chair. He studied Elizabeth's face, admiring again, as he always did, the fair complexion and the lively green eyes that decorated her heart-shaped face. "What's going on that I don't know about?"

Elizabeth said quietly, "We're going to have a baby, too."

For a moment there was another silence, then Hawk Spencer let out a whoop. Jumping from his chair, he ran over, pulled Elizabeth to her feet, and began to dance her around the room. He hugged her so tightly she gasped, "Hawk, you're going to squeeze me to death!"

"I'd like to almost," Hawk said. "When will it be here?"

"I hope it's another girl," Sarah chimed in.

"No, I want a brother this time!" Andrew protested.

"No!" Sarah said, reaching over and striking him with her fist. "It's time for another girl. That way there'll be three girls and two boys."

Hawk said with calmness in his eyes as he looked at Elizabeth, "I don't care what it is. I just hope it looks like you, boy or girl, and not me."

No one seemed to notice that Jacob had grown quiet. The news of an oncoming baby had stirred something in him again, and he did not understand it. Thoughts would arise in him from time to time that he seemed to have no control over, and now he was thinking, *Pa wants another son—one that will be like Andrew.* He looked at Elizabeth, whose face was filled with joy, and then the thought came quickly, *At least this baby won't be abandoned like I was.* For a moment he felt ashamed for thinking that. He realized all that Hawk had tried to do to make him feel at home.

He was, however, caught by emotions that were too strong for him, and finally he slipped out of the cabin and walked for a long time through the woods, oblivious to the rain that was still falling lightly. It ran down his hair and down his back and soaked his clothes. Suddenly he looked up with a start, realizing what he was doing. He turned slowly and headed back for the cabin, thinking, *I wish I could get my head straight. Why do I have thoughts like this? Why can't I be happy like Andrew is?*

Celebration With the Cherokee

Twenty-Two

awk leaned over and picked up Joshua Spencer. The sight of the three-month-old made him smile, as always. "You're going to be a handsome man, just like your pa," he whispered. Joshua had been born in late January. Hawk had had to help with the delivery because Deborah Stevens had trouble getting to their cabin through the snow. Everything had gone fine and Hawk exulted in this new son of his.

Iris Taylor, who had come in to help Elizabeth get the children ready, smiled. "It's amazing how much that child has grown. I believe he'll be as big a man as you are, Hawk."

"I hope he'll be smarter," Hawk said. He cradled the baby in his arms for a while, listening as the women in the kitchen were running around trying to get the food ready to go. Finally, putting the baby down, he passed through the kitchen as they discussed the upcoming day of celebration and talked about seeing friends who had not been in the settlement for some time.

Stepping outside the door, he found Sequatchie, Andrew, and Jacob, who had hitched up the wagon and saddled the horses. "All ready?" he asked.

"Sure, Pa," Andrew said. His hair was wet from where he had stuck it under the pump, and now he stroked his horse on the neck, saying, "Are you going to enter the race, Pa?"

"No, I'll leave that to you young fellows."

Jacob was already seated on Molly. He leaned over and patted her on the neck, winking at Sequatchie. "How much have you got bet on me, Sequatchie?"

"I never bet on horse races," Sequatchie said. "It's a foolish thing."

"Wouldn't be foolish to bet on me," Jacob bragged. "I plan on winning."

Sequatchie shot a look at Andrew, who said nothing, but whose face was marked with quiet determination.

Soon the women came out, and all the food was loaded in the wagon. Hawk lifted Hannah up to Elizabeth, who took her, then held young Joshua as Iris climbed in the wagon.

As they pulled out, Andrew said, "I hope things go well today. It means a lot to the Indians."

"It means a lot to us, too," Hawk nodded. "We'll just pray that it does."

———

Zeke Taylor tilted the brown bottle and drank several swallows. He lowered it and coughed violently, and his face turned a raw red hue. He expelled air and gasped for his breath, saying in a coarse whisper, "That stuff's got a kick like a mule."

"Ahh, you ain't no man, Zeke!" William Isaac Crabtree tipped the bottle, sipped at it, and blinked his eyes. "Come to think of it, it has got a bite."

The two men were deep in the woods, where they had spent the night. Both of them were dirty and ragged, and they had not shaved in weeks. After Zeke had escaped from jail last summer, with Crabtree's help, they had fled the settlement and gone on an extended trip. Their money had played out, however, and now they had drifted back toward the Watauga settlement.

Crabtree was shaking his head in disgust. "Can't believe them people wantin' to be friends with a bunch of Indians! Only good Indians are the dead ones!"

Zeke sipped cautiously at the fiery alcohol again and then nodded, anger clouding his muddy eyes. "It's that Hawk Spencer and his kind that's done it! Can't mind their own business! They got to be in everybody else's!"

The two men drank until the whiskey was gone. By that time Crabtree had turned mean. "It wouldn't take much for me to go break up that celebration today!"

Zeke Taylor suddenly looked up. He was not as drunk as Crabtree, and now an idea had come to him. It lit his brown eyes, and he studied Crabtree carefully, at the same time egging the man on about the celebration. His talk began to get rougher and more urgent until finally Crabtree kicked at a sapling. With a curse, he said, "I'm goin' to go to that place! Sycamore Shoals, ain't it?"

"That's right, but you know Hawk will be there."

"I don't care who's there! I'm gonna kill me an Indian!"

Crabtree's threat shocked Zeke Taylor, but he was pleased with it. Both men were drunk enough so that their caution was lowered, and Zeke was thinking of how Hawk had humiliated him.

If a war starts, he thought, *some men are gonna get killed. And even if Hawk Spencer ain't killed by an Indian, it would be easy to shoot him from behind a tree and make it look like an Indian did it.* He felt big and brave as the whiskey blotted out his natural cowardice, and he said, "Come on! Let's go help 'em celebrate!"

"Celebrate nothing! I'm gonna kill me an Indian!" Crabtree slurred.

———

The celebration at Sycamore Shoals was in full swing. The settlers had come, all who could, including the Spencers and MacNeals, the Stevenses, the Baxters, the Fosters, the Taylors, and Sequatchie, of course. Paul and Rhoda Anderson were also there, showing off their two-and-a-half-month-old daughter, Rachel.

The leaders of the settlement were there, including William and Lydia Bean, who had founded Watauga, James and Charlotte Robertson, members of the Regulators, and John Carter, who had founded a settlement in Carter Valley and was now chairman of the Watauga court.

As Hawk ran his eyes around the crowd that was eating and drinking and laughing loudly, he noted Jacob Brown, who had founded the settlement at Nolichucky, and the Sevier brothers, John and Valentine, along with Charles Robertson, and James Smith, the clerk of the association. Turning his eyes, he saw that Daniel Boone had attended with Chief Attacullaculla, the Little Carpenter. Along with the Little Carpenter was Chief Ostenaco and Chief Oconostota.

"Are you having a good time, Billie?" Hawk asked, stopping beside a tall Cherokee.

Cherokee Billie, who was the brother-in-law of Ostenaco, grinned at him. "Good time. Plenty of good food."

Slapping the tall young brave on the shoulder, Hawk left and passed through the crowd. He spoke to William Bean and also to Bean's young son, Russell, who was the first white child born in the settlement. He passed among the crowd and finally glanced over to where the women had congregated to serve the food. They were all working hard, for an enormous number of Cherokee had come. *I guess I ought to go help 'em,* Hawk thought. When he went over, Elizabeth said, "You just stay out of our way, Hawk."

Sweat was running down her face, and he reached over and wiped it off, saying, "You sure get fussy when you're cooking for a celebration." He grinned and left her then. Hearing a sound of cheering, he moved over to where he found some of the men talking about the afternoon horse race. He saw that Andrew, Jacob, and Sarah were there, along with Abigail, Amanda, Joseph and Helen Foster, and Philip Baxter. He stood back and listened to Jacob talk about how he would win the race, then moved away.

He came to where Sequatchie was talking with the Little Carpenter and the chief's niece, Nancy Ward. Nancy was married to a white man, Bryant Ward, and her face was strained as Hawk heard her say, "It's going to be hard, Sequatchie. Dragging Canoe is all for war."

"He always has been," Sequatchie said. "He's a man of blood."

The Little Carpenter spread his hands out. He was a small man, not at all impressive, and yet his ability to bring people together and work out terms was phenomenal. "We will have to be sure that he does not shed blood. The old ways are changing."

"I know," Nancy said. She was quiet for a moment, then shook her head. "I hate to see them go, but we must change with them."

"Yes," Sequatchie agreed, "or the Cherokee will cease to be a people. The white men are like a mighty river coming in, and we must learn to live with them or we will perish."

When the time for the meal came, John Carter, as chairman of the Watauga Court, called them all together.

"We welcome you, Chief Attacullaculla, as the representative of all the Cherokee. You and your people are welcome!"

The Little Carpenter responded, and then Paul Anderson rose to ask a blessing on the meal. He had become highly respected— respected by most of the Cherokee, except the warmongers. He had traveled for the last two years in the very heart of Cherokee country, living among them, and had won many to the Lord during that time.

He showed respect for their way of life, while at the same time showing them their need for a Savior. He ended the blessing by saying,
"May the Lord bless us, Cherokee and white men alike. In the name
of Jesus. Amen."

———————

Finally the meal was over, and it was time for the horse races.
Jacob came up to Abigail and was laughing. He was happy and con-
fident that he would win the race. His Molly had never failed him,
and now he said, "Give me a token, Abigail, to take into the race."

"A token? What's that?"

"Why, back in the days when the knights were around, they
would ask a lady for a token. She would give her knight a scarf, and
he would tie it on his lance, wear it while he went jousting."

Abigail smiled and reached into her pocket and gave him a
handkerchief. "I hope this will help."

"I can't lose," Jacob grinned. "I'll be back to claim my reward."

There were seven horses in the race, and all of them were good
ones. George Stevens started the race by firing a gun in the air, and
loud shouts went up as the horses all lunged forward.

Jacob leaned over, talking to his mare with excitement. He led
the race all the way to the sycamore tree, which had been set as a
halfway mark, and rounded it in the lead.

Halfway back, however, he caught a glimpse of someone to his
right. He took his glance off of the finish line long enough to turn
his head and saw that it was Andrew!

Andrew had ridden a good race. He had let Molly keep the lead,
wearing herself out, and now with the finish line no more than two
hundred yards ahead, he kicked his horse in the side and let out a
wild yell. The yell startled Molly, and she jerked off stride as she
bolted in fright.

By the time Jacob had gotten her under control, Andrew had
crossed the finish line and was surrounded by the crowd who had
closed in to congratulate him.

His face burning, Jacob slid off the horse and stood there thinking, *It wasn't fair! That shout he gave threw you off stride!*

Andrew received the reward from Abigail, a kiss on the cheek,
which Jacob saw. He turned to go away, but suddenly Hawk was in
front of him. "You rode a good race, son."

Jacob looked up quickly, for he was suspicious that Hawk was exulting over Andrew's win.

"I lost, and that's all that counts."

Turning abruptly away, he led Molly off to tie her to a sapling. When he turned around, he saw Amanda, who had come up. She was smiling and said, "You did fine, Jacob."

"No. I lost."

Amanda said, "In my mind you'll always be a winner, Jacob, no matter what anyone says."

Jacob suddenly felt better. He shrugged and said, "I'll have to learn to swallow my medicine with less fuss."

"Come on. Let's go watch the next race. The Cherokee are going to have one."

Jacob agreed and the two of them walked over to where a group of Cherokee were mounted and ready to begin the race. Cherokee Billie was one of them that Jacob knew, and he said, "Good luck, Billie!"

Billie looked around and waved his hand and then gathered the halter of his horse. The Indians had trouble getting their horses to be still, and just when they were in a roughly irregular line, a sudden shot came and Billie fell off his horse.

Hawk was standing at the end of the line, and at once he leaped to Billie's side. A bullet had taken the brave directly in the heart, and he was already dead.

"That way!" Sequatchie said. "Come!"

He and Hawk took off at a dead run. They were both agile, fast men, and soon they were close enough that Hawk caught a glimpse of two figures.

"That's Crabtree!" he panted to Sequatchie.

"Yes, and the other man is Zeke Taylor."

Neither man had brought a gun, but both had knives. However, even as they strained to catch up with the two, they saw them swing on their horses and disappear.

"We can't catch them without horses," Hawk said. "Come on! We'll get mounted and go after them!"

When they returned to the scene, they found the Cherokee gathering up the body of Billie and tying it on a horse. They said nothing, but there was something in their eyes that was disturbing.

Attacullaculla came to stand before the group of the white leaders. "I will do what I can to prevent retaliation."

William Bean said, "Chief, you can depend on one thing. We'll catch those men, and they will die for what they have done to your friend."

The Little Carpenter thought hard and then said, "I think some of you should come and meet with the chief to show good faith. War may be avoided for the time being, but Dragging Canoe and his hotheads have plenty of ammunition, and this gives them an excuse."

Hawk and Sequatchie remained standing together as the Cherokee filed out. "I'm afraid of what's going to happen now."

Sequatchie said nothing. His brow was furrowed, and sadness filled his eyes. He knew better than Hawk how bad things now looked, and how Dragging Canoe would stir the Cherokee up to war.

———————

The next day, in an emergency meeting, the Watauga court offered a reward for the capture of William Isaac Crabtree. They also decided that some of them should meet with Attacullaculla and the other chiefs to try to prevent a full-scale war.

James Robertson spoke up, saying, "Hawk, we will need you and Sequatchie to go."

"All right," Hawk said. "I feel that I failed by letting those two get away, but they hid their tracks in the river. I can go after them if you think best."

"No, that will wait," Robertson said. "Now we have to do all we can to stop a war." He turned to Paul and said, "Reverend, let's pray for peace."

Paul lowered his head, and all of the men removed their hats as Paul said quietly, "O God, we are helpless in this situation. We ask for a miracle. Keep the peace among our two peoples."

As Hawk left the room, he murmured to Sequatchie, "That was a good prayer."

"Yes, it was, and Paul is right. It will take a miracle to stop a war now."

PART III

Brothers

June 1774 – March 1775

Have we not all one father? hath not one God created us? why do we deal treacherously every man against his brother, by profaning the covenant of our fathers?

Malachi 2:10

Jacob Goes Courting

Twenty-Three

*E*lizabeth rose early to do her cooking. June had brought a heat that rose in waves, and by noon the cabin would be stifling. Before dawn she had slipped out of bed, leaving Hawk sleeping with his head buried under a pillow. She often wondered how he could sleep like that, thinking, *I'd suffocate if I tried to do it.*

After she had washed her face and slipped on a cool cotton dress with a white apron over it, she checked on Hannah and Joshua, who were both still sleeping, and then moved into the kitchen. Skillfully she built up the fire until it roared in the fireplace. Heating water in a kettle, she made herself a pot of tea, then stepped outside to watch the sun creep up over the horizon as she sipped from the china cup. She liked the early hours of the morning, savoring the coolness of it, and the silence that lay over the homestead. Even as she finished the cup, the clarion call of the big red rooster shattered the morning silence. She smiled quietly and spoke aloud, "Right on time. I wonder how you know to do that."

Moving back inside the cabin, Elizabeth was startled as she moved across the puncheon floor. A clatter of pots and pans falling in the fireplace made her blink, and she ran to see the green sapling that Hawk had wedged across the back of the fireplace had burned through.

"Oh no!" she muttered under her breath and quickly made efforts to pull the different utensils out of the fire.

"What's going on?" Hawk entered the room, wearing only a pair of trousers, his hair ruffled and his eyes crinkled with sleep. "Sounds like the house fell down."

"I told you that green sapling wouldn't work, Hawk!" Elizabeth said with exasperation. "It burned through! Now I can't get the utensils out!"

"Let me do it." Hawk crossed the room and, using the poker, managed to extricate all the utensils. "I'll go by the forge in the village and get an iron rod. That won't burn through," he said.

"That would be fine." She sighed and shook her head. "It seems like the harder we work on this place, the more things there are to do."

Laughing, Hawk came over and put his arms around her. The smooth muscles of his back and chest tightened as he held her closely. "Don't worry about it," he said. "If the worst thing that happened to us would be some pots falling into the fire, I'd say we were fortunate."

"I know you're right," she said. She leaned against him, putting her cheek against his chest, her arms around his back. They stood there quietly for a moment, then she shoved him back with a laugh, saying, "You go get shaved. I've got to fix breakfast."

"Fix a big one. I'm pretty hungry." Hawk returned to the bedroom to shave while Elizabeth turned back to her cooking.

"What do you want for breakfast?" she called through the door.

"Dressed eggs and johnny cakes."

Elizabeth was a good cook, having learned from the other frontier women, and she quickly made the preparations for the dressed eggs. When she was done, she made the johnny cakes. She had made them so often that she did not even have to think. She heated water and butter in an iron saucepan, and when it was bubbling, she poured in cornmeal, salt, and sugar. She did not even have to measure them exactly. Afterward she added milk and stirred the batter until it was well mixed.

Her movements were methodical as she reached over and got a black skillet, which she set over the fire on a spider—an iron contraption designed to hold a skillet over the hot coals. As soon as the skillet was hot, she took a wooden spoon and dropped six spoonfuls of the batter in the skillet. While the johnny cakes were cooking to a golden brown, she boiled the eggs. Before she started, she heated her long-handled shovel, which everyone called a salamander, in the fire until it was red-hot. After the eggs were cracked and cooking, but not hard, she held the red-hot salamander over the eggs to cook the tops. When they were cooked, she set them out on a plate, covered them with a cloth, then turned again to the johnny cakes, which were now a golden brown.

Knowing her family's appetite, she made double portions and then cut up parts of a ham and fried the slices over low heat. She poured the grease out into a small saucepan, then poured cold water over the grease and heated it until the gravy was bubbling hot.

By the time she had finished the breakfast, the family had gathered, and Hawk sat down at the head of the table, where he asked a blessing.

"What happened at the meeting?" Elizabeth asked at once.

Along with Paul, Sequatchie, James Robertson, and William Faulin, a trader among the Cherokee who was highly respected by the Indians, Hawk had attended a meeting with the Cherokee chiefs. He smeared one of the johnny cakes with apple butter and took a huge bite. Chewing around it, he said, "It was a fairly close thing. Wars have been started over smaller things than what happened at the celebration. Cherokee Billie was very popular, and I thought for a time that even Attacullaculla wouldn't be able to stop the hotheads among the Cherokee."

Andrew piped up. "You think they'll try to get even—for the murder of Cherokee Billie?"

"Dragging Canoe would."

"That's Attacullaculla's son, isn't it?" Jacob asked.

"That's right. He's got a temper like I've never seen. Nothing at all like his father."

"What did he want to do, Pa?" Sarah asked. She was stuffing eggs in her mouth despite her mother's admonitions and could hardly be understood. "Will there be a war?"

"No. Attacullaculla and the older chiefs prevailed. There won't be a war, right now, at least." He picked up his tea and sipped it, his eyes thoughtful. "James Robertson says we've got another problem."

"You mean with the Cherokee?" Elizabeth inquired. She got up and refilled the cups with tea, then sat down again, listening as Hawk explained.

"We found out that the Shawnee, down in the Ohio country, are trying to get the Cherokee to join them. They are making a war against Lord Dunmore, the Lieutenant Governor of Virginia. Dunmore claims the whole region the Indians call Can-tuc-kee. He says they got a treaty with the Iroquois."

"Do you think the Cherokee will do it?" Elizabeth asked as she fed Joshua the last of his breakfast.

"No. Dragging Canoe would, and the younger warriors, but the older ones do not want a war."

As they sat around the table, all of them knew that the idyllic peace that had been in the Watauga area could be broken in one day. All except Jacob and the youngsters had heard the screams of maddened Indians, and also the moans of the dying, and in the quiet that followed Hawk's words a solemnity prevailed.

"No one has seen William Crabtree," Hawk said, changing the subject. "I hope he's left the area. He's a bad one."

"Do you think he's left?" Elizabeth inquired.

A doubtful look clouded Hawk's eyes and his lips grew tight. "No, I don't think we've seen the last of him. Well, fine breakfast, wife! Now it's time to get to work."

———

Jacob pulled up in front of the Stevenses' cabin early in the afternoon. He had worked hard all morning with Hawk and Andrew but had asked for some time off, which Hawk had readily granted. Now as he dismounted and tied his mare to a post set in the front of the cabin, he was greeted by George Stevens, who nodded and smiled. "Hello, Jacob," he said. "I bet you didn't come to see me." A sly humor in the man surfaced from time to time, and he laughed as Jacob showed some embarrassment. "I'd be surprised if you did, and maybe even disappointed. You'll find Abby over there in the back helping her mother in the garden."

"Thank you, sir."

Jacob walked quickly around the cabin and found the two hoeing weeds.

"Hello, Abby. Hello, Mrs. Stevens."

"Why, hello, Jacob." Deborah smiled. "Did you come to help us with the garden?"

"Well, I guess I could, but to be truthful I had about enough gardening for one day." He looked at Abigail, who was looking pretty, as usual, even in a plain gray dress. "I thought you and I might go for a walk down by the river."

Deborah intercepted Abigail's quick look and nodded. "Go ahead. Will you be staying for supper, Jacob?"

"That'd be mighty fine, Mrs. Stevens."

Abigail, putting her hoe down, turned to the path that led down to the river. As they walked along between the trees that sprang up fifty yards from the cabin, she said, "It ought to be cooler down by the river."

"It has been hot. I'm glad your mother asked me to dinner."

They spoke quietly as they walked along the path. The trees overhead shaded them from the hot afternoon sun, and when they reached the river, Abigail said, "I like to sit over there under that chestnut tree."

"It looks like a good spot," Jacob murmured. He watched as Abigail sat down, tucking her feet under her and spreading her skirt over them, then plopped down beside her. Taking off his hat, he tossed it down and stared at the water, which made an elbow, forming a deep pool. Even as he watched, small fish broke the surface, and he said idly, "I'd like to fish for a while, but I'm too lazy."

Abigail brushed her hand across her hair and smiled at Jacob. "Pa's been catching catfish at night, but the mosquitoes are too bad for me. They leave big welts on me."

"Don't do it, then," Jacob said quickly. "You've got the prettiest skin I've ever seen. It's just like peaches and cream." He smiled and Abigail flushed, then for some time he flirted with her in a light-hearted way. Finally he asked, "What are you going to do on your birthday? I remember last year. It was the biggest birthday party I've ever seen."

"I hope this one will go a little bit better, but I won't have a party this year." She leaned back, pressing her hands into the moss that lined the bank, letting the faint breeze blow through her hair. She was very attractive as she sat there. Finally she turned to him and asked, "Are you going to the service that Brother Anderson's going to hold next Sunday?"

"I suppose so. Everyone will be there."

"Ma and Pa are glad about the preacher's and Rhoda's new baby. She is a sweet thing."

"She sure is. I wonder what they will do about going back to the Cherokee? They can't take a baby with them."

"I don't know. Pa says he hopes that they'll stay here in Watauga and pastor a church here, but I think Reverend Anderson will go back to the Cherokee." She hesitated for a moment, then asked,

"How's your new baby brother, Joshua?"

A cloud seemed to descend over Jacob, and he shook his head slightly. "He's fine," he said. "He's wonderful, according to my father."

"I'm sure Hawk must be very proud of his new son."

"Yes, he is."

Something in Jacob's voice caught at Abigail. She turned to him and studied his face intently. "You don't sound very happy. Aren't you proud of your new brother?"

"Oh, I suppose so." Jacob seemed disturbed by the conversation and said, "Can I ask you a personal question, Abby?"

"Why . . . I suppose so."

"How do you feel about Andrew?"

Jacob's abrupt question caught Abigail off guard. She lifted her hand to her cheek involuntarily and blinked her eyes with surprise. When she spoke, her voice was somewhat unsteady. "I . . . I'm very fond of him. We're very good friends."

"Is it anything more than that?"

"What more could there be? He's such a nice young man. Naturally I like him—everybody does."

"Well, that's good," Jacob said, looking satisfied. "I mean," he said, "it's good that you're just good friends." Then his mind seemed to veer. "How do you like it out here on the frontier?"

"Why, I love it. Don't you?"

Jacob picked up a stick and traced a design in the loose moss. He seemed to be thinking about her question, and finally he tossed the stick into the water and watched as the current swirled it around, then carried it away. "It's all right, but someday I want to go back to Virginia." His eyes grew bright and he leaned forward, saying with some suppressed excitement, "One of these days, Abigail, I'm going to start my own plantation right in the Tidewater area. My grandfather promised to help me get started." He leaned back then and thought back to the time when he was younger, then said, "That's always been a dream of mine as long as I can remember."

Abigail was surprised. She had never thought but what Jacob would stay on the frontier. "I'd hate to see you go back. You'd be missed here. Especially by your family."

"I haven't told you all my dream yet."

"What's the rest of it?"

"I've got to find someone to share that dream with me. Would you ever leave the frontier, Abby?"

"Why, I never thought about it, Jacob."

"I bet you would if . . . if the right man asked you to."

Abigail was disturbed by the direction his conversation had gone. "I think the right man might want to stay on the frontier." She stood up rather abruptly and he stood before her. She was apprehensive somehow.

Suddenly he said, "Abby, you're the prettiest thing I've ever seen." He put his arms around her, pulled her close, and kissed her.

Abigail was taken by surprise. She had been kissed before, but somehow this was different. This was not a childish thing, for she was becoming a woman and Jacob had reached the threshold of manhood. His lips were firm on hers, and for a moment she found herself surrendering to him. Then she pushed him back and murmured, "I've got to go back and help Mother."

"All right, but can I come and see you?"

Abigail understood, of course, that he was asking if he could come calling, and she said quickly, "Why, you can come and see us anytime. Ma and Pa are always glad to see you."

"Will you be glad to see me?"

Abigail was more disturbed now. She had mixed feelings about the young man and said, "I'm always glad to see all my friends."

She turned and walked quickly to the cabin, but somehow Jacob knew that it would take more than this to win Abigail's hand in marriage.

He ate supper with them, and as he rode home that night, all he could think of was, *Somehow, someday, I'm going to have that big plantation and a fine wife. Then Pa will be proud of me, and Andrew will see what it's like to have a brother who's rich and has a pretty wife! I don't need any help, either. I can do it all by myself.*

Hearts

Twenty-Four

*V*ery few activities appealed more to Andrew MacNeal than squirrel hunting, and he took advantage of every opportunity to go into the woods after the game. He had set out at noon and, as usual, found the woods thick with fat red squirrels. Now as he arrived back at the cabin, he moved at a smooth trot toward the area in the back devoted to cleaning game. At the age of seventeen, his chest had deepened and there was a sturdiness to his frame that most young men his age lacked. He wore a pair of moccasins, which he had made out of the deer that he himself had slain. He wore a thin cotton shirt tucked into a pair of loose-fitting gray trousers and a coonskin cap pushed back on his head. It was too hot, really, for a coonskin cap, but he was proud of it, since Hawk had given it to him.

Leaning his gun carefully against the back wall of the cabin, he set to work cleaning the squirrels with an ease that comes with much practice. Picking up a squirrel, he cut through the tail up through the skin of the back, then reversed the animal and cut slits down each ham. Putting his foot over the tail, he gave a sudden, hard pull, and the skin was stripped in one smooth, easy motion. The whole job was done in less than a minute, and he whistled softly under his breath as he worked on the bag full of squirrels at his feet.

"Looks like you found where they were."

Andrew looked up quickly to see Jacob, who had exited from the back door of the cabin. He was somewhat surprised to see his brother so dressed up in the middle of a working day and said, "I didn't know we were having church tonight."

"We're not," Jacob whistled. He ran his hand over his dark, wavy hair and shrugged. "I'm going over to call on Abby." He was wearing a pair of new brown trousers, a white cotton shirt with a string tie, and a pair of dark brown half boots that he had brought from Williamsburg with him. He only wore the boots, as a rule, to church, but now he cleaned the toes by rubbing them on the back of his trousers. "It's her birthday," he observed, then turned toward the small corral where his horse was grazing.

"I didn't know anyone had been invited," Andrew said. "I thought she was just celebrating her birthday with her family."

Jacob looked over his shoulder, replying casually, "She invited me to come calling anytime."

Andrew dropped the squirrels and put his hands on his hips. "What do you mean to 'come calling'?"

Jacob turned and a grin made a slash across his tan face. He settled his soft brown hat on his head and winked. "I guess you know what it means." He laughed at the expression on Andrew's face, then turned and entered the corral, where he quickly saddled his horse and rode out. It gave him some sort of satisfaction to see that Andrew had not gone back to cleaning the squirrels but had watched him, and now he took his hat off and waved it. "You take care of things here!" he yelled. "I'll take care of Abigail!"

It was a fine day, June 17, in the year of 1774. As Jacob rode along toward the Stevenses' house, he felt a rush of excitement, as he always did, when he anticipated seeing Abigail. He sat the horse well and thought how he had changed since leaving Williamsburg. It was not only that he had grown older—nineteen on his next birthday—but his muscles had hardened, and the softness that had been a part of his makeup had now turned into firm flesh. Now he slapped his horse on the shoulder and yelled, "Get up, Molly!" He felt exultant as the mare lifted him into a fast run. The wind caught his hat and he nearly lost it, but he managed to snatch it before it was blown off. The hot air blew his hair back, and he finally pulled the horse back to a walk. It felt good to release some of the energy he had pent up inside. He had discovered that he could only go so long without breaking out like this, and now he began to sing a tune under his breath as he moved along the trail.

Come, all ye fair and tender ladies,
Take warning how you court young men.
They're like a star in the summer morning.

They first appear and then they're gone.

By the time he reached the Stevenses' cabin, he had sung several songs. As he swung off his horse and greeted Abigail, who had stepped outside the cabin, he was filled with a quiet confidence that things were going his way.

"Happy birthday, Abigail." He held out a bouquet of wild flowers that he had stopped to pick along the way and tied together with a piece of string that he always carried in his pocket. "They're not as pretty as you, but they're the best I could do."

"Why, thank you, Jacob." She took the flowers and smelled them, then turned her head to one side. "Didn't expect to see you today."

"I couldn't pass up your birthday. You're looking mighty pretty. How does it feel to be seventeen years old?"

"No different from sixteen. Come on and I'll fix you some cider." She led him inside the house, where she poured him a glass of cool apple cider.

"Where are your folks?" he asked as he drank gratefully.

"Oh, Papa took Mama out to show her the new calf. It was born last night. Do you want some more cider?"

"Don't mind if I do. That's really good."

"What's Andrew doing?"

Jacob had lifted the glass halfway to his lips, but the question caught him off guard. "Why," he said quickly, "I think he's gone over to see Amanda." As he saw a slight look of disappointment touch Abigail's eyes, he thought to himself, *All's fair in love and war. Andrew will have to do his own courtin'. A man who won't tell a lie for a girl just doesn't want her bad enough.* Aloud, he said, "Those two are spending a lot of time together."

"Oh!" Abigail tried to appear unconcerned, but it was obvious she was not.

"Would you want to go for a walk?" Jacob asked.

"I'd better not. My folks wouldn't know where I was. Come on. You can see the new calf."

Actually Jacob felt he had seen enough calves in his life, but he had no choice but to agree. Following Abigail to the barn, he found himself having to make the most of the conversation. The calf was like all other calves, but that was not why Jacob had come to the Stevenses'. He was greeted by Abigail's parents charitably enough, but somehow there was not an ease in Abigail's manner. Finally, after a short stay, he made his excuses and left.

As he rode back toward the house, he felt a twinge of conscience. "Shouldn't have told Abby about Andrew and Amanda," he muttered. The mare pitched her ears forward at hearing Jacob's voice, then continued on a fast trot down the winding path that led to the Spencer cabin. Jacob stayed deep in thought most of the time and finally managed to shrug it off. He sang another verse or two of a song he had learned recently, and then thought, *Well, she was in bad spirits today, but it's just a matter of time until she realizes that I'm the man for her.*

Jacob did not want to go directly home, for there might be work to do, so he made a side trip, stopping off at the Andersons' cabin. He was greeted warmly by Rhoda, who said, "Paul's not here, but you can see the baby."

"Just what I wanted. Nothing like a brand-new baby to cheer a man up," Jacob grinned. Actually, he did like babies, and he found the infant rather charming. At Rhoda's invitation, he held the child on his knee as he sat on a cane-bottomed chair and drank the glass of fresh milk that Rhoda put before him. "She's gonna be a charmer," he said.

"You think so?" Rhoda was at that stage of motherhood where she was hungry for compliments for the new baby. Now she looked wistful and said, "I think she looks more like her father."

"No, I don't agree with that. She looks like you. Look at that dark hair, and pretty eyes, too. Just like yours."

"Why, thank you, Jacob."

Jacob sat in the cabin for a time, listening as Rhoda told him of the last trip they had made to evangelize the Cherokee. He was interested, but mainly he stayed because he liked Rhoda and knew that it pleased her to be told that her baby was pretty. Finally, however, he rose and said, "Well, I'll have to see the Reverend the next time through."

"Did you want to see him about anything in particular?"

"No. I was just on my way home. Besides, I had to see this little lady."

"Come back anytime, Jacob."

"Sure. Good to see you, Miss Rhoda."

By the time Jacob had arrived back at his own home, the sun

was dropping behind the low hills to the east. Looking up, he saw the pale disk of the moon and said out loud, "I wonder how come you can see the sun and the moon at the same time? I'd think they'd be on opposite ends or something."

Stepping off his horse, he led the mare into the barn, unsaddled her, then turned her loose in the corral. He spotted Amanda outside the cabin she shared with her mother and walked over to speak to her. "Hello, Amanda," he said.

"Hello, Jacob. How was Abigail?"

"Why, she was fine. How'd you know I was there?"

"Oh, Andrew mentioned it. Did she have a good birthday?"

"Not as good as last year. You remember that big party?"

"That was a good time, wasn't it, Jacob?"

A smile touched Amanda's soft lips, and suddenly Jacob was aware of the developing maturity and the youthful curves of the young woman. *She's fifteen now,* he thought. *Going to be young fellows come courting her pretty soon.* He admired the sheen of her long, dark brown hair and teased her a little bit. "I'm surprised Joseph Foster's not here. I saw him making eyes at you in church last week."

"Oh, he did not!" Amanda flushed and shook her head firmly. "He's just silly!"

"I hope you don't think it's silly for a young fella to like to look at a pretty girl."

He saw that his compliment had turned Amanda speechless. She was a painfully shy and unconfident girl. Jacob's anger seethed inside at the thought of what Amanda's father had done to her to make her feel so worthless. *That rotten pa of hers ought to be hung,* he thought, *for the way he's treated this girl.* He liked Amanda a great deal and now took the time to talk with her a little longer.

"Abigail's a wonderful person, isn't she?"

"Anyone that would get her would be very lucky, Jacob."

"I agree with that, too." Then he reached out and patted her shoulder. It was firm and warm beneath his touch, and he smiled as he said, "Anyone that gets you is going to be a lucky fellow, too, Amanda. You're growing up so fast I can't keep up with you."

Amanda looked down at the ground. The compliment brought such a sudden warmth to her that she could not speak again. She had long known of her attraction to Jacob Spencer, but she had not breathed a word of it to a living soul, not even to her mother. Finally she whispered, "Thank you, Jacob."

Then he patted her shoulder once more and walked away. "I'll see you later, Amanda."

"All right, Jacob." She thought for a long time about what he had said. It was the most complete compliment he had ever paid her. *"Any fellow that would get you would be lucky, Amanda."* She knew she would treasure those words and think of them for a long time, maybe for the rest of her life. Few enough good things had been a part of this young girl's life who had such capacity for love and so little outlet for it.

Now as she moved back and sat inside the cabin, Iris asked, "Was that Jacob?"

"Yes. He just got back from Abigail's."

"Oh? That's nice. I expect those two will be getting serious one of these days."

"I expect you're right, Mother."

As soon as Jacob got home, he went into the new section of the cabin that he shared with Andrew and found his brother reading a book. Andrew looked up to say, "How was Abigail?"

"Oh, fine." Then he fabricated the truth somewhat by telling Andrew what a good time the two had had. He had been disappointed at the visit and now found himself lying again. When he saw Andrew just listening with a strange expression on his face, he began to despise himself. "Well," he said, "that was about all there was to it."

"I'm glad you had a good time," Andrew said quietly.

Jacob shot a quick glance at Andrew's face and saw nothing but a quiet honesty. He, however, felt he had not behaved well, and as he removed his good clothes to put on older ones, he said to himself, *I've got to stop acting like this. I don't have to win Abby away from Andrew by telling lies.*

"Did you have a good time on your birthday?" Deborah Stevens asked as Abigail stood before her.

"Oh yes, Mama."

The two had been sitting together listening as George had read to them. Finally George yawned and said, "It's getting late for me.

I've got to get up early in the morning." He rose to kiss Abigail on the cheek and gave her a hug. "Happy Birthday, Abigail."

"Thank you, Pa."

"It wasn't much of a birthday," he observed, studying her face. "Last year we had a big celebration."

"It was all right. I enjoyed being with just you and Ma."

"Next year we'll have a big party again," Stevens promised. He left the room and for a time the two sat there talking quietly.

Noting that Abigail had little to say, Deborah asked tentatively, "Is something wrong, Abby?"

"I was only wishing that Andrew had come over to wish me a happy birthday."

"Well, we didn't really invite him. It was your idea."

"I know. I just thought . . . I thought he might drop by."

"I guess he got too busy and lost track of the time until it was too late."

"Maybe," Abigail said with a lack of enthusiasm. She rose and said, "I think I'll go to bed, Mother. I'm a little tired."

This set off a small alarm in Deborah Stevens, for Abigail was rarely tired. The girl had a great deal of inner strength and physical endurance. Now Deborah asked abruptly, "Why does it matter so much to you that Andrew didn't come? Are you interested in him?"

"Oh no! It's just that I've always liked him so much. We've been good friends for a long time. I just thought he might come."

Deborah rose and gave her daughter a kiss on the forehead. "I'll tell you what," she said. "Why don't you ask him over to supper one night this week? Not for a birthday or anything, just to spend some time with us all."

"Oh, that would be nice, Mother!" Abigail's eyes lightened, and she kissed her mother, then turned and went to bed.

She undressed quickly, slipped into a cotton nightgown, then blew out the candle and lay down. Outside, the stars made a sparkling canopy over the earth, and the moon was a huge silver disk. The pale light filtered in through the window and lit the room brightly. Abigail lay awake, not being sleepy. She thought once about getting up and lighting a candle to read for a while but decided not to. Finally she grew drowsy, and just before she dropped off to sleep, she found herself thinking of Jacob Spencer and Andrew MacNeal. *They're so different,* she thought just before she drifted off into a deep sleep.

Lord Dunmore's War

Twenty-Five

All of the trouble between the Indians and the settlers on the frontier had stemmed from the same source: the Indians had no concept of the ownership of land. They roamed over it killing their game, raising their families, moving from point to point when food became scarce—but as for owning the land, any attempt to explain this to them was usually futile. Therefore, as settlers began to filter across the Appalachian Mountains, inevitable conflicts arose. One of these conflicts was given the grandiose name of Lord Dunmore's War, after Virginia's military commander who was claiming the Indian lands of Can-tuc-kee for the British.

The events leading up to this conflict began in the late spring of 1774. The Cherokee were still angry over the murder of Cherokee Billie during the horse races on the Sycamore Shoals. Only the firm hand of Little Carpenter and a few of the other older chiefs kept war from breaking out right then. However, when another senseless killing took place along the Ohio River, the flood of war could no longer be contained.

A small party of Mingo were camped by the mouth of Yellow Creek at a spot called Bakers Bottom. Two men, both rather unsavory characters, Greathouse and Tomlinson, formed a motley crew of some twenty-seven men. The two hated Indians and let no opportunity escape to kill whenever they thought the time was right. Greathouse formulated a plan and moved across the river, where they were greeted by an Iroquois chief named Shikellimus. Greathouse was fluent in the Iroquois language and told the old Indian that they would like his band to join them for some rum and a marksmanship contest. Shikellimus declined but said he would send over five or six good marksmen to represent the Mingo.

Among the marksmen that went over was a pregnant Indian woman who was the daughter of Shikellimus and also the sister of Chief John Logan. Her brother, also called Talgayetta, was the Mingo chief of the Cuyahoga Indians, one of the five tribes grouped with the Iroquois. Logan was friendly to whites and had flatly refused to take part in the French and Indian War. He was a notable peacemaker and a valuable ally of the white settlers.

Early in the afternoon the small party of Mingo joined the whites and sat for some time drinking rum and engaging in sharpshooting. It was Logan's sister who suddenly uttered a piercing cry, leaped up, and ran toward the river.

By this time the Mingo were half drunk and looked around in confusion at the white men bearing muskets who had leaped out from hiding in the weeds. The Indians fumbled for their own weapons, but a volley of shots rang out, and all the Indians fell dead or dying. Knowing that the remaining Mingo across the river would come quickly to investigate, the entire party of whites fled after killing the Indians who had ferried the other victims across.

It was a senseless crime, and it changed the heart of the mighty Mingo chief, John Logan, who had never struck out at the whites, despite provocation. The next day, however, Chief Logan stood over the scalped and mutilated bodies of his kinsmen and great anger rose in him. He was transformed almost instantly into a man set on vengeance, and he vowed that he would not rest until the murderers of his people were dead.

Chief Logan's band fell upon the settlers almost instantly. Those who survived fled for safety, and by midsummer there was not a white settler left in all of Can-tuc-kee.

Logan visited the Cherokee, encouraging them to join him and drive the white man out of their native lands, but Oconostota and the Little Carpenter told Logan they had given their word not to retaliate for the murder of Cherokee Billie. The Cherokee nation would remain neutral, although some of the younger, more violent warriors, no doubt, joined Logan.

Disappointed and angry at the refusal of the Cherokee to join in the war, Logan turned toward the Clinch and Holston rivers. He and his marauding warriors rode with a vengeance, stealing, burning, scalping, and ravaging the frontier settlements and the thin line of forts along those rivers. At each place after the raid, Logan left a war club behind as a threat and a challenge. War clouds hung over Watauga and other settlements in the area, and unless something was done, no whites would be safe in the territory. It was a time for action, and unless something changed, the whites of the Colonies would be kept pinned to the small strip along the eastern seaboard, and the great westward migration would stop before it actually began.

————————

As soon as Elizabeth saw Hawk's face, she knew something was wrong. Rising from her chair where she had been sewing a new garment for the baby, she came to him at once. Her voice was breathless, as it sometimes got when she was under stress. "What is it, Hawk?" she murmured, reaching up to lay her hand on his chest.

Covering Elizabeth's hand, Hawk shook his head. He had left early that afternoon, and now a vague, troubling expression reflected in his eyes as he said, "Lord Dunmore has called for the militia of the Holston Territory to join him in fighting the Shawnee."

Elizabeth's heart suddenly beat faster, and her hand trembled under his. "Will . . . will the Watauga militia join?"

"Some will."

Elizabeth knew him very well, and a small shiver of fear gripped her heart as she asked, "That means you, doesn't it?"

"Yes, I'll have to go."

Elizabeth had endured the rumors of the outbreaks of the Shawnee with fortitude. Now, however, that the moment had come for her husband to put himself under the threat of the vicious and bloodthirsty tribesmen, she felt terribly weak. She suddenly had a frightening memory of her husband, Patrick, his bloody body as he had been cut down by Indians, and something in her protested, *No . . . no, not again! Once was enough!* Despite her resolutions, tears gathered in her eyes. She blinked them away quickly, however. *I must be strong. I can't let him see me like this.* "When will you leave?" she asked quietly.

"At first light. We have a long way to go." He put his arms around her, and for some time they stood there, not moving. A quietness filled the room and both of them were saddened by the sudden interruption of their lives. Hawk knew better than Elizabeth the dangers that lay ahead, but he knew that her fears were greater than his.

"I'll come back to you," he whispered and then kissed her cheek. He stroked her hair and was filled with the surprise that always came to him at the blessing of this woman whom God had sent into his life.

Elizabeth wrapped her arms around him, clinging to him as a drowning swimmer clings to a log that comes floating by as the last hope. He was strong and vital, and the life in him was powerful, yet she well knew that one arrow, one musket ball, or one blow of a tomahawk could end all that in an instant. She buried her face against his chest and shut her eyes tightly. "Come back to me, Hawk," she whispered, then lifted her arms and pulled his head down to take his kiss.

———

Hawk had explained to the children all of the news that he had given Elizabeth the night before. Now as he put on his hunting shirt and picked his rifle from the pegs over the door, he thought how hard it had been. "It's different for a married man," he had told Elizabeth. "Especially for one with children." It had been Sarah who had taken it the hardest. She had been afraid and unable to conceal it. The boys had done better, but he saw the looks of apprehension in both of their faces.

Now as Hawk slung his gear together, preparing to load his horse and join the others, he looked up to see Andrew come in through the front door. He was wearing buckskins with his coonskin cap and holding his rifle firmly in his hands.

Taken somewhat by surprise, Hawk said, "You going hunting, Andrew?"

"I'm going with you, Pa."

Hawk blinked with surprise and turned to face the young man. He had half expected Andrew to do something rash. As mildly as he could, he said, "Andrew, you've got to stay—"

"There's no sense talkin', Pa. I'm old enough to be in the militia, and I'm going. It would be better," he said quietly, "if you took it well. I'd hate to have to sneak around and join behind your back. You can say anything you please, but my mind's already made up."

"Have you told your mother about this?"

"Yes, I told her just now."

"What did she say?"

Andrew hesitated, then shook his head. "She's afraid for me, of course, just like she's afraid for you. But this isn't a thing that I can put off."

At that moment Elizabeth came in from outside, and Hawk saw that she was keeping her composure only by a distinct effort. Her face was usually in repose, but now there were lines of strain, and a panic appeared in her eyes that she could not hide. She stood beside Andrew and shook her head slightly. "Must you do it, son?"

"I've got to, Ma. I couldn't call myself a man if I didn't do what I could for this place and for our neighbors."

"Son, you have to think—"

"I know what you're going to say, Pa. Somebody's going to have to stay here and take care of Ma and Sarah, Hannah, and Josh, but Jacob will be here to do that."

For a few moments they stood there, Hawk trying to persuade Andrew to change his mind, but finally Hawk saw that it was useless. He went over and put his arm around Elizabeth and fixed his eyes on the strong figure of his stepson. "I'm against it," he said quietly, and then he found himself smiling. "But I have to tell you, in all honesty, I'm proud of you, Andy. You've become a man."

Elizabeth knew there was no persuading him to stay. She gave one final look of half desperation to her son, then said, "Hawk, watch out for him."

Andrew laughed. He felt better now that both his parents had agreed and said in a teasing fashion, "I'll look out for *him*, Ma."

At that moment both Sarah and Jacob came in the door, and Sarah said, "You're not going, too, are you, Andy?"

"Yes, I am."

Sarah had already seemed about to cry, and now tears formed in her large eyes.

Andrew stared at her with astonishment. "Well, I can't believe that you're going to miss me!" He went over and put his arms around Sarah and kissed her on the cheek. "Don't worry, sis. I'll be all right."

Jacob had watched all this with astonishment. Andrew had said nothing at all to him about going, and it came as a shock. Somehow he felt that he must do something to equal his brother, and he said quickly, "I'll go, too."

"No, son. Someone has to stay behind with Elizabeth and the children."

"Then Andrew should stay," Jacob said, his face flushed.

Andrew was the younger of the two, but somehow he seemed more mature. He turned to face his half brother and said quietly, "I guess you got more reason to stay than I have."

At once Jacob understood that he was referring to Abigail. He opened his mouth to speak, but nothing came to him. Somehow he felt that he had been amiss not to have volunteered to go with his father. After all, he was older. And now as he looked at the pride in Hawk's eyes as he gazed at Andrew, Jacob felt a tinge of misery but saw that it was useless to protest. *I should have done what Andrew's done,* he thought, watching his father's face carefully. *Then he would have been proud of me instead of his other son.*

Sarah did not sense the interchange between her two brothers, and now she piped up, asking, "Are you going to go tell Abigail good-bye, Andrew?"

"No reason to," Andrew muttered. Then he forced himself to smile. "You tell her good-bye for me, all right?"

"All right. I will."

Hawk hated good-byes and now said, "Well, the quicker we go, the quicker we'll get back." He embraced Elizabeth, kissed her, then went over to the cradle and picked Joshua up. "Son, you be a good boy. Grow up while I'm gone. Put some meat on your bones." He then turned to Hannah and held back the tears as he kissed her good-bye.

Andrew embraced his mother, then said, "I guess I'm ready, Pa."

Hawk picked up his rifle and his gear, and when he reached the door, he suddenly turned and looked at his family. "I'll miss all of you," he said simply.

Elizabeth moved outside, holding the baby and watching as the two men arranged their gear on their horses, then swung into the saddle. "God go with you," she whispered and waved as they turned and left at a fast gallop. "I think it would be good to say a prayer for them," she said. "Jacob, you're the man of the house now. You pray."

Taken off guard, Jacob managed to mumble a few words, asking for a safe return. When he had said the "Amen," he found himself wishing for the first time that he could have prayed to God as he should. He watched his father and brother disappear, and something cold grew in his stomach and he found himself more miserable than he would have imagined. He had not realized how his feelings for his father had begun to change, and even how close they now felt, despite their problems. Now as he turned to begin the chores, he felt a heaviness he knew would not soon pass away.

Almost at the same time that Chief Logan had tried to entice the Cherokee to join his rebellion, Virginia's military commander, Lord Dunmore, began to pull his forces together. Sending out an order for the militia to gather, he formed a plan to divide his army into two wings. The southern wing, under the command of Colonel Andrew Lewis, would be composed almost entirely of mountain men from the western counties. The other wing Dunmore himself would command, and many of the northern frontiersmen were gathered at Fort Pitt. Dunmore's initial plan was to build a fort at the Kanawha River at Point Pleasant on the Ohio. Then the two forces would combine to strike the Shawnee villages along the Scioto River near the Pickaway Plains.

It was only in the later days of August that the Watauga militia met the rest of the command at Shelby's Fort. From there, the entire force set off for the Ohio River, a march of some two hundred miles. They reached Point Pleasant on October 9 and set up a camp.

Unknown to Lord Dunmore, or any of the militia, Chief Cornstalk, the most powerful of the chiefs that formed the enemy army, had been watching both wings through his spies. It became obvious to Cornstalk that the large army was still faraway. He summoned the Shawnee warriors and the allies—the Mingo, Delaware, and Wyandot to arms, and they rushed to the call in large numbers. Cornstalk's aim was to destroy the smaller force under Colonel Lewis, which included the Watauga militia, then attack the larger force.

The attack began when Cornstalk's forces halted just above the mouth of the Kanawha River. After dark they crossed the Ohio River, and just as dawn was breaking, the large force of Indians waited the signal to attack the white men who camped below in a valley. The warriors were painted for war, hungry for scalps and for revenge. As the first gray light of dawn touched the hills to the north, they crouched hidden in the forest, gripping their muskets and testing the edges of their tomahawks, their eyes glowing in the early-morning light.

"It's been a hard trip, Andrew," Hawk remarked. He was sitting in front of a small fire roasting a squirrel, and now he took it out and tested it with the tip of his knife. "Not quite done," he remarked.

"Mine is," Andrew said. He was also roasting a squirrel, and now he pulled it back and tried to pull it off of the green stick of wood. "Ow!" he yelled. "It's hot!" He juggled the brown bit of meat until it grew cooler, then began tearing at it hungrily. "Sure tastes good. I just wish squirrels were as big as coons."

"Would be nice, wouldn't it?" Hawk was more patient, and finally his meat cooled. He began to pull it off, chewing thoughtfully as he studied Andrew. He was pleased with the young man's endurance, for it had been a hard march down to the Pickaway Plains. They lay now in the fork of two creeks, and dawn was only minutes away.

"Wish I had some of your ma's flapjacks and johnny cakes and fried ham," he said.

"Ah, you're just soft, Pa," Andrew grinned. He chewed the tough meat, then smiled and nodded. "I wouldn't mind havin' some of that myself."

Hawk looked over the forces and tried to estimate how they would do in a pitched battle. Almost all of them were experienced frontiersmen, but at least a fourth of the men had never heard a shot fired in anger. They were new to the frontier, untested and untried, and as Hawk lifted his eyes, trying to peer through the darkness, he wondered how many Indians lay out there somewhere. A vague feeling of unease moved through him, and he thought, *Am I getting old or am I afraid of a fight?* He stood up, holding the remains of the squirrel in his hands, cocked his head slightly to one side, and listened intently.

"Do you hear something, Hawk?" The speaker was a young man named Tom Feller, one of Hawk's neighbors. He was just married, with a baby on the way, and his wife had cried and begged him to stay home. Feller, however, had merely laughed, telling her, "Don't worry, Edna. I'll be back."

Now Feller was watching rather anxiously. He was a good shot, but he had never been in any sort of battle, having arrived in Watauga from North Carolina only a few months earlier. "What is it?" he asked nervously.

"Nothing. That's what bothers me."

"How can nothing bother you?" Feller demanded.

Hawk did not know how to explain it. It was something that was built up in a man over long periods of time in the wilderness. Sometimes silence meant as much as a noise. For example, he knew that right now there was an absence of the usual animal cries that one would have expected to begin at dawn. Perhaps it was nothing—but he well knew that the birds and the animals quieted when there was human movement, and the unnatural silence troubled him.

At that moment Captain Lewis came walking rapidly out of the waning darkness. "You all right, Spencer?"

"Yes, we are, Captain," Hawk replied.

Lewis was a short, muscular man with a deep chest and a full beard, rich brown but beginning to be speckled with gray. His deep-set eyes swept the territory as he peered into the darkness. "I don't feel good about this. We'd better pull ourselves into tighter ranks."

"All right, Captain," Hawk said. He liked Lewis and had confidence in the man who had survived more than one Indian war. Now he murmured, "Some of the men haven't ever heard a shot fired."

"That's right. Have 'em scattered out among your more experienced men."

"All right, Captain. I'll do that."

But he had no time to carry out the order, for even as the two men stood there speaking, a broken cry rose up and was cut off abruptly. It was a cry of fear, of terror, and it ended with a slight gurgling noise.

Hawk knew that sound. It was a knife slitting the throat of an unwary militiaman. "Indians!" he yelled at the top of his lungs. "Heads up! Make every shot count!"

His father's cry caught Andrew MacNeal off guard. He had just bitten off a huge bite, but at the scream that split through the morning's silence in an eerie, ghostlike fashion, and his father's urgent warning, he spat it out and made a wild grab for his musket. Shots suddenly rang out up ahead at the joining of the creek, and he heard his father calling out to form a line of battle.

"Find yourself some cover. They'll be coming in soon," he yelled. Then he turned and said, "Andrew, get behind that log over there."

"Yes, sir!" Andrew threw himself behind the log, checked his priming, and quickly put his powder horn and cartridge box beside him. He was surprised to find that he was calm. One part of his brain was screaming out that he might be dead, but he found himself able to override the fear as he watched the experienced mountain men find cover. He had no time to think for long, for a flicker of movement caught his attention and his father's musket suddenly exploded, almost in his ear. Andrew heard a muffled cry, and the movement suddenly ceased.

"You got that one," Tom Feller grinned. "Now I'll get me one."

Straining his eyes, Andrew saw little to shoot at. He had thought that a battle would be where two forces would come together, both in plain sight, but he soon discovered that the Indians were too wily for that. They flitted from tree to tree, almost invisible, so that all he ever got was a glance. Three times he shot, and three times he was bitterly disappointed, knowing that he had missed.

The battle had not gone on for more than five minutes when suddenly Jude Satterfield, who was standing behind a tree to Andrew's left, stepped out to get a better shot, but he never got it off. Andrew heard the sound of the bullet as it made a dull thud, and he saw Jude driven back. He fell to the ground, and Andrew sprang to him, crying, "Are you all right?" But looking down, he saw that the bullet had taken the man directly in the throat and blood was spouting like a fountain. Jude was trying to speak, but he could not. As he bent over the man and pulled him half up, he tried to stop the flow, even though he knew it was hopeless. He saw the frantic light of fear in Jude's eyes, and then the eyes dimmed, and with a cough Jude kicked twice, clawing at his throat, then stiffened and drew still.

"Andy, watch out!"

Andrew heard his father's cry and leaped for his musket, which he had just reloaded. This time he did see an Indian, a coppery figure painted with lurid colors who had burst out of the trees and was running straight for the line. He was joined by others, but Andrew could only see this one. His eyesight seemed to play him a trick so that the fierce visage of the Indian swelled and grew enormous before his eyes. He could even see the markings clearly on the face. Lowering his rifle, he put the bead right on the man's chest and pulled the trigger almost without thinking. The spark hit the frizzen and the rifle exploded, the shock of it striking hard against Andrew's shoulder. Involuntarily he closed his eyes, but at once he lowered his musket and saw that the Indian had stopped, as if he had run into a tree. He stood for one moment, looking down at the hole that began to leak red blood down the war paint, the blues and greens and ochres on his chest, and then he fell forward, his fingers clawing at the ground.

With trembling hands, Andrew grabbed his powder horn and poured a fresh charge down the barrel. He put some of the powder in the pan after shoving a ball down covered with a patch. His heart was beating and he tried to think, but his mind was racing with the instinct of survival. He knew he had just killed a man, a fellow human being, and somehow even in the midst of the screams and explosions of the muskets up and down the line, a deep sadness settled on him like an ominous shadow.

There was no time to grieve, however, for the battle raged furiously. At times the Indians would attack, and sometimes Lewis would direct the men to move forward.

Hawk's face was black with powder, but he paid no heed. He was worried about Andrew, and more than once warned him to stay behind in cover. "We're going to be moving up," he said, throwing himself down behind a log and peering out into the morning light. It was later now and the sun was hot as it beat down upon them. Licking his lips, he shook his head. "We're gonna be thirsty if we get away from this water. Be sure your canteen's full."

"All right, Pa."

Hawk hesitated, then said, "You're doing a man's job. Does it bother you?"

"I reckon it does, Pa."

Hawk suddenly reached over and squeezed Andrew's shoulder. "I'm glad it does. It bothers me, too. It bothers any man who thinks, but we don't have any choice."

For three full hours the battle raged. From time to time parts of the line engaged in hand-to-hand combat. The screams of the wounded and the dying were ugly and scraped on Andrew's nerves. He moved forward when told to do so by the leaders, fell behind cover, and at times retreated when the Indians threw their strength into another attack. It was a matter of wonder to him that he could fight like this. Somehow he knew it had something to do with Abigail. It seemed far away now, but once when the fighting slacked off and he sat panting, his back to a tree, taking a sip of the precious water, he knew the battle madness had something to do with his loss of Abigail. He felt he had lost her to Jacob, and it was this loss that sent him forward into the fierce fighting. He was not anxious to die, but somehow there was a calmness and a coolness in his spirit, and his great regret was losing the girl whom he now realized he loved more than life itself.

The day moved on inexorably, and finally the settlers pushed the Indians back. As they did so, the lines became scattered and broken and fragmented. Before he realized it, Andrew found himself cut off from the rest. He could still hear the shouts from both sides, and as he tried to move back toward the main action, he crossed a narrow, sluggish creek half buried in mud. The gumbo tugged at his feet, and he lost a moccasin, then wasted precious time in pulling it out of the dripping mud.

As he moved toward the sound of fighting, the smell of ferns rose in wild fragrance as he trampled them under his feet. Frantically, he hurdled dead logs matted with berry vines, and once a covey of quails, flushed from cover, drummed away in low flight from him.

Andrew grew winded, and as he drew closer to the raging battle where the fighting was hardest, bullets whipped by, and a chunk of bark flaked from a tree struck him on the cheek. He pulled himself back and fired at an Indian half hidden in the brush not fifteen feet away. The Indian swayed as the bullet struck him. The warrior turned and looked with wild eyes as the round spot on his chest bubbled and grew larger and the blood made a bright streak down his chest. Andrew watched as a dullness clouded the eyes of the Indian, then he fell back and lay without movement.

Andrew tried to reload his musket, but even as he pounded the ball down the barrel, a musket ball stung his side. He was not hit hard, but he looked up to see a Mingo coming for him at a dead run. He had a musket in his hand, but apparently it was not loaded. He was not twenty feet away, and with a wild, savage cry, he dropped the musket, snatched a tomahawk from his belt, and threw himself forward toward Andrew.

The sight of that glittering tomahawk, caught by the afternoon sun, sent a chill of fear through Andrew. There was no chance of reloading. He knew he could not outrun the Mingo, so he did the only thing he could. Grasping his musket close to the end of the barrel, he waited, his feet firmly planted. His heart seemed to be slogging with a slow, regular beat, and he found himself distinctly shocked that he was not filled with panic.

The Indian was not large but sinewy, and as he threw himself forward, Andrew forced himself to ignore the glittering tomahawk. One of them would die; he recognized that.

Swinging the musket in a wild arch, he saw the tomahawk descending. The musket caught the Indian on the shoulder and destroyed his aim. He was driven to one side, and the tomahawk went sailing through the air, but before Andrew could move, the Mingo had pulled out a wicked-looking knife, and with a wild cry, he leaped at Andrew.

Andrew dropped his musket and caught the Indian's wrist with both hands. He was not as strong as the Indian, he knew, and the blows from the Indian's free fist caught him in the face. Suddenly the Indian moved quickly and was behind him, and Andrew felt a hard form pressed against his throat, squeezing his windpipe.

Frantically Andrew threw himself to one side. He smelled the Indian and heard the guttural cries in his ear. Reaching over his head, he grabbed the Indian by the first thing he could touch, his scalp lock. With a mighty pull he heaved and heard a cry of pain break from the Indian's lips. The pressure on his throat eased for just one moment, just in time, for he had begun to see the world through a red haze.

He swung around and the Indian lost his grip, but he retained his knife. As he rolled over and came up again, Andrew snatched at the musket. The glittering eyes of the Indian seemed to be frozen, and then Andrew swung the musket. It caught the Indian on the side of the head. It made the sound of a hammer striking a watermelon, and the Indian's eyes glazed over as he was driven to one side.

Seeing that the Indian still clutched the knife, Andrew raised the musket and brought down the butt with all his force on the Indian's face.

Andrew's breath was coming in great gasps as he stood over the dead Indian. He stood still for a moment, then swayed, his vision blurred, and his hands shook as he drew them across his face.

"Are you hit, Andrew?"

Andrew turned to see his father come running up, his face contorted with anxiety.

"No, I'm all right."

"I was . . . I was afraid for you," Hawk said, breathing hard.

"I'm all right, Pa." Andrew forced himself to look at the gun butt, which was bloody, and a shudder went through him. "I ruined my gun."

Hawk barely glanced at the broken musket. "Guns can be fixed," he said.

"Are we winning?"

"It's pretty much over," Hawk said. "We beat 'em off. They're on the run."

"I'm glad you're all right, Pa."

Hawk squeezed the boy's shoulders hard and was unable to speak. He had not been afraid for himself, but he had vivid fears of finding Andrew with a bullet in his chest. Now he led Andrew back to where the forces were regathering.

Andrew stopped to see the body of Tom Feller lying still. His throat had been cut and his scalp taken.

"Edna will have a hard time living without him, won't she, Pa?"

"I guess she will," Hawk said grimly. "But we all have to go on. God will be with her if she'll turn to Him. I know that better than most."

"What will happen now, Pa?"

"I think this about finishes Cornstalk's rebellion. Colonel Lewis said if we could whip 'em here that they'd disappear. It'll open Cantuc-kee, that's one thing for sure. Daniel Boone will be glad."

The two moved along helping the wounded, and finally when they had done what they could, they fell exhausted into their blankets, and the last thing Hawk said was, "This will make the Watauga settlement safe. Now you'll see settlers come pouring in from over the Misty Mountains like they never have before. . . ."

The Heroes Return

Twenty-Six

*E*lizabeth moved around the kitchen preparing the evening meal, preoccupied with thoughts of Hawk and Andrew. Since they had left to go to the war, she had been concerned for their safety every waking hour, praying for them. Now as she bent over the heavy iron pot that contained beans that bubbled up and sent a savor through the room, a stab of fear came to her. *What would I do without Hawk or Andrew? I've already lost so much. Be with them, Father, and help me to be strong in you, no matter what.*

Adding a little salt and some peppers to the beans, she resolutely put the matter out of her mind and moved outside the cabin, where she made her way to the smokehouse. The November sky was gray, and as the breeze bit at her face she knew winter was coming on. The pale sun overhead seemed to give no warmth but simply hung in the sky, its feeble light washing across the clearing and the garden that was now dead and brown.

Reaching the smokehouse, Elizabeth stepped inside and critically examined the supplies. Hawk had done a good job of providing, as he always did, and now she lifted a haunch of venison and hefted its weight. The smokehouse was dark and filled with the smells of meat, smoked, cured, and salted. It gave her a good feeling to know that the provision was there for many meals.

As she stepped outside she heard a voice. Thinking it was Iris or Amanda coming, she turned to face the path that led to the settlement. When she saw two men, she dropped the smoked venison to the ground heedlessly and cried out, "Hawk—Andrew!" and flew across the cold ground toward them. When she reached them she took one glance at their faces wreathed in smiles and flung herself at Hawk, who swung her around, laughing. Then when he put her down, Andrew did the same with the same ease of strength.

"You're back!" she exclaimed and was embarrassed to find tears gathered in her eyes. She blinked them away quickly, and hearing Sarah call, she turned and said, "Look who's come home!"

"Let's get in out of this cold and have something to eat," Hawk grinned, holding Sarah as if she were a child.

"Put me down, Pa! I'm not a baby!"

"You are to me," Hawk said. He laughed and ignored her protests and kissed her cheek, then finally set her on the ground, saying, "You're growing up on me, Sarah. Getting plump, too."

"I am not!" she protested.

"Yes, you are," Andrew said. He reached down and scooped Sarah up, laughing at her screams, and squeezed her until she began to squirm too much.

The four stepped inside, and as they did, Jacob entered from the dog trot. He had seen them outside and now came forward quickly and put out his hand.

Hawk ignored the hand, reached out and squeezed Jacob's shoulders, and said, "Good to see you, Jacob."

"Good to see you, Pa—and you, Andrew."

"Tell us about the war," Sarah chirped, almost dancing around.

"I will," Hawk promised. "But I want to see Hannah and Joshua first."

They all watched with a smile as Hawk bent down and put his arms out to Hannah. She had hung back shyly at first, hiding behind her mother's skirt, but now she ran into his waiting arms and looked up at him with owlish eyes. She giggled loudly as he tickled her stomach and put her arms around his neck. He carried her over to the crib near the fireplace, where Joshua was taking a nap. Hawk set Hannah down on the floor and, despite the fact that Josh was asleep, picked him up and cuddled him in his arms. When he looked across at Jacob, he said, "I'm glad you were here to take care of things, son."

"Me too, Pa."

Elizabeth's heart filled with gratitude as she stood beside Hawk. Her husband and her children were safe, the men were home from the wars, and she did not need to lie awake anymore worrying about them.

"I know you're both starved. I've got beans, and I'll get some of this smoked venison. Oh—I dropped it when I saw you! Go get it for me, will you, Sarah?"

————

The cabin was full of laughter and talk as Hawk and Andrew ate ravenously.

"Tell us about the war. Did you kill any Indians?" Sarah demanded.

"I'll let Andrew tell you about it. He was a real soldier."

Andrew shifted nervously and shrugged his shoulders. "It wasn't so much," he muttered.

"None of that," Elizabeth said. "We want to hear all about it. Don't leave out anything."

Andrew then began to tell the story of the hard journeys and the battles. He was embarrassed at first and stumbled, but as the tale spun itself out, he found himself thinking back, and some of the fire of battle that had come to him in the midst of the action was reflected in his eyes. He sat there loosely at the table, his bronze, strong hands toying with the pewter mug. As he spoke there was a new maturity in him that had come in the past few weeks.

Finally he glanced up and saw everyone listening quietly, and it was as they would listen to a man, not a boy. A feeling of pride swelled in his chest, but suddenly he felt he had been bragging too much and he shook his head. "It wasn't much, but we had some good leaders."

Jacob listened with envy as Andrew related the story of the battle. Even more he wished that he had gone with his father. He was taken by surprise when Hawk said abruptly, "I'm glad to get home for your birthday, Jacob."

Jacob blinked, thinking that his father would have forgotten it, but Hawk asked with a smile, "What are you planning on doing to celebrate?"

"Oh, nothing much, I don't think," he mumbled.

"I know what he's going to do," Sarah piped up. She grinned broadly and winked at her father. "He's going to see Abigail. Why, he's about worn a pathway over to that place since you've been gone, Pa."

Andrew glanced quickly at his stepbrother. He picked up his cup and drank some of the sassafras tea that Elizabeth had made, not responding visibly, but it had bothered him more than he showed.

"Well, I think we ought to invite the Stevenses to dinner," Hawk said. "We haven't seen them for a while, and they'll want to hear about the battle." He winked over at Jacob and said, "And I guess it'll be all right if they bring Abigail along."

He did not see the expression on Andrew's face, but Elizabeth did and it troubled her. She said nothing, however, and when Hawk went back to get Joshua out of his crib and bounce him on his knee, she moved over and put her arm around Andrew, saying, "Your father would have been proud of you, son, as I am."

The words warmed Andrew, and he squeezed his mother's waist. "I still miss him, Ma."

"So do I," Elizabeth said, then she looked into the bright eyes so much like the ones she still remembered as her first love and whispered, "So do I, son."

The day passed quickly as Hawk walked around the homestead with a sense of wonder. He had not fully realized how deeply he had put down roots here. After the wanderings of his life he felt pleased and profoundly content to know that this piece of bountiful land was his in a particular way. A sense of pride filled his heart as he looked out across the land, marked with his sweat and toil and occupied by his wife and his children. *This land is mine*, he thought. He and Elizabeth had walked a great deal, then finally he had gone back and spent the evening playing with Hannah and Joshua with a deep satisfaction until bedtime.

When he was in bed with Elizabeth, he reached for her, drew her close, and felt the fullness of her body against his. "I missed you," he said lovingly.

"Hawk," Elizabeth said, then hesitated. She could not find the words to let him know how much she had missed him. So now she simply moved against him, pulled his head down, and kissed him with a fierceness that was at once possessive and loving and wonderful.

"Tell me some more about the battle," Jacob said as he and Andrew lay in their bunks in the upper room.

"Well, it wasn't like I thought it would be," Andrew said. He was still thinking of what had been said at supper concerning Abigail, but he mentioned nothing to Jacob about this. "Somehow I always thought war would be men lined up in neat lines, but it wasn't like that at all. It was almost like every man fought his own battle."

"Did it bother you to kill that Indian?"

"Yes, it did."

"It wouldn't bother me," Jacob said. "After what they've done to the settlers, I think I could kill every one of them!"

"They've got their ways, and we've broken their ways up," Andrew said. "Before we came here they had their wars with each other. Now they see us as taking what's theirs. Wouldn't you fight for what was yours if someone tried to take this place?"

Jacob was somewhat surprised. He sensed a new maturity in Andrew that had not been there before, and after a while he said, "I reckon you're right. It's hard to see it that way sometimes."

The two lay there quietly for some time, and then finally Jacob said, "I'm glad you're home, Andrew."

It was a simple statement, but somehow Andrew felt good about it. He had felt alienated from his stepbrother, and now he sensed that Jacob truly was glad he was back. Finally he said, "How are things going with Abigail?"

For a moment Jacob hesitated. The room was so quiet that both boys could hear the sound of leaves scraping as they blew across the shake roof. Outside the single window the walnut tree they had left for shade clawed at the roof with bare branches like bony fingers. It was a lonely, haunting sound, and both boys listened to it for a time. Finally Jacob said, "Fine. I . . . well, I guess we're going to be engaged soon."

The words struck at Andrew, but he covered them up by saying quickly, "Why, that's fine. You're getting a good girl, and she's getting a good man."

"Thanks, Andrew. Good to hear you say that."

Both young men then lay on their bunks listening to the sounds of the night, but both were thinking of Abigail Stevens and neither of them slept soundly that night.

A Proposal

Twenty-Seven

*J*acob's birthday party proved to be a good time of fellowship for the men, sharing their war experiences with their friends in Watauga who had not been able to join the militia. They sat around on the porch, enjoying the sunny and mild November day, probably one of the last warm days of the season. The women were all crowded into the cabin, preparing the meal and looking after the smaller children.

Looking out the window, Elizabeth saw George Stevens listening with respect to Andrew as he related his experiences in Lord Dunmore's War. She glanced across the kitchen where Amanda and Sarah were taking care of Hannah, Joshua, and Rachel Anderson. Even as she looked, the Fosters and the Baxters arrived, and she noted that Philip Baxter went at once to Sarah. Elizabeth smiled, for she liked the Baxter boy very much, and thought, *Someday he may come courting when Sarah is old enough.*

Abigail Stevens greeted Jacob warmly, wishing him a happy birthday. She turned to Andrew and smiled at him brightly, saying, "I'm so glad you're home safe, Andrew. I worried about you."

Jacob had taken this in, and as the two stood there talking, he was mildly concerned at the way Abigail seemed to light up in Andrew's presence. He had once moved closer to her, and the two of them had stayed close together ever since.

Outside the cabin Hawk was listening as George Stevens spoke of the events that had transpired since he had left the settlement to go to the war. Stevens seemed to have grown somewhat older, but he was healthy and wiry, his tall figure leaning up against the side of the cabin as he spoke slowly. There was a solidity about the man, and the gray at his temples added a touch of dignity to him.

"This fellow, Richard Henderson—he's that North Carolina man who ran the Transylvania Company. Daniel Boone seems to think a lot of him."

"Boone's in this business, is he, George?" Hawk inquired. He was sitting down on the porch, his legs crossed, his eyes half closed against the sunshine that filtered down on his face, casting his features into shadow.

"Yes, him and Henderson are trying to strike a new deal with the Cherokee for the purchase of western Can-tuc-kee, now known as Kentucky."

"You think it will work?" Hawk asked, his eyes opening with surprise.

"I think so," Stevens shrugged.

Sequatchie was standing upright, leaning against one of the supports of the lean-to roof that shaded the porch. "It might if the older chiefs prevail."

"You think they'll go along, Sequatchie?" Stevens asked eagerly. He valued the Cherokee's opinion, for no one knew the Cherokee as well as Sequatchie.

"It all depends on what the younger braves will do." A cloud passed across the dark face of Sequatchie, and he shrugged almost imperceptibly. "As the white men come farther and farther into the Indian lands, there's bound to be trouble. Dragging Canoe wants a war almost as much as he wants anything."

"I wonder why he's so different from his father?" Hawk pondered. "He's not at all like Attacullaculla."

"No, he is like his grandfather. He was a warrior, too, and a fiery one," Sequatchie said. "In a way," he said after a pause, "it may depend on how much hold the gospel has taken."

The men talked quietly, enjoying the peace and the sound of the women and children inside the cabin. The smells of cooking were drifting out, and there was a harmony and a sense of leisure that allowed the men to momentarily set aside their worries over marauding Indians and the problems of survival.

Finally Hawk said, "Maybe we ought to pay them for this land that we're on. Sooner or later the lease runs out, and then it'll have to be done anyway." He leaned back and stared thoughtfully across the yard and noted that Jacob and Abigail were walking down the path that led to the creek. It caught his interest, and he lost track of the conversation between Sequatchie and Stevens as his eyes followed them. *Something going on there,* he mused. *They're mighty young, but people marry younger out here.*

———————

Jacob had tired of the conversation among the men and had stepped inside to ask Abigail to go for a walk. The two young people had left the cabin and had taken the path leading down to the creek. When they reached the bank, Jacob touched the water with the toe of his boot. "It's going to be cold soon," he murmured. "This will be frozen over. I knew a fellow once," he said, "that came from up north. He said they cut holes in the ice and caught fish through them."

"It would be pretty uncomfortable, wouldn't it?"

"I suppose so, but if a fellow wants to catch fish, he has to do it any way he can."

Abigail was wearing a thin sweater she had knitted the previous winter. It was too small for her now and not warm enough, and she shivered. "I'll be glad when spring comes," she murmured. "I love the spring best of all with everything budding and the earth coming to life again."

Jacob listened as Abigail spoke of the spring. He had planned this moment for some time, but now that it had come he was hesitant. Still, he began resolutely and caught Abigail off guard when he suddenly reached out and touched her. She was facing the creek, and when he swung her around and looked, he saw surprise in her eyes.

"Why, Jacob, what is it?"

Jacob said quickly, "I think maybe you know what it is. You surely know by this time how I care for you, Abby." Then, as if he were afraid to slow down his speech, he stumbled over the next words. "I . . . I want us to get married, as soon as we can."

Abigail was shocked. She had expected that someday Jacob would ask her to marry him, but she had thought it would be far off in some distant time. Now as they stood there under the pale November sky with the rustling of dry branches overhead and the dead leaves underfoot, she could not answer for a moment. Like all young girls, she had thought about the day when some man would ask her to be his wife, but now that the moment had come she found herself reluctant to speak her heart. In truth she did not know her heart, and as Jacob continued to speak, telling her what a great life they could have, she finally knew that she had to say something.

"Why, Jacob, that's the greatest honor any man can give to a woman, and I am fond of you. But—"

"But what?" Jacob said, his tone somewhat strident. He saw doubt in her eyes and grew somewhat panicky. "What's the matter? Don't you care for me at all, Abby?"

"Why, I'm very fond of you, but it's caught me by surprise. I . . . I need some time to think it over."

Jacob suddenly reached out and pulled Abigail into his embrace. She did not resist, and as he bent his head and let his lips fall on hers, the pressure of her firm young body against his stirred him. Her lips were soft and yielding, and there was a sweet fragrance about her that seemed to go to his head, causing him almost to be dizzy. She was all that he thought a woman should be, pretty and yielding, soft and warm, and he held her tightly, his lips pressing harder against hers.

As for Abigail, she gave herself to his embrace with a willingness that surprised her. She felt the pressure of his arms drawing her ever closer and added her own pressure to the kiss, letting her hands go behind his neck. She held on to him for a moment, then pulled back, somewhat embarrassed by the stirring of her heart.

"I have to have time, Jacob."

"That's all right. I can wait."

The two walked along the creek, saying little but holding hands. Jacob's hand was strong and held hers tightly, and finally, when they turned to go back, she was thinking, *He'd probably make a very good husband—and he's so handsome.* She squeezed his hand and Jacob once again leaned forward. She kissed him lightly, then put her hand on his chest. "That's enough now. This might get to be a habit."

Jacob smiled at her, saying, "I hope so. That's what I had in mind."

The two made their way back to the cabin, and a warmth came to Jacob, and a happiness, and he felt that after all these lonely years his life was now complete. *Eventually,* he thought, *she'll say yes, then everything will be all right. . . .*

Plans for the Future

Twenty-Eight

*D*aniel Boone looked over the small group that had gathered in January 1775 to listen to what Richard Henderson of the Transylvania Company had to say. He had arrived with Henderson at Sycamore Shoals to meet with the Cherokee, and now as he looked over the Watauga Court, he said, "We've already met, Mr. Henderson and I, with Attaccullaculla."

"That's right," Henderson said quickly. He was a wiry man of about forty-five with alert gray eyes and a pleasing smile. Now he waved his hand, saying, "We went to the Overhill towns and brought the Little Carpenter and his wife to North Carolina to see the trade goods that would be part of the purchase of the land."

"How did the Little Carpenter react?" Sequatchie asked.

"Oh, very well!" Henderson smiled at the Cherokee. "He's asked the leaders of the tribes to meet there to work out the details of the sale." He shifted uneasily for a moment and cleared his throat, then asked, "I wonder if it would be possible for you gentlemen to encourage the settlers in this area to feed all the people who'll be gathering?"

John Carter answered for the group. Stroking his chin thoughtfully, he said, "Well, it's short notice, but we had a good crop last year. I think we could work out something."

John Carter, Jacob Brown, and James Robertson were sitting together, and it was Robertson who said after a time, "Mr. Henderson, do you think it would be possible to arrange to buy our land here around Watauga? Since the chiefs are here and they're in a good mood, I'd like to get this thing settled."

Henderson thought for a moment, then nodded. "I don't see

why not. I'll tell you what. Let us make the rest of the arrangements, and then after that's done, you can make your deal separately. How will this be?"

"It sounds good," Carter said. "Well, we need to talk about the price to be paid."

"I've got to go on home," Hawk said. "Whatever you decide will be fine by me."

Hawk left the meeting and swung onto his horse, then rode at a fast gallop toward his own place. When he reached home, he stepped inside and Elizabeth greeted him with a kiss.

"I hope you feel like cooking," he said.

"Why, don't I always?"

"Well, it's going to be a little bit more than that. Mr. Henderson wants all of us to pitch in to feed the Indians as they come to talk about selling us their lands."

"Oh, we can do that," Elizabeth said cheerfully.

"I hope it goes through. I'd like to buy this place. I don't feel quite settled just leasing it. It's like someday somebody could say, 'Okay, it's time for you to move on.'"

"Do you think it's possible to buy from the Indians? Will they sell?"

"I think so."

The two sat down before the fire talking and watching Hannah and Joshua play, and the children came in. Finally, after Hawk explained what was going to happen, he said, "I've got to go tell the Stevenses."

"Why, I'll do that, Pa," Jacob said at once.

Hawk grinned and winked at Elizabeth. "Oh, I wouldn't want to put you to all that trouble, Jacob."

Jacob flushed, for he knew his leg was being pulled. "Come on, Pa. Let a fellow alone, will you?"

"All right. You go pass the word along to George and Deborah— and give Abigail a kiss for me, will you?"

Sarah giggled, and Jacob plunged out the door, grabbing his coat from a peg and slipping into it as he stepped off the porch.

When he reached the Stevenses' house, Jacob found George and Deborah inside, and after he spoke to Abigail, he turned and gave them the news. George Stevens listened intently and nodded. "That's good sense. We've got to keep the Indians happy, though it will be a lot of work for you, Deborah, and the other ladies."

"I wouldn't mind, especially if we could buy this place, George."

Abigail said, "Sit down and I'll fix you something to eat, Jacob."

Willing enough to spend any time with Abigail, Jacob sat down and watched as she prepared some johnny cakes. When they were cooked, she sat down with him and watched him eat. Afterward, he glanced over at Abigail's mother and said abruptly, "Did that old cat of yours ever have kittens?"

"Yes, they're out in the barn. Would you like to see them?"

"Sure."

He and Abigail got up, put on their coats, and made their way out to the barn. Abigail led him to a corner where the gray tabby was lying sleepily with seven kittens that were crawling all over her.

"Aren't they precious?" Abigail crooned, picking up one and holding it to her cheek.

"*You* are," Jacob grinned. "I don't think about cats being too precious. They're just cats to me."

"You have no romance in your soul, Jacob. They are precious."

Jacob was content to watch Abigail as she picked up each kitten and spoke to it. Her smooth complexion was reddened by the cold, which made her that much more attractive. Finally, when every kitten had been addressed, she turned to him and said, "We'd better go back."

"Abby," Jacob said and reached out to put his hand on her shoulder. "I don't want to rush you, and I think I've been patient, but have you made up your mind about us?"

Abigail had known that Jacob had come for this purpose. Ever since he had asked her to marry him, she had thought of little else, and now she took a deep breath. Looking up at him she said, "Jacob, I'll be honored to be your wife."

At once Jacob reached out and hugged her, kissed her thoroughly, and said, "I'd like to whoop like a wild Indian."

"Don't do that," Abigail laughed. She was pleased that he was happy and then said quickly, "You'll have to ask Pa."

"Does he know about us?"

"I think he's got a pretty good idea, although I haven't said anything to him. I talked to Mama, though, and she's probably told him by now."

"Well, if he says no, I'll have to steal you away," Jacob grinned.

"He won't say no," Abigail said confidently as she took his arm. She was happy now that it was settled, and the two made their way into the cabin, where Jacob at once spoke of his desire to marry Abigail, then stood there waiting somewhat nervously.

"I'm afraid you didn't catch us off guard, Jacob," George said. He put his hand out and said, "I'd be glad to have you as a son-in-law. You're getting a good girl."

Deborah came over and reached up to Jacob and gave him a kiss on the cheek. "You'll be a good husband, and you two will be very happy."

Soon Jacob left, and as Abigail watched him, she suddenly was confounded to find herself, after the thing was done, unsettled and uncertain. It was not the first time she had felt like this, but she had thought it had passed away. Now she thought, *I bet all young women feel a little shaky and nervous after they have taken a man.* She went inside and began talking with her mother about her plans—what would be done, the dress to be made—and a peace came to her again, and she was happy.

The buying of the land and the coming of the Cherokee elders occupied everyone in Watauga in one way or another. Everyone wondered what would happen, and Sequatchie grew weary of telling the settlers that he could not speak for the rest of this tribe. Finally he left to get away from some of the pressure. He didn't go far, but he sought the seclusion of the wilds, as he often did.

At the end of the week, a large group of the settlers had gathered at Watauga to make plans for the upcoming events. The Spencers greeted the Stevenses. "Welcome to the family, daughter," Hawk said as Abigail entered with Jacob. He took her hand and patted it and smiled warmly. "Our family is getting so big I'm going to have to make different plans, but if Jacob doesn't treat you right, you just let me know."

Abigail had always admired Hawk, and now as Elizabeth came up and gave her a kiss, again she felt warm and secure.

"Come along," Elizabeth said. "You and your mother and I are going to have to talk about this wedding. We're going to make it the best anyone ever had in Watauga."

Andrew had been standing off to one side saying little, but now he came to Abigail and said quietly, "Congratulations, Abby."

"Why, thank you, Andrew." She tried to think of something else to say, but someone caught her attention and she turned away, missing the hurt and disappointment that showed on his face.

Sarah had come, along with Amanda, and Sarah whispered, "Come on. We want to hear all about it."

Amanda followed the two as they went into Sarah's room. She forced herself to appear interested, but her heart was heavy. She had known for some time that she was in love with Jacob Spencer, but it was useless to think of such things now. She watched the beautiful young girl before her and thought, *I'm so plain and homely. Even if Jacob weren't in love with Abigail, he would never look at someone like me.*

"Come on, Abby," Sarah was saying. "Tell us all about it. When did he ask you? What did he say?"

Abigail laughed and went into the details of the courtship. Finally Sarah said, "You know, I always thought you and Andrew might fall in love, and then we'd be sisters."

Abigail stared at the younger girl with surprise and then she smiled. "We'll be sisters anyway." She reached out and took Amanda's hand and said, "And you, too. We'll all three be sisters together."

"Yes," Sarah smiled. "Won't that be good, Amanda?"

"Yes, it will. I never had a sister before, and now I have two of them."

Finally, after a great deal of talk and gossip and cooking on the part of the women, Paul Anderson rose to speak to the group. As soon as they were all gathered, he grinned and said, "I suppose all of you have learned by now that when three or more people get together I'm going to preach a sermon." He waited until the laughter had died down and then said, "I think it's important at times like this that we stop and see where we are. All of us are making plans for buying land. Some of you are thinking of building a bigger house for the children that are going to be born. I want to preach to you about making plans, but first I would like for Rhoda to sing."

Rhoda did not move, but from where she stood, she suddenly began to sing softly the folk hymn *What Wondrous Love Is This?*— a favorite of the Appalachian frontier. She sang the first verse in

Cherokee, which brought a smile to Sequatchie's lips, and she sang the second verse in English. As the words rang out over the crowd, reminding them all of what Christ endured so that all might be forgiven, there was a sweetness and purity, not only in her voice, but in her eyes, as she stood there singing:

> What wondrous love is this, O my soul, O my soul,
> What wondrous love is this, O my soul!
> What wondrous love is this that caused the Lord of life
> To lay aside His crown for my soul, for my soul,
> To lay aside His crown for my soul?

The sound of her voice rose over the clearing, and everyone stood transfixed, listening to the minister's wife. Elizabeth, especially, was pleased. *She's come so far,* she thought, *and now I know at last she's found her place.*

After Rhoda sang, the congregation sang several songs together, and then Paul began to preach. His sermon was very simple. He quoted the scripture "Prepare to meet thy God" from the Old Testament. Then he continued to speak of making preparations. He first of all repeated what he had said about how many worldly preparations there were to be made, then he paused as he looked over the group. Finally he said, "But I want to remind myself and to remind you, friends, that there are other preparations, too, that are far more important than buying land or building a house. We must prepare for the day when we will stand before God. One day you will be there as I will be there, and we will look into the face of God, and He will look into our hearts, and only one question is important: What did I do with the Lord Jesus Christ?"

The sermon was simple but powerful, and finally, when Anderson said, "If there is one here who is not prepared to meet God, who does not have Jesus Christ and His precious blood covering his sins, now is the time to do that. Is there anyone who wants to meet the Lord and be converted?"

A sound of sobbing came, and Iris looked around with shock to see her daughter go forward. Tears filled her eyes as she saw Amanda greeted by Rhoda and Reverend Anderson. The two wrapped their arms around the young girl, and Iris could see Amanda weeping as the two prayed for her.

Abigail was happy to see Amanda go forward, then she whispered, "Look, Philip's going, too, Sarah!"

Sure enough, when Sarah turned to look, she saw Philip Baxter go forward, and she was happy. She whispered back, "Isn't that wonderful?"

Abigail suddenly turned and watched Jacob. The two of them had not said much about God. They were both always at every service, of course, but as she watched Jacob's face, she saw it reflect some sort of a struggle. *Why, he's under conviction!* Abigail thought. She began to pray for him, but then she saw a hardness come to his face. He dropped his head, bit his lip, and stood there staring at the ground.

As the others began to go forward to wish Amanda and Philip well, she saw Jacob turn and walk away quickly, as if fleeing the place. A troubling thought sent a chill through Abigail. This man would be her husband, and yet he was not sharing in the joy of seeing others come to Christ. *What if I've made a mistake?* she wondered. She had no time to think on it, for she was caught up in the celebration, but the thought would not go away. The happiness that had been hers when she had risen that morning now fled, and she felt alone and disturbed.

The Transylvania Purchase

Twenty-Nine

$\mathcal{R}$ ichard Henderson had moved very quickly after Lord Dunmore's War. Late in January 1775, he loaded six large wagons with trading goods and took them to Sycamore Shoals, where he stored them in specially built huts. The settlers and the Cherokee began to gather during the middle of March. After several days of festivities and talks, the underlying business of the meeting began to surface.

It was Henderson's determined proposal to buy outright the whole Cumberland Valley and the southern half of the Kentucky Valley. He offered to pay ten thousand pounds of English money, two in cash and eight in merchandise. Not everyone approved of Henderson's plan, for the land had already been sold by the Iroquois in 1768 and had been claimed by Virginia. Many said it would be foolish to pay the Cherokee for land already relinquished by the Iroquois. Still, the leaders in the area knew that it was the Cherokee who would have to be pacified.

During the preliminary period, Hawk and Sequatchie watched carefully so that there would be plenty of food for the gathering. The settlers contributed generously, and as the two of them stood talking on the day of the most important meetings, Hawk said, "I'm glad it has gone so well." He looked around at the food that had been prepared and at the women who were working so cheerfully, then added abruptly, "I'm glad Crabtree didn't show up."

"Probably miles away," Sequatchie shrugged, "like Zeke Taylor."

"I'm not so sure of that," Hawk replied reluctantly. He looked over at the Indians who were watching the preparations carefully and shook his head. "I just want this meeting to go well—no one to get hurt."

"I don't think they're in this part of the country. Boone has been looking for them, and he says he hasn't even heard anything about them."

"I wish Boone were here," Hawk remarked. "But he's working on that trail to Kentucky. He's so sure that this is going to work he wants a road ready."

"I believe he likes Kentucky best."

"I think so. If this land deal goes through, I think he'll settle there." Once again he looked around at the crowd of settlers and Cherokee and shook his head. "We'd better pray that this thing goes all right."

All of the great Cherokee chiefs had come to Sycamore Shoals, including Oconostota, the Little Carpenter, and others. Most of them did not wear their native dress but were wearing matching coats with ruffled shirts above their leggins. Several of them wore British medals, or more than one. Dangling from their earlobes were bangles, while around their necks gadgets of metal or beads hung low. It was a crowded gathering, for over twelve hundred braves, marked with colorful tattoos, some with slashes on their cheeks or forehead, crowded as closely as they could. Many of them, like Dragging Canoe, the son of Attacullaculla, were pockmarked from the ravages of smallpox.

The settlers poured in from everywhere so that over six hundred Wataugans gathered for the meetings. Finally Henderson and his associates brought out the merchandise that had been carried by wagon over the mountains, but it was not yet time.

Festivities and games had to take place first with much feasting, but finally the heart of the matter was reached. The Little Carpenter eloquently spoke for the merger. At the age of eighty he still had power in his voice and in his eyes and he swayed many.

As soon as he finished, Chief Oconostota vehemently spoke against the sale, but it was Dragging Canoe who was by far the most hostile of all the Indians. He began by depicting the ancient glories of the Cherokee before the advent of the white men. Finally he cried out, "Where are all our grandfathers, the Delaware?" A murmuring went around the many braves, and he cried dramatically, "Will all of these goods satisfy the white men? No! They will simply want more, and sooner or later they will have all of the land that is ours!"

Finally the Indians demanded time to speak among themselves, and it was at this meeting that Attacullaculla persuaded the older chiefs to comply with the sale.

Dragging Canoe stood up abruptly. "I will never yield another foot of our land to the white men!" He turned and moved his hand to encompass the land, and his voice was loud and clear as he said, "A dark cloud will hang over this land. It will be a dark and bloody ground for those who come to settle in it!" Whirling, he turned and stalked away, leaving the council.

Hawk said quietly to Sequatchie, "We will hear from him again. It will be bloody indeed, my friend."

Sequatchie shook his head sadly. "He is a man of blood, and your people will pay the price for coming over the mountains."

Finally the sale was done, and on March 19, Elizabeth and Hawk made their way back toward their homestead. They had come in a wagon, bringing as much food as they could spare, and now as Hawk slouched, holding the lines easily, he was thinking over what had taken place.

"Is the land really ours, Hawk?"

Turning to Elizabeth, he nodded. "Yes. It's ours." He smiled at her then, put his arm around her, and drew her close. "You were worried about it, weren't you?"

"Yes, I was."

They rode on for a while saying nothing. The children were in the back of the wagon, exhausted from their long days, while Jacob had ridden home with Abigail, and Andrew had disappeared.

Elizabeth suddenly turned and put her hand on Hawk's arm. "It's all come true—Patrick's dreams." When he looked at her with a slightly puzzled expression, she said, "It was back over the mountains that he first told me he wanted a place for me and for his children. He's not here now, but the place is here, and Patrick's dreams are coming true."

"That's good," Hawk murmured. He held her close then, but he was thinking not of Patrick MacNeal's dreams but of the bitter words of Dragging Canoe: *It will be a dark and bloody ground.*

PART IV

The Young Lions Roar

July 1775 – July 1777

The young lions roar after their prey,
and seek their meat from God.

Psalm 104:21

Revolutionary Fervor

Thirty

*E*ver since the end of the French and Indian War, trouble had been brewing between England, and her colonies spread out along the eastern seaboard of America. These colonies were vastly different in many ways. In effect, the southern planter on a tobacco farm in Georgia had very little in common with a merchant in Boston. They were, however, united in one respect—they were all Englishmen who had become accustomed to having a firm say in their own destiny. Somewhere between the time that Queen Elizabeth I drew her last breath as Queen of England, and King James I drew his first as Sovereign of England, the British people lost their taste for absolute monarchy. And so it was in America. As England pressured the Colonies to pay what they considered their fair share of the French and Indian War, more and more of these transported Englishmen felt they were being turned into a community of serfs and slaves.

Firebrands such as Samuel Adams began to proclaim the injustices that England manifested toward the Colonies and to agitate for a united country separate from England. England, however, was far away and the Hanoverian king, George III, was determined to rule under divine law. He felt that God had appointed him to draw the kingdom of England together, and any evidence of a revolution was enough to touch off his rather placid temper.

In effect, most of the colonists understood little of the political and philosophical struggles that moved the English nobility and the leaders of the Colonies. Years after the beginning of the struggle, one of the men who took part in the first battle at Concord, Captain Preston, was asked, "Did you take up arms against intolerable oppressions?"

"Oppressions?" the old man replied. "I didn't feel them."

"But certainly you were oppressed by the Stamp Act."

"I never saw one of those stamps. I certainly never paid a penny for one of them."

"What about the tea tax?"

"Never drank a drop of the stuff. The boys threw it all overboard."

"Then I suppose you have been reading John Locke, about the eternal principles of liberty?"

"Never heard of him. We read only the Bible, the Catechism, Watts' Psalms, and hymns, and the almanac."

Rather perplexed, the interviewer asked, "Sir, what was the matter? What did you mean in going to the fight?"

Captain Preston replied, "Young man, what we meant in going for those Redcoats was this: We always had governed ourselves and we always meant to. England didn't mean that we should." Captain Preston was typical of the men who touched off the American Revolution. They had always had some hand in governing themselves—and they always meant to.

The English Parliament and King George could not seem to grasp this spirit of autonomy. Even Governor Gage of Massachusetts, who had spent many years in America, should have known that America would rather fight than submit. He did feel apprehensive enough in early April of 1775 to send out a spy to feel out the temper of the colonists. John Howe made a long ride and found that the temper, indeed, was high. Stopping on his way back, Howe records in his diary how he stopped at a small house beside the road and spoke with an elderly man, who was cleaning a gun. "I asked him what he was going to kill. As he was so old, I should not think he could take sight in any game. He said there was a flock of Redcoats at Boston that he expected to be coming along soon. He also said he intended to hit one of them, and he expected they would be very good marks." Rather shocked at the old man's fiery words and obvious intentions, Howe asked if there were any Tories in the neighborhood.

"Aye," the old man replied. "There's one Tory house, and I wished it were in flames." Then turning to his wife, the man said, "Old woman, put in the bullet pouch a handful of buckshot, as I understand the English like an assortment of plums!"

Gage did not heed the warning of his own spy. He decided to destroy the patriots' munitions at Concord, and on one night in mid-April he dispatched a strong detail under Major John Pitcairn to perform this duty.

The patriots, however, were watching every move Gage made. That night Paul Revere and William Dawes galloped along the countryside, stopping only to inform their fellow patriots and minutemen that the British were coming, and by the break of day, minutemen were on the march as far away as New Hampshire and Connecticut.

By the time Major Pitcairn had marched his Redcoats all night and reached Lexington, he found a grim band of men lined up on the village common parallel to his line of advance. They were armed, and when the British halted, the major cried out loudly, "Disperse, ye rebels! Disperse!"

No one knows who fired the first shot of the American Revolution, but it was fired, and when the action was over and the minutemen had faded away, eight men lay dead on the green.

The British advanced and discovered that the munitions had been moved. After they were stopped at Concord by a body of determined patriots, they started back on the long march toward Boston. It was a long march indeed for the English. The Americans gathered now and stung them like wasps. From behind trees and stone walls they sent shot after shot into the orderly ranks of the British grenadiers. The march became a nightmare, and only the arrival of a relief party stopped the American forces from completely obliterating Major Pitcairn's forces.

All the news of the revolution filtered slowly to the inhabitants of Watauga. They were cut off by trackless forest over which there was no regular mail, and only bit by bit were they able to piece together what was happening. Some of them had even ceased to consider themselves as Englishmen and were doubtful of their true identity.

———

Hawk paused and wiped the sweat from his brow and grinned over at Andrew and Jacob, who were caulking the sides of the new addition to the cabin. "Now that the babies are getting older," he said, "I reckon we're going to have to keep on building."

Andrew grinned abruptly and took a deep breath, causing the heavy muscles of his chest and arms to stir. "How many more young'uns you intending to have, Pa? Seems to me like you're trying to repopulate the earth."

Hawk merely smiled and shook his head. "That's up to you, Andrew—and to you, Jacob. I'm kind of looking forward to being a grandpa."

Jacob picked up a gourd and filled it with spring water in a wooden bucket, took three swallows, then threw the rest of the water out. He, too, managed to smile and said, "I'll keep that in mind, Pa."

The three worked steadily for thirty minutes, then Hawk said, "I reckon that's enough for a while."

"It's enough for me," Jacob said, looking down at his hands. They were tougher now, of course, than they were when he had come to Watauga. He thought about how soft he had been and was suddenly proud of his strength and endurance.

Andrew had been quiet all morning, but now he suddenly said, "Pa, what do you think we should do? About the Redcoats, I mean? Are we going to get in this war?"

Hawk shook his head and a weariness passed across his face. "I never thought it would come to this," he admitted. "I think the colonists are right in wanting to govern themselves. We know how they feel out here in Watauga. I guess we've gotten so used to doing for ourselves that we want everybody to have that privilege." He picked up a straw from the ground, put it in his mouth, and chewed it slowly. "Better be careful, though. Samuel Adams may be biting off more than he can chew."

"Oh, Pa, that ain't so!" Andrew protested. "We can whip them British. All I want is a chance, and, Pa, you heard about how down in Fincastle County in Virginia they already formed their own committee of safety. And the North-of-Holston settlements in Virginia, but they're way off, just like we are."

Indeed Hawk was aware of the Fincastle movement. Evan Shelby had been made chairman of this "Pendleton District," named after a Virginia patriot and statesman, Edward Pendleton. He had owned a large tract of land in the vicinity of the Long Island of the Holston River, and now it appeared that this district was aligned with Virginia in the revolution.

"What about you, Jacob?" Andrew asked abruptly. "Don't you

want to get off a shot or two at them Redcoats?"

"I don't see that the fighting will come out here in these hills."

"Well, that could change fast, Jacob," Hawk replied quickly. "The British will probably try to get the Cherokee and the other Indians to fight with them, and that will mean they'll be coming against us here on the frontier."

"Why, the Little Carpenter and Sequatchie will stop that, Pa!" Andrew protested.

"I don't think they'll be able to this time, son. Dragging Canoe and Akando are swaying more and more of the Cherokee to their side. You've got to remember, too, that the Cherokee have come to rely on British goods. They may have to go along with them to keep up their good relations. Also, you know the British have promised to leave their lands alone."

"Well, I can understand that," Jacob said. "I think this war's foolish."

"The British wouldn't keep their word," Hawk said, shaking his head. "They'll eventually want the land. They don't understand the Indians nearly as well as most of us do. Sequatchie knows that and so does Attacullaculla, but they may not have a choice."

"Well, what will we do, Pa?" Andrew demanded.

"Who knows?" Hawk said simply. "These are awful times we are living in."

At that moment Elizabeth and Sarah appeared with a pitcher of cider that Elizabeth had gotten from the root cellar.

"It's cool," she said, smiling, as Sarah held out the pewter cups and poured them full.

As the men drank, Elizabeth looked with pride at her husband and her two tall sons. She never thought of Jacob in any other way than as another son, and now as they drank thirstily, she thought, *How much they've become like Hawk, and they've become men of the mountains. Even Jacob.*

Sarah handed Jacob his cup and grinned up at him. "You ought not to be wasting time building a room here, Jacob. You need to be building a house for you and Abigail."

"Guess I need to be doing something about that, Sarah." Andrew frowned but said nothing, and Jacob added, "Just haven't settled on a date yet."

"I don't see what you're waiting for." Sarah, as usual, had no patience to spare. Her red hair caught the gleam of the sunlight, and as she cocked her head to one side, the light brought out the few freckles that speckled her nose. "What *are* you waiting for?"

Jacob, aware that the others were watching him rather curiously, felt uncomfortable. "Why, there's plenty of time," he said.

"I thought you were in a hurry to get married," Sarah prodded.

Elizabeth, seeing Jacob's discomfort, said, "Sarah, stop your meddling!"

Sarah's eyes gleamed with fun. "When Brother Paul preached about spiritual gifts last Sunday, I decided what mine was."

Hawk knew the element of humor in this stepdaughter of his. "What is your gift, Sarah?"

"My spiritual gift is *meddling*."

The others could not help laughing, but as they stood there enjoying one another's company, for the moment Hawk thought, even as Sarah had, *I wonder what he's waiting for.* He studied Jacob's face a moment, and a surge of gratitude for all that God had done touched him. *It's been a miracle,* he thought, *that Jacob has learned to forgive me—at least partly—and I'm thankful for it, but something's wrong with Jacob. He says he loves Abigail, but yet one or the other of them is hanging back. I hope it's not trouble.*

Later that afternoon Jacob cleaned up after work and climbed on his horse.

"Where you going, Jacob?" Sarah yelled after him.

"None of your business."

"Tell Abigail I'd like to see her and be sure to give her a kiss!" the irrepressible girl yelled.

Jacob merely tried to ignore her, but the peals of her laughter followed him.

As he made his way along the familiar trail, his thoughts were troubled. He had been stirred by the prodding that Sarah had given him earlier, and he had seen the pointed curiosity in his parents' expressions. By the time he reached the Stevenses' place, he was determined to get an answer from Abigail.

As he approached, he found her standing beside the small corral where the sheep were kept. Riding up and getting off the horse, he tied the animal, then walked right over to her.

"Hello, Abigail," he said and reached over and kissed her cheek.

"I didn't expect to see you today, Jacob. I thought you'd be working on the addition."

"We did. All day. It's going to be finished pretty soon."

Abigail was wearing a dark red quilted skirt and a white blouse that laced up the front and was sprinkled with dainty flowers. As usual, Jacob admired the fresh glow of her cheeks and the sparkle of her eyes. Impulsively he said, "I think Christmas would be a good time to get married, don't you?"

"Why . . . I don't know, Jacob. I'm not so sure."

"Why not? What's wrong? I'm beginning to think you don't want to marry me, you've put it off so many times."

Absently Abigail patted his arm and shook her head, but she did pause. Finally she said, "I don't know. I guess I just think I need to help my parents since I'm the only one at home."

"Why, you'll have to leave as soon as we're married."

"I know." Abigail, indeed, was troubled, and it showed on her face. She had a sunny disposition, but now she was serious, and in an absentminded way, she bit her lower lip, a sure sign that she was agitated.

She took a deep breath and reached up and touched his cheek gently. "I'll decide soon. I promise." She reached up, pulled his head down, kissed him, then took his arm and said, "Come on. You can take supper with us tonight."

Jacob felt that somehow he had been defeated again. He had come to get a specific date, but there was something in Abigail, a reluctance to be pinned down, that he could not understand. He did not know a great deal about young women, and as he enjoyed the fellowship of the Stevenses that evening, his happiness was not complete, and he could neither explain it nor speak of it to anyone else.

Decisions

Thirty-One

The low-ceilinged room used by the settlers of Watauga for meetings was crowded to the walls. A rank smell of tobacco smoke hung in the air, but more of the men were prone to chew than to smoke. Hawk, who did neither, found the stench distasteful and carefully avoided, as far as possible, the amber stains that had splashed on the puncheon floors. He had come to this meeting in September of 1775 with apprehension, for he well knew that the decisions made in this relatively small group would alter the destiny of all who lived in Watauga and even farther westward.

John Carter, a tall, heavyset man, had been speaking for twenty minutes. He was a forceful man with a visionary gleam in his eye, and now he concluded his speech in ringing tones.

"We've talked about which way we should go in this war that's been forced upon us. I've listened as some of you have spoken of our loyalty to King George and the British Empire. No man has been more loyal than I have in this area, but times change. Nations take new pathways, and we must not destroy ourselves by hanging on to old ideals. You can't put new wine in old wineskins as the Scripture says. Therefore, I see we have no choice." He paused here and looked around the room. Every man's eyes were fixed upon him, some with apprehension, some with anger, but most, he saw, were following his line of reasoning.

"If we join with the king's forces, where will that leave us? If the British win, they have already informed us that they will force us to give our lands back to the Indians, so we will be paupers."

"We don't know that," a tall, hulking settler said. He clawed at his reddish whiskers and shook his head. "I've always been a king's man. I'll not fire a shot against my sovereign's forces."

"Then, Charles, that puts you in a precarious position," Carter said quietly. "You and I have been friends and neighbors, but as the Scripture says, 'Choose you this day whom ye will serve.' This land is merely a colony to England, but to me and to others it is a new nation. If England had been fair and allowed us to have a voice in Parliament, sending our own representatives, I would fight to the death for her cause. But she has refused to heed our reasonable requests, and now we have no other choice."

Hawk sat back while Carter listened patiently to those who were not ready for revolution. *He handled it well*, Hawk thought. *I couldn't do anything like that, but he's not going to satisfy everybody.* The meeting went on and on, and finally, after many hours of argument, Carter skillfully had persuaded most of the men who called themselves Tories to abandon their loyalty to the Crown and throw their lot in with the colonists.

"We are agreed, then," Carter nodded. "And I propose that this day we form a committee of safety, and I also propose that we name it the Washington District after the new commander in chief of the colonial forces."

"I second the motion," William Bean said, "and I also propose that John Carter be appointed chairman—and colonel of the militia."

Excitement was high around the room now, and Carter was elected almost unanimously. The other members of the committee included William Bean, Charles and James Robertson, John Sevier, Jacob Brown, George Russell, John Jones, Robert Lucas, Jacob Womack, James Smith, and Zachariah Isbell.

It was Isbell, a short, heavyset man with piercing black eyes, who asked, "What will we do with the Watauga Court, Carter?"

"We will keep it in place. It will continue to function," John Carter said instantly. "No British governing body will take over as has happened in the Colonies."

Hawk listened as the preparations were made, and he knew a feeling of gladness that the Wataugans had decided to go with the colonists. The idea of a new nation where a man could be free and have a say in his government excited him. He might have felt differently if he had been reared in England, but all he had ever known was America. As he thought about the future, however, a sense of despondency came over him, for he knew what brutality could come if the Cherokee decided to go on the warpath. The thought troubled him, and he rose and left the meeting, saying nothing to anyone. He knew he had to speak to Sequatchie.

All the way back to his homestead he thought of the burden that would lie upon his friend. "It'll be hard on him," he murmured. "He has Cherokee brothers, and yet I'm his brother, too. I'd not want to be in his place and have to make this decision."

The sun was nearly down when he pulled up at the small hut that Sequatchie had constructed for himself. Slipping off the horse, he called out, and Sequatchie stepped around the corner and nodded his greeting. "Well," Hawk said, "it's over." He spoke quickly, informing Sequatchie of the decision made at the meeting, and finally he stopped. The air was quiet, and already he could see a lamp glowing in his own house in the window, but no one was stirring in the yard. He looked over to the tall Cherokee and said, "I hope this won't come between you and me."

Sequatchie's face was grim, but he managed a smile. "We are brothers and always will be, but I will not raise my hand against the Cherokee. They are my own flesh and blood."

Hawk sensed the tension in Sequatchie, and impulsively he said, "We can only pray, my brother. Let us do so now."

Instantly Sequatchie nodded, and a warm light came into his eyes. "Yes, God is the only one," he said, "who can see us through all the coming days."

The two men stood and prayed together in the growing darkness as the sun dropped behind the low-lying hills. They clasped hands, and each seemed to draw strength from the other. When Hawk looked up after they were finished, he saw tears in his friend's eyes, and with an impulse he could not control, he embraced Sequatchie, held him tightly, and said, "God will watch over us, my brother."

———

Bright yellow pumpkins dotted the hills in the Watauga area as October came on. The other crops might fail, but it seemed as though pumpkins never did. And as Deborah Stevens moved around the kitchen preparing to use some of the succulent orange delight, Abigail stayed close beside her, watching every move she made.

"What are you going to make out of this pumpkin, Mama?"

"I think I'll bake a pumpkin pudding."

"Teach me how to make that, please. I can't seem to master some of your recipes yet," Abigail stated. "I'll never be as good a cook as you are, though."

"I wouldn't say that. It's all a matter of practice." The older woman moved toward the table, where she began mixing the ingredients.

Abigail watched as her mother cracked four eggs into a bowl and beat them with a wooden spoon. Then she dumped some pumpkin in and mixed that also.

"I never know how much of anything to use, and you don't ever measure it out," Abigail complained as she watched her mother add cinnamon, ginger, and several other spices, and then pour in some molasses and milk. "How do you know how much to put in there?"

"I don't know, Abby. I just do it."

"Well, that's not much help."

"You grease the pot with butter," Mrs. Stevens said, smiling at her daughter. "It will all come to you when you've done it as long as I have."

Abigail greased the cast-iron pot and poured the mixture in. Setting the lid on it, she hung it by one of the iron rods over the hot coals and then moved over to the window and gazed out pensively.

"What's wrong, Abigail?"

"Wrong? Why, nothing's wrong, Mama."

"Yes, I think there is." Deborah came over to stand beside her, and taking her arm, she turned her around. She studied Abigail's face, reached out and brushed a lock of her thick brown hair back from her forehead, then said gently, "You're not very good at hiding your feelings. What is it, now?"

Abigail dropped her eyes and was very quiet for a moment. She heard the ticking of the clock on the mantel across the room that punctuated the silence with its regular cadence. Finally she looked up and said in a voice that was almost a whisper, "I . . . I'm not quite sure, Mama . . . about getting married."

"Do you think it might be nerves? Young women sometimes get that way before the wedding."

"I don't think so."

For a moment Deborah stood quietly, then she asked, "Have you prayed about it, Abby?"

Abigail seemed surprised by the question. "Well, I think I have, but we've already decided."

"Every decision needs to be prayed about, I think."

"Why, I thought just spiritual things. Not everyday things, Mama."

"No, I don't think that's right. God is concerned about every aspect of the lives of His children. He longs for them to be happy, and He knows that the only way this can happen is for them to live for Him." She thought hard for a while, and said, "And I think, really, the only way to do that is to go to Him for all of life's decisions. Come over and sit down."

The two women went and sat down at the table. Deborah first glanced at the cooking utensils over the fire to be sure the meal was under control. Satisfied all was well, she turned to say, "Some things are just there that we must do—like eating and drinking and working and sleeping. We don't need to pray about those. They just have to be done. And then there's some things in the Word of God, such as warnings against lying or stealing. Like being kind to each other. We don't have to pray about these things, do we?"

"No, Mama. I don't think so."

"But there are some things that are not spelled out specifically in the Bible, and these things have to be prayed about."

"You mean like who we're to marry? God doesn't say specifically that I'm to marry Jacob."

"Exactly. And I know you have prayed, and so have your father and I."

"Maybe," Abigail said slowly, a pensive light touching her fine gray-green eyes, "I haven't prayed enough."

"Often that's the case. The Scripture says, 'You will find me when you seek for me *with all your heart.*' It's not enough just to ask once. We need to go again and again and again."

The two women sat there talking quietly as the smell of the food cooking at the fireplace filled the room. Once Deborah got up and stirred the fire and added a log, then she picked up a Bible and came back, and the two read Scriptures together. It was something they had often done, and somehow the very act of her mother's calm and quiet confidence came as a soothing bond to Abigail. Finally they prayed together, and her mother prayed more fervently than Abigail had ever heard her. She herself felt such an urgency for God's guidance that her voice was breaking when she called upon Him.

When she had finished, Abigail looked up with shock on her face. "You know, Mama, how you're always telling me that God gave you a Scripture?"

"Yes?"

"Well, I think that God just gave me one."

"What is it? What did God say?"

"The Scripture just came into my mind as we were praying—that believers are not to be yoked with unbelievers."

Somehow this did not surprise Deborah Stevens. It was a thought that she had shared with her husband, and the two of them were not happy with Jacob's spiritual condition, although they never said so to Abigail. But now that Abigail herself had brought it up, Deborah quickly responded. "It's the most important decision you'll ever make, next to choosing Jesus as your Savior. If you're not satisfied that Jacob is following after God, and that he would be a Christian father and a Christian husband, as your own father has been, then I think you need to be *very* cautious."

Abigail sat quietly for a moment, thoughts racing through her mind. She was a calm and rather thoughtful young woman, and now a sense of peace descended upon her. She had not realized how agitated she had been until suddenly that passed away, and she knew what she had to do.

————

A brisk wind stirred the dead leaves at Abigail's feet as she made her way along the path that led to the Spencer homestead. All the glaring reds and yellows and golds of the maples had come and gone now, so the bare trees seemed to be lifting their branches toward the sky in prayer. Lifting her face, Abigail relished the sharp gust of wind and the smell of the forest that pressed against the settlement from all sides. Somewhere over the peaks winter was lurking and would come down one day, touching the valley with a freezing hand, turning the earth to cold stone and the running brooks to ice, but now there was a refreshing quality in the air after the heat of summer.

Turning toward the final bend in the road, Abigail saw the smoke rising from the Spencer cabin, and also from the smaller one where

Iris and Amanda had come to live. A week had passed since she had talked with her mother, and every day she had gone about her work praying for guidance. It had been in her mind that Jacob would come, but he had not, and she had heard from one of the neighbors that he had gone out on a hunting trip with Sequatchie but had now returned. The peace that had come to her had not left, but now she felt a strain because she knew what she had to say to Jacob would not be well received.

She paused at the edge of the homestead and wished there were some way to speak to Jacob in private. She stood there for ten minutes, and finally, to her surprise, Jacob stepped out of the house and started toward the barn.

"Jacob!" Abigail called out. "Jake, over here!" She saw him as he heard her voice and turned quickly, then a smile came to his face. He ran across the yard lightly, and she realized again how he had become swifter and stronger since coming to the frontier. *He looks so much like his father,* she thought. *The same dark hair, the same dark blue eyes, and as tall as Hawk Spencer.*

"Abby, what are you doing here?" Jacob asked. He paused and looked down at her, a pleased expression in his dark eyes. "I was coming over to see you later this afternoon."

"I wanted to see you. Can we take a walk?"

"Why, sure." Jacob turned, but he took his full view of her, appreciating the slender but maturing form of the young woman who walked alongside him. He was pleased with her appearance and said so.

When Abigail did not respond, Jacob realized there was something wrong, and he asked, "What's the matter? Is someone sick?"

"Oh no." Abigail turned to face him, and for a moment agitation showed in her eyes. But she took a deep breath and said, "I came over to ask you to pray with me, Jacob."

Whatever Jacob Spencer had expected, it was not to be asked to pray. He frowned slightly, and two vertical lines appeared between his eyes, and his lips grew tense. "To pray? What about?"

"Why, about us. I've been thinking so hard about our engagement, and I know we need to pray about it."

Jacob stared at her hard and then shook his head. "I don't need to ask God for permission to marry you."

Something in Jacob's voice disturbed Abigail, and she said hurriedly, "It's not like that, but we need to make sure that it's right. That it's what God wants us to do."

Anger flared inside Jacob, and he could not explain it. His voice was hard when he answered. "I'm not going to ask a God that let my mother die and my father desert me what He thinks about who I'm going to marry."

The harshness of the reply grated against Abigail, and she was silent for a moment. Then she said evenly, "Why do you want to marry me, Jacob?"

"You know."

"No, I don't know. Tell me."

Jacob shifted his feet uncomfortably. He was not good at talking about things like this, although he wished he were. Now he thought briefly before answering. "I want someone by my side, to be with me."

It was not an answer that Abigail wanted. Finally she straightened her back and asked more directly, "Jacob, do you love me?"

"Why, of course I do!"

"You never told me."

"All right, then. I love you."

Suddenly Abigail knew that there was something terribly wrong in her decision to marry Jacob Spencer. "You have such a hard time saying that, Jacob," she said mildly.

"It's hard for me to talk about things like that."

"I don't think it's hard for us to talk about things we like, things we love. And I think what the trouble is, is that you don't love me in the right way."

Jacob blinked with surprise. "What do you mean, 'in the right way'?"

"I mean, you care for me after a fashion but not in the way you need to. A man who wants to marry a woman should love her in a very special way. Not like anything else in this world, Jacob. Just like a woman should have that same kind of love for a man. And for a week I've been praying. . . ." She paused and took a deep breath. "I don't think either of us has the sort of love a man and a woman should have to be married."

Jacob reacted immediately. "You're wrong about that! It's right that we should get married! I know it is!"

"I don't think so. We're not right for each other."

Suddenly Jacob's lips grew into a tight line, and he reached out and took Abigail by the upper arms. He almost shook her, and he exclaimed, "I know what's the matter! It's Andrew! That's what it is!"

Shocked and hurt by his accusation, Abigail replied instantly, "It's not Andrew. That's not the reason I'm doing this. Andrew has nothing to do with you and me, or my decision."

"That's not so. He's gotten to you, and now you want him instead of me."

Abigail knew then that she was right in her decision. She shook her head regretfully and said, "We can't talk about this now. You're upset—and you're wrong, Jacob." She suddenly reached out, laid her hand lightly on his chest, and in a very gentle tone said, "I know this hurts you. It hurts me, too, to think that I could have been so wrong about something so important. But I know it's best for both of us."

She stood there for a moment, then whispered, "Forgive me, Jacob," and tears gathered in her eyes. She turned and walked blindly back down the path, stumbling, and then broke into a light run.

Jacob stood there watching her. It was as if the heavens had fallen, and anger began to rise in him—anger that was so harsh it startled him. He found himself wanting to strike out at someone, or something, and as he whirled around and strode away in the opposite direction, he knew his life had been turned upside down. And he was certain it would never be put right again.

The Wounded Lion

Thirty-Two

Jacob could not seem to control the rage that boiled up inside of him. He walked rapidly for fifteen minutes, stalking blindly along the trail that led outward from the homestead. Once when a branch struck him in the forehead, he angrily pushed it out of the way. He was not given to bouts of blind anger, but Abigail's announcement had taken his reason from him, and all he could think of was how he had been set aside in favor of someone else once again. "First my father abandons me and then takes up with Andrew—and now Andrew takes the girl I want to marry!"

Abruptly he turned and moved back toward the homestead. He went directly to the barn, where he found Andrew inside, hanging up the harness for the horses on a peg.

"Hi, Jacob," Andrew said, barely looking up. Glancing over his shoulder, he hooked the harness over the peg, then turned and said, "What do you think—" He broke off abruptly when he saw the thundercloud on his stepbrother's face. "What's the matter?" he asked quickly.

"You're the matter!" Jacob stopped directly in front of Andrew, his feet spread apart and his fists tightly clenched. "You've done it, haven't you?"

"I don't know what you're talking about! What's wrong?"

"You've stolen my girl, that's what! You stole my father's love first, and now you have to have Abigail!"

"That's not true!" Andrew protested. He had been taken completely off guard by Jacob's accusations, for he had no idea of what had been happening between the two. He started to speak but never got the words out. Jacob suddenly caught him in the mouth with a blow that drove him backward. He sprawled out on the floor and saw that Jacob was coming at him to fall on him. Raising his feet, he shot them out and caught Jacob in the chest, driving the breath out of him and knocking him to one side. Scrambling to his feet, he said, "Wait a minute, Jacob. Let's talk about this."

But Jacob Spencer was past talk. A red curtain of rage had fallen over him, and he threw himself forward, striking out with all his force. The blow grazed Andrew's cheek but did not strike solidly.

Andrew grabbed Jacob by the arm and made a full sweep so that Jacob lost his balance. When Andrew released him, he crashed headlong into the side of the barn, practically rattling the rafters. With a cry of rage, Jacob scrambled to his feet and threw himself forward. He caught a blow high on the temple that stunned him for a moment, but blindly he moved forward, throwing blows from every direction.

Andrew saw that there was no reasoning with Jacob and defended himself as best he could. An anger grew in him, for Jacob stung him with his blows, and he began to fight harder.

The two were suddenly halted when a figure came between them and Jacob shoved at him, muttering in a guttural voice, "Get out of my way!"

Sequatchie reached forward and pulled Jacob away from Andrew. "What's the matter with you two?" When Jacob did not answer, Sequatchie turned and said, "What's going on, Andrew?"

"I don't know," Andrew panted. He reached up and wiped a smear of blood off of his face and shook his head. "He came in here and accused me of breaking him and Abigail up. I don't know what he's talking about."

Jacob stood stubbornly, his chin thrust forward, and his voice revealed the hot anger that remained in him. "He did it, and I'm going to pound him for it!"

"You're not going to pound anyone," Sequatchie said harshly. "This is not a way for grown men to act, and it better not happen again. Andrew, please leave. I need to talk to Jacob."

Without a word, Andrew stomped out of the barn, his face flushed, and at once Sequatchie said, "Now, what's the matter? What's this about you and Abigail?"

"He stole her! That's what he did!"

"What makes you think that?"

"Because she told me she wasn't going to marry me!"

Sequatchie paused for a moment, then said, "Was it because of Andrew? Is that what she said?"

"Well, no. She didn't exactly say that."

"Then, what did she say?"

Jacob dropped his head. Reason was beginning to return to him, and with it a measure of shame. He did not answer for so long that Sequatchie demanded again what she had said, and finally Jacob threw his hands apart. "She says that God doesn't want us to marry."

"Well, does He?"

"How should I know? What do I know about God?" Jacob ran his hand through his hair and shook his head, then said abruptly, "It's time for you to keep your end of the bargain, Sequatchie."

"You mean take you back to Williamsburg?"

"Yes. Now."

Sequatchie shook his head at once. "I cannot do it now. The Cherokee could go on the warpath anytime, and it would not be safe. Hawk would never forgive me if anything happened to his son."

"Who cares what he thinks? He doesn't care about me anyway." Again the anger and bitterness rose in him, and he added, "I'm going whether you take me or not!"

Sequatchie suddenly reached out and grabbed Jacob by the front of his shirt. His dark eyes were glowing now, and Jacob, who had never seen the Cherokee angry, knew that this was a dangerous man he was confronting. He tried to pull away, but Sequatchie held him easily and began to speak in a voice as hard as flint.

"You need to grow up! You're nothing but a papoose! Yes, your father was wrong in leaving you, but he's done all he could to make it up to you these last few years! Everyone makes mistakes, and Hawk has tried to make up for his—which you have not done!"

Jacob flinched at the severity of Sequatchie's words. He wanted to turn and leave, but Sequatchie held him firmly, and there was almost a merciless quality in his tone. "I'm tired of hearing you complain of what's happened to you! You think you're the only man that ever had a hard time? You need to get over it and forgive!" Sequatchie suddenly released Jacob and said in a milder tone, "You need the Lord Jesus in your heart. I can understand why Abigail won't marry you. All you ever think about is yourself. You never show love or concern for anyone."

"Is that all you've got to say to me?" Jacob said bitterly.

"No!" Sequatchie hesitated for a moment and took a deep breath. "If you really want to keep on living the kind of life you are living, go ahead and try to get home. It would hurt your father, especially if you were killed—which will probably happen! But I will not help you to hurt him anymore!" He took a deep breath again and said, "I am sorry to be harsh, for you need God's help. You are like the wounded lion in the Bible who needs to return to his Creator to be healed." He started to say something else, then shook his head sadly, turned his back, and walked away, leaving Jacob totally confused and deflated.

———

After supper Hawk rose and followed Jacob, who had said not one word during the meal and had left the table, having eaten practically nothing. Sarah had come to Hawk earlier and said, "Pa, I found out what the fight was about between Andrew and Jacob. Jacob thinks Andrew has stolen Abigail from him."

Stepping out on the porch, Hawk squinted his eyes in the darkness and turned to see Jacob standing with his back to the house, looking up at the skies. He approached his son, saying, "Jacob—?"

Jacob turned and stared at his father in the darkness. Only a few stars burned overhead, throwing a feeble light over the yard. Jacob was glad for the dark, for he did not want his father to see his expression. He said nothing but waited.

Finally Hawk spoke. "I heard about you and Abigail. Anything I can do, I will."

"You can do one thing. That's take me home."

Hawk said at once, "I can't leave the family now. You know that." He tried to find some way to put his love into words but finally said only, "It's a bad time to travel, Jacob. Cherokee could be surrounding us right now. I don't want anything to happen to you." When Jacob did not respond, Hawk said quietly, "I'll pray for you, son, and I'll be here if you need anything." He turned and went back to the cabin, troubled in spirit and under a cloud of despair.

Later that night when they were alone, Elizabeth asked, "What about Jacob? What's he going to do?"

"He wants to go back to Williamsburg."

"Abigail's refusal has hurt him terribly. His pride is shattered, but

I hope he doesn't go back. You can't turn your back and run from a thing like this."

"No, I think that's right." Hawk was silent for a moment, then he said almost grimly, "The only thing we can do is pray for him—because I think he's going to go through a very rough time."

Preparations for War

Thirty-Three

$\mathcal{A}$s the revolution heated up in May of 1776 along the eastern seaboard, the Watauga settlers concluded that there was a need for a stronger fort in the area. All of the men took time out from the work on their own homesteads to help build the new fort at Sycamore Shoals.

George Stevens and Hawk were lifting one of the final logs on the eastern end of the fort, and both men gave a sigh of relief as it fell into the notches at the end, fitting perfectly.

"Well," George said, wiping the sweat from his face, "this is beginning to look like a real fort."

Hawk leaned back against the logs. "We needed a new fort. The old one was too small to hold everyone in case of an attack." He moved over and took a drink from the bucket, using a small gourd for a cup, then shook his head. "I was hoping it wouldn't come to this, George."

"I suppose we all were, but now that the Cherokee have sided with the British, we don't have any choice. Did you hear about John Carter?"

"I don't reckon so."

"Carter got word from the British authorities that all of us here are illegal squatters and we've got to move on."

"Where do they suggest we move?" Hawk asked caustically. He was becoming more and more angry with the British for their treatment of the Colonies. "They want us to move to the moon?"

"Not quite that far." A wry expression touched Stevens' face, and he ran a hand through his graying hair, his voice filled with disgust. "The Redcoats say that everyone who complies with the Crown will receive free land—in Florida Territory."

"Florida? That's way down south past Georgia somewhere. What did Carter say?"

"He asked for time to think it over."

"I don't see what there is to think about. I'm not moving that far away and out of the Appalachians. None of us will."

"Of course not. John knew that. He was just stalling until we could figure out what to do."

The two men talked quietly about the tense political situation. The danger was real, for they were surrounded by angry and powerful Indian tribes, and there were no trained troops to call upon in case of an attack, which was almost sure to come. Finally Hawk said, "I think it might be time for us to talk to Virginia. Maybe they'd accept us as part of their colony."

"Maybe," George said doubtfully. He pulled a piece of dried deer meat from his pocket, bit off a small portion, and began to chew it thoughtfully. "I'm worried about the division here. The new clerk of Watauga, Felix Walker, took some of our militia to serve in a South Carolina regiment against the British forces. I don't see why he had to do that. We need every man we can get."

"Yes, we do, but God will be with us."

George suddenly looked embarrassed and wiped his hands on the front of his shirt in a rather strange fashion. "How's Jacob doing, Hawk?"

Looking up quickly, Hawk met Stevens' eyes and shrugged. "About the same. He goes through the motions of living, but he doesn't have anything to say. It's like he's withdrawn, George."

"I'm rightly sorry about the way it turned out, Hawk. Abigail was brokenhearted about it, but there was nothing else she could do."

"Well, if Abigail felt that way, it was best they didn't marry." He paused, then added quickly, "Elizabeth and I hold no ill will toward you or the family. You know that, I hope."

"I appreciate hearing it. Abigail's been afraid to come to your place. Afraid she wouldn't be welcome."

"I wish she would. Sarah misses her, George. She needs all the friends she can get."

The men were putting another log into place, and as he moved toward one end and Stevens took the other end, Hawk said, "All we can do is pray for Jacob, which Elizabeth and I have been doing for a long time." He leaned over and put his weight behind the log as it was hoisted into place by men on top pulling with ropes, then he said just loudly enough for Stevens to hear him, "I know God will send an answer if we will just wait on Him."

Abigail had spent considerable time at the building site, helping her mother cook for the men who came in from the outer settlements. Now that the fort was finished, her father said one morning, "I think you ought to go over and visit the Spencers, Abby. They might think you don't feel right toward them, staying away like you have."

Abigail agreed at once and began to make her way toward the Spencer homestead, wondering how she would be able to behave acceptably toward Jacob. She had slept badly ever since the breakup, and Sarah had told her how Jacob was refusing to say more than a few words to anybody.

Now as she entered the clearing she found herself apprehensive, and when she saw Jacob plowing in the garden patch, she forced herself to go to him.

"Hello, Jacob," she called out and stood waiting to see what he would say.

Jacob pulled the horse to a stop with a curt word and turned to face Abigail. His face was expressionless, and he said merely, "Andrew's in the barn."

"I came over to see Sarah."

"She's with him, and Amanda, too. Get up, Flossie!"

Abigail was hurt by Jacob's abrupt manner, but there was no way she could make things any better. She turned and walked quickly to the barn, where she found Sarah, Amanda, and Andrew admiring the newborn calf. "Hello," she said.

At once Sarah came over and gave her a hug. "I missed you."

"I missed you, too," Amanda said. "Come and look at the new calf. Sarah wants to name her Jezebel."

"You can't do that, Sarah. She was an awful woman," Andrew protested. He was smiling at Abigail, leaning back on one of the beams that held the roof in place. At nineteen he was in the prime of manhood, strong and fit. He seemed pleased to see Abigail and asked, "How are your folks?"

"They're fine. It's good to see you all."

The four stood there admiring the new calf, with Sarah doing most of the talking. She was now sixteen and already a beauty. Her red hair was fixed neatly for a change, plaited behind her back, and her pale green eyes were flashing with excitement as she spoke.

They talked about the fort and other things of interest in the community, but all the time Abigail was thinking primarily of Jacob. She was unaware that he had halted his horse and had come to stand outside the barn, listening to their conversation.

Even as he stood there, Jacob had an impulse to move inside, for he missed the camaraderie that he had had with all of the young people. He was twenty years old now and realized that he was acting like a small child. If he had been more honest with himself, he might have realized that he was at times reverting to the days of his childhood—striving to become again the small boy who desperately missed the father who had abandoned him. For a while he listened, then tore himself away and went silently back to the horse and began plowing again.

———

The coppery faces around the campfire were sullen, and dark eyes were bright with bitter anger. Most white men saw all Cherokee as being more or less alike, but the members of the tribes who had gathered to plan their strategy were similar and yet vastly different. From the north there were the Mohawk, the Delaware, the Ottawa, the Nancuta, the Mingo, and the Shawnee. Others of the Iroquois Federation sat around the circle. The meeting had been long, and all of these tribes were determined to enlist the aid of the Cherokee, the strongest tribe of the south. Now it was Dragging Canoe who stood before the representatives of all the tribes and made an eloquent plea. His pockmarked face was alive with excitement as he said, "We must support the British. We must drive the long knives back across the mountains, then we will have our land back."

The old chief Attacullaculla had reluctantly agreed to support the British. Now, however, he drew himself up and stared across the fire at his son. He studied him carefully and said, "You cannot trust the British. They claim that they will let us keep our lands, but they will not keep their treaty."

"We do not know that, Father," Dragging Canoe spoke up at once. "We do know that the long knives from across the mountains will take all that we have. We must fight for what is ours."

A rumble of agreement went around the circle, and Attaculla-culla knew a moment of deep despondency. For years he had been the friend of the white men, and now that the white men themselves had divided into two groups, he knew he could not support both. He sat silently while the debate went on, and finally, when he was forced to speak again, he rose and made his decision.

"I will support the king's cause, but I do not want the Cherokee to fight in this war."

"We must fight," Dragging Canoe said instantly. He made a passionate plea, and finally the battle cries broke out from the throats of all of the warriors.

Attacullaculla knew that he had lost. He sat down and stared at the dirt floor before him and said no more.

Henry Stewart, the king's representative, knew a surge of joy, for he had accomplished his aim to enlist the Indians to kill every settler in the area. But now he stood up and said quickly, "My brothers, you have done well to come to support the king, and you will be well rewarded, but I must ask you not to kill those white people who are still loyal to the king." He knew, in effect, that this was a useless plea, for when Indians went blind with battle rage, a scalp was a scalp. None of the Indians had the slightest notion of British politics, but he was constrained to say so. He knew now what would happen. He would go back to Mobile to the south in Alabama Territory and the northern tribes would leave, and the Cherokee women would begin to prepare their men for the war that was certain to come.

Washington, Lincoln, and Nancy Ward

Thirty-Four

$\mathcal{B}$y the spring of 1776 the flames of revolution were burning higher and higher. Across the sea King George III made his final mistake. The Colonies had made a peace overture called the Olive Branch Petition, which the monarch rejected out of hand. He pressured Parliament to send an army of fifty-five thousand men in order to crush the revolution. He soon discovered, however, that his subjects were not in sympathy with the British cause. Indeed, there was much more sympathy for the Americans!

The British soldiers and sailors who had always been ready to answer the call to battle turned a deaf ear to the king's invitation to crush their fellow Englishmen. Faced with such a lack of response, King George III went looking for hirelings.

Germany was a fruitful ground for those seeking hirelings, and eventually some thirty thousand German mercenaries served under the English colors in the American war. Since most of them came from Hesse-Cassel, they were all simply called Hessians. The German sovereign paid thirty-five dollars for each soldier killed, twelve dollars for each one wounded, and over five hundred thousand in cold cash.

This was King George's final indignity, which convinced most Americans that there was nothing left to do but declare their independence.

The thirteen Colonies then drew themselves together and eloquently drafted their statement of independence from British tyranny forever. Thomas Jefferson was selected as the chairman for the committees to vote for independence. At thirty-three he was the youngest of the delegates at Philadelphia and not nearly so universally known as Adams or Franklin.

The pathway to the Declaration was not simple, for although nine of the thirteen Colonies could be counted on to vote for independence, both New York and Pennsylvania had been instructed to oppose it, while South Carolina and Maryland were not firm in their decisions.

Finally, however, Thomas Jefferson was commissioned to write the Declaration, and he did so, thus making himself immortal. On July 1, John Adams declared publicly that the Colonies were free and independent, but still only nine Colonies would support the measure. On July 2, Congress convened after a tremendous battle between the Colonies. It was a toss-up as to whether the Declaration of Independence would take place—indeed, whether independence itself would come. Tension rose among the delegates. A driving rain came up, and those in favor of independence searched the rain-soaked streets. The decision might lie in the hands of a Delaware delegate named Caesar Rodney, who was known to be a friend of independence, but who was at the bedside of his ailing wife. Finally Rodney arrived and flung himself off his horse. He was splashed with mud and soaked to the skin. His small, round face, hardly bigger than a large grapefruit, was livid from the ordeal. He was rushed into the chambers and put Delaware into the affirmative column, after which Pennsylvania came into line, and South Carolina then followed.

On July 4, all the delegates to the Congress were present, except John Dickinson, and approved the Declaration of Independence. John Hancock, President of the Congress, signed first with the great strokes of his pen, which would make his name synonymous with flamboyant signatures, and declared, "There, I guess King George will be able to read that!"

They all signed then, the Lees of Virginia, Charles Carroll of Carrolltown, a Catholic in the midst of a Protestant sea, and finally it was Ben Franklin who wryly said, "We must all hang together or assuredly we shall all hang separately."

The Declaration of Independence was printed and sent all over the Colonies with tremendous effect. Savannah burned King George in effigy, New York pulled down his statue, and Connecticut melted it down for bullets, while Boston tore George's coat of arms from the State House and burned it in an exultant and defiant manner. Thus it was that America was born, and the independence that burned in the hearts of the colonists was put into the immortal words of the Declaration of Independence.

————

Isaac Lincoln had not been an outspoken member among the Watauga leaders. A small man with a full gray beard, he was faithful to the court and to the settlement but had taken almost no part of the leadership. He was a distant relative of Daniel Boone and had come to the area on his recommendation in November 1775.

Isaac Lincoln now sat quietly listening while the leaders discussed what to do. James Robertson had brought the news that Virginia had refused to accept them as part of their state, and William Bean had spoken up, saying, "I think it might be best to send a petition to North Carolina. I have reason to believe that they will be glad to accept us as part of their colony."

"I'm for that," Hawk spoke up quickly. "Now that the Declaration of Independence has been made, we've got to make our position clear. I'm for petitioning to join North Carolina as Washington County."

It was then that Isaac Lincoln spoke up, saying, "We must make one thing clear, gentlemen." He looked around at their surprised faces, for he had never spoken so firmly before, but it was clear in his mind what he wanted to do. "Whatever else, they *must* accept the fact that the purchase of our lands from the Cherokee is legal."

A murmur of agreement went around the room, and immediately the messenger left with the petition, the ink almost wet upon it. Hawk came over to stand beside Lincoln and said, "That was a good point, Isaac. It wouldn't do much good to fight for liberty if we had no lands of our own in the end."

Isaac smiled slightly, then grew sober. "I wonder what the Cherokee are doing," he mused.

"Nothing for our good. You can be sure of that," Hawk murmured.

————

Indeed, the Cherokee were making plans to go to war. They had met with all of the chiefs, and now the decision had been made.

Chief Old Abram was there, as well as Chief The Raven. But it was Chief Dragging Canoe who acted as spokesman for the group.

"We must strike and strike at once!" Dragging Canoe stood before the others. A large crowd of braves had gathered, and even some of the squaws stood in the background. All knew that war would come and they were hungry for it—at least the young men were.

Far in the background Nancy Ward, the niece of Attacullaculla, stood listening quietly. She allowed nothing to show on her face, but her heart was saddened because of the deaths among both whites and Cherokee that soon would come. She listened, hoping to find some mitigation in the views of Dragging Canoe, but the more she listened, the more she knew there was no hope of averting war.

"Chief Old Abram will lead four hundred warriors against the Watauga and Nolichucky whites," Dragging Canoe said loudly. "I will lead that many against the Long Island settlement, and then move to Virginia. Chief The Raven will take a group of braves and attack the settlement at Carter's Valley, and then join me in attacking Virginia. We will wipe the white men from the face of our land! They will never return, for we will soak the earth with their blood!"

For some time the meeting went on, and Nancy Ward stood listening to all that was said. Finally she knew that although her heart was with the Cherokee, and she was called the "Beloved Woman" of the tribe, she could not allow the slaughter to take place. Turning, she walked quietly away. No one paid heed to her as she disappeared, mounted her horse, then rode out of the Cherokee camp.

Shadows were growing long by the time Nancy had reached the home of her cousin, Wurteh. Wurteh was married to a Virginian named Nathaniel Gist, and she met Nancy with her seven-month-old baby in her arms. The child was named George, but called Sequoyah by the Cherokee.

"My sister," Wurteh smiled. "You are welcome." Then seeing the expression on Nancy Ward's face, she said, "What is the matter?"

"Where is the trader Isaac Thomas, Wurteh?"

"He is with Nathaniel and with some other traders outside the town. What is wrong?"

Nancy hesitated. "It is war. I will tell you later, but now I must go find Thomas." She left at once, guiding her mare until she found Isaac Thomas speaking with William Faulin and Jarrett Williams, who turned to greet her. All had great respect for Nancy Ward, and after greeting her, they waited until she spoke.

"You must get the settlers away. Dragging Canoe and the other warriors will attack very soon now."

Nancy's statement electrified Gist, and at once he began to make plans. "I'll get you some horses," he said to the traders, "then you'll have to get out of town. We've got to warn the settlers of what is to happen."

Nathaniel turned to Nancy and put his hand lightly on her shoulder. "You have saved many lives, Nancy. All of our people will be grateful to you."

Nancy did not return Gist's smile, for she was a woman caught between two destinies. She loved the Cherokee, but she also loved her husband and the white people in the valley. Now she knew as she turned away that there would be dead men, women, and children on both sides of her heritage.

Hawk made a final trip out to the wagon to toss in the feather mattress. It was goose down and represented the labor of many months. He himself had always been satisfied with corn shucks, but Elizabeth had not only plucked her own geese but traded for feathers from everyone in the area. As he put the mattress down he thought, *Well, I don't think there's any danger of Indians making off with this, but I will admit it's pretty nice on a cold winter night.*

As Hawk turned away he bumped into Andrew, who had brought out the last of the clothes stuffed into a cotton sack. He tossed it up on the wagon, waited to see if it would roll off, and when he turned to Hawk, his eyes were bright with excitement. "Do you really think there'll be fighting, Pa?"

Hawk made a slight grimace at the look of expectation on Andrew's face, but he knew that young men thought differently about war. He looked with affection into Andrew's face, thinking, as he often did, how much he looked like his father, Patrick. "I calculate there will. That's why we're going to Fort Caswell."

"Why did they name it Fort Caswell? It seems they'd have named it Fort Bean or after one of our people."

"Richard Caswell is the Governor Elect of North Carolina, son. Now, we'd better get ready. I wouldn't put it past the Cherokee to attack at any time." He looked up as Jacob came out the door carrying the large black pot that was Elizabeth's pride and joy and said, "Jacob, would you go see if Iris and Amanda are ready to go? And finish helping them load up."

"All right," Jacob nodded briefly, then turned toward the smaller cabin. He stopped long enough to put the pot in the wagon, then moved quickly until he came to stand before the second wagon, where Amanda was just putting a sack of something inside.

"Let me help you with that, Amanda." Reaching down, he lifted the sack and grunted. "This is heavy. What is it?"

"It's our cooking pots and an iron that Mr. Smith made for us at his smithy."

"Are you almost ready to go?"

"Almost. Just a few more things."

"All right. Pa says we've got to leave in a hurry. I'll come back and drive the wagon for you."

Amanda had been working hard on loading the wagon. If an attack came, it was likely that the Indians would burn the cabin, so all the settlers were taking everything they could into the fort. Now, however, as she looked at Jacob, she saw something in his face that made her call out impulsively, "Jacob?"

Jacob turned and asked impatiently, "What is it, Amanda?"

"I . . . I was just wondering what was wrong with you. I've been meaning to talk to you, but it seems there's never time."

"I'm all right. There's nothing wrong with me," Jacob snapped.

Amanda shrank as Jacob spoke sharply and she turned back toward the door. However, before she entered the cabin, suddenly her face changed. She was a mild-mannered girl, never challenging what her elders said, but something seemed to come to her and she whirled and said, "Wait a minute!"

She moved quickly and lightly across the ground and stood in front of Jacob. She was breathing rather quickly, and she fingered the buttons on the bodice of her dress nervously. A wave of panic came over her, but gathering her strength together, she said, "Jacob, this may not be my place, but . . ." She hesitated for just a moment, then said firmly, "I think you've been behaving terribly."

Jacob's face flushed and he nodded, saying curtly, "You're right. It's not your place!"

"I thought we were friends."

"We are friends, but you're getting into my business!"

"I don't think I am. It's not just your business the way you treat your father. And friends tell each other things and even have to correct each other sometimes."

"You don't know anything about it, Amanda!" Jacob had never spoken harshly to Amanda. He had always been a faithful friend to her, partly out of compassion over the severity of her life and the difficulties she faced with a harsh father, but also because she was growing up to be a handsome young woman he found pleasing. Now, however, he was not himself and snapped, "You don't know anything about me and about my family! My father abandoned me!"

Amanda stared at Jacob for a minute, then with a sudden burst of inner strength, she spoke up, and her own voice was tinged with something as close to anger as she would ever have toward this young man. "You had a father who abandoned you, but that's better than . . . but that's better than having one who beat you!"

Whatever Jacob had been expecting Amanda to say, it was not this. He stood there with the sunlight beating down on his face, feeling the warmth of it, but his eyes were locked onto Amanda's. She had beautiful brown eyes, almond shaped and expressive, and now suddenly he found he could not meet her gaze. He was struck with the truth that he was speaking to someone with more problems than he had. He stood there quietly as she spoke, wishing to turn and run away from her words, but unwilling to retreat.

"Your father left you, Jacob, but he came back, and he's been trying to make it up to you."

As he glanced up when she stopped speaking, her face suddenly seemed very vulnerable to Jacob. There was a softness and a gentleness about this girl that he had always admired. Somehow she had none of the sharpness or the quickness of other young women, and he had always admired her for this.

Finally she whispered, "Jacob, my father always mistreated me terribly and . . . and I hated him! You can't know how I hated him! Why, I would lie in bed at night and wish that he would die!" Here she turned her eyes upward and her lips trembled as dark memories swept back over her. "But after I gave my heart to God, I had to ask forgiveness for all those feelings."

Jacob was moved by her words and even more by her open honesty in being willing to share this with him. It was a quality he admired, for he himself had never been able to share his innermost thoughts with anyone. It was as if he kept a room somewhere with all of his deepest feelings and his dreams locked up securely. Even now, as he felt a yearning to speak out about those things that had troubled him for years, he found himself unable to mention them to Amanda. "God doesn't care for me," he muttered.

"God gave you a family, Jacob. Even when your father left, you had your grandparents. They took wonderful care of you obviously."

"Well . . . maybe so."

"Instead of being upset, you ought to be thankful."

"I don't want to listen to this, Amanda. . . !" Jacob turned to go, but suddenly his arm was grasped and he turned around, surprised to see Amanda's eyes were suddenly angry.

"I think everyone's getting tired of you feeling sorry for yourself," she said, and there was a strength in her voice that he had never heard before. "You've had a hard time, but that's no reason for you to behave like you're doing now. All that's in the past! You need to put everything behind you and go forward! Jacob, can't you see you're hurting yourself even more than you're hurting others?" She waited for him to speak and when he did not, she said, "Try to understand. Hawk left you without a father for many years—but he has changed, and now you're robbing yourself of a father who really loves you! Can't you see that, Jacob?"

The words of the young woman struck at Jacob with a stronger force than he let show. Jacob kept his face immobile, though his heart was crying out at the truth of what Amanda was saying. He could not answer, for he knew if he did, he would have to share hurts and deep disappointments that he could not talk about. Feeling like a coward, he said brusquely, "I'll come back and drive the wagon, Amanda."

Amanda watched as Jacob whirled and walked rapidly away, his back straight. She felt a sense of failure and frustration and fought to keep back her tears. For a long time she had been secretly attracted to Jacob Spencer, although she would never have admitted it to anyone. After his engagement with Abigail failed, a ray of hope had shone into her heart, and she had waited for Jacob to notice her. Many times she had tried her best to do her hair a different way and had dressed more carefully, but all for naught. Now she turned blindly and moved back into the cabin, hearing her mother call.

"All right, Mother. I'm coming," she said, and as she did, she quietly closed the door on her feelings for Jacob Spencer.

———

Fort Caswell was little different from any of the other forts in the wilderness. Some were small, while others were quite large and stockaded. The log fort was the most common type of fortification on the Appalachian frontier. They could be built by unskilled labor, for the walls were made of upright pointed stakes with the tops sharpened, embedded deeply in the ground to prevent them from being pried out of place. Long horizontal stringers fastened with wooden pegs held the palisades in place, and heavy log blockhouses that overhung the second stories were built at each corner. Usually the forts comprised a single acre, rarely any larger, and along the inside walls small log cabins, sometimes joined to each other using a single inner wall, provided living quarters. As a rule, they had two rooms with puncheon floors, but many were simply hard-packed dirt. Often the clapboard roofs were held in place by lengths of long, heavy saplings.

Inside the fort the courtyard served as a stock pen, but at Fort Caswell an enclosure had been built at the north end to shelter the horses and cattle at night. A single large, heavy folding gate faced the outside, which was critically balanced so that a single strong man could close it without difficulty. Outside the fort all trees and undergrowth had been cleared away for about three hundred feet. The Spencers arrived at the fort and at once were aware of the stir of people within the stockade. Men were moving in and out constantly, and the fear of invasion could be seen in the eyes of some of the women. Others were cheerful, insisting that there would be no war.

Hawk had rented one of the small cabins built against the inner wall of the fort, and Elizabeth and the other women who came in soon learned how to adjust. Elizabeth made a broom by shredding a hickory pole grain by grain, then swept the earthen floor each day. She cooked game meats over the fireplace, or baked corn pones there, using the iron vessels she had brought with her. Life was reduced to a few simple things, and although Elizabeth soon realized that a long stay in such close confinement would be aggravating, they would have to endure it. She settled down and grew accustomed to the hum of people who came and went inside the walled town. She learned quickly every element inside the fort. The smith's shop was set up inside the center square, and men brought their tools and guns to be mended. She went often to the hominy block, where corn was pounded free of the husk, and then would wait at the spring while the women in turn dipped water into their piggins.

Amanda and Iris, the Stevenses, the Andersons, the Fosters, and the Baxters were all close friends, so the young people often got together and talked of the excitement that had come into their rather undramatic lives. Jacob mostly stayed away, keeping to himself. He went out each day with the hunters to bring in game for those confined to the safety of the fort.

Sarah was happy, for she was a girl who liked the bustle of activity. Sometimes life out on the homestead grew tiresome for her, but now she rose early and talked almost constantly with someone, usually Philip Baxter. Young Baxter was obviously taken with her and told her so. They often went outside the walls of the stockade, never going far, for Hawk and others had put out pickets so that by day, at least, the fort was safe from attack.

Rhoda Anderson soon grew fond of Ann Robertson, the sister of James, and Catherine Sherill, a single woman who was more outgoing than most.

Elizabeth, missing Lydia Bean, asked William when his wife was coming in, and she received a rather strange answer.

"Oh, she'll be in when she sees the Indians coming. Our house is so close that we wouldn't have any trouble getting into the stockade."

Hawk, who was standing nearby, narrowed his eyes. "I don't much care for that, William. Those Indians can sneak up on a man before he knows they're even in the country."

Bean grinned. "I been dodgin' 'em for some years now, Hawk. I reckon I can do it for a while longer."

Later that day Hawk spoke to Elizabeth of Lydia Bean. "I don't like it. I'm going to talk to William again."

"She just doesn't like living in the stockade."

"Neither do you. None of us do, but it's a thing that has to be done. I'll speak to William about it later. It's too dangerous out there for a woman."

On the Warpath

Thirty-Five

John Sevier looked up from his work on the stockade at Fort Lee on Limestone Creek. He had been instrumental in having the fort built on the Nolichucky River and had hurried the construction as quickly as possible. However, there were not enough hands for the work, and the fort was far from ready for any sort of defense.

"Who's that?" the man asked Charlie Denvers, who had also stopped. Denvers had the sharpest eyes of any man at Fort Lee, and now he peered carefully at the approaching rider.

"Don't know, but he's shore to kill that horse. Must be Indians on his trail or somethin'."

The two men moved out, picking up their muskets as they went and calling a warning to the men down the line. They all waited while the horse staggered into camp and a man fell off.

"Hello, stranger. Your horse is about gone."

"I'm looking for Sevier."

"I'm John Sevier."

"My name's Catlin. Josh Catlin. I've got bad news." Catlin's face was strained and his lips were chapped with the heat of the sun. "You got some water for a man?" He waited until one of the men brought a bucket of water, drank from it noisily, then shook his head. "You better pull out of here. Them Cherokees is on the move."

"How do you know that?" Sevier asked quickly. He had been fearing such news, and now he was almost certain that it had come.

"Nancy Ward. She was at the Cherokee council. She managed to slip away unnoticed and got word to Isaac Thomas, and he broke away and brought the news. You gotta get out of here right now. I 'spect there'll be around five hundred of them red devils comin'!"

The messenger was exhausted and was surrounded at once by men and women who were startled by his news. Sevier took one look around and knew there was no hope. A near panic broke out as the people of Nolichucky fled in a mass exodus. Sevier was left with fifteen men and shook his head. "We'd better get over to the fort at Watauga. I expect they'll need all the help they can get."

The day after Sevier and the inhabitants of Fort Lee fled, the Cherokee arrived with Dragging Canoe and Old Abram leading the combined tribes of warriors. Finding the fort deserted, they did not even bother to destroy the crops or the animals. They burned the fort, and here the main force divided. Dragging Canoe led his forces toward Long Island, and Old Abram continued his march toward Watauga.

Dragging Canoe was burning with a fierce anger and assumed that he would have an easy time with the helpless settlers. But he did not know that five companies of militia, warned by the message brought by Isaac Thomas, had assembled at Eaton's Station near Long Island.

The militia, led by Colonel William Preston, prepared to meet the attack. Instead of staying inside the fort, they chose rather to fight on open ground. The two forces were about equal in number and met in a fierce battle on Island Flats. The hand-to-hand combat lasted only an hour, but the Indians were defeated. Many warriors were killed or wounded, among them Chief Dragging Canoe, suffering a broken thigh. The Indians fled the field, carrying their wounded with them—thus the first battle of the American Revolution west of the mountains was over. The defeat of the Indians gave the white leaders confidence that they could meet the Indians on equal terms. To the Cherokee the battle meant loss of faith in their strength. Dragging Canoe's forces moved back in a retreat, but Old Abram moved steadily toward Fort Watauga.

John Sevier looked around the inside of the fort and nodded grimly. He was a tall, dark-haired man with piercing gray eyes and now said, "Well, Hawk, it looks like we're as ready as we'll ever be."

Hawk was molding bullets and looked up long enough from his

chore to nod. "I'm glad you came, Sevier. It sounds like we're going to need all of you."

"What's the date?" Sevier asked idly. He was watching a tall young woman who was laughing and playing with several of the younger children. They were playing some kind of a game that involved running, and he noticed that she ran like a deer. The sun caught her dark hair, and he was intrigued by her.

"July twenty-first," Hawk answered. He looked up to see Sevier watching the young woman and smiled. "You know that young woman?"

"No, but I'd like to. What's her name?"

"Catherine Sherill. They call her Bonnie Kate." Hawk was amused at Sevier's open admiration. "Sometimes I think she can outrun, outshoot, and outride any man in the settlement."

"Wouldn't be a bad woman to have on your side," Sevier said.

Sevier left Hawk and moved over to stand closer to where the game was taking place. The young woman noticed him and stopped and smiled at him. She had eyes the color of a blue cornflower, and they were striking in her tanned face. "Maybe you'd like to join the game," she smiled.

"Not likely. I don't think any man could catch you—in a race, that is."

"No man ever has."

"That doesn't mean no man ever will," John Sevier said. He stood there speaking to the young woman, pleased by her openness and frankness, then said, "Maybe we'll have a dance here after we get these Indians taken care of. I dance a little better than I run, I think."

Catherine Sherill laughed and said cheerfully, "I wouldn't mind that."

"Maybe we could go for a walk early tomorrow sometime outside the stockade. A man gets crowded in here."

Catherine only smiled at him and went back to the game.

That night there was an uneasiness in the air, and Hawk crowded into the small cabin with his whole family and was holding Joshua, entertaining him, by the light of the single lamp. Elizabeth was holding Hannah, humming a little song to put her to sleep. "You look worried, Hawk."

"I think we're in for a hard time."

"You think they'll come soon?"

"Yes. They have to do it quick. Indians don't stay together like white men. They'll come together for a while, but they don't seem to have the ability to fit together in a federation of any kind."

"Be careful when the fighting starts."

Hawk smiled and shrugged. "The Lord will have to keep us all safe."

The next morning at daybreak Hawk strolled along the inside of the fort, speaking again to Sevier. He had learned to know the man and liked him considerably. "I saw you speaking to Bonnie Kate yesterday. You got something on your mind, John?"

"I might. I never saw a woman like her. I wish—" He broke off suddenly and turned his head, and Hawk also did. "That's a musket shot," he said. "Come on." The two men climbed on top of the cabin roofs where they could fire over the walls of the stockade, and at once both men saw the red bodies of Indians gleaming in the early-morning sunlight.

"There's women out there!" Sevier exclaimed, and his eyes caught the athletic form of Catherine Sherill. She was running hard for the stockade, but the door was shut.

"Here, you're a better shot! Take my rifle, Hawk!"

"What are you going to do?"

"She can't get up these walls and the door's shut. Make every shot count!"

Hawk watched as the young woman raced across the open space. Some fleet Indians were chasing her not far behind. He chose one in front, drew a bead on him, and squeezed the trigger. The shot drove the brave backward, and Hawk instantly picked up Sevier's musket. He turned to see Sevier leaning down over the top of the palisades trying to dodge the sharp edges of the logs. He was holding on with his left hand and had stooped down so far that he had appeared to fall.

Hawk said, "Hang on, John! When you get her I'll help!" He waited until the young woman was almost to the wall, then shot another Indian in the chest. He had no time to reload, so he grabbed Sevier's legs and lowered him an extra foot. "Can you get her, John?"

Sevier leaned over the wall. He heard the striking of musket balls into the solid logs beside him but only cared about Kate. His eyes were fixed on the young woman's face, and he called out, "Here,

Kate! Take my hand!" He leaned and stretched as far as he could, and when the young woman reached the wall, she made a tremendous jump, farther than any woman could possibly leap, he thought. It was well that she did, for her hand barely reached his. He grabbed her wrist, squeezed it, and said, "Pull us up, Hawk!"

Hawk gave a tremendous pull at Sevier's legs, and Sevier, using both hands on Kate Sherill's wrists, hauled her up. The two fell together, and she landed directly across Sevier's chest.

Sevier looked up into her eyes and smiled. "This wasn't the kind of dance I thought about."

Catherine looked directly into Sevier's gray eyes and, despite the danger, smiled. "We'll have time for a better dance another day."

The fight started in earnest then, and there were many occasions of heroism as they all fought for their lives. Ann Robertson, James' sister, poured boiling water from washpots on a group of braves trying to set fire to the fort walls. She was wounded by one of the arrows but stayed at her post until the scalded Indians gave up and scampered back to safety.

During the heat of battle Hawk kept his two sons beside him, both of them firing and reloading with a furious activity. He looked over at Jacob and said, "That was a good shot, son."

Jacob flushed with pleasure and then shook his head. "They're brave men."

"They always were," Hawk nodded. Then he looked over at Andrew and said, "Keep your head down."

"Right, Pa, and you, too."

Finally the action ceased, and as the Indians pulled back beyond musket range, Hawk said as he stood up, "I think we won this time."

"You think they'll come back, Pa?" Andrew asked eagerly, his eyes alight with the excitement of battle.

"They may, but I doubt it. I think they've had enough. They lost quite a few braves."

There was rejoicing in the fort but sadness, too, for there had been several killed and many wounded, and Hawk learned from Elizabeth the next day that Lydia Bean had been captured. "I was afraid it would happen," she said and bit her lip nervously. "Poor Lydia."

One bit of heroism that the defenders of the fort only learned later was how Lydia Bean's life was saved. After being captured, she was taken to Togue, where she was condemned to be burned. She was tied to the stake and the fire lighted, when Nancy Ward appeared. She kicked the burning embers and stomped out the fire, glaring at the braves who were staring at her. After she untied Lydia Bean, she turned and said with scorn, "It revolts my soul that the Cherokee warriors would stoop so low as to torture a squaw!" She took Lydia away from the angry stares of the braves and kept her safe at her own home, where Lydia taught the Indian squaws how to make butter and cheese before she was returned to the settlement.

Dragging Canoe was defeated. He set up his camp and sent out raiding parties, but he himself was unable to carry on any more of the fighting. He was a bitter man, and as the Cherokee pulled back, he was already plotting other raids on the white settlements.

One of the raiding parties was under the leadership of Akando, who was as violent as Dragging Canoe. Akando led his small band of warriors through the countryside, murdering and butchering every white person found, except for two. Creeping up with three of his warriors early one morning, he captured two white men. They were in a drunken stupor and easy prey for the silent Indians who crept into their camp like ghosts.

Zeke Taylor and William Crabtree had been drinking all night. They had heard of the ravages of the Indians, and Zeke was worried about his family, while Crabtree was simply rejoicing in what might be the deaths of some of his enemies.

Zeke Taylor woke when something sharp touched his throat, and when he opened his eyes and saw the coppery face marked with war paint, he knew he was a dead man. He heard Crabtree, who lay a few feet away, begging for his life and knew it was hopeless.

Akando laughed at the pleas of Crabtree and shook his head. "We will not kill you quickly. We will see how much pain you can stand."

"No, don't do that!" Crabtree begged. "We'll help you! Don't kill us!"

"How can you help us?" Akando asked, his cruel eyes glittering.

"You know Hawk Spencer?"

"Yes, I know him. He is my enemy."

"Let us live, and we'll help you get him. He's at Watauga. It won't be hard to trap him. Just let us live. . . !"

Akando used his knife on Crabtree but not seriously. An idea was forming in his mind, and finally he said, "You can live until you help us catch the Hawk. If you do not, then you will go through the fire!"

The Lion's Heart

Thirty-Six

Hawk had come to Jacob's room and now stood watching quietly as the young man pulled his things together and packed them. Sequatchie had come to him three days earlier, saying, "Jacob holds me to my bargain. I promised to take him home when he became a man, and I think I must go."

"Do you think it will be safe?" Hawk had asked.

"Yes. My people have had enough. They have gone back to the Overhill towns."

Hawk sat down on the bed, half his mind analyzing the risk that Sequatchie and Jacob would have on their trip back through the mountains toward Williamsburg. The militias of Georgia, South Carolina, North Carolina, and Virginia had poured into the country to fight the Cherokee. They had pushed them back to the Overhill towns so that the frontier was safe. North Carolina had also accepted Watauga as Washington County, and there would be more protection for the area from now on.

"I don't need to say how much I'll miss you, Jacob."

Jacob did not turn around but muttered, "Well, it's been good of you to have me, Pa." He finished his packing and turned around, and his father stood up. The two of them were almost the same height, and although Hawk was much heavier, they appeared to be looking into a mirror.

"Jake, be careful about Sequatchie. As a matter of fact, I really wish you weren't going. You know the feelings against the Cherokee are pretty hot right now, so watch out for him."

"Well, I think it'll be all right, Pa, but I'll be careful."

A silence then filled the room, and Jacob said awkwardly, "I guess I'll move my stuff to the door."

"I'll help you."

The two men went to the main room, and as Jacob turned to say good-bye to the rest of the family, Hawk stood back. He watched as Elizabeth, Sarah, and Andrew came to bid Jacob good-bye, and noted that Andrew bore no ill will, for which Hawk was grateful.

Jacob said good-bye to Hannah and Joshua, then looked up at Elizabeth, saying, "I'm going to miss these two."

"They'll miss you, too, Jacob. They really love you—but then we all do."

Sarah said, "You're going to say good-bye to Iris and Amanda, aren't you?"

"Sure I am."

"I'll saddle your horse and put your things on the packhorse, Jake," Andrew said.

"Thanks, Andrew."

Actually, Jacob was glad to get outside the cabin. He felt a strange sense of depression and had hardly slept at all. He had thought it would be a pleasure to get away from Watauga, especially to distance himself from Abigail. Now that the time had come, however, a great emptiness welled up inside him. He kept his head down as he crossed the path and looked up in surprise to see that Amanda was coming to greet him.

His lips were stiff and he tried to speak naturally. "Hello, Amanda."

"You mean good-bye, don't you?" Amanda seemed rather unnatural and her face was pale. "You want to take one look at the yearling before you go?" She did not really want Jacob to see the calf, but she wanted to say her good-bye in private. She had been praying all night, and now she knew that this might be the last time she would ever see Jacob Spencer.

"I guess so."

The two walked to the barn and stepped inside, and Jacob glanced indifferently over at the calf, saying, "She's a fine calf."

"Jacob, I didn't come in here to look at the calf. I just wanted to talk to you." She had prepared the speech all night long, but now that it was time to say it, she hardly knew how to find the words. "I . . . I've been wanting to tell you how sorry I am."

"Sorry for what, Amanda?"

"You know—for what I said to you about your being selfish."

"You didn't go far wrong. I am selfish."

"I felt so bad about it."

"Don't worry. It's all right."

Jacob turned to leave, but she took his arm, and when he turned around, she swallowed hard. "I'll miss you, Jacob."

Jacob looked down at her and was struck again with how she had grown up. He remembered how thin and frightened she had been when he had first seen her. She would not even hold her head up then, so afraid she was of her father and so intimidated by his abuse. But something had happened to her, and he knew it had something to do with her surrender to God. He forced a smile and said, "I'll miss you, too. I won't have anyone to go fishing with me."

It was not what he wanted to say, and he felt he was babbling like an idiot.

Suddenly Amanda said, "Jacob, you don't really want to go!" Her voice was urgent, and she reached up and held the loose fabric of his cotton shirt. It was as if she would hold him there and keep him from going, and her lips were trembling. "No, you don't want to go! I know it!"

"Yes, I do. I've got to go."

"No, Jacob, you don't have to go. What you're looking for you won't find in Williamsburg any more than you could right here."

"What are you talking about, Amanda?"

Taking a deep breath, Amanda whispered, "Jacob, you need the Lord. You're not ever going to be happy until you find Jesus. Until He's inside of you as He's inside your father and your mother."

Jacob shook his head and was aware of the deep longing for something inside his heart. "I've heard all that before," he said.

"I know you have, but you haven't listened, Jacob. You're miserable, and there's no happiness unless you let God take it away."

The simple honesty in her words and the emptiness of his heart struck hard at Jacob. Perhaps it was the accumulation of sermons that he had heard all of his life from his grandparents, and then from Paul Anderson, from his father, and now from Amanda. He was shocked to find out that he was trembling, and for once he voiced what he really felt.

"Amanda—I feel so *alone*!"

"If you'd just let God fill you with His love and forgiveness, you'd never be alone again. He loves you, Jacob, and He wants you to know joy and happiness, but you have to humble yourself and ask for it."

The trembling in Jacob's body increased, and he looked down at his hands and whispered, "Look, I can't hold my hands still." Fear took hold of him then, and he said desperately, "I can't go on like this, Amanda! I . . . I think I'm going crazy sometimes!"

Amanda whispered, "Jacob, will you pray with me and just ask Jesus to come into your heart? Will you do that?"

So many times Jacob Spencer had wondered why he could not say yes to God. He knew that God had dealt with him all of his life, but somehow the loss of his mother, and then the loss of his father for so many years had put a wall about his bitter and angry heart. He could not let God in, and he could not get out of the dark prison that held him captive. Now, however, something was happening inside the half darkness of that barn. As he looked down into the brown eyes of the young girl, he saw her heart revealed in the depth of her gaze and realized with a shock that she loved him. It suddenly came to him how many people had loved him and how little love he had given in return. Guilt and shame washed over him, and to his horror he felt tears brimming in his eyes. He was embarrassed and humiliated and dashed them away with the backs of his hands, but Amanda reached out and held his hands.

"Don't be ashamed of your tears! God is dealing with you. Jacob, let's pray! Kneel here, and let's ask God to give you what you've longed for."

And then Jacob Spencer found himself dropping to his knees. He was vaguely aware of Amanda praying urgently. He was more acutely aware that a revolution was taking place in his own heart. Guilt, such as he had never known, welled up in him, and he saw clearly how he had become bitter and had lashed out at a father who loved him and had ignored the call of God on his life. He began to sob, and finally in desperation he cried out, "Oh, God, I've been so wrong! I've gone the wrong way! I ask you in the name of Jesus to forgive me and to help me be the man you want me to be!"

Amanda was sobbing now, and finally the two of them clung together. Slowly Jake struggled to his feet and pulled Amanda up. He looked down and saw the tears running down her face.

"You'll never be alone again now," she said, a smile on her tear-streaked face.

Jacob was aware that something drastic had changed. There was a peace in his spirit, and he felt utterly drained—but filled with a sense of completeness he had never known in all of his life. "I feel so different . . . so clean," he whispered.

"Jacob, you now have a personal relationship with a heavenly Father who loves you and will always be with you wherever you go. But you have an earthly father who is still waiting to be forgiven by a son he loves very much."

A determined look followed by a smile came to Jacob's face. "Will you please tell Sequatchie that I won't need him to take me to Williamsburg?"

Amanda could hardly keep from shouting as she said, "Of course!"

Jacob barely heard Amanda answer as he began to walk toward the cabin. His steps quickened with every stride until he was running, calling louder and louder, "Daddy! Daddy!" as the tears coursed down his face.

Hawk appeared at the door with an anxious look on his face. Before he could ask what the trouble was, Jacob threw himself into his father's arms, sobbing, oblivious to anything except his father and himself.

Jacob finally looked at his father. "Will you please forgive me for how I have acted?"

"I am the one who needs to be forgiven, son. I left you when you needed me the most."

"That's all in the past. Just as my sins are now!"

Hawk grabbed his son in another strong embrace as he sent a prayer of thankfulness heavenward.

Jacob then looked at his father again and smiled. "I love you, Daddy!"

Hawk answered as tears now began to flow from his eyes, "I love you, too, son!"

Akando's Attack

Thirty-Seven

The hot summer passed away and with it the memories of the Cherokee war faded. Not for everyone, however, for there were fresh graves, and some carried wounds to the end of their lives over the brief but fierce struggle. A sense of peace descended over the hills and valleys of the frontier as the Cherokee pulled back, and the militia grew stronger day by day. As the leaves of the hardwoods turned to a riotous yellow and gold and red, and the air brought an invigorating crispness to it, the Spencers all grew closer together in a way they had all dreamed of.

The creek that wound around the Spencer homestead made a serpentine shape as it meandered over the lowlands. Each fall it grew shallow, but there was one spot hollowed out by years of erosion, where a large pond swelled over nearly half an acre. Some strange force of nature had cut out a disk-shaped indentation in the earth, and the water had entered it, filled it, then left to wind its narrow way toward the Watauga River. It was a favorite fishing spot for the Spencers, and one Thursday afternoon Jacob, Andrew, and Philip Baxter had formed a party with Abigail, Sarah, and Amanda. The six had made the trip, bearing baskets of food that were packed by the young women, while the young men carried the fishing gear. They had been fishing at the pool now for some time, and as usual, Andrew had caught the most fish. Jacob had caught a monstrous snapping turtle, which had occupied them for a time. It was a frightening-looking thing with its mossy back, fierce old eyes, and, most of all, the curved beak. The boys had discovered that it could break a stick in two and enjoyed themselves letting it perform this trick while the girls wrinkled their noses and said, "Turn that old thing loose. He's so ugly!"

Jacob, upon hearing Amanda say this, grinned broadly. "Why, how do you know that? He may be the handsomest snapping turtle in the world."

Amanda was wearing a chocolate brown dress with a square neckline, elbow-length sleeves edged in white lace, and the waist encircled with a white sash. She looked very pretty. "I don't think so."

Jacob laughed and said, "He may be the Romeo of the turtle world. Somewhere there's a Juliet waiting for him to come back."

"Well, let him go back to Juliet, then," Amanda insisted.

"No, we're going to eat him," Andrew said, winking at Philip, who was sitting next to Sarah. He had become a regular member of the little group that took every opportunity to get together, and now he grinned, saying, "Nothing like turtle soup, is there, Sarah?"

Sarah reached over and pinched Philip on the side, saying, "I ought to make you eat it for talking like that."

"Ow!" Philip yelled. "Watch what you're doing! You pinched a plug out of me!" He reached up and pulled at Sarah, and she struggled to get away but could not. Philip's eyes gleamed, and he winked at Andrew, saying, "Let's see if that turtle can bite a girl's finger through."

"Don't you dare, Philip Baxter!" Sarah wrenched away and picked up a stick, saying, "Your pa should have taken a switch to you a long time ago! It's not too late to start!"

"I reckon I'm a little bit large for that," Philip said.

The playful spirit went on for some time, and finally Philip went downstream with Andrew to see if they could catch a few more fish. "You know what, Andrew? I think your sister is wonderful."

Andrew laughed, and with a big brother's mentality, said, "Must be love because you're not seeing what's really there. She drives me crazy."

Philip, however, was unembarrassed. He watched Sarah, who had left the other girls and was moving upstream from them. She had taken off her shoes and was wading in the water. "I'm going to go ask if she'll go to the dance with me over in the settlement next week." He seemed not to mind the taunts of Jacob and Andrew, who teased him unmercifully, as he made his way a hundred yards upstream. He glanced up and saw that Abigail and Amanda were sitting down on a grassy spot talking about something, and as he approached, he said, "You look mighty pretty, Sarah."

Sarah had seen him coming and now smiled. They had been friends for a long time, and she knew that someday, when they got a little older, he would actually come courting her. He reached out to take her hand and help her over the rocks, which were slick with green moss, and said, "Sarah—"

Sarah was waiting to hear what he would say but saw that his hand suddenly stopped and his mouth opened as if in surprise. She thought for one moment that he was about to sneeze or cough, and then she saw a small dot on the left side of his chest grow larger as crimson blood gushed forth.

"Philip—!" she screamed and leaped toward him. He was falling forward, and she fell under his weight. "Philip, what is it?" Then she realized that she had heard the sound of a musket, and she saw that the water was turning scarlet around her and that Philip was lying facedown. Desperately she turned him over, but she knew he was dead. She heard Andrew calling and looked up to see the boys rushing down the side of the creek. "Come on!" Andrew shouted, and as he came up to her, she saw that he had blood on his side, but he jerked her to her feet.

"Come on! They're coming!" Jacob yelled.

They made a wild dash away from the creek, and Sarah gasped, "We can't leave Philip there!"

Andrew said grimly, "He's dead, Sarah," and pulled her along so that she nearly stumbled.

They reached the cabin and Andrew collapsed. Abigail and Elizabeth helped take him inside. Elizabeth looked with fear at Abigail as they both saw the wound in his side that was bleeding heavily.

Jacob began shouting, "Pa—!" as he emerged from the cabin with his long rifle.

Hawk, who was chopping wood, dropped his ax and snatched up his rifle. He ran forward, yelling something that Jacob could not understand.

The sound of footsteps came to Sarah, and as everything became confused she was aware that Jacob and Hawk were firing at a group of grotesquely painted Indians. But she was also aware that Amanda, who had turned toward her own cabin, was suddenly seized by a bronzed Indian in buckskins.

He's going to kill her! Sarah thought wildly and cried out even as the men moved forward. Somehow Sequatchie had appeared, and

Sarah heard him calling out in the Cherokee language to the attackers.

And then out of the woods a figure came running. At first Sarah thought it was another Indian, but she saw at once that it was a white man—and then she saw that it was Zeke Taylor.

He was yelling, and she heard him say, "That's my girl! Let go of her!"

Akando whirled and was evidently surprised that one of his own was coming for him. A scream emerged from his lips and he leveled his rifle to fire at Zeke, who was running straight at him. The rifle was knocked upward as Amanda turned to see her father coming. She reached out and tilted the rifle—but not quickly enough.

Sequatchie had seen all this, and he saw Zeke fall, grasping his stomach as the blood poured through his fingers. As he collapsed, Sequatchie sped across the open ground and headed for Akando. The Indian released Amanda and yanked the tomahawk out of his belt, warning Sequatchie in the Cherokee dialect.

It seemed they were frozen like that when Jacob, who had come from the side, launched himself in the air and threw his arms around Akando, knocking him to the ground. The Indian swung his tomahawk, and the haft of it caught Jacob in the head and made him lose his grip. Sequatchie yanked Amanda up, and Jacob leaped to his feet, pulled his knife from his belt, and threw himself at Akando.

Akando was a strong, wiry man with tremendous physical strength. He caught Jacob's wrist and held it, and the two rolled on the ground. Jacob's whole mind and heart were set on freeing his hand, but the grip of the Cherokee was powerful. He looked up to see William Crabtree, who had suddenly appeared and was coming to help Akando. He had his musket loaded, apparently, and as Jacob stared into the muzzle, it seemed as big as a dark tunnel. At that instant of time he was very glad he had taken Christ into his life. He waited for the musket to fire and for death to come—but it did not happen.

A shot did ring out, and Crabtree was driven backward. Akando jerked himself free from Jacob and ran in a crouched position, fleeing to the trees. The other Indians who had not been killed by Hawk and Jacob followed. When Jacob turned around, he saw Hawk lowering his rifle, and he got to his feet and moved over to stand beside him. "You saved me that time, Pa!" he gasped, his breath coming in spurts.

"I'm glad I was there. Let's see how Zeke is."

The two hurried over to where Amanda had come to kneel beside her father. When Hawk leaned over and looked at the stomach wound, he shook his head slightly, a gesture that Jacob did not miss. Both men knew that stomach wounds were the worst kind.

Iris Taylor had observed all that had happened from the door of her cabin. She had been frozen as she watched her daughter get captured and then her husband shot as he tried to save her. As the others knelt over Zeke, Iris left her cabin and hurried toward her husband. "Carry him into the cabin. I will see to his wound."

Sequatchie was amazed at the strength of this woman who was offering to help the man who had abused her so terribly. He helped Hawk and Jacob carry Zeke into the Taylors' cabin. Iris and Amanda immediately began to try to help Zeke as the others moved to the door.

Hawk turned to Jacob. "Please stay here with Iris and Amanda. They will probably need someone to help them."

"Sure, Pa. But let me know how Andrew is doing as soon as you can. Philip didn't make it."

Hawk grasped the shoulder of his son. "I'm sorry, Jake. And I'll let you know about Andrew as soon as I find out something." His expression told Jacob everything else, pride for a son who had acted so bravely to save another and worry for another son who lay injured and hurting.

Hawk and Sequatchie walked outside and saw Crabtree lying where he had been shot. As they moved toward him, Hawk saw that his bullet had only hit Crabtree in the arm, but that he had hit his head on a rock when he fell. "Take him into Watauga, Sequatchie. He'll need to be tried for what he has taken part in today. And please stop by the Baxters' and tell them about their son. Tell them we are praying for them and will do anything we can for them."

"Of course, my brother. I will also pray for Andrew while I am gone."

"Pray for Zeke Taylor, too. Unless a miracle happens, he is in far greater danger than anyone else. He has an eternity at stake."

Sequatchie nodded grimly as he watched Hawk turn and hurry to the cabin to see about his son.

Amanda's Father

Thirty-Eight

*H*ow is Sarah?" Hawk asked anxiously. He had been talking to Elizabeth about the attack, and now an anxious look came into his eyes as he glanced into the bedroom.

"I put her in our bed and gave her some tea. She's very upset."

"I think she was fonder of Philip than any of us knew."

"Yes," Elizabeth agreed. "She'll always think of him, I believe, as her first love."

"He was a fine young fellow," Hawk said quietly. "I'll miss him."

"What about Zeke?"

"I don't think he's going to make it."

"What a shame! It must be hard for a man like that to face death."

"I think it is," Hawk said. He hesitated, then said, "I guess I'll go look in on Andrew."

Elizabeth smiled, and a pixyish look came over her face. "You'll have to get around Abigail. She hasn't left his side since we put him to bed."

"Well, it wasn't a serious wound, just painful. I thank God for that." He grinned, then reached out and hugged Elizabeth. "God was with us. We came through it all right."

"Go along, now. Go and see Andrew."

Hawk, however, did not actually go into the room. He stopped at the door that led to Andrew's room, and seeing Abigail sitting beside him, leaning over him with an anxious look in her face, he simply returned to the main room. *I reckon he would rather see her as me*, he thought, and somehow it pleased him to think that Abigail held such concern for Andrew.

Andrew shifted uncomfortably on the bed and looked up at Abigail, who was seated on a chair and was bending over him. "Much obliged for taking care of me, Abby."

"It was nothing. I'm just so glad it wasn't worse."

Andrew gazed at her face and studied her for a moment, then muttered, "You don't have to stay. I'm all right."

"I want to."

For a moment a memory flashed back, and she knew it would be with her for a long time. She had seen Philip as he had been killed with a single shot, and then she had seen Andrew suddenly straighten up and clutch at his side. Her heart had seemed to die within her, for she was certain that at that moment Andrew was mortally wounded. She had rushed forward, crying his name, and then he had held his hand over his bloody side and urged her to flee.

Now she took a deep breath and whispered, "When I saw you get hit with that musket ball, Andrew, I thought I'd lost you."

"Lost me? Why, Abby—"

Suddenly Abigail reached out and put the tips of her fingers across his mouth. "No. Don't say anything, Andrew. I . . . I've got to tell you something." She held her hand over his lips for a moment and summoned up her courage, then said, "I couldn't bear the thought of losing you when I've never told you . . . how I felt."

Reaching up, Andrew took her hand from his lips and kept hold of it. It was warm and soft, and he asked, "What do you mean, Abby?"

"I love you, Andrew."

Andrew MacNeal stared at the girl. He had loved her for so long that he had forgotten how it had first come into his heart, but now as she bent over him and he could see the clearness of her eyes and the smoothness of her cheeks, he could not believe what he was hearing. "I can't believe that," he said quietly.

"I've been so foolish that I don't blame you for not believing me. I thought I was falling in love with Jacob. I really did, but I wasn't. All the time, as long as I've known you, I've always felt something in my heart, but I didn't know what it was. . . ."

Andrew listened as Abigail continued to speak, then finally he interrupted, saying, "I guess you know that I've always loved you, Abby."

"Why didn't you tell me?"

"I thought you were in love with Jacob. I thought I'd lost you because I hadn't fought for you, but I'll never let that happen again."

A great joy filled Abigail Stevens' heart. She leaned forward, whispering, "You're right about that." She leaned against him and her lips were soft and yet possessive as she kissed him. She leaned forward still harder, and suddenly he groaned, for she had leaned against his wound.

Laughter danced in his eyes as he grimaced, but he did not release her hand. "I didn't know your kisses hurt so much."

Abigail laughed and said, "If you don't like them, I won't do it anymore."

"A little pain never hurt anyone," he said and drew her down again eagerly. He put his arm around her and held her close and knew that she had come into his life to stay.

———

Hawk entered the cabin of Iris and Amanda and saw Jacob standing beside Amanda on one side of the bed where Zeke Taylor lay, with Iris on the other. He studied Jacob's face as he turned toward him and saw his son shake his head. He knew it wouldn't be long.

The silence was broken as Zeke, in a faint, raspy voice, called out, "Hawk. . .!"

Quickly Hawk moved across the room. Amanda moved back, and Jacob put his arm around her and held her tightly as Hawk knelt down by the bedside. "I'm here, Zeke. What is it?"

"Reckon . . . I've treated you . . . purty bad."

"Don't think about that now, Zeke."

"Guess maybe . . . it's the only time . . . I got. I'm right sorry."

Hawk's heart went out to the dying man. He had never liked Zeke, and yet now he felt pity rise in him, and he said quietly, "I'd like for you to be asking God for forgiveness, not me. You've got mine, for what it's worth."

"Too late for that!"

Iris bent over and brushed the hair away from her husband's forehead. "It's never too late to ask God, Zeke."

A faint ray of hope crept into Taylor's eyes, and his lips trembled. "You reckon it's so?" he whispered.

"Yes, it's so," Hawk said quickly. "The Bible is full of promises that God's ready to forgive. All we have to do is know we're wrong and ask."

Zeke listened as Hawk continued to speak quietly, quoting Scriptures on God's love and mercy. Finally the dying man shook his head with despair. "Not me. I've been too mean ... to my wife and young'un."

Inspiration came to Hawk then, and he said, "If you really want to do something for Amanda and Iris, then get right with God. Then one day they'll come and be with you. You'll all be together. A real family."

Iris watched as tears filled Zeke's eyes. *I never saw him cry, not once, in all the years we were married,* she thought. She knelt down beside him, took his hand, and said, "Ask God to forgive you in Jesus' name, Zeke!"

Zeke mumbled and his chest heaved. His voice was growing weaker, but they all heard him say, "Oh, God, I ask for forgiveness in the name of Jesus."

Amanda then sobbed and pulled herself away from Jacob. She knelt beside her father, took his free hand, and said, "Oh, Pa, I love you!"

"I'm sorry I treated you ... so bad," Zeke gasped.

Amanda barely caught the words, and her tears fell on his hand as she kissed it. "It's all right, Pa. It's all right now."

Zeke Taylor only had time to reach up and touch his wife's cheek. "Iris, I'm sorry." Then he whispered, "You was always ... the prettiest woman ... I ever saw."

They stood around the bed of the dying man and he did not speak again. Just before he died he looked up into the faces of those around him and strength seemed to return to him. He raised his hand as if in a farewell wave, then he smiled. It was a smile such as none of them had ever seen on his lips, then he closed his eyes, and his chest ceased to move.

"He's gone," Iris whispered, tears flowing down her face.

Amanda put her arm around her mother, and her voice was choked as she said, "He's gone, Ma, but he went to be with the Lord. We'll see him again someday!"

America's First Birthday

Thirty-Nine

Get up, woman! You're going to miss your son's wedding day!"
Elizabeth had been lying in the bed, coming out of a deep sleep. She sat bolt upright and stared at Hawk, who was standing over beside the washstand, his razor in his hand, his eyes laughing at her.

"Oh me! What time is it?"

"Time for you to get up. Here it is July 4, 1777, your son's wedding day and America's first birthday. You'd better jump to it."

Elizabeth slipped out of her nightgown at once and began pulling her clothes out of the chest beside the wall, saying, "Hurry up! I need to wash my face!"

Hawk was lathering up and said, "Your face doesn't need washing. You washed it just three days ago." He laughed as she picked up a moccasin and threw it at him and then began raking the blade down over his tough beard. His eyes watered, and he gritted his teeth. "Indians ought to try shaving for a torture," he said. "It's about the worst thing I know."

Elizabeth was slipping into her undergarments, and she stopped long enough to stare at him. "Don't talk about things like that. Not today—well, not ever, really."

"All right." Drawing the blade down his other cheek, Hawk said, "Life's real funny sometimes. Here we are getting ready for Andrew and Abigail's wedding. Just seems like yesterday you and I were getting married."

Elizabeth pulled the shift over her head and then moved over to begin combing her hair. "God's always working things out in His own time," she remarked.

Hawk said nothing until he had finished shaving, then he bent over and sputtered into the water, washing the lather away. As he dried on a coarse towel and picked up the basin to get rid of the water, he said, "I was proud of Jake offering to stand up for his step-brother."

"I think he's gotten over Abigail pretty well. He was never in love with her anyway. He didn't love her as he should, but she's going to make a good sister-in-law for him."

Hawk moved away and sat down as Elizabeth poured fresh water into the basin and began to wash her face with soft soap. "Things are going well with the settlers, aren't they?"

"Couldn't be better." Hawk thought about the treaties that were signed in June, ending the war with the Cherokee. It had come about when William Christian had led a force of militia against the Ov-erhill towns in October. He had defeated the Cherokee and forced them to surrender—all except Dragging Canoe. He thought about that fierce warrior and the rumor that he had fled into the Chick-amauga area. Aloud he said, "I wonder if we'll ever see Akando again? Nobody saw him after the attack."

"I hope not. Don't talk about that, Hawk."

"All right." He came over, leaned over and kissed the back of her neck, then put his arms around her. "I'll talk about how beautiful you look."

Elizabeth turned, put her arms around his neck, and drew his head down. She kissed him firmly, then said, "I've got two small ones to attend to. Now, you get dressed. I want *you* to look beautiful today."

"I always look beautiful," Hawk grinned, then turned to begin dressing.

————

The wedding of Andrew MacNeal and Abigail Stevens was being held at Fort Patrick Henry near Long Island. It was a part of a large celebration that was being held at the fort to commemorate the first birthday of the new United States of America. Settlers from all parts of the frontier were to be in attendance to see troops parade from Virginia, North and South Carolina, and Georgia, as well as militia companies from Watauga and Nolichucky. They were even being joined by more than five hundred Cherokee warriors, including twenty chiefs. To show good faith, the Indians were even going to perform a dance for the settlers in their dress costumes.

As soon as Elizabeth and Hawk arrived at the settlement, they looked up to see William and Lydia Bean.

Elizabeth, at once, went to Lydia and put her arm around her. "I'm glad to see you. Are you all right?"

"Oh yes," Lydia smiled. She had indeed survived being taken prisoner by Old Abram, but she had spread the word throughout the settlement that it was Nancy Ward who had saved her.

"Did you hear about Nathaniel Gist? He's going to join Washington's Continental Army. He's given his land to Joseph Martin, the new Indian agent from Virginia. He's the husband of Betsy Ward, Nancy's daughter."

"Yes," Hawk nodded, "and James Robertson has been made the Indian agent for North Carolina. That's a good choice. He's a good man."

Hawk then smiled as he said to William, "Are you ready to give your speech?"

Bean smiled ruefully as he replied, "I'm not too sure about this. I knew when they asked me to speak that I should have said no. You should be up there instead of me. How about it?"

"No, I don't think so. I'll leave the speechmaking to people like you, Robertson, and Sevier. My wife is better at making speeches, anyway—at least to me she is."

Elizabeth poked Hawk in the side. "You're pretty good at it yourself, you know."

Bean chuckled, then sobered as he said, "I'm sure glad to see the Cherokee here. We all need to get along now and learn to share this land. There's plenty for everyone."

Hawk seemed to look far in the distance as he replied, "I hope you're right, William, but some people think the frontier should belong only to the settlers. I'm afraid there may be more trouble ahead, especially with the revolution going on. It's only a matter of time till the British come over the mountains, too."

Elizabeth felt the conversation needed to be changed to a lighter note. She turned to her husband. "Come on, Hawk," Elizabeth whispered. "We've got to get inside. We'll miss the wedding."

"Well, the groom's mother ought to have a place right in the front," Hawk laughed. "Come along. We'll see them off in style!"

The wedding was held outdoors in the central square of the fort. The guests simply gathered around, while Paul Anderson stood in front of Abigail and Andrew. Jacob and Sarah stood up with them as Anderson said the old words, and they promised to love each other "till death do us part." Finally Paul Anderson said, "I now pronounce you man and wife. You may kiss your bride."

Andrew turned and gave Abigail a resounding kiss, at which there was great laughter and a few teasing remarks by his young friends. Abigail flushed, then laughed, and the two stood beaming as the neighbors and relatives came up to greet them. A trio of musicians—on fiddle, banjo, and dulcimer—struck up a lively tune, and the crowd gathered around the refreshment table.

As Hawk and Elizabeth stood eating some wedding cake and drinking apple cider, they watched Sarah carefully.

Hawk said abruptly, "What would you say if we sent Sarah back to stay with my folks in Williamsburg?"

Elizabeth turned, her eyes wide. "How did you know that was what I was thinking?"

"I didn't," Hawk admitted, "but she's not getting over seeing young Baxter die. She's not eating, and she mopes a lot. That's not like Sarah. She's always been so lively."

Elizabeth sighed. The Baxters had moved away from the area after burying their son, but she knew that Hawk was right. Finally she said, "I think it might be best if she did get away from here for a while. How would she get there? Would you take her?"

"I'll ask Jacob. He's been wanting to go back and see his grandparents. If that doesn't work, she can go to Boston to your family."

"I hate to see her go, but she needs to get away, and we've been praying about it. Why don't you ask Jacob?"

"I'll do it right now."

Hawk approached Jacob and drew him off to one side. "Son, I want to ask a favor."

"Sure. What is it?"

"Sarah's not doing well. I guess you've noticed."

"Yes, I have. It worries me. What are you thinking about?"

"I think it might be well if you take her to Williamsburg. Go with her. You've been wanting to go back. Introduce her to some young people. Take her to some parties. Get her mind off Philip if you can."

"Why, I'd be proud, Pa."

"Good, I'll send word to my parents that you're coming." Then an apprehensive look crossed his face, and he reached out and took Jacob's arm, squeezing it hard. "This doesn't mean I want you to stay there, you understand?"

Jacob grinned and suddenly slapped his father on the chest. "It'll be nice to see my grandparents after all these years, but I've got a father to come home to now, and a family."

Hawk smiled and the two suddenly put out their hands and held on as they smiled into each other's eyes.

Jacob moved away from his father, coming to stand beside Amanda. She looked at him with surprise and then smiled at him. "The wedding was beautiful, wasn't it?"

"Sure was." He looked over and saw Iris standing beside Sequatchie and noted that she was smiling up at the tall Cherokee.

I wouldn't be surprised if something didn't come of that one of these days, he thought, but he said nothing to Amanda.

After the wedding, everyone gathered to watch the Cherokee perform. Jacob and Amanda were amazed by the intricate movements of the Indians. After the performance, Jacob turned to Amanda and said, "Let's take a walk. I want to talk to you."

"All right."

They walked along under the fading sun that was already growing crimson. Jacob stopped her as soon as they were out of sight of the cabin and turned to her. "I'm taking Sarah to Williamsburg."

"I didn't know that."

"Pa and Ma just decided it'd be good for her to get away."

"I think it will. She misses Philip so much. When will you go?"

"Right away. Probably next week."

"I'll miss you, Jacob."

Jacob took her hand and held it, then said, "I'll miss you, too."

She did not answer. There was a quietness in her, and her eyes were expressive as she looked up at him. He could not read her thoughts, and he said, "How much will you miss me?"

She smiled more broadly. "Enough," she said.

"Enough to wait for me to come back? You won't go running off with one of these young fellows?"

"No, I won't do that."

There was a sweetness and a gentleness in her at that moment. It had always been there, perhaps, but Jacob knew that he had missed it somewhere along the way. She had grown up to be a very pretty young woman, with beautiful doelike brown eyes. He reached out and pulled her forward, waiting for her to resist, but she did not. She came against him, and her face was in repose with an expression that stirred his curiosity. He found himself trying to find a name for it. It was something like the gravity that comes when someone has seen a great deal, and there was a shadow of hidden sadness and yet there was a joy. She always had a curtain of reserve, but now he sensed the great vitality and imagination kept under stern restraint. He knew suddenly that there was a fire in this young woman that made her lovely, and he bent and touched the coolness of her lips. She had the power to stir him and she did so now, deepening his love for her and arousing a sense of loneliness. One powerful flash of emotion touched them both then. Her lips were soft, and she yielded herself to him wholly, completely, and he knew that something had happened to them both.

As he lifted his head, Amanda whispered, "I'll wait for you, Jacob."

"I'll come back," he whispered. "I couldn't do without you, Amanda!"

Sounds of gunfire caused the couple to turn back toward the crowd. They watched as the new nation's flag was raised over the fort while the guns continued their salute.

As Jacob kissed Amanda again, the promising future of America seemed to symbolize the promising future of its brave pioneers.

Epilogue

Thomas Denton stepped into the library to stare at his sister, Annabelle. She fit into the rich surroundings of the room in a mauve-colored silk dress with a large gray bow hanging down the back. Her beautiful figure was enhanced by the close-fitting bodice and waistline, and the three-quarter-length sleeves that ended just below the elbow with a white frill. She turned toward him and smiled in a rather disturbing fashion.

"You'll never guess who I just heard from, Annabelle."

"No, I can't guess," Annabelle said. "Who is it?"

"Jacob Spencer."

"You heard from Jacob?" she said abruptly. She held her head higher, and an interest came into her eyes.

"Yes, I saw James Spencer, his grandfather, you know. He'd gotten a letter from Jake's father. You remember Hawk Spencer, the long hunter?"

"I remember. What about him?"

"Jake's coming home for a visit and bringing his stepsister with him."

"His stepsister? I wonder why?"

"Mr. Spencer just said that the girl has had a hard time. He thinks the trip will help her." He studied Annabelle carefully. "You never really quite got over Jake, did you?"

"Don't be foolish, Tom."

"I know you pretty well. You shed your suitors like a tree sheds leaves in the fall."

"That's a very poor metaphor."

"It isn't a metaphor. It's a simile," Denton laughed, "and I'm right, too. I'll tell you what. We'll have a party for Jacob when he gets here, and for his sister, too. Maybe she'll be a pretty, virtuous young lady that I can pay attention to."

Annabelle was only half listening. She waited until Tom had finished teasing her, and after he left the library, she turned and went to stare out the window. It was hot outside, and hardly a breeze was stirring. The grass was green, however, and she watched distractedly as a white cat with emerald green eyes strolled by outside and disappeared around the corner of the house.

"Jacob Spencer," she whispered to herself, and her mind went back to the days when she had fancied that young man somewhat. "He's grown up now. He ought to be rather interesting. He won't be a backwoodsman. He's got a good education—and he always was a handsome thing."

As the brilliant summer sun beat down on the city of Williamsburg, Annabelle Denton remained in front of the window staring out. Once, she reached up and drew her hand across her lips at some memory, then a half smile came to her face.

"Jacob Spencer," she murmured, and then smiled as if some secret thought passed through her mind.

Notes to Our Readers

Well, here we are again at the close of another chapter of THE SPIRIT OF APPALACHIA. We want to thank you, the readers, for making the first book such a success! God has blessed us both so much with this collaboration. Thank you also for all of the kind letters you sent about *Over the Misty Mountains*. We appreciate every one.

We hope you have enjoyed this second journey, *Beyond the Quiet Hills*. We have really enjoyed telling the story of Jacob. Many of you wrote that you hoped there would be more about him and Hawk, so we hope you were pleased. We wanted to wait until the second book to deal with their relationship, as a quick resolution would not have been true for the situation. Jacob needed to deal with his feelings about being abandoned. He portrayed himself as a victim until he was faced with someone who had gone through worse circumstances. He was then able to see how God had worked to bring good out of the wrongs that had been done.

Once again we felt that you might want to know the real events of the book. The history of this area is so rich and fascinating. If you have enjoyed these books, you might want to check your library for books about the real people who settled in Watauga.

The settlers of Watauga did meet with the Cherokee in 1772 and did lease the land from them. They had set up their own governing body to make this contract legal. Even though they did not declare themselves independent of any colonial ties, they did govern themselves, and for all practical purposes, they were the first self-governing group on the continent.

The members of the Watauga Court given here are the true members. The name of the first sheriff was not given, so we thought it would be fun to make Hawk the sheriff. Many of the challenges Hawk dealt with as sheriff really happened. A man named Shoate did steal a horse and was hanged for his deed. Other punishments for horse stealing consisted of branding the guilty with an "H" and

THE SPIRIT OF APPALACHIA

a "T" on the cheeks. The "Bread Rounds" incident also is real, although the name of Hiram Younger is fictitious.

There really was a celebration with the Cherokee in the spring of 1774 to mark the agreement between the two groups. William Crabtree did shoot and kill Cherokee Billie at the festivities, which led to bad feelings toward the settlers by the Cherokee. This tragedy did lead some of the Cherokee to participate in Lord Dunmore's War later that year. The settlers' victory did open Kentucky for settlement, led by Daniel Boone.

The Transylvania Company negotiated to buy the lands of western Can-tuc-kee, now Kentucky, from the Cherokee in March 1775. The Wataugans used this meeting to negotiate the purchase of their own lands. Chief Attacullaculla led the Cherokee in agreeing to the purchases, but his son, Tsugunsini, Dragging Canoe, was vehemently opposed. At the meeting, he did make his famous "bloody ground" speech. He helped his prediction come true by going on the warpath with other Cherokee warriors the following year when the British did elicit the help of the Cherokee against the frontier settlers during the beginning of the American Revolution.

The Wataugans did form a committee of safety known as the Washington District. This was the first area named after George Washington. This allied the settlers with the colonists against the British and the Cherokee. Knowing that if the British won they would be forced off their lands, the Wataugans established Washington County and made themselves a part of North Carolina. They prepared for war by building new forts and fortifying the old ones.

Nancy Ward proved her friendship with the settlers when she warned them of the planned attack by the Cherokee. Her warning gave the settlers time to take refuge in the forts, and many lives were saved. The stories of John Sevier, Catherine Sherrill, Ann Robertson, and Lydia Bean around the siege of Fort Caswell are all true. Mrs. Bean was saved by Nancy Ward and returned to her family after teaching some of the Cherokee women how to sew and do other things that the settlers did. The Cherokee chief Old Abram withdrew from the fort after hearing of the defeats of the other bands of Cherokee. Dragging Canoe did set up raiding parties after his defeat. After the Cherokee were defeated by the forces of William Christian and they signed a peace treaty on June 20, 1777, Dragging Canoe refused to honor the peace and took his followers to the Chicka-mauga area.

The celebration at Fort Patrick Henry on July 4, 1777, was held to honor America's first birthday. Many Cherokee warriors did attend and join in the festivities. The frontier had been secured for the new nation, and now the settlers could turn their attention toward the East. They would come to play a major role in the struggle for freedom against the British, as will be seen in future volumes of the series. We hope you will join us for the future expeditions. Again, write and let us know what you think of our book. And keep reading!

Gilbert Morris &
Aaron McCarver